Praise for Brenda Novak's
Taking the Heat

"Vivid…intense…compelling.
You have not read many books like this one."
—Amanda Kilgore, *Huntress Book Reviews*

"Novak's story is richly dramatic,
with a stark setting that distinguishes it nicely
from the lusher worlds of older romances."
—*Publishers Weekly*

"This story started out with a bang
and believe me, it didn't stop…. I eagerly look forward
to Brenda Novak's next book."
—Kathy Boswell, *The Best Reviews*

"Terrific! Ms. Novak always comes up with
something different. Her characters are three-dimensional
and riveting. Don't miss this one!"
—Suzanne Coleburn, *Reader to Reader Reviews*

"With *Taking the Heat*,
Brenda Novak has written exactly the kind of story
that readers want to read…. Spellbinding."
—Diane Tidlund, *Writers Unlimited*

"The story is compelling…
a good mix of romance and suspense."
—Judith Flavell, *The Romance Reader*

"Ms. Novak always writes a wonderful story,
whether it's her Superromances or her single-title books.
I know when I pick up something she's written,
I'll be totally satisfied."
—Allyn Pogue, *Old Book Barn Gazette*

BRENDA NOVAK

is a two-time Golden Heart finalist. (The Golden Heart is a prestigious award given by the Romance Writers of America.) Brenda has sold seventeen books to Harlequin, many of which have placed in contests such as the National Readers' Choice and the Booksellers' Best. Her first single title, *Taking the Heat* (published in 2003), received high praise from readers and reviewers alike.

A busy wife and mother of five, Brenda—who lives in Sacramento, California—calls herself the typical "soccer mom." She juggles her writing career with daily car pools, helping her kids do homework and driving them to baseball, basketball and soccer games, depending on the season.

brenda novak

COLD FEET

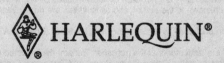

HARLEQUIN®

TORONTO • NEW YORK • LONDON
AMSTERDAM • PARIS • SYDNEY • HAMBURG
STOCKHOLM • ATHENS • TOKYO • MILAN • MADRID
PRAGUE • WARSAW • BUDAPEST • AUCKLAND

ISBN 0-373-83600-7

COLD FEET

To my mother, Lavar Moffitt. I come from a long line of mentally tough women, and my mother is one of the toughest. As I grow older, I recognize more and more the foundation she has built for me, and the debt of gratitude I owe her. I pray I will live up to the character she has tried to foster in me and, for my own children's sake, that I'll pass on her legacy….

ACKNOWLEDGMENT

Many thanks to Detective Tom Bennett of Colorado for his help with the police and forensic details of this novel. Tom has spent more than thirty years in public service, working for the Arvada Police Department, and has investigated approximately 2000 felony cases. The recipient of numerous departmental honors, including the Medal of Valor, the highest honor the Arvada P.D. bestows on a police officer, Tom is a gifted detective and an honorable man.

Dear Reader,

Like many of you, I'm a big fan of Court TV. But through every criminal profile I watch, I can't help wondering about the friends and family associated with the perpetrator—especially the friends and family of those guilty of the more heinous crimes. Certainly someone, somewhere, loves or has loved these twisted individuals. At some point they must seem somewhat "normal." They live among us, go to school with us, work with us.... Or did their mothers/fathers/sisters/brothers have an inkling that they were capable of such violence? What went wrong inside their psyches? What caused one brother to become a rapist and the other to be a law-abiding citizen? How does the wife of a serial killer not know that she's married to a monster? And how does she live with what has happened once she learns?

My curiosity in this area definitely provided the creative seed for this story. Poor Madison Lieberman has grown up refusing to believe what the police and the media insist is true about her father. In *Cold Feet* she faces the trial of her faith in him, a man she loves and has always admired. It's a study of relationships I found intriguing. I hope you'll agree!

I love to hear from readers! Please feel free to contact me via my Web site at www.brendanovak.com, where I routinely give away great prizes and post information about my backlist and upcoming books. Or write to me at P.O. Box 3781, Citrus Heights, CA 95611.

Here's hoping you know your loved ones as well as you think you do....

Best wishes,

Brenda Novak

CHAPTER ONE

"CALEB, SHE'S GONE. Disappeared. Vanished," Holly said.

Caleb Trovato could hear the distress in his ex-wife's voice, but he wasn't about to respond to it. Everything seemed to affect her far more acutely than it would anyone else, and by virtue of the fact that they were divorced—for the second time—he didn't have to ride her emotional roller coaster anymore.

He propped the phone up with his shoulder and swiveled back to his computer to check his e-mail, so the next few minutes wouldn't be a total waste. "Your sister's what—twenty-six? She'll turn up."

"How can you be so sure?"

"Susan's disappeared before. Remember that time she met some rich guy on an hour's layover in Vegas and let him talk her into a wild fling? We were positive something terrible had happened to her. Especially when the airline confirmed that she'd boarded the flight out of Phoenix."

"That was different," Holly retorted. "She called me the next day."

"Only because loverboy had started acting a little scary. She finally realized it might be a good thing to let someone know where she was. And she needed money to get home."

"That was almost five years ago, Caleb. She's changed.

She has a steady job at Nordstrom's cosmetics counter and she's kept her own apartment for almost a year.''

The high pitch of Holly's voice brought back memories of the many outbursts he'd been forced to endure while they were married, and put his teeth on edge. "Listen, Holly, I'm sorry Susan's giving you a scare, but I'm really busy," he said, determined to escape this time. "I've got to go.''

"Caleb, don't do this to me," she replied, openly crying. "I haven't bothered you for anything since our last divorce.''

Caleb rolled his eyes. Wasn't that the general idea? It wasn't as if they had children together. And contrary to her claim of not bothering him, she called often. She called to borrow money. She called to ask how to file her income tax returns. She called to see if he could remember what happened to the X rays that had been taken of her leg when she'd had that waterskiing accident. She even called to see what his plans were for certain holidays.

"I don't understand what you want from me," he said in frustration.

"I haven't been able to reach Susan for almost a week. Mom and Dad haven't heard from her. Lance, the guy she's dating, hasn't heard from her. She hasn't called in at work—''

"Skipping work is nothing new for Susan, either," he pointed out.

"Caleb, she was living near the university.''

At this Caleb sat forward, feeling his first flicker of alarm. Eleven women had been abducted and killed near the University of Washington over the past twelve years. Holly had lived right next door to one of them. That was how he'd met her. He'd been working for the Seattle Police Department, canvassing the apartment building of the strangler's ninth victim, looking for leads, and he'd knocked on Holly's door to check if she'd seen or heard anything.

But Caleb was certain the man who'd committed those murders was now dead. He should know. He'd spent three years on the task force investigating the case and another four continuing to help after he'd quit the Seattle PD. "Holly, the Sandpoint Strangler shot himself in his own backyard over a year ago."

She sniffed. "If you're so sure, why didn't you ever finish the book you were going to write about him?"

"There wasn't enough hard evidence to connect Ellis Purcell to the killings," Caleb admitted. "But you saw him drive away from your apartment building the night Anna was murdered: You're the one who gave us the partial plate number."

"But you could never place him inside the apartment."

"That doesn't mean he was innocent, Holly," Caleb said, making a halfhearted attempt to organize his desk while they talked. "Purcell couldn't account for his whereabouts during several of the murders. He failed two different lie-detector tests. The geographical profile done by the FBI indicated the killer lived within a five-block radius of him and his family. And he was secretive, kind of a recluse. I talked to him twice, Holly, and it always felt as though he was hiding something."

"I know all that, but when you worked for the department you searched his place three different times and never found anything."

"Some of the task force searched it. I was young enough, and new enough to the force, that I did what Gibbons told me, which was mainly behind-the-scenes grunt work. Gibbons was lead detective. He always dealt with the really important stuff. But the murders have stopped since Purcell's death,'' Caleb said. ''That should tell you something.''

''They stopped for several years after Anna's body was discovered, too,'' Holly argued.

''That's because the police were watching Purcell so closely he could scarcely breathe. The murders started up again as soon as that custodian, John Roach, killed a kindergarten teacher at Schwab Elementary downtown and almost everyone on the force, including Gibbons, suddenly believed we'd been barking up the wrong tree. But it was only wishful thinking.''

''Then what about the woman who went missing from Spokane a couple of months ago?'' Holly asked. ''How do you explain that if the strangler's dead?''

''I haven't heard anything about it,'' he said.

''I just read an article the other day that said the police found some of that date rape drug on the floor of her car. Roach is in prison and Purcell is dead, but that sounds like the strangler to me.''

Caleb still had several close friends on the force. If anything interesting had developed, Detective Gibbons or Detective Thomas would have called him. This case had meant a lot to all of them. ''Have they found her body?''

''Not yet.''

''Then they don't know anything. Roofies are only about two bucks per tablet, and they're easy to buy. We saw them in that pharmacy when we were in Mexico, remember?''

''So what about Susan?'' she asked, with more than a hint of desperation.

She was baiting him, trying to tempt him back into her life. But it wasn't going to work this time. He no longer felt the same compulsion to rescue her that had drawn him to her in the first place. "I don't know what you want me to do."

"You used to be a cop, for God's sake! A good one. I want you to come out here and find her, Caleb."

Shoving his mouse away, Caleb turned in his new leather office chair to stare out the picture window that revealed a breathtaking view of San Francisco Bay. A panorama of blue-green, undulating ocean dotted with at least twenty colorful sailboats was spread out before him. "I live in California now, Holly." As if to prove how necessary it was that he remain in his current surroundings, he added, "I have someone coming to lay new carpet next week."

"This could mean Susan's life!" Holly cried.

Another over-the-top statement? Given Holly's penchant for theatrics, he figured it was.... "I'm not a cop anymore. I write true crime books. I don't know what you think I can do."

"I *know* what you can do," she said. "I married you twice, remember? It's almost uncanny how you turn up whatever you're looking for. It's a talent. You're...you're like one of those journalists who'll stop at nothing to uncover a story."

Caleb wasn't sure that was such a positive association, but he let it pass because she was still talking.

"You could come if you wanted to. Lord knows you've got the money."

"Money isn't the issue," he replied.

"Then what is?"

His hard-won freedom. He'd had to leave the Seattle area to get far enough away from Holly. He wasn't about to head back now, even though his parents still lived on Fidalgo Island, where he'd grown up, and he loved the place. "I can't leave. I'm in the middle of another book."

She seemed to sense that he wasn't going for the panicky stuff, and made an effort to rein in her emotions. "What's this one about?"

"A girl who murdered her stepfather."

She sniffled again. "Sounds fun."

At her sarcasm, he felt his lips twist into a wry grin. "It's a living. *Somebody* I know hated being a cop's wife and encouraged me to go for my dream of becoming a writer."

"And is that so bad? Now you're rich and famous."

But still divorced. No matter how much Holly professed to love him, he couldn't live with her. She was simply too obsessive. He'd married her the first time because he'd thought they could make a life together. He'd married her the second time because his sense of honor demanded it. But beyond their initial few months together, their relationship had been fractious at best, and they'd spent more days apart than they'd ever spent as a couple.

"You should come back here and do some more work on the Sandpoint Strangler," she said in a pouty voice.

"No, thanks. I've learned a bit since the early days." Caleb started doodling on an empty message pad. "Now I typically write about crimes that have already been solved—by someone else. It's a hell of a lot easier."

"You helped the police solve the murder of that one young runaway, then wrote a book about it, remember?"

He remembered. *Maria* had been the most satisfying project he'd worked on to date, because he felt he'd made a real difference in achieving justice for the victim and everyone involved. "That one happened to work out," he told Holly. "But it's always a gamble, and I don't think my publisher would appreciate the increased risk of having each book languish for years while I search high and low for a satisfying resolution."

"But you were fascinated by the Sandpoint Strangler."

He'd probably been more obsessed than fascinated. Even after leaving law enforcement, he'd continued to work the case, pro bono, with the hope of eventually putting it all in a book.

"You've said yourself, a hundred times, that working the investigation gave you an insider's view you simply couldn't achieve when you were writing about someone else's case," she went on. "I know a book about him would really sell. Nobody's done one yet."

"There're still too many unanswered questions to make for interesting reading, Holly. People like a definitive ending when they purchase a true crime book. They like logical sequences and answers. I can't give them that with the Sandpoint Strangler."

"Things change."

"I doubt there's enough new information to make much of a difference," he said.

"So you won't come?"

"Holly—"

"Where does that leave me with Susan, Caleb?" she asked, her veneer of control cracking and giving way to a sob.

Caleb pinched the bridge of his nose. He didn't want to let Holly's tears sway him, but her distress and what she'd said were beginning to make him wonder. Susan had been his sister, too, for a while. Although she'd been a real pain in the ass, always getting herself into one scrape or another, he still felt some residual affection for her.

"Have you called the police?" he asked.

"Of course. I'm frantic!"

He could tell. What he didn't know was whether or not her state of mind was justified. "What'd they say?"

"Nothing. They're as stumped as I am. There was no forced entry, no sign of a struggle at her apartment, no missing jewelry or credit cards—at least, that we could tell—and no activity on her bank account. I don't think they have any leads. They don't even know where to look."

"What about her car?"

"It's gone, but I know she didn't just drive off into the sunset. We would've heard from her by now. Unless…"

"Stop imagining the worst," he said. "There could be a lot of reasons for her disappearance. Maybe she met a rich college boy, and they're off cruising the Bahamas. It would be like her to show up tomorrow and say, 'Oh, you were worried? I didn't even think to call you.'" He rubbed the whiskers on his chin, trying to come up with another plausible explanation. "Or maybe she's gotten mixed up in drugs. She was always—"

"She left her dogs behind, Caleb," Holly interrupted. "She wouldn't leave for days without asking someone to feed them. Not for a trip to the Caribbean. Not for the world's best party. Not for anything."

Holly had a point. Susan adored her schnauzers, to the tune of paying a veterinarian six thousand dollars—money she didn't really have—for extensive surgery when one darted across the street and was hit by a truck.

Caleb rocked back and draped an arm over his eyes. He didn't want to face it, but this wasn't sounding good. Even if the Sandpoint Strangler was no longer on the prowl, *something* had happened to Susan. And the longer she was missing, the tougher it would be to find her.

"When was the last time you saw her?" he asked in resignation.

"Six days ago."

Six days... Caleb propped his feet on the desk and considered the book he was writing. It wasn't going very well, anyway. After piecing the whole story together, he was actually feeling more sympathy for the girl who'd committed the crime than the abusive stepfather she'd poisoned.

"All right, I'll fly out first thing in the morning." He hung up and looked around his crisp, modern condo. *Shit. So much for putting some space between me and Holly.*

Somehow she always managed to reel him back in....

MADISON LIEBERMAN STARED at her father's photograph for a long time. He gazed back at her with fathomless dark eyes, his complexion as ruddy as a seaman's, his salt-and-pepper flattop as militarily precise as ever. He'd only been dead about a year, but already he seemed like a stranger to her. Maybe it was because she wondered so often if she'd ever really known him....

"Madison? Did you find it?"

Her mother's voice, coming from upstairs, pulled her away from the photograph, but she couldn't help glancing at it again as she hesitantly approached the small door that opened into the crawl space. She'd been raised in this home. The three-foot gap under the house provided additional storage for canned goods, emergency supplies, old baskets, arts and crafts and holiday decorations, among other things.

But it was damp, dark and crowded—perfect for spiders or, worse, rats. Which was one reason Madison generally avoided it. When she was a child, she'd been afraid her father would lock her in. Probably because he'd threatened to do so once, when she was only four years old and he'd caught her digging through the Christmas presents her mother had hidden there.

It wasn't the fear of spiders or rats, or even the fear of being locked in, that bothered her at age twenty-eight, however. Ever since the police and the media had started following her father around, suspecting him of being involved in the terrible murders near the university only a few blocks away, she'd been terrified of what she might find if she ever really looked....

"Madison?" Her mother's voice filtered down to her again.

"Give me a minute," she called in annoyance as she opened the small door. "It's a twenty-dollar punch bowl," she grumbled to herself. "Why can't she just let me buy her a new one?"

The smell of moist earth and rotting wood greeted her as she flipped on the dangling bulb overhead and peered inside. Years ago, her father had covered the bare, uneven ground with black plastic and made a path of wooden boards that snaked through the clutter. These makeshift improvements reminded her that this was *his* domain, one of the places he'd never liked her to go.

It didn't make the thought of snooping around any more appealing. Her half brothers, Johnny and Tye, her father's children by his first wife, stored things here occasionally, but she did her best to forget the dark yawning space even existed. She certainly didn't want to spend any portion of what had started out as a relaxing Sunday afternoon scrounging around this creepy place.

She considered telling her mother the punch bowl wasn't there. But ever since her father's suicide, her mother seemed to fixate on the smallest details. If Madison couldn't find it, she'd probably insist on looking herself, and Annette was getting too old to be crawling around on her hands and knees. Besides, Madison and her mother had stood by Ellis Purcell throughout the investigation that had ended with his death. Certainly Madison could have a little faith in him now. The police had searched the house about four years after the killings began and never found anything.

She wasn't going to find anything, either. Because her father was innocent. Of course.

Taking a deep, calming breath, she resisted the fresh wave of anxiety that seemed to press her back toward the entrance, and crawled inside. The punch bowl couldn't be far. It would only take a second to find it.

A row of boxes lined the wall closest to her. Some were labeled, others weren't. Madison quickly opened the ones that weren't labeled to discover some things her father had owned as a young man—old photo albums, school and college yearbooks, military stuff from his stint in Vietnam.

The photos and letters seemed so normal and far removed from the articles she'd read about Ellis in the newspapers that she finally began to relax. A lot of cobwebs hung overhead, almost iridescent in the ethereal glow of the dim lightbulb, but if there were spiders, they were off in the corners. Nothing jumped out to grab her. She saw no indication that anyone had been underneath the house since Johnny had come by to get his summer clothes out of storage two years ago.

Her father might have ended his life with one heck of a finale, but his death and the investigation, if not the suspicion, were behind them now. She could quit being afraid. She could move on and forget....

Shoving the memorabilia off to one side, she rummaged around some more and eventually came up with the punch bowl. She was about to drag it to the entrance when she remembered the box of Barbie dolls she'd packed up when she was twelve. They were probably down here, too, she realized. If she could find them, she could give them to her own daughter, Brianna, who'd just turned six.

Following the curve in the wooden path, Madison came across some leftover tiles from when they'd redone the bathroom, a dusty briefcase, an old ice-cream maker, and some of her baby things. Near the edge of the plastic, where bare dirt stretched into complete darkness, she found a few boxes that had belonged to her half brothers, along with the denim bedding her mother had bought when Johnny and Tye came to live with them.

As she pushed past Johnny's old stereo, she promised herself she'd write him again this week, even though he never answered her letters. He'd been in and out of prison for years, always on drug charges. But he had to be lonely. Tye stayed in touch with him, but her mother pretended he didn't exist. And he hated his own alcoholic mother who, last Madison had heard, was living somewhere in Pennsylvania in a halfway house.

She squinted in the dim light to make out the writing on several boxes: "Mother Rayma's tablecloths…" "Mother Rayma's dishes…" "Aunt Zelma's paintings."

No Barbies. Disappointed, Madison rocked back into a sitting position to save her knees from the hard planking, and hugged her legs to her chest, trying to figure out where that box might have gone. Brianna had had a difficult year, what with the divorce, their move to Whidbey Island thirty-five miles northwest of Seattle, her father's remarriage, and the expectation of a half sibling in the near future. Madison would love to have fifteen or more vintage Barbie dolls waiting in her back seat when she collected her daughter from her ex-husband's later today. Danny certainly lavished Brianna with enough toys.

Maybe she needed to dig deeper. Pushing several boxes out of the way, she slid the old mirror from the spare bedroom to the left, and the avocado bathroom accessories that had once decorated the upstairs bathroom to the right, to reach the stuff piled behind. She was pretty far from the light at the entrance, which made it difficult to see, but she was eventually rewarded for her efforts when she recognized her own childish writing on a large box tucked into the corner.

"There it is!" she murmured, wriggling the box out from behind an old Crock-Pot and some extra fabric that looked as if it was from the sixties and better off forgotten. "You're gonna love me for this, Brianna."

"Madison, what could possibly be taking so long?"

Madison jumped at the unexpected sound, knocking her head on a beam. "Ow."

"Are you okay?" her mother asked. Annette stood at the mouth of the crawl space, but Madison couldn't see her for all the junk between them.

"I'm fine." She batted away a few cobwebs to rub the sore spot on her forehead. "You can tell Mrs. Howell I found the punch bowl you said she could borrow."

"I use that punch bowl every Christmas. What's it doing all the way back there?"

"It wasn't back here. I've been looking for my old Barbies."

"Don't waste another minute on that," her mother said. "We gave them to Goodwill a long time ago."

"No, we didn't. They're right here."

"They are?"

"Sure." Madison pulled open the top flap of the box to prove it, and felt her heart suddenly slam against her chest. Her mother was right. There weren't any Barbies inside. Just a bunch of women's shoes and underwear, in various sizes. And a short coil of rope.

CHAPTER TWO

STUNNED, MADISON BLINKED at the jumble in the box as the pictures the police had shown her years earlier flashed through her mind—grotesque, heart-rending photos of women after the Sandpoint Strangler had finished with them. It made her dizzy and nauseous to even think about those poor women; it made her feel worse to believe her father might have—

No! Surely there was some mistake. The police had searched the crawl space. They would've found this stuff.

Steeling herself against overwhelming revulsion, Madison used a towel rod to poke through the box in hopes of finding some evidence that would refute the obvious.

In the bottom corner, she saw something that glittered, and forced herself to reach gingerly inside. It was a metal chain. When she pulled it out into the murky light, she could see it was a necklace with a gold locket on the end. But she was too terrified to open it. Her heart hammered against her ribs and her hands shook as she stared at it until, finally, she gathered the nerve to unhook the tiny clasp.

Inside, she saw an oval picture of Lisa and Joe McDonna. Lisa was victim number two. Madison knew because she'd memorized them all—by face and by name.

Closing her eyes, she put a hand to her stomach, attempting to override her body's reaction. But she retched anyway, several dry heaves that hurt her throat and her stomach. She'd hung on to her belief in Ellis's innocence for so long. She'd stood against the police, the media and popular opinion. She'd stayed in the same high school even after the kids had started taunting her and doing vengeful things, like throwing eggs and oranges at the house or writing "murderer" in the lawn with bleach. She'd held her head high and attended the University of Washington, just as she'd always planned. Through it all, she'd refused to consider the possibility of her father's culpability in the murders, even when the police produced an eyewitness who said she saw Ellis driving away from a neighbor's house the night that neighbor was murdered. The witness was old and could have been mistaken. There were a lot of blue Fords with white camper shells in Seattle. All the evidence was circumstantial.

But if he was innocent, how could such a personal item belonging to one of the victims have found its way inside the house?

"Ellis saved those Barbies, after all?" Annette said, her words suddenly sounding as though they had an echo. "I could've sworn we took them to Goodwill."

Madison couldn't breathe well enough to speak. After those hellish years in high school, she'd expected the scandal to die down, especially when the police couldn't find any DNA evidence. But the suspicion and hatred had gone on long after that, until it had destroyed her marriage. Her husband wanted to be seen as upwardly mobile and a man who had it all. Not the man who'd married the daughter of the Sandpoint Strangler.

"Madison?" her mother said, when she didn't respond.

She took a few bolstering breaths and managed an answer. "What?"

"Are you going to bring those Barbie dolls out or not? I'm sure Brianna will be thrilled to have them."

Madison wasn't about to let her mother see what the box really contained. Annette had been through enough already.

Wiping away the sweat beading on her upper lip, Madison struggled to distance herself from the whole tragic mess. She hadn't hurt those women. If her father had, she'd been as much a victim as anyone.

"It—it looks like there've been some rats in the box," she said. "I d-don't think we can give them to Brianna."

"That's too bad. Well, drag them out here anyway, and I'll get rid of them once and for all."

Madison breathed in through her nose and out through her mouth, struggling to remain calm and rational. "If it's okay with you, I'll just leave them here. They...there's a sticky web all over and I'm afraid there might be a black widow someplace."

"Oh boy, we wouldn't want to drag that out. You're right, just leave them. I'll hire someone to come down here and clean this out when I move."

When she moved... Ever since her father had shot himself in the backyard, Madison had been trying to talk her mother into relocating. Madison had a difficult time even coming to the house, what with all the bad memories; she couldn't imagine how Annette still lived here.

But now she wasn't so sure she wanted her mother to go anywhere. If Annette sold the house, Madison would either have to come forward with what she'd found, which was unimaginable, or she'd have to destroy it—something she wasn't sure her conscience would allow.

God, she'd thought the nightmare was over. Now she knew it would never be....

HOLLY MET CALEB at the airport on Monday morning. With her long, curly blond hair, he noticed her in the crowd almost as soon as he entered the arrivals lounge, and steeled himself for the moment she'd come rushing to meet him. Two years his senior, she was taller than most women, thin, and had a heart-shaped, angelic face. She looked good. She always *looked* good. But looks didn't matter with a woman whose emotions swung as widely as Holly's did.

He saw her pushing through the crowd as she made her way toward him. And then she was there, smiling in obvious relief. "Caleb, I'm so glad you came." She reached up to hug him, and he allowed it but quickly moved on, following the flow of the other passengers toward the baggage claim.

"You haven't heard from Susan?" he asked, glad to finally stretch his legs. First class had been full. He was too big for the narrow, cramped space allotted him in economy, but without advance booking he'd had to take what he could get.

"Not a word. I check my answering machine every hour, just in case. But…" She blinked rapidly, and he hoped she wasn't going to cry again. He hadn't come to be her emotional support. He just wanted to find Susan and get back to San Francisco.

"Have the Seattle police assigned any detectives to the case?"

"Two. Lynch and Jones. Do you know them?"

"I know Lynch better than Jones."

"They're driving me nuts," she said. "They keep talking about searching for fiber evidence and what not, but it doesn't seem like they're doing much of anything."

"This isn't television, Holly. Fiber evidence takes a long time. You have to track down all the people who visited Susan's apartment, and collect samples before you can send them to the lab for comparison. And you generally don't have a lab tech sitting there, twiddling his thumbs while waiting to help you. You have to take your place in line.''

He dodged a woman who'd stopped right in front of him to dig through a bag. ''Have you talked to your parents again?'' he asked. Caleb knew relations between Holly and her adoptive parents were strained. They had been for most of her life. She hated her birth mother for giving her up, even though her birth mother had been barely sixteen. She hated her adoptive mother for not being her birth mother. And she was frequently jealous of Susan, who'd been born with the assistance of fertility drugs when Holly was seven.

''I called them last night to tell them you were coming,'' she said.

''What did they have to say about Susan's disappearance?''

''At first they said the same thing you did—she's done this before, she'll turn up. Now that it's been almost a week, they're worried. They're willing to hire a private investigator, if you think that's the best way to go. They wanted me to talk to you about it.''

''I think we should do whatever we can as soon as possible.''

''Okay.'' She scratched her arm through her sweater, looking uncertain. ''You know how we were talking about the Sandpoint Strangler?''

''Yes?''

''There was something on the news earlier....''

They'd reached the luggage carousel. He slipped through the crowd to grab the small bag he'd packed in San Francisco. Besides a few clothes, he'd brought only his cell phone, his day planner and his laptop, so he could work if he got the chance. "What?" he asked, when he had his bag slung over his shoulder.

"Someone desecrated the grave of Ellis Purcell."

Caleb stiffened in surprise. "How? From what I remember, his widow and daughter went to great pains to keep its location a secret."

"I don't know. I just caught a clip while I was eating breakfast."

Caleb rubbed the stubble on his chin. He hadn't showered or shaved this morning. He'd had such an early flight, he'd simply rolled out of bed, pulled on a Fox Racing T-shirt, a pair of faded jeans and a Giants ball cap and headed south to the airport.

"It's probably just a coincidence," he said. But he had to admit it was strange that a woman would go missing from the Sandpoint Strangler's old hunting grounds a year after Ellis Purcell was dead. That she'd be related to Holly. And that Purcell's grave would be desecrated in the same week.

ALTHOUGH MONDAY AFTERNOON was warm, with a rare amount of sun for Seattle in September, the mortuary was cool. Too cool. It smelled of carnations, furniture polish and formaldehyde, which dredged up memories of every funeral Madison had ever attended—Aunt Zelma's, Grandma Rayma's, the skeletal-looking man who'd lived next door when she was five. She couldn't think of the old guy's name, but she remembered staring at his waxy face as he lay in his coffin.

Fortunately, she didn't have to deal with any memories of her father's funeral. They hadn't given him one. She, her mother, Tye and Johnny had simply sent out notices of his death to the few friends and family who'd remained supportive, and buried him without any type of viewing or wake. Because of the ongoing investigation, and the damage he'd done with his old rifle, it seemed prudent to handle things as quickly and quietly as possible.

Lawrence Howell, the manager of Sunset Lawn Funeral Home and Memorial Park, had helped make the arrangements. He sat across from Madison and her mother now, his short blond hair neatly combed, his face wearing the same somber expression he always wore.

Fortunately, Madison had been able to reach Joanna Stapley, a senior at South Whidbey High School who often baby-sat for her, in time to have her pick up Brianna from school, so she didn't have to cope with a wriggling six-year-old during such a difficult meeting.

"How could this have happened?" she asked when Mr. Howell had finished explaining what he'd told her on the phone when he'd reached her at her office earlier—that someone had dug up her father's coffin last night. "How could anyone have figured out where he was buried?"

Howell rested his elbows on his mahogany desk and clasped long white fingers in front of him. "As I told the gentleman who called me this morning—"

"What gentleman?" Annette demanded.

Madison put a comforting hand on her mother's arm. "Tye, Mom. I phoned him as soon as Mr. Howell contacted me. I thought he might want to be part of this."

"Is he coming?" she asked, obviously not pleased that Madison had included him.

"No, he said he has to work."

"What about his wife? Is she going to be here?"

"Sharon and the kids are visiting her mother in Spokane."

"Ellis never could count on his boys," Annette said, her lips compressed in disapproval. She didn't want Tye or his wife involved, yet she sounded affronted by their lack of support.

Mr. Howell, who'd waited politely through their exchange, cleared his throat. "As I was saying, I have no way of knowing how this happened. There was no headstone or anything else to mark your father's grave, Ms. Lieberman, just as you requested. Our files are kept private and are always locked up at night. There was no sign of forced entry into the mortuary here, where we keep the files. And it's been a year since the burial—a year in which we've had no hint of trouble."

"That's what I don't understand," Annette said, her eyes filling with tears. "Why now? What would anyone want with Ellis's body after all this time?"

"A year's not so long, Mom," Madison said before Howell could respond. "Whoever it was wants the same thing we've encountered before, to express their anger and contempt for…for what happened."

"I just want my husband to be able to rest in peace," her mother said. "Ellis was innocent. He never hurt those women."

Madison wished her mother's words didn't sound so hollow to her. She still wanted to believe them. But the locket she'd discovered under the house yesterday threatened the last of her faith, was leaching away the righteous anger that had sustained her so far. Without a strong conviction that her father was innocent, she had nothing to cling to, except the desire to protect her mother and Brianna from what was, most probably, the truth.

"Of course he was innocent," Howell said, his tone placating.

Madison was willing to bet Howell believed more in the extra money they'd paid him to keep her father's burial place a secret than he did in her father's innocence.

Just as she thought the call he'd made to them this morning, and what he might shortly suggest for her father's reburial, would come with a hefty price tag. They should've gone ahead with the cremation Madison had suggested from the first. But her mother wouldn't hear of it. Annette had never known anyone who'd been cremated. It seemed foreign to her—certainly nothing she was willing to do with her beloved husband's body.

"Fortunately, our security guard frightened the culprit away before he could open the casket," Howell added.

Madison rummaged through her purse to get her mother a tissue. Annette didn't used to cry so easily, but the past twelve years had taken quite a toll. "Why didn't the security guard catch him sooner?" she asked.

Howell politely turned his attention her way. "As you know, this is a big cemetery, Ms. Lieberman. Anthony, our security guard, circles the entire area several times a night, but he focuses mostly on the outer reaches. We buried your father close to the mortuary here, to throw off the media and anyone who might be looking for a fresh grave. Most folks buried near the mortuary have been dead sixty or seventy years, which means they're pretty well forgotten." He propped his fingertips together. "The lights on the building also serve as a deterrent."

"Did your security guard get a look at this guy?" Madison asked, handing the tissue to her mother.

"Anthony said he was wearing jeans and a blue jacket with a red Chinese dragon on the back, and he looked small, maybe a hundred and sixty pounds. But that's all he could see. As soon as Anthony started toward him in the security cart, he threw down his shovel and ran off." Howell bent to one side to cover a small cough. "We gave these details to the police this morning, of course."

"So this…guy, he—he just unearthed the coffin?"

Madison asked, her muscles aching with anxiety. How many other people had to deal with such a parade of unsettling incidents? "That's it?"

"He made a few pry marks on the coffin, but Anthony came along before he was able to get it open. We could have reburied your father easily enough, but I thought I'd better check with you and your mother to see if you'd like him moved now that...well, now that the media and everyone else seem to have taken a renewed interest."

"The media? How did the media find out?" Annette asked, her eyes wide with panic.

Howell unclasped his hands. "They must've heard the call go out when Anthony phoned the police."

Madison was still thinking about the guy in the Chinese dragon jacket. "So the police are looking for whoever did this?"

"We've made a report, as I said. Technically, there's a chance this...*disturbance* would be classified as a felony. Individual plots are personal property. But..." he hesitated, and this time his glance seemed to hold real compassion "...if you want the truth, Ms. Lieberman, I can't imagine the police will waste much time chasing down the crazy guy who did this when they're already so overworked and understaffed. I think you and your mother would be better off to simply move the coffin and put this unfortunate incident behind you."

Along with everything else, Madison thought bitterly. Only nothing from the past ever seemed to stay there.

CALEB STOOD AT THE ENTRANCE to Susan's bedroom Monday evening, surveying the clothes littering the floor, the perfume bottles and makeup strewn across the dresser, and her unmade bed. The place smelled like the expensive perfume so typical of Susan, which brought her back to him more clearly than he'd remembered her so far, and caused worry to claw at his gut. She hadn't been seen for a week, since last Monday. Where could she be?

Crossing to the dresser, he smoothed out a crinkled piece of paper to see that it was only a quick thank-you from a friend at work, then rifled through some change. He wasn't sure what he was looking for. Anything, really. Anything that might lead him to Susan.

Holly hovered behind him. "What are you doing?" she asked. "Why aren't you checking for pry marks on the window or something?"

He caught his ex-wife's eye in the mirror. It felt strange to be inside Susan's apartment with everything so quiet, so motionless. Even when Susan wasn't around, her dogs had always been here, barking and wagging a welcome. Now Holly had the schnauzers at her place, and other than a few visits from police, the apartment had been shut up. "I'm sure the detectives have done all that."

"So?"

"I'm focusing on my personal knowledge of Susan's behavior and habits."

"Which means…"

"I'm trying to figure out what she might have been wearing and doing the night she disappeared. When I talked to Detective Lynch a few minutes ago, he said you were the last person to see her on Monday afternoon. But she wasn't reported missing until Wednesday, when she didn't show up for work. That's a lot of time to change clothes."

Holly rearranged the slew of bottles and cosmetics on the dresser, putting them in some semblance of order. "There's no way to tell what she was wearing. For all we know, she was abducted in the middle of the night dressed in a pair of boxers and a T-shirt."

"I doubt she was taken from here."

Holly gave up on the mess and raised her eyebrows in surprise. "Just because there was no forced entry? Maybe someone came to the door," she said. "Maybe she knew who it was so she opened up. She might have even left with him. Detective Lynch seems to believe that's most likely what happened."

"Except that her car's gone," Caleb said.

Holly shrugged. "She and whoever she was with could have used her car."

"Susan wouldn't have wanted to drive if she had a man at the door with his own transportation. This was a woman who spent every dime she had on clothes and makeup and—" He indicated the perfumes, body lotions, mascara and eye shadow that covered almost every horizontal surface "—judging by the looks of this place, that hasn't changed over the past two years."

Holly pulled her hair into a ponytail. "I still don't think we can figure out what she was wearing. When I saw her on Monday, she was telling me about some hot new outfit she was going to buy. How are we supposed to place her in something we might never have seen?"

Caleb turned to study the room again, taking in the pajama bottoms draped over a chair, and noticing underwear on the floor near the bathroom. "Maybe we can't. But to me it looks like she took a shower, got dressed up and left for an evening out."

Holly frowned at his assessment and toyed with the hem of her turtleneck sweater. "What makes you say that?"

"I can still smell perfume in the air, as if she sprayed it last thing, and those panties look as though she just stepped out of them. If she was expecting someone, she would've at least tossed the underwear in the hamper, don't you think?''

"Susan was never much of a clean freak.''

Caleb crossed to the closet, which was crammed full of blouses, slacks, suits, dresses, jackets, jeans and sweaters. There were even a few wigs and hairpieces on the shelf above. ''Knowing Susan, she'd be anxious to wear the new clothes she told you about. Did she describe them to you?''

"Of course, but I wasn't really listening. She's always telling me about some new shade of eye shadow or clothes bargain.''

He fingered a black sweater with faux fur at the wrists and collar. ''Have you looked through her closet for anything with the tags still on it?''

"I haven't looked specifically for tags, but I know there are a few new things.''

"Where are they?''

Holly started examining clothes at the back of the closet, but Caleb stopped her.

"Forget it,'' he said. ''She wouldn't shove a hot new outfit all the way to the back. If she's got any new clothes that far back, she's never found an occasion to wear them, and they've probably been there for some time.''

"So now what?''

"Maybe we could call Nordstrom to see what she's purchased lately. She'd probably put it on her charge card, wouldn't she?''

Holly didn't seem hopeful. ''Except that her charge card's been maxed out since her first two weeks at work.''

Of course. He hadn't taken Susan's spending habits into account. Still, there had to be some way to figure out what she'd bought and whether or not she was wearing it....

Caleb took another turn around the room, thinking. She

would've carried her purchase inside from the car, possibly tried it on, admired herself in the mirror and cut off the tags.

The tags...

Moving to the small garbage can on the other side of the nightstand, he found a crumpled Nordstrom bag with two tags inside. "Bingo," he said.

Holly took the tags from him. "What's so exciting about these?"

"We can use the SKU numbers to find out what Susan bought. Maybe she was wearing it when she went missing."

"What if she wasn't?"

He rubbed the back of his neck. "We have to start somewhere. Susan always liked the unique and ultratrendy. Maybe she wearing an outfit that really stood out."

Holly smiled up at him. "I knew I was right to have you come out here, Caleb."

"Slow down, Holly. We don't even know if this means anything."

"I'm sure you'll be able to help me," she said, and he hoped to God she was right.

CALEB GOT HIS WISH—at least in one regard. The short, worn-looking denim skirt and leopard-print halter top the Nordstrom saleswoman draped across the counter thirty minutes later was certainly conspicuous. He doubted that scrap of fabric the saleswoman called a skirt would cover much, but he had more to worry about than Susan's general lack of modesty.

"You're positive these items match the tags?" he asked.

"Check for yourself," the saleswoman—Deborah, according to her badge—held them up for comparison.

"Did you see anything like this in her apartment?" he asked Holly.

"No. I've never seen a halter top like this before in my life," she told him. "And I'd definitely remember it."

"I know Susan bought this because I sold it to her," Deborah insisted. "Just last week. She comes up here from cosmetics all the time or—" she looked slightly abashed "—she used to, anyway. And it was on clearance, so she got a great deal."

A great deal? Caleb touched the flimsy material. "Would someone really wear something like this in mid-September?" he asked. "Seattle doesn't exactly have beach weather."

"She was going clubbing," Deborah volunteered, trying to be helpful. "And it's so hot in those places. Especially when you're dancing, you know?"

Caleb knew all about clubs, but not because he'd visited one recently. He'd quickly grown tired of them after his divorce.

"It's too much of a long shot," Holly said. "Let's go."

She started for the door, but Caleb pulled her back. "Not so fast. It's better than nothing. I say we take a picture and add it to the flyers, just in case."

Holly studied the outfit with a critical eye, then sighed and shrugged. "If you say so."

"We'll take it," he told Deborah.

While he was paying for it, Holly looped her arm through his the way she used to while they were married. "This is just like old times," she murmured.

Caleb carefully extricated himself. "I'm not going to be in Seattle long," he said, and was determined to make sure she remembered that.

MADISON WAS EXHAUSTED by the time she returned home, but she felt a definite sense of relief the moment she drove off the Mukilteo-Clinton Ferry, which had brought her across Puget Sound from the mainland. After the unwelcome media attention she'd received during the past twelve years, and the crushing disappointment she'd experienced for her daughter's sake when Danny announced he was leaving her, she'd wanted to relocate as far from Seattle as possible. Start over. Forget. Or go into hiding until she was strong enough to face the world again.

But her divorce agreement stipulated that she couldn't move more than two hours away from Danny, who had joint custody of Brianna and lived on Mercer Island. And she felt too much responsibility toward her mother to leave without a backward glance. Annette was talking more favorably about moving than ever before, but she was still set in her ways and didn't want to go very far from the city where she'd been born and raised.

Whidbey became the compromise Madison had been searching for. With the island's sandy, saltwater beaches, damp, green woods, towering bluffs and spectacular views of Puget Sound and the Cascade Mountains, it felt remote. Yet it was still basically a suburb, with eateries and fast food, gas stations and convenience stores. And it was…familiar.

"Brianna!" Madison called as she let herself into the small cottage she'd used her divorce settlement to buy, along with her new business, the South Whidbey Realty Company. Located just off Maxwelton Beach, tucked into a stand of thick pine trees, the house itself reminded Madison of something from a Thomas Kinkade painting—romantic to the point of being whimsical. Built of redbrick and almost completely covered in ivy, the house was more than fifty years old. But it had always been well-loved and well-maintained, and the previous owners had done a fabulous job with the garden. The garage, which was detached, resembled an old carriage house and had been converted some years ago into a sort of minicottage.

"Hey? Where's my girl?" she called again, putting her briefcase next to the hall tree.

This time the television went off and Brianna came running, clutching Elizabeth, her stuffed rabbit, in one arm. "Mommy, you're home!"

"Yes, sweetie, I'm home." Madison gave her daughter a tight squeeze. "I'm sorry I had to be away. Grandma needed me. And then I had to swing by the office to pick up all the paperwork I didn't get around to today."

"Why couldn't I go with you to see Grandma? She loves it when I come to visit. And Elizabeth misses her."

"You and Elizabeth see her at least once a week, kiddo, and you weren't out of school yet," Madison said. But she wouldn't have taken Brianna to the Sunset Funeral Home and Memorial Park even if she'd been available. Madison tried to shield her daughter as much as possible from the taint of her grandfather's legacy.

Joanna Stapley appeared behind Brianna, toting a backpack. "Your timing's good," she said. "I just finished my homework."

"Perfect." Madison gave her a grateful smile and dug through her purse for the money to pay her. "Did anyone call while I was gone?"

"You had an ad call on the rental place."

"An ad call?" Brianna echoed. "What's an ad call?"

Madison shook her head. Her daughter was only six years old, but nothing slipped past her. "I'm trying to rent out the carriage house. Did the caller leave her name?" she asked Joanna.

"It was a he."

"Oh." For safety reasons, Madison had been hoping for a female tenant. But at this point, she knew she'd take anyone with good credit and solid references.

"What does it mean to rent out the carriage house?" Brianna asked.

"It means someone else will live there," Madison said. "Why?"

To help her financially. When she'd purchased the house and her business, she'd planned for the eight months it would take her to learn what she needed to know and get her broker's license. But she hadn't expected business to be so slow once she actually took over. And she'd already lost her top agent, which meant she was down to three. It wasn't going to be easy to survive if the real estate market didn't pick up.

"Because it might be fun to have some company once in a while, don't you think?" she said to Brianna, even though company was really the last thing Madison wanted. She'd dealt with enough curious strangers to last her a lifetime.

Brianna scrunched up her face as though she wasn't quite sure about company, either, but Madison was more interested in what Joanna had to say. Danny had made some comments that led her to believe he and Leslie might sue for custody of Brianna *again*. Madison wanted to be ready for him. She needed to save what little money she had left from the divorce for a good attorney.

"Did he leave his name and number?" she asked.

Joanna frowned as she tried to remember. "Dwight… Sanderson, I think. His number's on the fridge."

"Good. I'm having trouble finding a tenant. Everyone wants to come for a visit, but the ferry can take as long as two hours, so we're not exactly in a prime location for people who work on the mainland."

"This guy definitely sounds interested."

"Thanks."

"No problem. If you need me again, just call my cell." The door slammed behind Joanna, then Madison heard the distinctive rattle of her Volkswagen bug as she pulled out of the drive.

"Dwight Sanderson," Madison mumbled to herself, heading straight to the kitchen.

"I don't want a man to live in the carriage house, Mommy," Brianna complained, trailing after her. "That's where you draw, and me and Elizabeth play."

"It's nice to have the extra room, but we can do without it," she replied.

"Daddy said we live in a closet."

Daddy doesn't know everything, Madison wanted to say, but she bit her tongue. "Our house isn't as big as his, but I like it here, don't you?"

Brianna nodded enthusiastically. "This is a cottage for princesses."

Hearing her own words come back at her from the day they'd moved in, Madison smiled. "Right. And we're princesses, so it's ideal."

"Will the man who moves in be a prince?" she asked.

Madison stared down at the Post-it note Joanna had stuck on the fridge, and thought about her father, her two half brothers and her ex-husband. She hadn't met very many princes in her life. She was beginning to believe they didn't exist.

"I doubt it," she said, and picked up the phone.

CHAPTER THREE

CALEB STOOD in the antique-filled living room of his parents' white Victorian, staring out the window at Guemes Channel and the wooded island beyond as he wondered what he was going to try next. He'd already spent three days doing everything he could think of to dig up some kind of lead on Susan. But he'd had no luck at all. Along with the police and the private investigator hired by Holly's parents, he and Holly had talked to Susan's friends, neighbors and work associates. They'd visited nightclub after nightclub with Susan's picture and checked her bank account again.

Still they'd come up empty.

"Holly called while you were in the shower," his mother said from the doorway.

Caleb glanced over his shoulder. Justine Trovato was in her early sixties, but she looked at least ten years younger. Today she'd pinned up her white hair and was wearing a tasteful pair of brown slacks and a silky blouse, with pearls at her neck and ears.

"If she calls back, tell her I need to do a few things on my own today," he said.

"If she calls back? Aren't you going to respond to her message? She thought you might need a ride somewhere."

Caleb didn't want to talk to Holly. They'd lost their tempers yesterday while canvassing the apartment building, and she'd stormed off for a couple of hours. She came back when she'd cooled off, but they were both pretty tense. He thought they could use some time apart. Which was the story of their whole relationship. "I'll rent a car."

"You know you can take my Cadillac." Justine moved into the room to straighten a doily, and Caleb immediately recognized the lavender fragrance she'd worn since he was small.

"I don't want to put you out. I don't really know my schedule."

"I'm sure I could live without a car for the day. Your father's out back tinkering in his shed. He could drive me in his little pickup if I need to go somewhere. Or there's always your sister."

Tamara, Caleb's older sister, lived next door with her husband and twin boys in a home his parents had helped them buy. "I appreciate the offer, Mom, but I'll feel more mobile if I have a car of my own."

"If it makes you more comfortable, dear."

More comfortable? Caleb wasn't feeling very comfortable about anything. He'd already spent far more time than he'd hoped it would take to find Susan—and he wasn't any closer than the day he'd arrived in Seattle.

She'll turn up.... He'd told Holly that when she first called him. But those words seemed terribly glib now. He was beginning to think that if Susan did turn up, she'd turn up dead. Otherwise they would've found some trace of her.

"Where are you planning to go?" his mother asked.

"I spoke to Detective Gibbons this morning and—"

"Oh, he called here yesterday saying he'd received a message from you."

"He got hold of me on my cell."

"Can he help?" His parents were as worried about Susan as he was. They'd met her at his wedding—the second time, they'd eloped—and had seen her at a few family functions since.

"He doesn't know much about Susan's case. It's not his to worry about."

"Then why did you contact him?"

"He worked on the Sandpoint Strangler task force with me."

"Those poor women." His mother shuddered. "But you're not interested in the Sandpoint Strangler anymore, are you? I thought you put that book aside."

Caleb had always been interested in the Sandpoint Strangler. Probably because he'd been brand-new to the police department when the killings first started, so he'd followed them from the very beginning. The Sandpoint Strangler was the biggest case he ever worked, too, and the most frustrating. He felt as though they'd come within inches of unraveling the whole mystery—only to have Ellis Purcell check out before they could hit pay dirt. When the killings stopped and the case went cold, the task force disbanded and the police naturally changed their focus to finding those rapists and murderers who were still living and breathing and capable of violence. Caleb had given up the search then, too. But he'd never stopped wondering how, exactly, the strange Mr. Purcell had managed to kill so many women and dump their bodies in such public places without leaving more of a trail. He'd since done several books about murderers: on Angel Maturino Resendiz, who was convicted of murdering a Houston woman but was linked by confessions and evidence to at least twelve other killings nationwide. On Robert L. Yates, Jr., who admitted to fifteen murders, and Aileen Wuornos, a female serial killer convicted of murdering six men while working as a prostitute along highways in central Florida. Or Jeffrey Dahmer, who'd been convicted of seventeen homicides, most in Milwaukee. Caleb had written several other books, as well, mostly isolated cases where a husband killed his wife for the insurance, or a wife killed the man who'd been cheating on her. Whoever did the killing always took a significant misstep somewhere.

But not Ellis Purcell.

"Holly told me something at the airport that's bothered me ever since," he said.

"What's that?" his mother asked.

"Ellis Purcell's grave was disturbed the night before I arrived."

"I read that in the paper."

"I'm wondering how whoever it was found out where he was buried."

His mother twisted the clasp of the necklace she was wearing around to the back. "Maybe someone in the family let it slip."

"Maybe," he said, jingling the change in the pocket of his chinos. But when he remembered Madison Lieberman and her mother, and how staunchly they'd supported Ellis throughout the whole affair, he doubted they'd revealed anything at all.

THAT AFTERNOON Caleb pulled his rental car, a silver-and-black convertible Mustang, in front of 433 Old Beachview Road, the small brick house that corresponded with the address Detective Gibbons had given him for Madison Lieberman. Then he bent his head to look at the place through the passenger-side window.

It was small but charming, not unlike Langley, the closest town, which boasted the highest density of bed-and-breakfasts, country inns and guest cottages in the state.

An arched entry covered with primroses partially concealed the front windows. But he didn't see activity anywhere, and there weren't any cars in the drive. Chances were Madison wasn't home.

The dull-gray mist that shrouded the island made it seem much later than midafternoon. Caleb glanced at the digital clock on his dash to see that it was just after three, close to the time school let out, and wondered if he should wait. When he'd still been researching her father's case a couple of years ago, Madison had been working as a Realtor and living in a house not far from Bill Gates's mansion on Mercer Island. But Detective Gibbons had told him this morning that she and her husband had split and Danny Lieberman had bought her out. Now she owned a small real estate company with office space only a few miles away, in Clinton.

Caleb parked next to a stand of pine trees and got out to have a look around. He'd never approached Madison Lieberman in person before. When he was an officer on the task force, he was new enough that he'd been relegated to the work least likely to bring him in contact with her. And since he'd quit the department and started writing full-time, he'd seen too many news clips of Madison turning her face resolutely away from the camera, read too many comments spoken in defense of her father, to harbor any illusions that she might be willing to cooperate with him. But, using his pseudonym, he *had* sent her, as well as Danny, several letters over the years. Danny had responded a time or two, but it quickly became apparent that he didn't have the answers Caleb needed. Madison had finally replied by threatening him with a restraining order if he so much as tried to speak with her.

He hoped she didn't feel quite so strongly about the issue now that her father was dead.

Shoving his keys in his pocket, he strode up the walk. The yard was generally well-kept but had once known a more diligent hand; he could tell that right away. A couple of hummingbird feeders and a birdbath sat in a meticulously tended herb garden off to the right, but the trees and shrubs everywhere else were overgrown and the grass was a little too long. What with being a single mom and trying to run a small business, Madison probably didn't have the time or money to maintain what had been in place before she came here. No doubt money was the reason for the For Rent sign Caleb saw attached to the small cottage at the side of the main house.

For rent... He hesitated briefly at the arch before changing direction and heading toward what had once been a garage. It was renovated now. Through a mullioned window exactly like those in the main house, he could see a studio apartment, complete with kitchen-living room, a single bedroom and a bath. A brown wicker couch with giant yellow-and-blue cushions faced a television in the large main room, which had a wooden floor and lots of rugs. A chair that matched the couch and the drapes sat off to the side, next to a rack of magazines. White cupboards lined the kitchen in the corner, which contained a round wooden table with plaid place mats in the same blue and yellow as the couch and drapes.

He could see only a slice of the bedroom and bath through two open doorways, but he could tell the bedroom was furnished with a four-poster bed, a fluffy down comforter and more pillows—these in red, white and blue. The bathroom had an old-style sink with brass fixtures.

He liked the place, he realized. It had the sort of country charm his mother had taught him to appreciate.

Taking a narrow path that led through the herb garden, he crossed over to the main house, where he saw a similar decorating theme. Madison's home wasn't quite as light and airy as the garage, certainly not as new, but it had a warm, cozy atmosphere.

The sound of a car pulling up made Caleb jerk away from the window and start toward the drive.

A petite woman he recognized as Madison Lieberman jumped out of a Toyota Camry as soon as she cut the engine. "Oh, my gosh! I never dreamed you'd beat me here," she exclaimed, obviously flushed from hurrying. A thin, strawberry-blond girl got out much more slowly, clinging to an old stuffed rabbit. "The ferry must be moving quickly today."

Caleb hadn't taken the ferry. He'd come south over Deception Pass from Fidalgo Island, which was due north. But he didn't correct her. He was enjoying the warmth of this reception—especially when he compared it to the "Get off my property" he'd most likely receive the moment he identified himself as the crime writer who'd contacted her before.

"Did you peek in the windows?" she asked.

He cleared his throat. "Actually, I did."

"I think you'd be very comfortable here."

Madison was much more attractive in person. Maybe it was because this was the first time Caleb had ever seen her smile. Only five foot four or so, she had a gymnast's body, which made him believe she stayed active, and almond-shaped brown eyes. Her hair was auburn—not his favorite color—but it looked soft and swayed gently around her chin in a stylish cut. And other than a few freckles sprinkled across her nose, her complexion was smooth and slightly golden.

"I know you're worried about privacy," she was saying, "but we'd never bother you. It's quiet here."

The little girl with Madison glared at him. He could

definitely see a family resemblance, mostly through the mouth. They both had full, pouty lips. "Is this your daughter?" he asked.

"It is. Say hello, Brianna," Madison prompted.

Brianna said nothing. She folded her arms around her stuffed toy and jutted out her sharp little chin.

"She's not happy about renting out the carriage house," Madison explained. "She called her father last night and he told her—" she waved her hand "—oh, never mind. I've got the key right here. Why don't we take a look inside?"

Caleb realized that now was probably a good time to explain that he wasn't who she thought he was. But he didn't see any need to hurry. It certainly wouldn't hurt to catch a glimpse of what Madison Lieberman was really like. That could only help him understand her family and, by extension, her father.

"Sounds good," he said, following her to what she'd labeled the carriage house.

Brianna glanced back at him several times, as if she thought she could scare him away with her dark looks. But he merely smiled and, when Madison swung the door wide, stepped past her.

The place smelled like an expensive candle store, Caleb decided as he began to notice several things he'd missed before—the vase of fresh wildflowers on the kitchen table, the small shower in the bathroom he'd been unable to see from the window, the mahogany entertainment center in the bedroom that housed another television.

"You know, from your voice, I thought you'd be older," Madison said as she watched him look around.

Opening what appeared to be a pantry, he pretended not to hear her. "How soon did you want to get someone in here?"

"As you can see, it's ready. I've had a phone installed and everything. You could move in tomorrow."

The hope in her voice and the modest car she was driving reinforced Caleb's impression that, considering Danny Lieberman's wealth, she hadn't managed to get a very good divorce settlement. "How long has it been on the market?"

"A little over a month. But I've lowered the price." She tucked a strand of hair behind one ear in a self-conscious movement. "I'm only asking eight hundred."

He nodded and walked back into the living room, wondering how to turn the conversation to her father—while feeling a peculiar reluctance to do so. "This place is small but…nice," he said.

Brianna was sitting on the couch with her stuffed rabbit and had spread several sheets of paper on the coffee table in front of her.

"These are very good," he said when he realized they were sketches, and that she meant for him to see them. "Who drew them?"

"My mom."

He studied the first, a pencil drawing of an old, gnarled hand gripping a cane, then the second, a set of clasped hands—one male, the other female—and the last, an intriguing pair of eyes. Were they Ellis Purcell's eyes? Caleb could have sworn they were. They seemed to hold all kinds of dark secrets.

He wondered if Madison knew those dark secrets, and if he'd ever be able to get them out of her.

"Brianna, what are you doing with my sketches?" Madison asked, coming up from behind.

"I think she's proud of you," Caleb said. "And it looks as though she has reason to be. You're very talented."

Madison quickly gathered up her drawings. "Thanks,

but it's just a hobby.'' After setting them aside, she clasped her hands in a businesslike manner. ''So, do you like it? Do you want the place?''

He was about to explain that he hadn't really come to rent the carriage house when there was a knock on the door.

Brianna grabbed her stuffed rabbit and ran to open it. A tall, white-haired gentleman who looked to be in his late fifties stood on the stoop. ''Is your mommy here?''

Brianna turned expectantly, and Madison approached the door. ''Can I help you?''

''I'm Dwight Sanderson.''

''*Who?*'' she said.

Caleb watched the man's face cloud with confusion at Madison's startled reaction. ''I spoke with you a few days ago and then again this morning, remember? I'm here to see the house.''

''But—''

''I'm afraid you're too late,'' Caleb interrupted, joining them at the door. ''It's already taken.''

Madison blinked at him in surprise, and Caleb felt a good measure of surprise himself. What the hell did he think he was doing?

''I thought you were… Who *are* you?'' Madison asked, turning to him.

''Caleb Trovato.'' He stuck out his hand, fairly confident she'd never recognize his name. He wrote under the pseudonym Thomas L. Wagner, his mother's grandfather's name, and had signed the letters he'd sent her and Danny the same way, since they'd been written in a professional capacity.

''Caleb Trovato,'' she repeated, hesitantly accepting his handshake. ''If you called, my baby-sitter forgot to write it down.''

Her fingers felt slim and dainty, and she was close enough that he could smell a hint of her perfume. "I didn't call. I just happened to see the sign as I was driving by. I actually live in San Francisco, but business has brought me here."

"For how long?"

"That remains to be seen."

"Oh." She glanced from him to Sanderson. "So is either of you willing to sign a lease?"

"I told you on the phone that I can't commit long-term," Sanderson said. "My situation is too tentative right now."

"I'll sign a lease," Caleb said, even though he knew he was crazy to offer. He'd recently furnished his new condo in San Francisco and planned to return there. But he couldn't miss this opportunity. Maybe now he'd finally be able to crack the Sandpoint Strangler case and achieve some closure—for himself, the public, the force and, most importantly, the families of the victims. Maybe he could even ease the foreboding that had settled over him since he'd learned of Susan's disappearance. If the deceased Purcell was really the Sandpoint Strangler, she certainly stood a better chance of being found alive. Random murders were rare. Most homicides of women were the result of a love relationship gone bad and, according to Holly, Susan hadn't been involved with anyone for over three years. She'd only been seeing Lance, the guy she was dating before she disappeared, for a couple of months.

In any case, Caleb could look for Susan from here just as easily as his parents' place on Fidalgo, and simply buy out the lease when he was ready to head home.

"Do you have any pets?" she asked.

"Would that be a problem?"

"Not necessarily. One dog or cat would be fine. I'm

not sure I'd be happy with a whole houseful of Doberman pinschers.''

"No animals."

"Not even a hamster?"

"Not even a hamster."

"What about kids?" she asked.

He cocked an eyebrow. "You don't want a houseful of those, either?" He could understand it if they were all as sour as her daughter.

"I'd expect you to make sure they don't trample the flowerbeds."

"The flowerbeds are safe," he said. "I don't have any kids."

"Fine." She looked as though she wanted to smile but wouldn't allow it. "What kind of business brings you to Seattle, Mr. Trovato?"

He searched his mind, trying to come up with something that wouldn't give him away. "I'm a small-business consultant," he said, because it was the first thing he could think of.

"So you're regularly employed?"

"Definitely."

"And how long a lease are you willing to sign? A year?"

"Six months," he replied, letting her know by his tone that she wasn't getting any more out of him.

"And when would you like to move in?"

"Tomorrow morning, if that's okay with you."

"That's fine." Now she did smile, right before she turned back to Sanderson. "I've got your phone number, Mr. Sanderson," she said. "If Mr. Trovato's references don't check out, I'll give you a call."

Sanderson didn't appear too pleased with the situation, but there wasn't much he could do. Madison followed him out, probably to apologize for the wasted trip. Brianna stayed behind, still eyeing Caleb warily.

"You don't want me to live here?" he asked.

Her bottom lip came out. "No."

"Why not?"

"Because this is *our* house. My mommy draws here, and me and Elizabeth dance."

"I won't be staying long," he admitted. Then he remembered that Madison had started to tell him something out in the drive. "What did your dad have to say about the idea last night?"

Brianna tucked her stuffed bunny protectively under one slender arm. "He said you should never rent out part of your house."

"Why not?"

"Because you never know who might be moving in with you."

CHAPTER FOUR

POUNDING ON THE FRONT door dragged Madison from the depths of sleep.

She glanced, bleary-eyed, at the alarm clock on her nightstand. It was only eleven o'clock. Generally she wasn't in bed so early on a Friday night. She stayed up on weekends, handling paperwork, e-mail, or working on the computer. But this hadn't been a regular week. Ever since she'd found that box under her mother's house, she'd been so tired it felt as though someone had tied ten-pound weights to each limb. She'd climbed into bed a mere thirty minutes ago but was already sleeping like the dead.

Like the dead? Considering the recent disturbance of her father's grave, that seemed rather chilling. She rubbed her arms as she shivered and groped for her robe. The knocking continued.

"Mommy?" Brianna's confused voice came to her from the other room.

"Yes, honey?"

"Is it morning-time?"

"Not yet."

"Who's here?"

"I'm sure it's just our new renter. He probably can't find the remote for his television or doesn't know how to run the dishwasher or something." Madison tied the belt to her robe. "And he didn't bother to notice that our lights are out," she added under her breath.

"We shouldn't have let him move in," Brianna said, as if this incident proved the point she'd been trying to make from the start.

Brianna sounded like an echo of Danny. Sometimes Brianna also behaved a great deal like her father. Today she'd pouted and glowered at Mr. Trovato all afternoon while he was carrying in his belongings, which were rather sparse, along with a few groceries. "Try to go back to sleep, honey," she said.

Bang, bang, bang. The knocking was impatient. Demanding.

How could Brianna sleep with all that noise? "Give me a minute," Madison called out. As she stuffed her feet into the frumpy "housewife" slippers Danny had given her a year ago last Christmas, she pictured the diamond tennis bracelet he'd presented to his new wife the day she'd announced her pregnancy. After dropping out of college to finish putting him through school, Madison had come away from their seven-year marriage with probably a fifth of Danny's net worth, a real estate license and a pair of ugly house shoes, while Leslie was living in Madison's old mansion and dripping in diamonds. Somehow it didn't seem fair. But Madison didn't want Danny if he couldn't stand by her "for better or worse"—although she hated the fact that her daughter had lost the firm foundation of having both parents in the home.

"I'm coming," she said when she neared the door. "Who is it?"

There was no answer, but the banging didn't subside. It came in loud, staccato bursts that grated on Madison's nerves.

"Who is it?" she repeated more insistently, and

snapped on the porch light so she could peer through the peephole.

It definitely wasn't Caleb Trovato. She could see that right away. Mr. Trovato was probably six foot four, two hundred ten pounds of well-defined muscle. He was the kind of man who could turn a woman's head from forty feet away. This person was skinny to the point of looking emaciated. His hair was almost as dark as Mr. Trovato's, though not nearly as thick. And—

Her visitor moved and she caught a glimpse of his face. Oh, God! It was Johnny.

Unlatching the safety chain, Madison opened the door for her half brother. "Johnny! What are you doing here?"

He sniffed as though he had allergies and shifted on the balls of his feet, regarding her with red-rimmed eyes. Behind him, headlights from some kind of car bore down on her, but the engine was off.

"I need a few bucks," he said, point-blank. "Can you help me out?"

Johnny and Tye had come to live with Madison and her parents for the first time when Johnny was fifteen and Tye was sixteen. From the beginning, they'd been in and out of trouble with her parents, the school, even the authorities, and didn't bother much with a little sister who was only eight. But for the eighteen months Johnny was living at the house, Madison had liked him a lot better than Tye, who was far more remote. She'd sort of idealized Johnny, because he did sometimes do her a kind deed. He'd let her play with the stray cats he brought home occasionally—before her mother made him turn them loose again. He'd share whatever candy filled his pockets. Tye ignored her completely.

"Are you alone?" she hedged, caught completely off

guard. Last she'd heard, Johnny was supposed to be in prison for another three years.

"Yeah."

"It doesn't look like you're alone." She shaded her eyes against the headlights and squinted, making out a shadowy figure sitting in the driver's seat of what was probably an old Buick Skylark.

"So I'm with a friend. Does it matter?" More nervous energy. More restless movements. From the way he was acting, he had to be on something.

Evidently there wasn't much about Johnny's lifestyle that had changed over the years. "When did you get out?"

He sniffled again. "Couple weeks ago, I guess."

He was so strung out, Madison wasn't sure he could tell one day from the next. Maybe he *hadn't* been released at all; maybe he'd escaped, and whoever was waiting in the car was his accomplice.

She tightened her robe, wondering what to do. If she gave Johnny money, he'd only use it to buy more drugs. But she had to help him. Except for Tye, she was his only family. And she felt guilty for having had the love and support of their father and for having a good mother when theirs was so neglectful and abusive.

"I've got twenty bucks," she said.

"Is that all?"

"That's all."

"Then how 'bout a drink? You got a beer for your brother?"

Madison hesitated. Johnny had his better moments, but he could also be unpredictable and moody. And, for all she knew, the person waiting in the car was another ex-convict. But Johnny *was* her half brother and he'd never done anything truly threatening to her in the past.

"Come in and I'll get you a Coke." She opened the door wider, to admit him, then locked it against whoever was waiting in the car.

"When was the last time you ate?" she asked as she led him to the kitchen.

He didn't answer. He was too busy staring at something in the hall.

Madison turned to see what that something was, and felt her stomach drop when she realized Brianna was standing there. "Go back to bed, sweetheart," she said. She didn't want her daughter around Johnny. The fact that he had a drug habit didn't necessarily make him dangerous. But they hadn't spent any time together in years, and Madison didn't feel she knew him all that well anymore.

"Who's *he?*" Brianna asked, peering at Johnny with the disdain she'd practiced on Caleb Trovato.

Johnny hooked his thumbs in the pockets of his filthy, tattered jeans and smiled. "Don't you remember me, pip-squeak? I saw you once, just before your grandpa blew his brains out."

"Johnny, don't," Madison said.

"Mommy, how do you blow your brains out?" Brianna asked.

Madison sent Johnny a look that was meant to silence him. "Never mind, honey. Grandpa went to heaven. You know that."

Johnny gave a disbelieving snort when she said "heaven," but Madison ignored him. Brianna was too little to understand everything that had happened, and she saw no reason to explain the gritty details, at least, not while Brianna was so young.

"You never could stand the truth," he said, shaking his head.

"There's no need to upset her. She's only six," Madison replied. But she didn't blame Johnny for being bitter. He'd been the one to find Ellis, and everyone knew Ellis had meant it to be that way. Just before Madison and her mother went on an all-day shopping trip, he'd called Johnny and said he needed to talk to him.

A few hours later, Johnny had found what was left of their father in Ellis's workshop.

"She doesn't look upset to me," he said.

Brianna was clinging to Elizabeth while giving him a challenging glare. "My name isn't pipsqueak," she told him. "And I don't think my father would like you very much."

Horrified, Madison gaped at her. "Brianna!"

"It's *true*."

"I don't care if it is," she said. "Johnny's your uncle. You're not to be rude to him or anyone else. Now please go back to bed."

Brianna didn't budge, so Madison gave her a frown designed to let her know there'd be serious consequences if she didn't obey. Finally, she turned and walked resolutely down the hall.

"I'll be there shortly to tuck you in," Madison called after her.

Johnny's twitching seemed to grow more extreme. "You're gonna have your hands full with that kid."

"Brianna's usually very sweet. It's just been lately, after I get her back from her father's, that I've run into these attitude problems." Anxious for Johnny to leave, she handed him a can of Coke. "Sorry I don't have any beer. I don't drink it."

He accepted what she offered him. "You wrote me about your divorce," he said.

"I wasn't sure you got that letter. You never answered it." He'd never answered any of her letters.

"I wanted to believe you were still living the good life." He said the words accusingly, as though she'd had some choice in the matter.

"No one lives a fairy tale." She leaned against the counter. "Does Tye know you're out?"

The can hissed as Johnny popped the top and took a long pull. "I went by his place a couple days ago. No one was home."

"His wife's been visiting her mother. Maybe he drove to Spokane to get her and the kids."

"Visiting her mom?" Johnny chuckled, scratching his shoulder, then his elbow, moving, always moving. "You mean she left him. Again."

Again? This was the first Madison had ever heard of any serious marital strife between Tye and Sharon. "Why would she leave?"

"They haven't been getting along."

"Are you sure?" she said, disappointed that Tye hadn't trusted her enough to share this information with her.

"You know Tye has a temper. They've been on and off for years." Johnny downed the rest of the soda, wiped his mouth on his sleeve and tossed the empty can toward the garbage. When he missed, it hit the floor with a rattle, and Madison quickly bent to pick it up.

"About that money…" he said.

She glanced down the hall to see Brianna poking her head out of her bedroom, and knew she needed to get her half brother on his way. "Here you go," she said, handing him a twenty.

He frowned at the bill. "You sure that's all you've got?"

She told herself to remain firm. But when she took in the state of his clothing and the old tennis shoes on his feet, she immediately began to second-guess her decision not to give him more. He looked so needy, so desperate. She hated watching him ruin his life. "Are you okay, Johnny?"

He blinked at her as though surprised by the question. "Does it matter?"

"Of course." She searched through the bottom of her purse. "Maybe I can scrounge together another few dollars."

"Thanks."

"No problem." She gave him an additional fistful of change, and he started for the door.

She should have breathed a sigh of relief and let him go, but something made her call him back. "Johnny?"

He peered over his shoulder at her. "Yeah?"

Except in general terms, Madison had never spoken to her brothers about the crimes their father had been accused of committing. Neither Johnny nor Tye had good feelings toward Ellis, so Madison had never expected them to be supportive. Her brothers were too busy trying to recover from their unhappy childhoods to worry about what was happening to their father—a father who'd let them down so badly. But she suddenly felt the need to talk to Johnny now, before he disappeared for another five years.

"Do you think he really did it?" she asked softly.

For a moment, Johnny looked more lucid than she'd seen him in years. "You mean Dad?"

She nodded. She longed to tell him what she'd found beneath the house. She had to tell *someone*. The burden of keeping the secret was too heavy. And there was no one else....

He stared at the floor for several seconds. "He did it."

"How do you know?"

"I don't want to talk about it," he said.

"You never heard or saw anything…out of the ordinary, did you?"

He was moving toward the door again. "I wasn't around."

"You showed up every once in a while, for short periods of time," she said, following him.

"I never saw anything."

Madison wished she could erase from her mind the image of opening that locket in the dank atmosphere of the crawl space. "Did you hear what happened to Dad's grave?" she asked as he opened the door and stepped outside.

He turned, scowling at her. "I don't want to know."

"But—"

"Look at me, Maddy," he said, calling her by the nickname the kids in the neighborhood had given her when she was young.

She met his gaze.

"You see what I am," he said. "I can't help you. I can't even help myself. You want a shoulder to cry on, call Tye. He's the one who never flinched, no matter how bad it got."

Then he hurried to the car, the motor revved and he was gone.

CALEB LEANED CLOSER to the house to avoid being seen by the men in the Buick Skylark. Who were they? And what did they want? Judging by the late hour, the rattle-trap condition of their car and the "drifter" appearance of the guy who'd gone inside Madison's house, they weren't insurance salesmen.

He muttered the license plate number to himself a few more times, planning to have Detective Gibbons run a check on it in the morning, and started back to the cottage.

When he'd heard the car pull up, he'd been in bed watching television, and hadn't bothered to put on anything but a pair of jeans. It was chilly to be walking around without a shirt and shoes. But he hesitated when he passed Madison's window and glanced in to find her sitting at the kitchen table, her head in her hands. If he wasn't mistaken, she was crying. Even if she wasn't, there was something so weary, so hopeless about her posture....

Was she okay? His natural reluctance to intrude on her privacy warred with the desire to capitalize on a golden opportunity. After all, he'd moved in to get close to her.

Hurrying to the cottage house, he scribbled down the license plate number, put on a T-shirt and a pair of shoes and jogged back.

It took several seconds for her to answer his knock. When she finally came to the door, her cheeks were dry, but her eyes were red and damp.

Caleb studied her for a moment, wishing she were middle-aged and frumpy. That she was single and attractive only complicated matters. "Is something wrong?" he asked.

There was an insincere smile on her face and, when she spoke, her voice carried the high pitch of false cheer. "No, of course not. Why?"

He jerked his head toward the drive. "Those guys who were here. They didn't look very reputable. I thought maybe I should check on you."

"Oh." Her smile faltered. "That was just my brother Johnny."

Johnny Purcell. Caleb had come across that name years ago while he was researching Ellis. As a matter of fact, he'd interviewed Johnny once, in prison. But Johnny must have lost a lot of weight since then. Caleb hadn't recognized him.

"I know he doesn't look like much," she said. "But he's basically harmless. Fortunately, he doesn't come around very often. I'm sorry if he woke you."

"It's no problem. I wasn't sleeping. Is he in some sort of trouble?"

"No."

An awkward silence ensued, during which Caleb racked his brain for some other way to learn more about Johnny's visit.

Madison spoke first. "Did you get settled?"

"For the most part." He grinned, hoping to charm her. "I loaded up on the important things—peanut butter and bread."

"Well, if there's anything you need, a cup of sugar or an egg or whatever, feel free to ask."

"I appreciate that." He shoved his hands in the pockets of his jeans, wishing she'd invite him in for a cup of coffee. Other than moving onto the property, he hadn't considered *how* he was going to get close to Madison. Especially when she seemed so remote.

"Is Brianna asleep?" he asked.

"She's in bed. I don't know that she's asleep."

"I realize she feels I'm encroaching on her space, but with any luck she'll get used to having me around, don't you think?"

"I hope so," Madison said. "I know space shouldn't be an issue. She's got plenty of space. Especially at her father's. He lives in an eight-thousand-square-foot house, complete with a giant water fountain worthy of a casino."

"Sounds…ostentatious."

"It is." She finally gave him a genuine smile. "I hated living there. It felt like a mausoleum." She folded her arms, unwittingly revealing a fair amount of cleavage.

Caleb wished again that she was older, or significantly younger, or considerably overweight…

"Brianna's had a rough year," she was saying. "I'm guessing this is some sort of delayed reaction."

He pulled his attention away from the smooth skin of her breasts. "How long have you been divorced?"

"A little less than a year."

"It'll get easier."

"You sound as though you speak from experience."

"I went through a divorce two years ago." He didn't mention the first divorce. There'd been no one in between so it didn't count.

"I'm sorry."

"Don't be. Things are better now."

"They are for me, too," she said, but he didn't get the impression she really believed it.

Caleb considered being direct and simply asking if he could join her for a cup of coffee. With Susan missing, he felt the clock ticking. But he didn't dare come on too strong. If he frightened Madison or made her leery of him in any way, he'd only defeat his purpose.

"Well, thanks for checking on me," she said, and started backing up to close the door.

Caleb had no choice but to step off the porch. "Have a good night."

"You, too."

Reluctantly, he walked down the stone path that led to his new home, frustrated that he hadn't managed to wrangle any type of invitation out of her. Then he caught sight of her car. A nice car was important in the real estate business. He had no doubt that if she could afford it, she'd be driving a Mercedes instead of a Camry. "By the way," he said before she could close the door.

"Yes?"

"I'd like to hire someone to do my laundry and make me a few meals. I was wondering if you'd be interested."

"You're going to hire someone to cook and clean for you?"

He was if he could get her to take the job. "I'll be coming and going a lot."

"How much are you willing to pay?"

Caleb had always taken care of himself. He had no idea what such services should rightfully cost. But he wasn't afraid of being generous. He thought that helping her out financially might ease his conscience about having ulterior motives in befriending her. "Six hundred dollars a month sound fair?"

She coughed. "That's almost as much as you're paying in rent."

Evidently he'd been a little too generous. "That would include the price of groceries, of course."

Her teeth sank into the soft flesh of her bottom lip, distracting him again. "What constitutes 'a few meals'?"

"Dinner every night, unless you have other plans, and breakfast on the weekends." For a moment, he thought she'd refuse, and wished he'd asked her for less of a time commitment. She was trying to run a business and already seemed harried. But he needed to gain her confidence quickly. "I'm flexible, though. So if you think that's too much…"

"What kind of menu?" she asked.

"You can choose."

"Do you want me to bring it over to you?"

"If you'd prefer. But if you're open to company, I'd rather not eat alone."

She hesitated for another moment. "All right," she said at last. "I'm already cooking for Brianna and me. It won't take long to add an extra plate for dinner and do a few more loads of laundry each week. I think it might help Brianna adjust to having you here if she gets to know you a little.''

''My laundry isn't difficult,'' he told her. ''Mostly jeans and T-shirts.''

''Sounds as though you live a pretty easy life, Mr. Trovato,'' she said.

''Call me Caleb.''

''When would you like me to start, Caleb?''

He smiled as he moved away, feeling a sense of victory. It was only a matter of time before he knew everything Madison did. ''How about tomorrow?''

CHAPTER FIVE

"CALEB, WHERE have you been? I've been calling your cell for the past hour."

Holly. Again. Between Caleb's run to his folks' house for his things that morning, and his trip to the grocery store in the afternoon, he'd met her at the university and helped pass out flyers with Susan's picture and description. Every time his ex-wife had called since then, he'd jumped for the phone, thinking she'd heard from someone who'd seen Susan. Shortly before Johnny had pulled up outside, Caleb had finally realized she was just stressed and worried and wanted to go over the same things she'd been saying all day. Only he'd already done everything he could until morning and didn't want to hold her hand anymore. He was comfortable in bed, once again flipping through satellite channels on television and enjoying the solitude.

"It's after midnight, Holly," he said. "Can't this wait until we get together in the morning?"

"No, it can't," she replied. "Someone called me about the flyer a little while ago."

At last! Caleb hit the off button and sat up, giving Holly his full attention. "Who was it?"

"I'll tell you all about it when I get there. I have something to show you."

"*Show* me?"

"I'm on my way."

"Wait, I'm not staying at my folks' place," he said before she could hang up.

"You're not?"

"No, I rented a small house."

Silence. Eventually she asked, "Why would you rent a place? You could've stayed here for free."

"Holly, we're divorced."

"I know that, Caleb. It isn't as though I'm asking you to sleep with me. I only offered to put you up for a few weeks. You're helping me, after all. I feel it's the least I can do."

"There's no need," he said. "I'm fine where I am."

"And where is that?"

"Whidbey Island."

"Whidbey! What made you move there?"

"It's closer to the mainland."

"If you wanted to be close to the mainland, why didn't you rent an apartment *on* the mainland?"

Caleb considered telling Holly that he was renting from Ellis Purcell's daughter, but decided not to. He didn't want her badgering him for information until he was ready to share it. Just because he *might* come across answers no one else had been able to glean didn't necessarily mean he would. It was possible that Madison was too secretive to let anything slip. It was also possible that she didn't know anything. But he was willing to bet against both of those possibilities. She'd been living with Ellis during his killing spree. At a minimum, she should be able to tell Caleb bits and pieces of conversation she'd overheard between her parents, whether her father was really at home when he'd claimed to be, whether she sometimes heard things go bump in the night, whether she ever saw him

move something heavy that just might have resembled a
dead body....

"This place is nice," he said instead.

"How much is it costing you?"

"It doesn't matter."

"Waste your money, then. I don't care," she said.
"You're so stubborn. I don't know why I married you
once, let alone twice."

He thought she might hang up in a huff, but she didn't.
"Are you going to give me directions?" she asked after
an extended silence.

A quick glance at the clock told him it was even later
than he'd realized. But she'd said she had something to
show him. "What do you have?" he asked.

"You'll see."

If she had a lead, he needed to know about it as soon
as possible. He told her how to find him. Then he got up,
dressed and put on some coffee.

Across the yard, he could see that the lights were still
on in Madison's house, and he wondered what she was
doing. Earlier, it had looked as though she carried the
weight of the world on her shoulders....

Guilt about masquerading as a random renter flickered
inside him. He could already tell Madison wasn't the ice
princess he'd assumed from her television interviews and
that one strongly worded letter. Her behavior wasn't
strange, either, like her father's. Actually, she seemed
pretty...normal. And there was no question she'd been
through a lot.

Leaning against the wall, he stared out the window at
her light. She might be nice. She might even be one of
the most attractive women he'd ever met—but being nice
and attractive didn't change the fact that the truth had to
be told.

MADISON COULDN'T SLEEP. She was tired yet wound up, and didn't dare take a sleeping pill, for several reasons. Brianna could wake up in the night. Johnny, or whoever had been with him, could come back. And she wasn't yet comfortable with having a stranger living on her property. Especially one who knew she and Brianna were alone. Caleb Trovato's credit references had checked out; he seemed like a pretty solid citizen. But still...

Pulling out her sketchpad, she sat at the kitchen table and began to draw. She had tons of paperwork to take care of. She needed to review the purchase offers her agents had generated in the past week. As their broker, she was liable for any legal repercussions if they made a mistake. She also needed to revise the independent contractor agreement she was having her agents sign when they came to work for her, decide whether or not she was going to hire the young woman she'd interviewed this afternoon, and review the lease for the new copier she was buying for the office. But she was too tense to delve into work-related matters tonight.

Because she couldn't forget Johnny, she drew his eyes. Because she was worried about Brianna, she drew her daughter's full lips. She even sketched Danny's angry brow—something that had come to symbolize their relationship. The scratch of her pencil and her intense focus usually eased the stress knotting the muscles in her back and neck. But nothing seemed to help tonight. She still felt as though she were walking a tightrope with the ground frighteningly far below.

Her eyes slid to her briefcase. The urgency to make her business successful was part of the problem. Sales weren't going nearly as well as she'd hoped when she'd purchased South Whidbey Realty. She knew she was crazy to be wasting time while Brianna was sleeping, but Madison simply couldn't face the work she'd brought home with her.

Flipping to a new page, she considered drawing her mother's hands. But anything to do with her mother reminded Madison of her father, and she didn't want to confront her doubts about him. Not right now. Not in the middle of the night with the clock on the wall ticking and the rest of the house so silent.

She sorted through the faces she'd seen lately: an obese woman with beautiful blond hair she'd met at Brianna's school; a wiry, angular man who'd just started doing the janitorial work at the office building where she leased space; a baby she'd seen at the mall. None interested her enough to attempt them. But the gruff old man who worked on the ferry seemed to have potential—

A car pulled into the drive, and Madison's heart began to race. Was Johnny back? What could he possibly want now?

Dropping her pencil, she went to the window, but the car that parked behind Caleb's Mustang didn't look anything like the one Johnny had been riding in earlier. This car was a late-model Honda. And the person getting out of it was a woman—a tall woman who wasn't approaching her house.

A moment later, Caleb Trovato's door opened and he stepped out under the eaves. His broad shoulders blocked most of the light spilling from the cottage behind him, but Madison could see that his visitor was blond and most likely very pretty. Was she a friend? A lover? Coming this late she could even be a call girl.

No, Caleb would have no need to hire a prostitute, Madison decided. He probably had more female attention than he knew what to do with. He was ruggedly handsome. More than that, he carried himself with the sort of beguiling indifference most women found so appealing.

Most women, but not Madison. She'd trusted her father. She'd trusted Danny. She would have trusted Johnny and Tye, except they'd never let her get close enough. For some reason, when it came to men, she wasn't a very good judge of character. Which meant she was better off alone.

Even if she *wanted* a new love interest, how could she get close to anyone while guarding her father's terrible secret?

"THIS IS A CUTE PLACE," Holly said.

Caleb stretched out on the couch and flipped on the television. "Thanks."

"How did you find it?"

"I stumbled across the For Rent sign."

"So you leased it?" She snapped her fingers. "Like that?"

"Pretty much." He waved to the chair at the end of the couch. "Sit down and show me what you've got."

She didn't move toward the chair. "If you didn't want to stay with your mother or me, why not get a hotel? That's what most people do."

"Does it matter?" he asked, trying to head her off. She'd brought up the Sandpoint Strangler a number of times and was already frightened that Susan's disappearance might be connected. He didn't want to fuel her fears by admitting he suspected the same thing. At least until he had more to go on than gut instinct and a few wild coincidences.

She shook her head as she gazed around. "I just never expected it."

He buzzed past a commercial for dandruff shampoo.

"Don't make a big deal out of it, Holly. Now I have a place of my own while I'm here. That's it."

"And the downside is you're paying by the week?"

"*Forget* the cottage."

At the irritation in his voice, she propped her hands on her hips and faced him. "Why'd I have to fall in love with you?"

Caleb had asked himself the same question about her, many times. She'd just been so…lost when he met her. And he'd always been a sucker for a woman down on her luck. He liked feeling needed, liked taking care of others. Unfortunately, she'd exploited that tendency to its fullest. "I wish I knew."

"I'll never understand you or what happened between us—"

"That's the beauty of being divorced," he interrupted. "We no longer have to analyze what's wrong with us. No more teary talks that carry on through the night. No more debilitating guilt. Surely you're as relieved as I am."

"But we loved each other."

Caleb scrubbed a hand over his jaw. "We just hated each other more."

"I never hated you," she said.

"God, Hol, would you let it go?" He blew out a sigh, hoping some of his frustration would go with it. "We couldn't be together for more than two days in a row. Now, do you have something on Susan or not?"

It took her a moment to regain control. But she managed to do so, for a change, and Caleb relaxed.

Leaving the remote control on the arm of the couch, he went to the refrigerator to get a beer. "Well?" he said when he'd popped the top and drunk almost half of it.

She finally sat down and stared at the television, probably so she wouldn't have to look at him. "I'm not sure if it'll tell us much in the end, but a woman named Jennifer Allred saw Susan the day after she and I had our nails done."

"Where?" He leaned one hip against the kitchen counter, enjoying the smooth taste of his Michelob Light and letting it siphon off some of the tension he'd been feeling only moments earlier.

"At a vegetarian pizza place not far from the university."

"She's sure it was Susan?"

Holly reached into her purse and withdrew a photograph. "She gave me this."

Surprised, Caleb left his beer on the counter and walked over to get a better look. "*How* did she give you this?" he asked. "I thought you said she *called* you."

"She did. Then she asked me to meet her on campus because she had some proof to give me."

"And you did it? Don't tell me you went there alone, Holly."

"What else was I supposed to do? Drag someone out of bed and coerce him or her into going with me? You weren't picking up."

He'd been outside creeping around, trying to figure out what was going on at Madison's—not the type of errand on which he wanted to carry a cell phone. "Twelve women, if you count Susan, have been snatched from that campus or the surrounding area! What were you thinking, meeting someone so late?"

"Oh, don't pretend you care about me," she said, coming right back at him. "If you cared, you never would've given up on me."

"Damn it, Holly, would you quit twisting the knife? I wanted to be there for you. I married you twice, remember? We aren't a good fit. I don't know how much more proof you need!'' He hadn't planned on shouting, but she always managed to snap the control that was sufficient for every other situation and relationship.

She stared at him for several seconds, her glare challenging enough to make him believe they were going to end up in another of their famous rows. She was probably going to start in on the miscarriage. She always used that as some sort of trump card, as if he hadn't felt the loss of their baby just as deeply.

Instead, she covered her eyes and shook her head, obviously backing down. "Look at the picture, okay?"

Caleb felt the anger drain out of him. No one made him as crazy as Holly did. But this wasn't about their marriages or their divorces. This was about Susan, he reminded himself, gazing down at the picture. "I don't recognize any of these people," he said.

"That's because you've probably never seen them before. That's Jennifer and her two roommates. They're celebrating because the guy on the left just won an art grant."

"So what does this have to do with Susan?"

"Look behind them, in the background."

Caleb held the picture closer to the light, trying to make out the slightly blurred figure beyond the open door of the pizza place. It could have been any woman of Susan's general size, shape and coloring. But then he saw a slice of leopard print halter beneath a short black jacket and knew it was her.

"She's wearing just what I thought she was wearing," he said in amazement.

"Notice anything else?"

Caleb's blood ran cold. Next to Susan, parked at the curb, was a blue Ford pickup with a white camper shell. He cut his gaze to Holly. "Purcell's truck?"

"Or one just like it."

Another connection. At this stage, Caleb saw no benefit in keeping his reason for renting the cottage a secret. With the appearance of Purcell's truck in this picture with Susan, Holly's fears were already confirmed. "You wanted to know why I rented this place," he said.

"You're finally going to tell me?"

"Madison Lieberman lives next door. She's my landlady."

Holly's brows drew together as if she couldn't quite identify the name. "Madison Lieberman…"

"Ellis Purcell's daughter."

"Of course! I heard about her over and over when you were researching the Sandpoint Strangler. But she'd never talk to you. Has she changed her mind?"

"Not exactly. She doesn't even know that Caleb Trovato and Thomas L. Wagner are the same man. She was looking for a renter, and I happened to get here first. That's it." He tapped the picture against his palm. "Tell me how Jennifer came across one of our flyers."

"She's a graduate student at the university and saw it posted at the library."

Holly had insisted on putting her phone number on the flyer, which made sense because hers was local and not long distance. Also, Caleb knew a woman's name and number would seem less threatening. But Holly and this Jennifer woman had both been stupid to meet on campus so late at night—not that there was any point in arguing about it now. "What I don't understand is why she noticed something so obscure in one of her pictures," he said.

"Susan was involved in an argument that drew everyone's attention. When Jennifer saw the flyer, she looked through the pictures she'd taken that night and, voilà, there was Susan.''

With a truck like Ellis Purcell's in the same vicinity. Was it another strange coincidence? Or did the police have a copycat killer on their hands?

"Did Jennifer say what the argument was about?" he asked.

"She wasn't sure. She thinks Susan bumped someone's fender while trying to park or something like that. Jennifer and her friends weren't really aware of anyone else until Susan screamed a curse. Then they all craned their heads to see what was going on. A male voice answered by calling her a stupid bitch. Then Susan got in her car and peeled off.''

"What did the guy who called her a bitch look like?"

"He was beyond their view. After Susan left, Jennifer and her friends went back to their fun. She said if she hadn't seen the flyer, she probably wouldn't have thought about the incident again.''

Caleb returned his attention to the picture, trying to figure out what it meant.

Holly watched him closely, fiddling with the cuff of her long-sleeved, black cotton blouse. "This might or might not have any relevance to my sister's disappearance, though, right?" she said. "I mean, for all we know that truck's a coincidence and Susan was arguing with Lance, the guy she was dating.''

"At least this picture narrows down the time she could have disappeared," Caleb said. "Jennifer said this was taken on Tuesday?"

Holly nodded.

"She was reported missing when she didn't show up for work on Wednesday, which means she disappeared sometime Tuesday night or early Wednesday morning.''

"Do you think it was Lance she was arguing with at the pizza place?" Holly persisted.

"We've talked to Lance. The last time he saw Susan was when they spent the night together on Saturday, remember?"

"That's what he *says*. Maybe he's afraid to tell us about the argument for fear it'll make him a suspect in the case."

"He's already a suspect," Caleb said. "In any homicide, the police look at the husband or boyfriend first, then extended family members and friends. But Gibbons doesn't believe Lance is our guy."

Her eyes narrowed. "When did you talk to Gibbons?"

"Last night."

"You didn't mention it to me."

"I haven't had a chance."

"We were passing out flyers together all day!"

"It's a moot point," he said. "Lance has a good alibi."

"For when?"

"For Monday *and* Tuesday nights." And for Wednesday and Thursday, as well, but Caleb didn't want to go into that.

"Where was he?" she asked.

Caleb raked his fingers through his hair, wondering how to frame his answer.

"What is it?" she pressed when he didn't respond right away. "You know something you're not telling me."

What the hell, he decided. The truth was the truth. "Lance is engaged to be married," he said. "He's been living with his fiancée and seeing Susan on the side."

"What?" Holly scrambled to her feet. "Susan told me he was living with his sister."

"If it makes you feel any better, his fiancée didn't know about Susan, either. She kicked him out as soon as she learned. But she maintains that he was home by six o'clock both Monday and Tuesday nights. She works evenings and needed him to sit with her mother, who just had surgery to replace a knee. The mother confirmed that she and Lance watched television together for several hours both nights.''

"I can't believe it," Holly cried. "What scum! Men are all alike!"

"Hey, I never cheated on you," he said.

"You quit loving me. That's even worse." Burying her face in her hands, she dissolved into tears.

Her crying tugged at Caleb's heart, but he told himself not to feel any sympathy. He couldn't afford sympathy. Where Holly was concerned, the softer emotions always got him into trouble. But he couldn't stand to see her, or any woman, cry.

Leaving his beer on the counter, he went to see if he could get her to settle down. "Holly, you'll meet someone else," he told her.

She slipped her arms around his neck. His immediate impulse was to pull away, but she looked so crestfallen he couldn't bring himself to do it. "Someone who's more compatible with you than I am," he added, patting her awkwardly. "And we'll find Susan, okay? Don't give up hope. Not yet. She needs us to believe."

Holly clung to him, nestling her face into his neck. "What if we don't find her? I'll live my whole life never knowing what happened to my own sister. I've lost you already, Caleb. I can't bear to lose her, too. She's all I've got left."

Caleb thought of the other families suffering through the same kind of loss. He didn't relish the idea of lying to Madison Lieberman, but it seemed a small price to pay to resolve the mystery that had affected so many lives.

"I'm going to help you find Susan," he said. "Have some faith."

Holly shifted slightly in his arms, fitting her body more snugly to his. "If we don't find her, you'll eventually have to give up."

"We'll find her." He got the impression she was making her body accessible on purpose, and decided he'd given her all the comfort he could.

But when he tried to release her, she held on tight.

"Caleb?"

"What?"

"Is it *really* over between us? Because sometimes it doesn't feel like it is."

It had been more than two years since he'd made love to Holly. After his second divorce, he'd gone on a brief womanizing rampage, trying to repair what his failed marriage had done to his ego, he supposed. But he'd soon found the lifestyle too empty to bother with and had thrown himself back into his work. Now it had been ten months since he'd made love to *any* woman.

He had to admit he was beginning to feel his body's long neglect, but Caleb wasn't about to make another mistake with Holly. After their first divorce, a moment's weakness had left her pregnant and, for the baby's sake, he'd married her again. He certainly didn't want a repeat performance.

"It's really over," he said, putting her firmly away from him.

"Is there someone else?" she asked.

After tolerating Holly for so many years, Caleb suspected he wasn't naive enough to ever fall in love again. "No."

"You came back here to help me, even though we're through?"

He nodded. He had come to help her, and Susan. And because of Madison, he just might get lucky enough to solve the murders that had obsessed him for years.

CHAPTER SIX

MADISON WAS ON THE PHONE with Tye when Caleb knocked at her door for breakfast the following morning. Propping the receiver against her shoulder, she yelled for Brianna to let him in while she flipped the pancakes on the griddle.

"I can't believe Johnny's out," Tye said. "When did they release him?"

"He couldn't really tell me. I think he was on something."

Tye sighed. "That comes as no surprise."

Caleb knocked again. Evidently Brianna wasn't getting the door as she'd asked. Covering the phone a second time, Madison prompted her daughter to hurry.

Once she heard the patter of Brianna's feet finally heading down the hallway, she returned to their conversation. "I'm sorry. I thought you'd want to know," she said. "He tried stopping by your place before coming here. I guess you weren't home, but I'm sure he'll try again."

"Did he hit you up for money?"

Madison didn't want to admit that Johnny had asked for money, because she probably shouldn't have given him any. But letting him have what he wanted was the easiest way to deal with her conscience over everything that had happened—or not happened—in his life.

"He asked for a few bucks," she said.

"Did you give it to him?"

"What do you think?"

"Madison, we've talked about this before."

"I know." The emotions that made her give Johnny the money were so complex she couldn't have explained them if she'd tried. Especially because she felt some of the same guilt about Tye. He'd certainly turned out a lot better than Johnny, but he'd endured the same kind of childhood, and it had taken her years to get to know him well enough to feel comfortable calling him occasionally. "I won't give him any more," she said.

She could hear Brianna at the door, greeting Caleb with a chilly, "Oh, it's *you*." Momentarily distracted, Madison covered the phone to tell Brianna to mind her manners. But she was trying to get the pancakes off the griddle at the same time Tye was asking where she'd moved their father's coffin. She decided to have a talk with Brianna later. "He's at the Green Hill Cemetery in Renton," she told Tye.

Caleb's footsteps came down the hall and into the kitchen. She turned to wave a welcome, and ended up letting her gaze slide quickly over him instead. Not many men looked so good in a simple rugby shirt and a pair of faded jeans.

No wonder he had beautiful blond women visiting him in the middle of the night. The only mystery was that the woman hadn't stayed until morning and made him breakfast herself.

He gave her a devastating smile. "Smells great."

Madison told herself not to burn the food. "I hope you like pancakes."

"I like everything."

Suddenly remembering that she had Tye on the phone, she cleared her throat and told Caleb to have a seat. "I'll be with you in a second," she said. "I'm talking to my brother. I hope you don't mind."

"No problem." He removed the newspaper he'd been carrying under one arm and spread it out on the table.

Brianna sat directly across from him, twirling the fork at her place setting and glaring at him.

Madison threw her daughter a warning glance. Then she turned her attention back to Tye, because there was something she still wanted to ask him. Johnny had told her that Tye and Sharon were having problems, but Tye acted as though nothing had changed.

"Would you and Sharon like to drive over and have breakfast with us today?" she asked, trying to introduce the subject of Sharon as naturally as possible. Madison hoped, if he needed to talk, he might feel safe opening up to her. "It's nearly ready, but you don't live far. We could wait."

"Not today," he said. "The kids have soccer games."

"Oh." Madison poured more batter on the griddle, wondering what to say next. She wanted him to know he could trust her, but she didn't want him to think she was prying into his personal business. "Maybe Brianna and I could come and see them play."

"Next week would be better," he said.

"Next week" would probably never come. Madison wanted to see more of her nieces and nephews, but Tye was always so aloof. "Well, you know I'm here if you need anything, right? You'd call me if…if you ever felt like you wanted to talk, wouldn't you?"

"Of course," he said. But she knew he never would. Madison was fairly certain he still harbored some of the resentment he'd felt toward her when they were young. She had no idea what she could do to overcome it. She'd never mistreated Johnny or Tye. Some of the anger they felt toward Ellis for not being there when they needed him, and her mother for being such an unresponsive step-mother, had slopped over onto her.

"I'd better go," he said. "I don't want to make the kids late for their games. Thanks for telling me about Johnny."

"Sure." She hung up, feeling slightly hurt that Tye never wanted to include her in his life.

The rattle of the newspaper behind her reminded her that she had other things to think about.

She poured Caleb Trovato a cup of coffee and a glass of orange juice and motioned for Brianna to put down her fork and quit staring daggers at him.

"Thanks," he said, lowering the paper enough to look over it. He glanced at Brianna, grinned and went back to reading his paper.

Brianna's expression darkened the moment she realized her acute unhappiness at his presence caused Caleb no discomfort.

Madison decided she really had to talk to Danny about unifying their efforts to raise their daughter as a happy, well-adjusted child. "Did you sleep well?" she asked Caleb, cracking an egg into the skillet she'd just gotten out.

He folded the paper and set it to one side. "Very well. You?"

She was more than a little curious about Caleb's late-night visitor. But she wasn't about to mention it. She didn't want to seem like a nosy landlady—especially when she guarded her own privacy so carefully. "Fine, thanks."

"Was that the brother who came by last night?" he asked, nodding toward the telephone.

"No, that was Tye. He's a year older than Johnny."

"Do you have any other siblings?"

"Just the two brothers."

"They're both weird," Brianna volunteered, wrinkling her nose. "And Johnny stinks."

Embarrassed by Brianna's behavior, Madison grappled for patience. "Brianna, that's not polite. You're talking about your own uncles. And Johnny smells like smoke. That doesn't mean he stinks."

"He stinks to Elizabeth. And he stinks to Dad," she said smugly. "Dad says it's a wonder Johnny hasn't—"

"Let's not go into what your father has to say," Madison interrupted, knowing it wouldn't be nice. She added a pancake and a piece of bacon to Brianna's plate, and set the food in front of her in hopes she'd soon be too busy eating to speak.

But Brianna only stared at her food. "He doesn't like you, either," her daughter responded sullenly. "He said you couldn't see what was right in front of your eyes. He told Leslie that no-good son of a bitch father of yours nearly ruined his life."

Madison's jaw dropped. Brianna's words were obviously a direct quote, but that didn't make it any easier to hear them. "Brianna, you know better than to use that kind of language!"

"Dad says it," she said smugly.

"That doesn't make it right. Why don't you go to your room and see if you can remember what we talked about the last time you used a bad word."

Brianna spared her an angry glance before heading out of the kitchen, carrying Elizabeth smashed beneath one arm. She walked with her spine ramrod straight and her head held high, but it wasn't long before Madison heard sniffles coming from the direction of her bedroom.

Torn between going to her daughter and trying to remain firm, Madison closed her eyes and shook her head. "I'm sorry, Mr. Tro—"

"It's Caleb, remember?" he said gently.

"Caleb, I'm sorry. I'm afraid we're dealing with some…issues here. If you'd rather, I could bring your meals over to your place in the future."

"No, that's okay. Brianna doesn't bother me. I'm sure she's a great kid."

A lump swelled in Madison's throat. "She *is* a great kid. She's just a little out of her element right now. Her father remarried this past year, almost the day our divorce was final, which hasn't helped. The woman who's now her stepmother was already pregnant."

"That's a lot for a child to deal with."

Madison got another plate from the cupboard. "I'm afraid she's blaming me for all the changes, but I don't want to be too hard on her."

"A bright girl like Brianna will figure things out."

Madison scooped two eggs onto his plate. "I hope so."

"Here." Standing, he crossed the distance between them and guided her to Brianna's seat. "Why don't you sit down and relax a minute? I can get my own food."

Madison would have argued, but she'd been taking care of her mother and Brianna—and Danny before that—for so long, it felt good to let someone else take charge.

Using the fork Brianna had been so fixated on twirling, she began picking at the food she'd dished up for her daughter.

Caleb set a cup of coffee near her plate. "Sounds as though your ex-husband doesn't like your father much." Gathering his own plate, now heaped with food, he took his seat.

She put her fork aside and added some cream to her coffee. "My father's dead."

"I'm sorry to hear that." Caleb paused, his own coffee in hand. "When did he pass away?"

For her, Ellis had died just recently—the day she'd found that box. Somehow, letting go of the man she'd believed him to be felt worse than living without his physical presence. "It's been a year or so."

He took a sip. "That's too bad. How old was he?"

"Fifty-eight."

"Fifty-eight's pretty young. Did he have a heart attack?"

Normally Madison didn't like talking about her father. But Caleb was a complete stranger, which meant he had no stake in the situation. That seemed to make a difference. "He shot himself in our backyard."

His eyebrows drew together, and his gaze briefly touched her face. "That must have been terrible for you."

"It was." She remembered Johnny calling her the day it had happened. She'd felt shock and grief, of course, but also an incendiary anger. She'd believed the police and the media had finally badgered Ellis to the point where he could tolerate no more. She'd stood in the middle of the mall, her cell phone pressed tightly to her ear, her legs shaky as Johnny told her what he'd found. And once she'd hung up she had to break the news to her mother.

"Was he going through some type of depression?" Caleb asked. His attention was on his food, but the tone of his voice invited her confidence.

Madison wondered if telling him a little might bring her some solace. "My father was Ellis Purcell," she said.

Caleb set his coffee cup down with a clink. "Not the Ellis Purcell who was implicated in the killings over by the university."

"I'm afraid that's the one." Her father had been on the national news and in the papers so many times, it would've been much more surprising if Caleb *hadn't* recognized his name, but it was still a little disconcerting to have him clue in so fast.

Caleb didn't say anything for a moment, and Madison immediately regretted being so forthright. "I shouldn't have told you," she said.

There was a hesitancy in his expression that gave her the impression he agreed with her. But his words seemed to contradict that. "Why not?" he asked, stirring more sugar into his coffee before taking another sip.

She couldn't see his expression behind his cup. "Because I've spent years trying to escape the taint of it."

He put his coffee back on the table and finally looked at her. "I'm sorry," he said, the tone of his voice compassionate.

The ache that had begun deep inside her at the outset of the conversation seemed to intensify. She wanted to hang on to someone, to break away from her troubled past and be like other people. But it was impossible. Her father, or whoever had left those sickening souvenirs under the house, had seen to that. "That's what my ex-husband was referring to when he said what he did in front of Brianna," she explained.

"I see." Caleb cleared his throat. "How old were you when the first woman went missing?"

"Fifteen. I remember my mother talking about it one night. But it was just another story on the news to me then." She chuckled humorlessly. "Little did I know how much it would affect me later...."

He started eating his pancakes. "What was your father's reaction to the news?"

"He didn't really say anything. My mother was the one talking about it."

When Caleb had swallowed, he said, "Your father must not have been a suspect right away, then."

"No, he wasn't drawn into it until two years later, when some woman claimed she saw my father's truck leaving the house of her neighbor—who'd just been murdered. Then the police started coming over, asking questions. They contacted just about everyone who'd ever known us. They searched the house."

"What did they find?" he asked, pushing his plate away.

"Besides the fact that I was exchanging love letters with a boy my father had forbidden me to associate with, and I had just bought my first pair of sexy underwear?" She laughed. "Nothing."

Caleb's lips curved in a sympathetic smile. "They exposed all your girlish secrets, huh?"

"To this day I stay away from airports just in case security decides to rifle through my bags."

She'd meant her comments to sound flip but was afraid they didn't come across that way when Caleb remained serious. "So what do you think?" he asked.

"About what?"

"You probably knew your father as well as anyone." She could suddenly feel the depth of his focus, which seemed at odds with his casual pose. "Did he do it?"

She'd faced this question before, dozens of times. And she'd always had a ready, if passionate, answer. But that was before. Should she tell him what she'd believed throughout the investigation? Or should she admit that she might've been wrong all along?

She'd opened her mouth to tell him she didn't know *what* to think when the telephone interrupted.

"Excuse me," she said, and picked up the handset.

"Good news," Annette announced from the other end of the line, her voice cheerful.

"What's that?" Madison glanced down the hall toward Brianna's room, feeling as though she could use some good news at the moment.

"I've decided to sell the house."

"What?"

"I'm ready to move. I know it's taken me a while to come to this, but it's time."

A vision of her mother stumbling upon the shoes and underwear—and that locket and rope—flashed through Madison's mind. "There's no hurry, Mom," she said, turning away from Caleb. "Why don't you wait until spring?"

"Because I don't want to spend another Christmas here without Ellis. Do you think you can sell this house inside a couple of months?"

"I—I'm not sure."

"If not, maybe I'll rent it out. Now that I've made my decision, the memories are crowding so close."

"I understand. But…"

"But what?"

Madison looked at Caleb, wishing for the second time that she hadn't shared so many personal details with him. There was still a great deal to protect. She had to be more careful. "Don't start packing yet," she said.

"Why not?"

She groped for something that would sound logical. "Wait until I can help you."

"You're so busy. You just worry about getting this place sold. I'll have Toby next door help me."

"When?" Madison asked, her panic rising.

"He said he could do it the weekend following next."

The weekend following next…

She needed to move that box. And she needed to do it sometime in the next two weeks.

CALEB CURSED the untimely interruption of the telephone. He'd just had Madison talking to him about her father. She'd been open and warm, completely the opposite of what he'd expected her to be.

And then her mother had called.

He helped himself to another pancake and took his time eating, hoping they could return to their conversation as soon as Madison hung up. But when she got off the phone, she looked upset.

"How's your mother?" he asked, setting his napkin next to his plate as he finished.

"Fine."

"Does she live close?"

She gathered up the dishes. "Just beyond the university, for the time being."

"For the time being?"

She ran hot water in the sink. "She's talking about moving."

"Does that upset you?"

Madison glanced over at him and, if he wasn't mistaken, a wariness entered her eyes that hadn't been nearly as pronounced as when they were talking earlier. "No, why?"

"You seem a little tense, that's all."

"I'm the one who's been telling her to move," she said. "It's tough to stay in the same house where everything went so wrong." Suddenly, she turned off the water. "Will you excuse me, please?"

"Of course."

She disappeared down the hall and, after a moment, he could hear her talking in a soft voice to her daughter. "Do you understand why I wasn't happy with what you said at the table, Bri?... Do you think you could try a little harder to remember your manners?... Okay, come give

Mommy a hug…. I know things haven't been easy lately, princess, but they'll get better…. Are you ready to eat?''

Caleb felt he should probably leave. There were several people he still needed to interview. And he wanted to talk to Jennifer Allred, the woman Holly had met last night, just to see if he could jog her memory for details. But the odd change that had come over Madison made him believe there was more to that phone call with her mother than she was saying, and he hoped to figure it out before he left.

"Breakfast was great," he said when she came back into the kitchen holding Brianna's hand.

"Thanks," she responded. "Have you always had someone cook and clean for you?"

He almost admitted that he hadn't, but he wanted to make it sound as though this type of arrangement wasn't anything new, so she'd relax around him even more. "Occasionally."

"Must be nice."

Brianna glowered at him, still sulky, as he carried the cream and sugar to the counter, searching for an excuse to linger. It was the weekend. He could probably spend more time with Madison if only he could think of something menial to do for her. He could fix something, wash her car, mow the grass—

The overgrown grass. Perfect.

"Any chance you'd like to work in the yard this afternoon?" he asked. "I've got a few hours. I thought I could mow the lawn and maybe trim some of the bushes while you and Brianna handled the weeds."

Madison set the frying pan in the soapy water and let her hands dangle in the sink. "Really?"

When he heard the gratitude in her voice, he felt less than an inch tall. But he had to stay focused, had to make this work. "If you don't mind my help."

She shook her head. "I don't mind at all. I'll even take some money off your rent, or trade you a couple of meals. I'm falling behind out there. My business takes every extra minute. I just lost my top agent and I've been trying to find someone to replace her. And my office manager doubles as typist for the agents, but she's a much better typist than she is a manager."

"We can do the grass ourselves," Brianna said, out of nowhere.

"Brianna..." Madison used her tone as another warning.

"Or you could help us," she added grudgingly.

Caleb grinned. "There's no need to compensate me." He knew it would only make him feel worse. "I think it'll be good to get out. I cut my folks' grass for years."

"Where do your folks live?"

"On Fidalgo Island."

"Really?" Madison's eyebrows rose. "That's not far."

"Farther than I'd want to drive to reach downtown," he said, so she wouldn't wonder why he'd rented her cottage, instead of staying with family.

"Do you often work downtown?"

"Not often. Once in a while."

"I see." Madison glanced at the clock over the table. "I'm afraid I have to run a few errands this morning. What time do you want to do the yard?"

"One o'clock okay?"

"Perfect."

He smiled. "See you then."

CHAPTER SEVEN

MADISON WAS NEARLY thirty minutes late returning from her errands. She'd had to deliver some tax returns to a loan agent for a buyer who was trying to purchase a vacation home outside Langley, and had gotten caught up talking to him about another deal they'd been working on, which had fallen apart. She'd also drawn up a purchase offer for one of her own listings, a small two-bedroom, two-bath located just down the street, even though she knew the buyer was coming in so low the seller would probably be offended and not even bother to counter. She was so busy managing the other agents and running the office that she didn't have the chance to get out and sell much, but she was doing everything she could to turn her business around, which meant she sometimes had to act as a regular agent, too.

Fortunately, once she and Brianna left the house, Brianna's mood had dramatically improved. Madison talked to her about being polite to guests and how important it was that Brianna, Madison and Danny treat each other with fairness and respect even though they were no longer living as a family. But it was difficult to tell whether Brianna actually grasped these concepts. It was the sort of stuff older children had problems sorting out. How could Madison expect a six-year-old to understand?

Pushing back the sleeve of her gray suit, she glanced

nervously at her watch as she pulled into the drive. She hoped Caleb hadn't given up on her.

As soon as she cut the engine, she could hear the steady roar of the lawnmower coming from the backyard, and felt a measure of relief. She loved where she lived and was anxious to get the grounds cleaned up. Because the previous owner had taken such meticulous care of the place, with Caleb's help it would soon look as good as it used to.

"You ready to do some weeding?" she asked Brianna as she got out.

Her daughter didn't move.

"You like working in the yard," Madison said, leaning back inside the car. "Come on. It'll be fun. We'll probably find some snails."

Reluctantly, Brianna climbed out.

The lawnmower fell silent and Caleb came around the house, carrying the grass bin. At her first sight of him, Brianna's expression darkened, but Madison had trouble fighting an appreciative smile. He'd obviously been working for some time—long enough to get too heated for his T-shirt, which he'd taken off and stuffed in his back pocket. Sweat gleamed on his golden torso, making the contours of his muscular chest and arms seem that much more defined.

Madison had seen a lot of sweaty, muscle-bound men at the gym when she was married to Danny. But from a sketch artist's standpoint, there was something truly beautiful about the way Caleb Trovato was put together. He looked far more natural than any of those men at the gym. When he moved, she could tell his tan ended at the waist, as though he'd gotten it from working or playing outdoors instead of baking naked in a tanning salon. And he seemed unconcerned with impressing others. He put down the bin and shrugged into his T-shirt the moment he saw them.

"There you are," he said.

"Sorry I'm late." Madison tried to hold the mental picture of his bare torso in her mind so she'd be able to recall it later. After being relatively uninspired over the past few weeks, she suddenly felt a jolt of creative energy. "I had to do a few things that just couldn't wait."

"No problem. I'm nearly finished in the back."

"I really appreciate your help," she said, and meant it. Having Caleb around, pitching in, made her life suddenly seem fuller, almost...normal.

He picked up the grass bin and emptied it in the green refuse container. "I found something I think you and your bunny might like," he said to Brianna.

Brianna had already dropped to her knees and situated Elizabeth beside her. She was digging in the dirt with a stick and pretending to ignore Caleb, but Madison could see her peeking at him, trying to figure out what he was talking about.

"Do you want to see what it is?" he asked when she didn't answer.

"No." She continued to dig.

Madison opened her mouth to remind her daughter of the talk they'd just had in the car. But Caleb gave her a quick shake of his head, indicating that he didn't need her to get involved.

"I'll bet Elizabeth would like to know," he said.

Brianna pretended to converse with Elizabeth, but ultimately shook her head.

"Okay." He started toward the mower with the empty bin.

Brianna rocked back on her haunches. "It's probably nothing we'd like, anyway," she called after him.

He didn't bother turning. "Whatever you say."

She frowned at his retreating form. "So, what is it?"

"Never mind."

"You're not going to tell?"

"You're not interested, remember? Even Elizabeth doesn't want to know."

Grabbing her stuffed animal, she stood up and ran after him. "What if Elizabeth's changed her mind?"

Madison retrieved her briefcase from the car, smiling at how easily Caleb had engaged Brianna's curiosity. Then she headed to the backyard to find them both kneeling over a shoebox covered with a piece of plastic Caleb had slit in several places.

"What is it?" she asked, unable to see because their heads blocked her view.

"It's a praying mantis," Brianna breathed, as though she'd never seen anything quite so wonderful. "See, Mom? It looks just like a green leaf."

"That's how it camouflages itself," Caleb explained. "Most of the time it blends in with the trees."

"Will it bite me?" Brianna asked.

"No."

"What does it eat?"

"Other insects."

"Yuck!"

"That's a good thing," Caleb said. "It helps keep the bad bugs in the garden from eating all the vegetables."

Brianna's nose was still wrinkled in distaste. "Ooo."

"Don't you find gnats and mosquitoes particularly appetizing?" he teased.

"What's *appetizing* mean?"

He chuckled. "Never mind. Do you want to hold it?"

Brianna shrank away from him. "I don't think so."

"Come on." He pulled back the plastic and gently

withdrew the mantis. "It won't hurt you. It has spiny legs that feel a little funny, but it's harmless."

Brianna remained skeptical at first, but the longer Caleb let the praying mantis perch on his hand, the more confident she became. "Okay."

He carefully transferred the insect to her just as Madison's cell phone rang. The LED readout identified the caller as Danny.

Taking a deep breath, she stepped away from Brianna and Caleb. "Hello?"

"You left a message on my voice mail this morning that you want to talk about Brianna," Danny said without the courtesy of a greeting. "What's going on?"

"I do want to talk, but I'm afraid now isn't a good time."

"What could possibly be wrong? God, she's six," he said.

Madison lowered her voice. "I have some very legitimate concerns, Danny. Our daughter is going through a difficult time, and I'm hoping you'll cooperate with me for her benefit."

"She'd be fine if only you'd let her come and live with us. She's perfectly happy when she's here. Ask Leslie."

"I don't need to ask Leslie anything," Madison said, irritated by the way he constantly discounted her feelings. "I know my own daughter. And I'm not going to give up my rights to her."

"Well, I don't want to conference with you about every little thing."

"Every *little* thing?" she replied. "Our *daughter* isn't a little thing."

"I think you just like to bother me, although I can't imagine why. When we were married you certainly didn't give a damn about anything other than protecting your beloved father.''

Madison glanced up to see Caleb watching her. She didn't like him witnessing the discord between her and Danny, but she wasn't willing to end the conversation just yet. She was tired of Danny's unrelenting bitterness. He thought she'd ruined *his* life, but dealing with him wasn't easy.

''I'm going to pretend you never said that and say what I called to tell you in the first place,'' she said in carefully measured tones, thinking she might as well get it over with. ''You're expressing opinions and attitudes in Brianna's presence that aren't good for her to hear. It's as simple as that.''

''What opinions?''

''You're criticizing me in front of her, and I'm her mother.''

''I haven't told her anything that isn't true,'' he said, and laughed.

Rolling her eyes, Madison consciously tried to sidestep an argument. ''Just…just be careful of what you say in future, okay?''

''I'll do what I damn well please.''

Another glance at Caleb and Brianna told Madison that her daughter was still absorbed with the mantis, but Caleb was watching her intently enough to suggest he recognized that something was wrong.

''Listen, we'll have to talk about this later,'' she said. ''I've got someone here.''

''Someone? Don't tell me you're finally starting to date.''

She moved farther away from Caleb and Brianna and lowered her voice. ''Whether I'm dating or not is none of your business. Anyway, I'm not seeing this guy. I'm renting to him."

The tension between them turned palpable. "You leased the cottage house?" Danny said, all sign of levity gone.

"I told you I was going to."

"And I told you I didn't want you to. Do you even know this guy?"

Madison curled the nails of her free hand into her palm. He thought he could walk out on her and still have a say in her choices; his presumption tested her patience, but she was determined not to lose her temper. "I'm getting to know him," she said calmly.

"So he's basically a stranger."

"A lot of people live in homes that are built closer together than my house is to the carriage house, Danny," she said. "If it helps, think of us as having a new neighbor."

"I'm taking you back to court," he snapped. "You'll be sorry you didn't listen to me when I cut my child support in half."

Disgusted that he'd threaten her with something that would hurt Brianna, Madison let her true opinion of him ooze into her voice. "You're pathetic, you know that?"

"Be careful. You really don't want to piss me off," he said, and hung up.

Madison was shaking by the time she hit the End button. Caleb was talking about the praying mantis again, but Brianna had finally clued in to the drama unfolding on the phone, despite his efforts to distract her.

"Was that Daddy?" she asked, watching her mother with wide, uncertain eyes.

Madison shoved her cell into her purse. "Yes, but don't worry, honey, everything's okay."

Brianna shaded her eyes against the sun. "Your face gets all red when you talk to Daddy."

Madison started moving toward the house. "It's a little hot in this suit. I'd better go change."

"I'll bet some ice cream would cool you down," Caleb said before she could get very far.

Brianna immediately jumped to her feet and clapped and danced. "I want some ice cream! Elizabeth wants ice cream, too!"

"I've got a yes from Brianna," he said. "What about you?"

Madison didn't want to go out for ice cream. After her conversation with Danny, she didn't want to go anywhere. Especially with her handsome renter. Letting another man into her life was like embracing a tornado. But she knew Caleb was trying to help her, so she made a conscious effort to let him. "Ice cream sounds good," she said.

THREE HOURS LATER, Caleb sat at a table at a McDonald's not far from Holly's house in Alderwood Manor, a suburb between Whidbey Island and Seattle. He tapped his pen on his leg, waiting impatiently for Detective Gibbons to answer his call as Holly inched forward in line. He'd spent most of the afternoon with Madison and Brianna, but he hadn't been able to get anything new out of Madison about her father or the murders. Even while they were having ice cream, she'd been too preoccupied by that phone call she'd received from her ex.

Caleb couldn't blame her. From what he'd overheard, Danny Lieberman was an ass.

When Gibbons finally came to the phone, Caleb had to yank the receiver away from his ear before the loud, foul-mouthed, twenty-year police veteran blasted out his eardrum.

"Trovato, what the hell are you doing calling me at home on a Saturday?"

Chuckling, Caleb leaned forward as Holly momentarily disappeared behind some hanging plants. When he'd ordered, she'd refused to eat, but he'd finally talked her into getting a hamburger and wanted to make sure she was still in line to order it. As soon as they finished a quick dinner, they were planning to canvass Susan's neighborhood again, just in case they'd missed someone or something. They didn't have a lot of other options. The private investigator was supposedly hard at work doing background checks on just about everyone who'd ever been associated with Susan, and the police were digging, too, searching for Susan's car, but no one seemed to be finding anything.

"What, you only accept calls when it's convenient, Gibbons?" he teased. "If I didn't know you better, I'd say you're in it strictly for the paycheck, man."

"You don't know what the hell you're talking about, as usual," he grumbled, but the old affection was still there. Caleb could feel it beneath the surface of everything that was said. "What do you want?"

Caleb wadded up his hamburger wrapper and shoved it inside his empty cup. "I have some evidence that might connect the Sandpoint Strangler case to—"

"The Sandpoint Strangler case!" he interrupted. "I have a woman who looks like Catherine Zeta Jones on her way over to fix me dinner, less than five minutes to clean up this dump, and you call me, acting like there's some kind of emergency on a case that's totally cold?"

Caleb had a hard time believing Gibbons could get a woman who even *remotely* resembled Catherine Zeta Jones to cook him dinner. Short, balding and a little on the heavy side, he had a blockish head with bulldog jowls.

To make things worse, he had a disconcerting way of shouting almost everything he said. "Just listen to me for a second, Gibbons. I think there might be a connection between the Strangler case and the Susan Michaelson disappearance."

"Don't give me that, Trovato."

"Susan Michaelson fits the profile. She's small, she's in the right age range and she was abducted from the same area."

"That could just as easily be coincidence as anything else. Quit looking for something exciting to put in one of those damn books you're writing these days."

Holly moved forward in line. Dressed in a denim jacket with fake fur at the collar, she studied the lighted menu overhead as though she hadn't seen it a million times. "I'm not working on a book right now. I'm trying to find Susan."

"Then why are you calling me? I'm not assigned to the Michaelson case."

"I think you should get yourself assigned to it, because I'm telling you there's a connection."

"Listen," Gibbons responded. "I'd give my right nut to know how that bastard Purcell did what he did. But you know as well as I do that the Sandpoint Strangler is dead. So, if that's all you've got, call me on Monday."

The phone clicked and Gibbons was gone.

"Damn," Caleb muttered, and dialed him again.

Gibbons answered on the first ring. "She just pulled up," he complained. "What the hell is it *this* time?"

Caleb came right to the point. "I've got a picture of Susan the night she disappeared."

His words were met with a few moments of silence, then, "How? Where?"

A doorbell rang in the background. While Gibbons let

his lady friend into the house, Caleb explained how he and Holly had come across the photo.

"So Tuesday night's the last time anyone saw her alive," Gibbons said.

"Anyone we've found so far."

"I want to see that picture."

"I thought you were too busy with Catherine Zeta Jones to get involved in someone else's case," Caleb said. "It's Saturday night, remember?"

"Kiss my ass, Trovato. I was heading back to the office in a couple of hours anyway."

"*There's* the hopeless workaholic I know and love."

"Criminals don't only work nine to five."

"Well, I've got something that'll get your attention. In the background of this picture, there's an '87 or '88 Ford, blue, with a white camper shell. It's identical to the one Purcell drove."

Gibbons gave an audible sigh, hesitated as though weighing this information, then said, "That could be a coincidence, too."

"Too many coincidences usually means there's no coincidence," Caleb said. "What's this I hear about a woman who's gone missing from Spokane?"

"That's probably completely unrelated."

"Holly says there was an article in the paper detailing the similarities. Some Rohypnol was found in her car, along with a piece of rope."

"We haven't even found her body yet. You're a cop, for hell's sake. Or you used to be," he added. "Don't start jumping to conclusions like everyone else. For all we know, that Spokane woman could be languishing on a beach somewhere."

"Or the Sandpoint Strangler is back in business."

"I think the Sandpoint Strangler is dead."

Caleb didn't mention that at one point Gibbons had thought the janitor at Schwab Elementary was the strangler.

"I guess it's possible that we're dealing with a copycat," Gibbons said. "Spokane's not in our jurisdiction, but I'll talk to Lieutenant Coughman and see if I can't help out a little with the Michaelson case. I know the lead detective was expecting the preliminary findings on some of the hair and fiber evidence recovered from her apartment, but I haven't heard anything yet."

"You find out, and I'll drop by in a few hours." Caleb saw Holly making her way toward him with a child-size hamburger and the change from his twenty. "One more thing," he said.

"What is it?"

"Would you do me a favor?"

"That depends on what it is."

Caleb pulled out the license plate number he'd written down last night. "I need you to run a plate."

"Why?"

"Just covering a few bases."

"I've gotta have a better reason than that, Trovato. You're not on the payroll anymore."

"I saw Johnny Purcell last night. He was in an old Buick Skylark with this plate."

Another long silence. Finally, Gibbons muttered, "What the hell. This is probably a waste, but...get me something to write with, will you, Kitten?"

"*Kitten?*" Caleb repeated.

"Go f—" Catching himself, probably for the lady's benefit, Gibbons lowered his voice. "Screw you," he said. Then he took down the plate number and hung up.

WHY, AFTER DRAGGING HER feet at every mention of moving, did her mother want to sell the house *now?*

Madison paced the floor of her living room, with the movie *Chocolat* on her DVD player, wondering what she should do. She felt a headache coming on, was exhausted from her busy day and her lack of sleep the night before, but she couldn't let herself rest. Neither could she concentrate on the movie. She had to make a decision about that box before her mother's neighbor started clearing out the crawl space.

House for sale... Nightmare in the making...

Madison rubbed her temples, hoping to ward off her headache. Her mother's neighborhood was a mixed bag of brick, wood and stucco homes, the timeless and well-maintained next to the old and dilapidated. But it was close to the university, had appealing narrow streets, rows of tall shady trees and, like the ivy-covered, redbrick buildings of the campus, gave the impression of traditional values and old money. Her mother's place should sell right away—except for the fact that it was the home of an alleged murderer and the location of a suicide. That would draw more curiosity seekers and ghouls than serious buyers.

The telephone rang, startling her. Snatching up the receiver so the sound wouldn't wake Brianna, she murmured a soft "Hello?" She'd expected it to be Danny again. Brianna had called him before bed to tell him about the praying mantis. Caleb was letting her keep it in her room until Monday, when she planned to take it to school to show the class.

"Sorry to bother you." It was Caleb Trovato. Madison knew instantly because of the flutter of excitement in her belly. "I saw your lights on and thought you might be hungry," he said. "I just ordered a pizza. Would you like to share it with me?"

Instinctively, Madison moved toward the window to peer through the wooden shutters she'd closed when she heard Caleb pull into the drive an hour or so earlier. She saw him standing at his living room window, one hand holding the phone to his ear, the other propped against the wall as he gazed out. She knew he'd seen her peeking at him when he smiled and gave her a small salute.

Closing the shutters, Madison stepped quickly away. Attractive didn't begin to describe Caleb Trovato, which was a big problem. She couldn't afford to get involved with anyone right now, least of all someone so smooth. Earlier this afternoon, he'd neutralized Brianna's resentment of him in just a few hours. And he'd charmed them both at the ice cream parlor. Given enough time and privacy, imagine what he could do with a lonely divorcée....

"I've already eaten," she said. "But I appreciate the offer."

"I was actually looking for company more than anything," he replied. "It's Saturday night, after all, and I don't know anyone in the immediate area."

Plotting to cover up her father's misdeeds was by nature a rather solitary endeavor, Madison thought sarcastically. "It's getting late...."

"It's only ten o'clock."

She could tell that "no" wasn't an answer Caleb heard very often. But she wasn't particularly concerned about his potential loneliness. She was more worried about insuring her life and Brianna's remained on a calm and even course. No extreme ups and downs. Just thoughtful decisions, solid parenting and a strong work ethic—no matter how good he looked standing in that window.

"Let me be honest, Caleb," she said. "You've been

very nice, and…and I really appreciate all the work you did in the yard today and the ice cream and all that. But I'd prefer to compensate you for your time and effort in rent or meals rather than feel obligated to you in…other ways.''

"*Obligated* to me?''

He obviously didn't like the sound of that. Perhaps determination had prompted her to state her position a little too bluntly. "I feel bad turning you down after what you've done,'' she said. "But my life's a bit complicated. I'm a single mom, trying to run a business. I'm not interested in seeing anyone.''

"I'm not asking for a relationship,'' he said, his tone slightly affronted. "I'm moving back to San Francisco at the end of my lease, so I won't be around long, anyway. I was just hoping we could be friends while I'm here.''

She thought of how much she'd enjoyed their time together in the yard today and later at the ice cream parlor, and had to admit that being Caleb's friend was pretty tempting. Most of the friends she'd known growing up had either abandoned her or turned on her when the investigation destroyed her father's good name and reputation. Rhonda, her best friend since grade school, had hung in through the initial years—until the police became more and more convinced that Ellis was indeed their killer. Then she'd started pressuring Madison to assist in the investigation. She'd said she owed it to the women of Seattle. But when Madison had refused to do anything that could hurt her father, even Rhonda began to distance herself.

"You don't have any problems with being friends, do you?'' Caleb asked.

"Of course not,'' Madison said. "I just don't want to

mislead you. As long as you understand my feelings, I'm perfectly okay with hanging out once in a while.''

"Good. Sounds like we agree. So how 'bout a slice of pizza? It should be here any minute.''

Madison smiled, thinking a distraction might actually be good for her. She couldn't do anything about that box at her mother's house until Brianna was staying with her father next weekend, anyway.

"Bring it over whenever you're ready,'' she said.

CHAPTER EIGHT

THAT COMMENT HE'D MADE on the phone about being friends really bothered Caleb. He took friendship seriously. Most of his friends had outlasted his two marriages. But at this point he had to use every avenue available to him to get close to Madison. Susan's life was possibly hanging in the balance, and Caleb was getting desperate. After spending a couple of hours down at the station with Detective Gibbons this evening, he'd learned that, so far, the hair and fiber analysis from the samples collected at Susan's apartment had yielded exactly nothing. All the hairs belonged to Susan or Holly or someone else who had a reason to be there. No unusual fibers, foot imprints or fingerprints offered any clues. And the forensics team had sprayed the apartment with luminol and determined that there wasn't any blood there, either.

Whatever happened to Susan had probably happened elsewhere. That fact had to be established, of course, but it was a very small step forward when they had no body, no crime scene, no suspect and no leads. They hadn't even found Susan's car....

A knock at the door told Caleb that the pizza had finally arrived. He handed the deliveryman thirty bucks, grabbed the pizza box and a bottle of wine he'd purchased on his way home, and headed directly to Madison's. With Brianna in bed asleep, he hoped this might be a good time to talk to her mom. Maybe he could persuade Madison to have a glass of wine, relax....

The smell of sausage and pepperoni rose to his nostrils while he waited on the front stoop, but did little to tempt his appetite. Like Madison, he'd eaten earlier. The pizza was only an excuse to get together with her—which, when he thought of it, bothered his conscience, too. He generally didn't pretend to be something he wasn't.

"Hi," she said when she opened the door. "Smells good."

Caleb's smile when he saw her was genuine; he didn't have to pretend he was glad to see her. "I brought some wine. I hope you'll have a glass with me."

She hesitated. "Maybe... Come in."

He could hear the television as he followed her into the kitchen, where she grabbed napkins, plates and glasses before waving him into the living room. "Are you comfortable over at the carriage house?" she asked.

"Actually I am. It's going to work out pretty well." He sat down and put a slice of pizza on a plate, which he passed to her, then nodded toward the film that was playing. "Looks like I interrupted you. What have you been watching?"

"*Chocolat.* Have you seen it?"

"No."

"It's fabulous."

He could've said the same for the way she looked, even though she certainly hadn't dressed up on his account. With her auburn hair in a short, messy ponytail, she was wearing a white long-john top and plaid pajama bottoms. No shoes. She'd already removed her makeup, which made the few freckles across her nose seem more pronounced.

He appreciated her fresh-scrubbed face. Not many

women possessed the inherent beauty to go so natural. But what really caught his attention was that she wasn't wearing a bra. She wasn't particularly big-busted, but the sight reminded him of just how long it had been since he'd seen, let alone touched, a woman in any intimate place. He had to drag his gaze away and remind himself that now was not the time. "Do you watch many movies?" he asked.

"Not really." She turned off the television. "I bought a real estate business when I moved here, and it keeps me busy. I don't go out much, and I only own a few DVDs. Mostly romantic comedies."

He could certainly understand why she might not have any thrillers in her collection. Uncorking the wine, he poured them each a glass. "So how's Brianna doing with her new pet?"

"She's crazy about it." Madison raised an eyebrow at him. "But I hope you're planning on helping her feed it. Looking for bugs isn't one of my favorite pastimes."

"Sure, I'll help," he said with a chuckle. "It only needs to be fed twice a day."

"*Twice* a day?"

"Come on," he teased. "Didn't those brothers of yours teach you anything?"

She accepted the glass he gave her but set it on the coffee table, next to her plate. "We weren't very close," she admitted.

He took a slice of pizza and grinned. "Maybe that's not entirely a bad thing. When I saw Johnny the other night, I got the impression he's caused some trouble in his lifetime."

She sat on the edge of the overstuffed chair not far from the sofa, and Caleb allowed himself another glance at her chest as she picked up her plate. "He has, but—in his defense—he didn't have a very good childhood."

"What happened?" he asked, wondering if she'd had a bad childhood, too.

She shrugged and swallowed her first bite. "Nothing too unusual. My father got his girlfriend pregnant in high school. They got married."

"Then the baby came." That statement seemed to stem the sexual awareness humming through him.

"Exactly. And they had Johnny right after Tye. But the marriage was too dysfunctional to survive. My father dropped out of school to become a truck driver, so he was gone a lot, and Peg—his wife—started drinking."

"That's too bad," he said, concentrating on his own pizza so he'd keep his eyes where they should be. "When did they split up?"

"Only a couple years later, I think. I'm not really sure of the details. My father was never much for conversation, and he probably didn't want to believe all the stuff he heard about Peg. But Tye and Johnny came to live with us when they were teenagers, and they told some pretty hair-raising stories."

Caleb traded the pizza for his glass of wine. He wasn't having any luck redirecting his attention, and it was easier to watch her over the rim of his glass. "Like what?"

She waited until she'd swallowed again, but she seemed to be enjoying the chance to talk. He could tell he'd chosen the right approach—targeting peripheral subjects, moving the conversation along, giving her a chance to drink some wine.

She tightened her ponytail, but her hair was pretty much falling out of it, anyway. "They said their mother once had a boyfriend who used to slug them if they made him angry," she said. "There might even have been sexual abuse, although the boys never talked about that."

She picked up her glass, studied it and finally took a sip. "They said there was usually nothing in the refrigerator except vodka and some moldy fast-food leftovers. One time Johnny called Peg to get him after school, and she was so drunk she told him he couldn't come home. Another time, when they were only ten and eleven, she dropped them off at a mall and never came back. When the place closed, the police finally brought them home."

"There's no excuse for that." Caleb's disgust helped check the attraction he was feeling. Unfortunately, the wine did not. "Why didn't the state take Tye and Johnny away from her?"

Madison finished the last of her pizza and set her plate aside. "Because she always knew how to pull it together when she really needed to, and her mother would occasionally step in and clean her place, make her look better than she really was."

"Did she ever dry out?"

"Not for long." Madison tossed a lap blanket over her legs and leaned back with her wine, folding one arm beneath the perfect breasts he found so fascinating. "Bottom line, I think she resented Johnny and Tye. I think she blamed them because she never found another man who was willing to take care of her."

"Why didn't your father step in and take over?"

She raised her glass to her lips again. "This is good," she said.

He smiled, beginning to feel a little warm.

"I don't think he realized how bad it was at the time, not that that's any excuse," she continued.

"Did he pay child support?"

"I'm sure he did."

"Maybe he thought that was enough."

"Maybe."

The wine rolled gently down Caleb's throat, easing the tension he'd felt earlier in the day. "What did your mother have to say about the boys?"

Madison pulled her blanket a little higher. "I'm ashamed to admit she was probably the reason my dad didn't get more involved with them. He didn't think it was fair to expect her to clean up a mess she hadn't done anything to create."

"Wow." He poured a little more wine into his glass and lifted the bottle to her in question, but she shook her head. "So you didn't get to know your brothers until they came to live with you?"

"I didn't have any contact with them until then. Once Peg's mother died, Peg called my dad to tell him she couldn't handle the boys anymore."

Caleb leaned forward, resting his elbows on his knees. "How did it go once they came to live at your place?"

"They didn't stay long. Johnny got busted for drugs and went to a juvenile detention center within the first eighteen months. Tye shut himself up in his room and listened to stoner music for hours on end. He didn't do his homework or interact with the family. He didn't have friends. It drove my mother nuts that he could simply cut everyone off like that."

"Was he on drugs, too?"

"Probably," she said with a shrug, and surprised Caleb by accepting when he once again offered her more wine. "Dad and Tye argued constantly."

"Did it ever come to blows?"

She sat back and faced him, her expression thoughtful. "Occasionally. Usually over schoolwork. My dad didn't want Tye to end up without an education, like him. And he didn't like the way Tye treated my mother." She sighed. "On the other hand, Tye didn't think my father had the right to tell him anything. Sometimes I could see hate flickering in his eyes when he spoke to my parents, and it was almost—" she hesitated, seeming to grope for the right words "—frightening."

Caleb couldn't help marveling at how different Madison was from the woman he'd expected her to be—and wishing she wasn't so nice. Then maybe he wouldn't have to feel like such a jerk for taking advantage of her. "Did *you* get along okay with Tye and Johnny?" he asked, feeling a bit protective in case the answer was no.

"I was only eight when they came to live with us, so I didn't really have much to do with them. I felt like a spectator most of the time. I heard the yelling and watched the fighting, but I couldn't do anything to stop what was going on around me. So I tried to tune it out."

"You and your brothers make my childhood seem like a party," he said. "Between the situation with Tye and Johnny and the investigation, how did you survive?"

He'd switched topics as smoothly as possible, but when she didn't answer right away, he feared she was going to say something about calling it a night.

Instead, she drank a little more wine. "I don't know. It all seems like a bad dream—a bad dream that lasted a very long time."

Her answer was too vague. He needed more. "How did your father deal with the investigation?"

She threw the blanket aside and started clearing up the mess. "At first he tried to protect my mother and me by cooperating with the police. But when he agreed to take a lie detector test and they claimed he failed it, he wouldn't cooperate anymore."

"They *claimed* he failed it?"

She looked up at him. "There's no law that says the police have to be truthful during an interrogation. Did you know that?"

Caleb tried not to think how darn pretty she was....

What was wrong with him? This was business. If only she'd put on her damn bra. "I didn't," he said, feeling more like Judas by the minute.

"I guess once my father learned that they didn't have to be honest, he assumed they weren't and never trusted them again," she said. "He thought they were out to get him."

He could tell she was no longer enjoying the conversation, but he had to keep pushing. Partially because he refused to let her beauty distract him from his real goal. "What did *you* think?"

"I believed him," she said. "I saw how the police were acting, knew they were definitely out to get *somebody*."

"But why your father?"

She shrugged and shifted positions, but he kept an expectant expression on his face, and she finally said, "He worked on the third victim's house, doing a renovation. Her name was Tatiana Harris. She lived pretty close to us, so that shouldn't have been particularly unusual. But the lady across the street claimed she saw my father's truck leaving Tatiana's house the night she was murdered."

"You mentioned something about that before. But you don't believe she saw what she claimed she saw?"

"I think she could've been confused about *when* she saw my father's truck. Or mistaken it for someone else's in the dark. I tried talking to her about it once, and she seemed a little dotty to me. But the police thought they'd found the connection they'd been searching for, and kept digging. From there, circumstantial evidence made my father look even guiltier. And then another woman, years later, claimed she saw my father's truck leaving another crime scene.''

That was Holly, of course, who'd even managed to remember the first three digits of Purcell's license plate number. But Madison didn't add that license plate detail. Maybe she didn't want to face it.

''You don't believe her, either?''

''I don't know what to believe now.'' She toyed with her hair. ''At the time I thought the second woman was just jumping on the bandwagon. The media had publicized the details of the case so much, everyone knew my father's blue Ford had supposedly been spotted at one of the crime scenes. Anyone who'd seen him in town or simply driving down the street could note his plate number.''

So she did acknowledge the plate detail. Caleb set his glass on the table and leaned back. ''But the police didn't look at it that way.''

''No. Nine women had already been sexually assaulted and then murdered. Public pressure was such that they needed to solve the case as soon as possible.'' She gathered up the pizza box, on which she'd set their dirty plates, but before she could head to the kitchen, he stopped her with another question.

''Did your father ever think about hiring an independent specialist to administer a separate lie detector test?''

''Why would he bother?''

''To prove the police were wrong.''

''I don't think it would've made any difference.''

Caleb knew he should probably let the subject go—for tonight, anyway. She was growing agitated. But he needed answers, and he needed them fast. If only she'd tell him something he *didn't* already know… "Why wouldn't it?" he pressed.

"My father wasn't a very sophisticated man. He just wanted to be left in peace."

Just as she wanted to be left in peace. But she hadn't really answered his question. If Ellis *hadn't* been lying, why didn't he try to prove it?

Maybe winning her over would take too long. Maybe he needed to crack her cautious facade. "Do you ever think about the victims?" he asked.

She jerked as though he'd just poked her with something sharp, and he immediately realized he'd said what he'd said to remind himself of who she was. She appealed to him at such a gut level he regretted that he couldn't get to know her in any type of honest relationship.

"I try not to," she said.

"Did your father ever say anything about them?"

Ignoring his last question, she headed for the kitchen. "Thanks for the pizza, but I'd rather not talk about this anymore. It's hard enough to forget what happened to those poor women without dragging it all out in the open."

"I'm sorry," he said, following her.

She didn't answer.

"Madison?"

"It's late."

His calculated risk hadn't paid off. She hadn't given him any new information and was most definitely shutting him out. "Are we on for breakfast in the morning?"

"I don't think so. I promised Brianna I'd take her to the zoo, and we should probably get an early start. Maybe we'll just prorate your payment for meals by the number of days I actually cook."

"No problem," he said, because he didn't have a choice.

She led him down the hall and flicked on the porch light as soon as they reached the front door. "Watch that first step," she said politely as she held the door open for him.

Caleb started to go, then turned back to face her. "I don't want to go home like this," he said. It was probably the most honest thing he'd said so far.

"I don't know what you mean."

"What's wrong?"

"Nothing."

"You're upset."

"I'm not upset," she said.

"Then what?"

"I'm—" she lifted her hands helplessly "—disappointed."

Caleb leaned against the doorframe, wishing he could go back in time and take the evening a little more subtly. He'd grown impatient and pushed too hard. And he'd become frustrated by the fact that he *really* liked her when he didn't want to like her at all. "Are you going to tell me why?"

She sighed and folded her arms. "I guess I stupidly thought that when you offered to be my friend, you meant it."

His conscience wouldn't let him say he *did* want to be her friend, even though, on some level, it was true. If there'd never been a Sandpoint Strangler... If Susan weren't missing... "And now?"

"And now I know you're just like everyone else. You're only out to satisfy your morbid curiosity at my expense." She lifted her chin. "Well, I hope you were entertained."

Caleb didn't know how to respond. He let the silence stretch, torn between his duty and how he would have handled the situation if circumstances were different. "I owe you an apology," he said at last, but that sounded trite, even to his own ears. So he stepped close and ran a finger lightly over her soft cheek. "I'm really sorry, Madison."

She swatted his hand away and blinked several times in rapid succession, as though battling tears, and Caleb couldn't help pulling her into his arms.

She resisted at first, but he murmured, "It's okay, come here," and she finally relaxed against him. Only he didn't feel he'd improved matters. He couldn't promise to be a better friend. He couldn't declare his innocence. He was still living a lie.

He held her for several minutes—until he felt her tears fall on his forearm. Then he leaned away to wipe her cheeks and said what had been going through his mind all evening. "You're so beautiful, Madison. You know that?"

She stared up at him, her dark eyes luminous in the porch light. His gaze lowered to her lips. Then his heart began to pound and he did something he knew he was going to regret—he bent his head and kissed her.

CALEB'S KISS WAS SOFT and lingering, gentle. Letting her eyes close, Madison slipped her fingers into the hair at the nape of his neck and refused to think about anything. Not all the arguments against what she was doing. And certainly not her father. It was late, and they were completely alone. She felt as though she'd stolen this moment out of time and could do with it as she pleased. If she wanted only to *feel*—to feel and forget the shadow of violence in her life—she could do it right now.

Breathing in, she caught his slightly musky scent and liked it. When his arms tightened around her, she liked that, too. For the first time in a very long while, she seemed to be drowning in a sea of warm, pleasant sensations. She'd been cold for so long; she hadn't even realized how cold, until now.

His hand came up to brace her head as he parted her lips. She hesitated briefly as she remembered his pointed questions. But most people were curious about her father, and her disappointment in Caleb's earlier insensitivity was swept away by his touch. All of a sudden, she wasn't a rejected wife. She wasn't a single mother trying to run a struggling small business. She was young and wanton and desirable again....

You're so beautiful, Madison.

Sliding her other hand up over the muscles of his chest, she leaned into him as he kissed her more deeply. She wanted him to go on and on but, without warning, he pulled away.

"I shouldn't have done that," he said, closing his eyes as though he'd just made a huge mistake. "I had no idea."

She cupped his chin and made him open his eyes. "No idea of what?"

His breathing was a little erratic, giving her the impression that whatever had come over her had affected him just as much. "That you, of all people, could do this to me."

"Me, *of all people?* What's that supposed to mean?"

"Nothing," he said and left.

THE FOLLOWING MORNING, Caleb started packing. His big strategy had been a bust. He'd spent nearly the entire night thinking about Madison, and had decided he just wasn't cut out to use her. He was the guy who'd married a woman twice just to be sure he'd given her a fair shake. What made him believe he'd be able to divorce himself from the personal betrayal involved in what he had planned for Madison? She might be Ellis Purcell's daughter, but she was as deserving of loyalty and respect as anyone else.

He'd just have to find Susan without her. He wasn't *sure* there was any connection between the Sandpoint Strangler case and his ex-sister-in-law's disappearance, anyway. He'd only been working on a hunch. He'd buy out the lease and be on his way and never think of Madison Lieberman again.

Except that he knew he *would* think of her. After that kiss, he craved the taste of her—and wished like hell that they'd met under different circumstances.

His cell phone rang. He glanced over at it, reluctant to even check the caller ID, certain it was Holly or his mother. Yesterday he'd told Justine Trovato that he was renting a cottage from the daughter of Ellis Purcell. His mother knew what he wanted from Madison and hadn't liked his methods at all.

"*'What tangled webs we weave,'*" she'd quoted.

He should have listened to her.

Whoever had called simply hung up and tried again. Shoving the rest of his clothes into his bag with little regard for neatness, he finally grabbed his cell phone. The caller ID simply said "private."

"Hello?" he barked, curiously tense for someone who'd just gotten out of bed.

"There you are."

Gibbons. "Tell me you've found Susan," Caleb said.

For once the detective was noticeably reticent. "I'm afraid we have."

Dropping the tennis shoes he'd been trying to stuff into

his bag, which was nearly bursting its seams because he'd put his computer in there, too, he sank onto the bed. "But?"

"It isn't good news."

Those words seemed to echo through Caleb's head. He pictured his ex-sister-in-law coming toward him, grinning sheepishly, that time he and Holly had collected her from the airport after the stunt she'd pulled in Vegas, and closed his eyes, knowing instinctively what Gibbons was about to say.

"She's dead."

Jaw clenched, Caleb didn't bother to respond. His chest had constricted so tightly he could barely breathe, let alone speak.

"You there?" Gibbons asked after a few moments.

Caleb struggled to find his voice. "Have you or someone else notified the family?"

"Not yet. I thought maybe you should do it."

Thanks, he wanted to say. And yet he knew it was better for him to break the news than some stranger. "Right. I'll take care of it."

"Caleb?"

"What?"

"She was strangled."

Chills cascaded down Caleb's spine. "Then I was right."

"There's *something* going on. She was killed just like all the others, same fracture to the hyoid bone, same ligature marks, same..." He hesitated, obviously sensitive to the fact that because of the nature of his involvement, Caleb might not want to hear the gory details. "Same everything," he finished.

Which meant she'd been sexually assaulted with a foreign object and positioned for maximum shock value.

Caleb closed his eyes against the mental picture that was conjured up in his mind, and cursed. It felt as though he was living in some sort of alternate reality. How could the violence and horror he wrote about in the lives of others now reach out to touch him so personally? "Where did you find her?"

"Not far from where we found the others."

"Near the university?"

"Just off the Burke Gilman Trail, in some trees. A jogger saw a glimpse of white fabric—she was wrapped in a sheet—and went to investigate."

"How long has she been dead?"

"I don't have the coroner's report yet, of course, but looking at the body, I'd say at least ten days, maybe two weeks."

She'd been dead before Caleb ever reached Seattle. But what made the killer single Susan out?

"We'll know the time of death soon enough," Gibbons added, then covered the phone while he coughed. "Meanwhile, I need the next of kin to come down and ID the body."

Her parents were in Arizona, so Holly would have to do it. And Caleb knew, after two weeks, Susan wouldn't be a pretty sight. God, how was his ex-wife going to deal with seeing her sister like that?

"I'll bring Holly down to the morgue after…in a couple of hours," he said.

"That'll work."

Caleb sighed, wondering how to break the news.

"You get anywhere with Purcell's daughter?" Gibbons asked.

He'd nearly rounded first base, but that wasn't the kind of progress he'd been hoping for—and it certainly wasn't what Gibbons wanted to hear. "No, nothing that could help us."

"It's not too late."

"Too late for what?"

"We can catch this guy. There was a tire track at the scene."

"But do we have a vehicle to compare it against?" Caleb asked. Even DNA evidence wasn't any good unless the police could pinpoint a suspect and get a sample.

"Not yet, but according to a specialist on tire track impressions, it's probably from a truck."

"Oh, that narrows it down."

Any other time, Gibbons would have called him a smart ass. But he said only, "I want to check it against the tires on that blue Ford pick-up Purcell used to drive."

The blue Ford. There was a blue Ford in the picture Holly had acquired of Susan. And Susan had been strangled shortly after that photo was taken. "Do we know where the truck is?"

"I already checked with the DMV. It's still registered to the Purcells."

"So you're going to get another search warrant?"

"With Purcell dead, I don't think it's possible. Judges don't take the violation of people's constitutional rights lightly, and we both know Annette Purcell isn't capable of this murder. I was thinking it would be better to have you borrow the truck so I can take a quick peek."

"I can't borrow that truck," Caleb said.

"Why not?"

"Having me act as an agent for the police in order to obtain evidence could get you fired, for one thing. And I'm moving out of here."

"You're making this a bigger deal than it is," Gibbons replied. "I'm not going to touch the damn truck or its tires. The tread of this imprint is unusual enough that I should be able to get some idea from a visual inspection. If it checks out, I'll ask for a warrant. But I have to know I'm not out of my mind for wanting to see Purcell's vehicle when the man's already dead."

Caleb looked over at his packed bag. He'd been halfway out the door…. "Can't you see the truck's tires some other way?"

"I could if Purcell's widow ever drove it."

"Madison won't lend me her father's truck," Caleb said, remembering how difficult it had been for her to even talk about Ellis.

"She hasn't figured out who you really are, has she?"

"No."

"Then how do you know she won't do you a favor? You haven't asked her yet."

"She's trying to put her life back together. She's running a business, raising a kid. I can't—"

"Are you interested in solving this or not?" Gibbons interrupted.

"Of course." He wanted to solve it now more than ever. All the friends and family members of the various victims he'd met through the years suddenly seemed far closer to him. Instead of telling the story from a distance, he was now part of the actual picture—and the irony didn't escape him. To think that someone he knew, someone he cared about, had suffered as Susan must have suffered made him ill and showed him the difference between empathy and real understanding.

But he didn't want to use Madison. After last night, he knew that much.

"So what are you thinking?" Caleb asked.

"I don't know," Gibbons said. "Maybe we were wrong about Purcell. Maybe he wasn't the strangler, after all. Or maybe someone else has picked up where he left off. Someone close enough to know how he worked.''

"Like who?" Caleb asked.

"Remember that license plate you had me run? The car you said Purcell's son was riding in a couple of nights ago?"

"Yeah?"

"It came back as stolen."

Caleb scrubbed a hand over his jaw. "You don't think Johnny's somehow involved, do you? He was in prison when some of those women were murdered."

"Well, he's not in prison anymore," Gibbons said. "They let him out three days before Susan disappeared."

CHAPTER NINE

THEY'D LEFT THE VIEWING room fifteen minutes earlier. Caleb and Holly had stared at Susan's body through a small window; they'd been separated from her by a wall and a glass panel, so Caleb knew he had to be imagining that he couldn't rid himself of the sweet, cloying scent of death. But he still would've headed directly home, stripped off his clothes and taken a long hot shower—with plenty of suds and vigorous scrubbing. Except he couldn't leave Holly. She was in no condition to be on her own, and her parents' flight from Phoenix wasn't arriving until later this evening.

"You okay?" he murmured as they sat on a bench in the hallway of the morgue. Holly had wept since he'd told her about Susan, but she seemed to be coming to the end of her tears. Her skin was splotchy, her eyes red and puffy, her hair somewhat tangled, but her face had taken on a stark expression that conveyed the depth of her grief far more effectively than simple crying.

She didn't answer him. She just wrapped her jacket more tightly around her.

"Hol?" He gave her shoulders a gentle squeeze.

"How can you even ask me that?" she said dully, her voice barely a whisper. "Of course I'm not okay."

"You have to get through this," he said. "Susan wouldn't want you to fall apart."

"Susan." Tears welled in her eyes again, but she didn't

curl into him as she had before. She sat on her hands and stared blankly at the floor.

Down the hall, Detective Gibbons stepped out of the autopsy room. "You're still here?" he said when he saw Caleb.

Caleb hadn't been able to get Holly to leave. She couldn't bear the sight of Susan as she was now. But the battered and badly decomposed corpse was all that remained of her sister. For Holly, walking away would sever that one last tie.

"You got a minute?" Gibbons asked. Though Gibbons's language and manner were pretty rough, he did wear a suit. It was a rather cheesy, three-piece affair—a throwback to professional fashion in the seventies—but it was a suit. And the way he straightened and buttoned his coat told Caleb that Gibbons wanted to talk to him alone.

Caleb was reluctant to abandon Holly. She seemed so fragile. But when he hesitated, she lifted her gaze to his and the tears that had pooled in her eyes brimmed and rolled down her cheeks. "Go. I want this bastard caught."

With a nod, Caleb got up and followed Gibbons into the coroner's office, where the smell of fresh-brewed coffee heartened him. He'd received Gibbons's call so early, he hadn't showered or shaved, and he felt rumpled and dirty, as though he'd been sleeping in his clothes.

Turning the bill of his ball cap to the back, he glanced around the empty room before propping himself against the coroner's desk. "Tell me you've found something," he said.

Gibbons sighed. "Autopsies take time—you know that. And they haven't even started yet. But judging by the injuries to her forearms, this young lady put up a good fight."

Susan would, Caleb thought; she had Holly's spirit. "Which means we have a chance of finding biological evidence under her nails, right?"

"Or on the sheet in which her body was wrapped. The forensics team has found a drop of blood that definitely doesn't belong to Susan."

"What can I do to help?" Caleb asked.

Reaching into his breast pocket, Gibbons pulled out a copy of the picture that had been taken at the pizza parlor, and handed it to him. "Take this and go back to the pizza place tonight," he said. "Show it around and see if you can find out who was driving that truck. And who was arguing with Susan."

"So you're officially on the case?" Caleb asked.

"Because Susan was killed in the same way as the victims of the Sandpoint Strangler, I'm not only on the case, I'm lead detective. The department doesn't want to waste resources by rebuilding everything I've already put together."

"No one knows more about the Sandpoint Strangler than you do."

Gibbons raised his brows. "Except maybe you. You're the one practically living with Madison Lieberman. Think you can get hold of Purcell's truck?"

Caleb let his breath seep slowly between his teeth as he considered the question. He hated the thought of embroiling Madison and Brianna in another painful investigation, this one centering on Johnny. She'd already been through more than enough. But he couldn't let whoever killed Susan get away with it. Especially when chances were likely that the sick bastard would strike again. "I'll figure something out," he said.

Gibbons clapped him on the back. "Good man."

MADISON LEANED CLOSE to the window to peer out at the dark drive as she finished drying the pans she'd used to make dinner. She knew Caleb was still gone. She'd been listening for his car for several hours and hadn't heard anything beyond the wash cycle of her dishwasher.

Where was he? It was getting late. He'd indicated that his work schedule wasn't especially grueling, yet he'd been gone from dawn until ten or eleven at night four days in a row. He hadn't even wanted dinner. He'd left a brief message on her answering machine Monday through Wednesday saying that he had to work late and not to expect him.

It wasn't until this morning, when she'd bumped into him as she was leaving to take Brianna to school, that she'd actually spoken to him. He'd been dressed in a dark suit, seemed far more somber than the man she'd thought she was getting to know, and had very little to say, except that he didn't want dinner again tonight.

Maybe he was avoiding her. Maybe that kiss had bothered him even more than she'd assumed. *That you, of all people, could do this to me.* What had he meant by that? Was he as afraid of intimacy as she was? Was he worried she might fall at his feet and try to extract some kind of commitment—over one silly kiss?

She shook her head. If so, he didn't understand that she wasn't open to the possibility of falling in love. She couldn't deal with the hope, the effort, the risk. Too much was riding on the next few years, for her business and her daughter.

"Mommy, look what I found!" Brianna said, charging into the kitchen.

Madison glanced through the window once more to find the drive still empty, then turned to see her daughter carrying a large photo album. There was anticipation on Brianna's little face. But Madison had to bite back a groan when she saw that it wasn't just any album. It was the album she'd hidden under her bed.

"See? It's my baby book!" she announced proudly. "Come on, Mommy, let's look at it."

The album contained pictures of Brianna's birth and infancy, and a few photos of when she was a toddler. Madison and Brianna used to spend a lot of time poring over this particular book. Like most children, Brianna was fascinated by pictures of herself and the concept that she hadn't always been as she was now. But there were also photos of Madison's father in there that Madison didn't want to see. Not now. She'd just taken down every picture of him.

"It's getting late, punkin," she said. "Why don't we look at that tomorrow?"

"No," Brianna said. "You promised you'd read me a bedtime story. I want to look at my pictures instead."

"But—"

"Please, Mommy?" Brianna wore such a beseeching expression that Madison couldn't refuse.

"For a little while," she said.

Brianna rewarded her with a beaming smile and started pulling her into the living room. "Come on, let's sit down."

Madison took a deep breath, steeling herself for the moments to follow, but it didn't help. Once they were seated on the couch and going through the album page by page, Brianna not only insisted on pointing at every person in every picture, she demanded Madison tell her all the old stories. How the doctor had missed the delivery when she was born and the nurse had to step in. How Daddy had fallen asleep in the chair by the bed and nearly slept through what had almost turned into an emergency. How Grandpa used to stand her up in the palm of his hand before she could even walk. How Grandma had once dressed her up in a snowsuit and taken her to Utah to visit Madison's Aunt Belinda, or Aunt Bee, as Brianna knew her.

By the time they'd gone through several pages, the memories crashed over Madison like waves, hard and fast, threatening to drag her out to sea. Through it all, she couldn't help wondering—what had gone wrong? If her father *had* killed those women, what had been so incredibly different about him that he could harm others, seemingly without remorse? Surely there must've been some clue that she'd missed. But she couldn't figure out what it would be. Her father had been quiet and difficult to know because of that, but not every strong, silent male becomes a mass murderer.

She knew he'd had a difficult childhood, that he was brought up in a strict household where corporal punishment was sometimes taken to the extreme. But other than maintaining a rigid belief in the father as patriarch of the home, he didn't seem too affected by the past. He went to bed early, got up before dawn, worked hard and took care of everything in the house with a fastidiousness seldom seen in the American world of "easy come, easy go." He'd been a simple man. Or so she'd thought.

"What's wrong, Mommy?" Brianna asked, frowning when Madison didn't turn the page.

Madison closed her eyes, remembering. Her father had never been demonstrative, but he'd always had a roll of Lifesavers in his pocket for Brianna. Whenever they visited Grandma and Grandpa's house, Grandpa had let Brianna help him husk corn or snap peas or tinker in the garage.

That she'd trusted her father enough to let him get so

close to Brianna terrified Madison now, just in case he'd been what everyone said he was.

"Mommy?" Brianna asked, sounding worried.

Madison pulled herself out of the sea of memories long enough to force a smile for her daughter. "What, honey?"

"What's wrong?"

"Nothing. I was just thinking."

Uncertainty flickered in Brianna's eyes, but Madison easily distracted her with the next picture. "This is when Grandma baked you a Barbie cake for your second birthday, and Grandpa made you that playhouse in the backyard. Do you remember?"

Brianna's forehead wrinkled. "Daddy said he built the playhouse."

"No, it was Grandpa." Her father had come over to build the playhouse because the guy Danny hired didn't show. Madison remembered being upset because it was Sunday, a day Danny didn't have to work, yet he'd been gone anyway. Madison knew her father found it strange that Danny wasn't more of a support to her. She'd thought Ellis was going to say something about it as he left that day. Instead, he'd squeezed her shoulder—for him, the equivalent of a long conversation.

With her father, so much went unsaid. And yet she'd always known he loved her....

"Mommy, why are you crying?" Brianna asked.

Madison hadn't realized she *was* crying. Dashing a hand across her cheeks, she searched for words that might make things clear for her daughter. But she knew Brianna wouldn't understand even if she tried to explain. Madison herself didn't understand, at least not fully. The fact that someone she loved and trusted so deeply could ruin the whole essence of who he was for reasons she couldn't begin to fathom was simply confusing and painful. And that was before she considered the victims and their families and friends....

"That's enough for tonight," she said, closing the book. "It's time for bed."

A knock at the door stole Brianna's attention. She hopped off the couch to answer, but Madison caught her by the arm. "You know it's not safe to go to the door alone, especially after dark. I'll see who it is. You get your pajamas on."

"Mo-om," Brianna complained.

"You have school in the morning."

Her daughter's scowl deepened.

"Even princesses need their sleep," Madison said.

"But it might be Caleb."

Madison arched an eyebrow at her. "I thought you didn't like Caleb. I thought you didn't want me to let him move in."

"*I* don't like him," she said quickly, "but Elizabeth does."

If not for the spell cast by that darn photo album, Madison might have laughed. "Elizabeth isn't even here," she pointed out.

"She's in the bedroom. I'll get her."

Brianna scampered off and Madison set the photo album aside, trying to convince herself that *she* wasn't excited by the prospect of seeing Caleb.

She should've known Caleb was much too handsome and charismatic to fit smoothly into her life.

She tried telling herself their kiss was nothing as she headed down the hall, but it didn't feel like nothing when she opened the door. Caleb stood there, still wearing the same suit he'd been wearing this morning, with his tie loosened and his hair slightly tousled as though it had been a long, hard day.

"Are you okay?" she asked.

His gaze briefly lowered to her lips before he met her eyes, and Madison had the strangest impulse to slip into his arms and let him kiss her again.

That's crazy. I'm *crazy.*

"Yes," he said. "Everything okay here?"

"Fine."

"Good." He hesitated for a moment, nodded and started walking away. But then Brianna came running. "Caleb! Caleb, where are you going? I'm right here!"

He turned and gave her a half smile. "I thought you'd be asleep, half-pint."

"We were just looking at pictures," she announced.

He reached into his pocket. "Well, I'm glad you're up because I brought you something."

"A surprise?"

"Sort of."

"Did you hear that, Elizabeth? He brought us a surprise!" Hugging her stuffed rabbit, she twirled around.

"Just a small one," he said and, her curiosity piqued, Madison leaned forward to see him drop a large nugget of pyrite in her child's hand.

Brianna's eyes went round. "Is it *gold?*"

"Oh, no. Gold is nothing compared to this," he said. "Haven't you ever heard the story 'Jack and the Beanstalk?'"

"I've heard it," she said. "Mommy reads it to me all the time."

"Then you know about his magic beans."

She nodded enthusiastically.

"This rock is like those beans. It's—" he looked around as though he was afraid he might be overheard and dropped his voice "—magic."

"It is?" she asked, completely taken in. "What can it do?"

"It can remind you of important things."

"Like what?" Her voice was filled with the awe and reverence he'd inspired.

"When you're scared or worried about something, anything at all, and there's nothing you can do to make it better, you hold this rock tightly in one hand, like this." He took the rock from her and made a fist around it. "And if you close your eyes and listen, it'll whisper to you."

"What will it say?"

"It will remind you of all the people who love you and it will tell you that everything is going to be okay."

"*Really?*" she breathed.

"You have to listen hard," he said.

"Oh, I will."

Madison put a hand to her mouth to cover a smile. "It's time for you to take your magic rock to bed," she said when she'd composed herself.

"But Caleb just got here," Brianna complained.

"Maybe you can see him tomorrow."

Brianna was too busy examining her rock to move, so Madison gave her a gentle nudge.

"Thanks," Brianna told Caleb. "I won't lose it."

He winked at her, and she skipped down the hall, talking to Elizabeth the whole way. "Look, Elizabeth. It's magic...."

Madison leaned against the doorjamb, thinking Caleb looked so handsome with his loosened tie and unbuttoned collar that he could start a new fashion trend—rumpled chic. "You got a rock for me?" she asked.

His lips curved into a sexy smile. "You want one, too?"

"Only if it's magic."

He reached into his pocket and pulled out a fifty-cent piece. "Looks like a magic coin is the best I can offer."

"Will it whisper to me when I'm worried or afraid?"

"You bet," he said.

"What will it say?"

He took her hand and put the coin in the center of her palm. "To call me."

She curled her fingers around the metal, which was warm from his touch, and let that warmth travel through her. "You might be a little tough to get hold of," she said. "You've been gone a lot lately."

With a sigh, he loosened his tie even more. "This has been a tough week."

"You want to talk about it?"

"Not really."

She waited, hoping he'd change his mind, but he changed the subject instead. "What's been happening around here?"

"Same old stuff." She grinned. "None of it magic."

"Has Johnny been around?"

"No. For all I know he's back in jail. It generally doesn't take him long." She tucked her hair behind one ear. "What you did for Brianna was really nice. What made you think of her?"

"Thinking of you and Brianna isn't the problem."

"I didn't know there was a problem, at least where we're concerned."

He glanced over his shoulder at his dark cottage. "There isn't. I'm just tired."

She could see that from the small lines of fatigue around his eyes and bracketing his mouth, but she was hesitant to let him leave while he seemed so…somber and unsettled. "Would you like a glass of wine before you go? It might help you relax."

"I don't know." His eyes grew thoughtful. "You'd probably be better off to send me straight home to bed. You know that, don't you?"

Madison imagined Caleb lying in bed, the sheet pulled only to his waist, his chest and arms bare, and felt a flutter of excitement that told her he was definitely right. Yet she opened the door wider. "But my magic coin is telling me you could use a drink."

CHAPTER TEN

WHILE MADISON WENT to tuck Brianna in for the night, Caleb sipped the wine she'd given him and circled her living room. He knew he should head directly to the cottage, get a good night's sleep, gain some perspective on everything that had happened—including Susan's funeral earlier today, which had been almost surreal—and call Madison in the morning to see if he could somehow borrow her father's truck. If he was going to help Gibbons and still maintain his integrity, he needed to be careful not to get too close.

Unfortunately, that was easier said than done. Caleb had blown his plan to keep a safe distance the minute he'd pulled into the drive—by going to Madison's house instead of his own. He'd just needed to assure himself that she, at least, was all right. But he hadn't been able to walk away. The moment he saw her, he'd remembered the taste of her kiss and wanted to bury his face in her neck, let her surround him with her scent, the softness of her skin, the warmth of her heart....

"Almost done," she called.

He could hear the water running in the bathroom, where she was helping Brianna brush her teeth. He finished his wine, considered leaving, ignored what was best— again—and turned on the television.

The news came blaring into the room. Irritated by the noise, he turned it off and sat down to look through the photo album he found on the table. The words *Our Little Princess* were affixed to the cover, along with a 5x7 photo of Brianna as a baby, and he couldn't help thinking that Susan's parents probably had a similar album about her somewhere.

Pulling the book into his lap, Caleb opened it to pictures of Madison in a hospital bed, smiling proudly as she cradled a red-faced newborn. Standing next to her was a man who had to be her ex-husband, Danny.

Caleb stripped off his jacket and rolled up his sleeves, then scrutinized the man she'd been speaking to on the phone a few days ago. Danny wasn't anything like he'd expected. Short and balding, he looked too old for Madison. And even though he was *in* the picture, his body language suggested he didn't necessarily want to be. While Caleb read joy on Madison's face at the birth of her first child, Danny seemed far less interested.

"What a guy," he muttered, and turned the page to find more hospital photos, these featuring Madison's parents. Danny's backside or leg appeared here and there, so Caleb knew he wasn't the person behind the lens. But neither was he posing with the others. From the relative positioning of everyone in the room, Caleb got the impression that there'd been no love lost between Madison's parents and her husband, even while she was married.

The next few pictures were of Grandpa and the baby. Caleb held the book closer as he examined Ellis Purcell. What could Ellis have been thinking as he looked at his wife, daughter and brand-new granddaughter? Was he feeling any remorse for the women he'd murdered so brutally? Or was his mind a million miles away, anticipating his next victim?

If so, Purcell had outsmarted them all.

Or maybe he hadn't outsmarted anybody. Maybe they'd

set their sights on the wrong guy from the beginning. Gibbons was becoming more and more suspicious of Johnny. He thought Johnny might've picked up where his father had left off. Who else would have access to Purcell's truck? Gibbons had argued. Who else would have known exactly how to position the body except someone with inside information?

Caleb couldn't answer those questions. But *he* wasn't convinced that Johnny was their man. In Caleb's mind, Johnny didn't have the nerve to do what this killer did. This killer was cool and cunning, far more controlled than Johnny. Stealing a car was one thing. Sexually assaulting and strangling a woman was another. That kind of brutality took a deep-seated rage....

"She's finally asleep," Madison said, emerging from the hall.

"I hope you don't mind," Caleb said, indicating the photo album. "It was on the table."

She frowned slightly but crossed the room and sat on the sofa a few feet away from him, wearing the same jeans and tight-fitting T-shirt she'd had on when he arrived. "Brianna dragged it out."

"I take it this is your ex," he said, turning back to the picture of Danny on the front page.

She made a face and scooted closer to look. "Handsome devil, isn't he?"

Caleb smiled at her sarcasm. "I'm guessing he must've had other attributes."

"Not really."

He raised his brows in question.

"I've decided he was an escape," she said. "An escape from everything that was going on in my life at the time. I didn't realize it when I married him, of course. But I had to face the truth shortly after. Especially because my marriage didn't really change anything, at least not for the better.''

"You mean you couldn't get along with a guy who frowns at the birth of his own daughter?" he asked with feigned surprise.

Madison laughed. "That passes as a smile for Danny."

"How did such a love match unravel?"

"We weren't ever what you could call a 'love match.' Danny's persistence and his confidence that we were meant to be together finally won me over. He was five years older and had his life all neatly planned out. He was also pretty understanding about the investigation—at first. And I'd just lost my best friend, so I was particularly vulnerable."

She brought her legs up and wrapped her arms around them. "Most of all, I was longing to settle down, have a family of my own and live what I hoped would be a 'normal' life. He claimed he wanted those things, too."

Caleb still couldn't believe Danny had managed to get a woman like Madison to even look at him. "What changed after you were married?"

"Danny was a lot more complex and difficult than I'd ever expected. Emotionally, he was like a child—everything revolved around him. He could never see how what was happening with my father affected *me,* only how it affected *him.* And after the first few years, two more bodies were discovered and the investigation intensified, so he stopped being as understanding."

"How long were you married?"

"Seven years." She drew an audible breath. "But we had detectives following us around toward the end. So that probably made a big difference to his behavior."

Caleb got up to pour himself some more wine. "You knew the police were following you?"

"Sometimes the detectives would sit at the curb out front and wave to us as we went in and out. I think they were trying to intimidate us."

That must have been after Caleb quit the force, because he'd never seen Danny in person. Gibbons had always kept him busy taking care of the hundreds of peripheral people who had to be interviewed. "Did it work?" he called from the kitchen.

"It was intimidating, sure," she said. "It would be intimidating for anyone. But I don't think they were very smart to bully us."

"Why?"

She accepted the glass of wine he brought back for her. "Their tactics only made me more determined to remain firm. Not that it did me any good. When the killings started up again, the police felt so much pressure to solve the case, they transferred that pressure to us, including Danny. Pretty soon the neighbors were accustomed to seeing detectives coming and going from my house, but they certainly weren't happy about it."

She paused to take a sip of wine. "They formed their own opinions," she continued, "and hinted that if I'd only cooperate and 'do the right thing' it would all be over and my 'poor husband' could hold up his head again. They quit inviting us to neighborhood barbecue parties. They wouldn't let their children play with Brianna or come to our house." She sighed and shifted position so she could stretch her legs out in front of her. "Danny couldn't tolerate all the negative attention."

"Why didn't the two of you take your baby and move somewhere else? Somewhere the murders and the investigation weren't so publicized?" Caleb asked, thinking that if he were Danny, he would've done anything to protect his family.

"By the time we realized things weren't going to die down, Danny had landed a fantastic job at Waskell, Bolchevik and Piedmont. You've probably heard of them."

"The big engineering firm downtown?"

She nodded. "He wasn't willing to walk away from that. His job came before everything."

"Does he have other family in town?"

"His parents and one brother live in Spokane, so they're not far."

Caleb held his glass up to the light, studying the pale gold of the chardonnay. "What about you?"

"What about me?"

"Didn't *you* want to leave Seattle?"

"No, leaving was never an option. I'm my mother's only child. I had to stay here and support her and my father."

He crossed his feet at the ankles, finally beginning to relax and distance himself from the reality of what had happened to Susan, and her funeral, and the whole past week. "What about your parents? Didn't they ever consider moving?" he asked.

"No."

"Why not?"

"Toward the end, they were convinced the police would plant some sort of evidence if one of the detectives ever gained access to the house."

Caleb pictured Madison with a young baby, a bad marriage, a needy mother, a murder suspect for a father, and Gibbons and Thomas always at her heels, invading her privacy.

"I admire you for standing by your parents," he said, and was surprised by the fact that he actually meant it. At one time he'd thought her callous and irresponsible for refusing to cooperate with the police. But now that he understood her situation better, he could see exactly why she'd done what she had. Few women were as loyal as Madison Lieberman. She'd even hung on to Danny for seven years.

"I did what I thought was best," she said. "But now…"

Caleb finished the last of his wine and slid down so he could rest his head on the back of the couch. "But now?"

"Now I think I might have made a huge mistake."

"How so?" He glanced over at her, noting her grave expression.

"Can I trust you, Caleb?"

"Trust me?" he repeated, feeling numb. *Sure, you can trust me* was a little too blatant a lie, even if he told it for the right reasons. "That depends on what you're going to trust me with," he said, hedging.

She placed her hand on his forearm and let it slip down. Unable to resist, he turned his hand palm up when she reached it, lacing his fingers securely through hers.

She looked down at their entwined hands, and he could tell that, like his, her breathing had gone a little shallow.

"Sometimes I wish I'd never been born to Ellis Purcell," she said.

Mesmerized by the contact, by the delicacy of her slim fingers, Caleb was feeling a very powerful physical response. It didn't help that it was late, they were alone…and the last thing he wanted was to return to an empty house to brood about Susan.

On impulse, he lifted her hand to his mouth and brushed a kiss across her knuckles. "I thought you said he didn't do it."

She shivered as though a tingle had traveled through her body—through places he wished he could touch.

"I said I didn't *think* he did it." She swallowed visibly,

her eyes on his mouth as he rubbed his lips lightly across the back of her hand. "But I didn't know then what I know now."

What was she saying? He'd been so preoccupied with touching her that he hadn't been paying as much attention to her words as he should. Letting go, he sat up. "You want to run that by me one more time?"

She seemed a little startled by his abrupt change. "Nothing. It's the wine, that's all," she said, grabbing her wineglass. "I don't know what I'm saying."

"Madison?"

"What?"

"You said you didn't know then what you know now. What did you mean by that?"

She put the photo album on the coffee table. "Never mind. My heart still tells me there's no way my father could have hurt those women."

"But can you always trust your heart?" he murmured, cupping her chin so she had to look up at him.

She lowered her lashes, and he sensed that she was feeling the same attraction he was.

"I don't know," she said, "but I think everyone comes face-to-face with that question at least once in a lifetime. Don't you?"

Caleb was pretty sure he was coming face to face with it now. His heart was telling him to protect Madison, to let himself care about her. But his head was telling him he'd been right all along. She knew something she wasn't saying.

And for Susan, and Holly, and all the women in Seattle who deserved to be safe, he had to find out what it was.

WHAT HAD SHE BEEN thinking, nearly telling Caleb about what she'd found in the crawl space? Obviously she was lonelier than she'd realized. He just seemed so caring, so safe, she was tempted to open up to him about her father. And Danny. Throughout her marriage and subsequent divorce, she hadn't had anyone to talk to—not about personal matters. She couldn't burden her mother with the sad little details of her failing marriage. Not when Annette was already overwhelmed by having her husband accused of sexual assault and murder. And because of the investigation and her focus on Brianna, Madison didn't have any close friends.

After a good night's sleep, she'd do better at keeping their conversations centered on inconsequential facts, she told herself. But she wasn't sure she'd be able to fall asleep right away. Her body was still humming with the aftereffects of Caleb's lips grazing her knuckles. Every time she closed her eyes, she imagined his mouth and hands on other parts of her body....

The telephone rang, startling her as she headed down the hall to her bedroom. She halfway hoped it was Caleb, despite wanting to keep some emotional distance between them.

When she answered, her mother's voice came on the line. "We're vindicated," she said. "At last."

Madison pulled the phone away to look down at it before bringing it back to her ear. "Did I miss something?" she asked.

"It's true. Haven't you heard?"

"Heard what?"

"It's been all over the news."

"I don't watch the news or read the papers," Madison said. "I've had enough of the press for the next ten years. So you might want to tell me what you're so excited about."

"The police have found another victim," her mother said. "Another woman's been strangled."

Madison's breath seemed to lodge in her throat. "You sound as though you think this is *good* news," she said when she could speak again.

"It *is* good news, for us. Don't you understand what it means?"

"It means another person has suffered untold depravity and violence. It means some other family has been deprived of a loved one."

"I'm sorry for all of that," her mother said tersely. "But I didn't do anything to cause it. And this proves that your father wasn't the Sandpoint Strangler, just as we've been saying all along."

"How?" Madison asked.

"This victim fit the same profile the earlier ones did. She was strangled and positioned just like the others. It's obviously the same killer."

Her knees suddenly weak, Madison felt behind her for the couch and sank down onto it. She didn't know what to think or how to feel. Relieved? Fearful? Doubtful? Hopeful? Somehow she seemed to be experiencing them all at once. "How do you know it's not a copycat?" she breathed.

"Because Ellis didn't kill those women, so there's nothing to copy. And now that it's happened again and he's gone, the police will have to turn their attention to finding the real killer, and the truth will finally come out."

"This doesn't make sense," Madison muttered to herself.

"What did you say?"

She swallowed hard. "Nothing. I— Where did they find her?"

"A few miles from the house."

"Who was she?"

"A twenty-six-year-old single woman who lived near the university and worked at Nordstrom. I think her name was Susan."

Susan. Madison closed her eyes. What if there was something in that box she'd found under the house that could've saved that woman? What if there was something that might help the police now? She had to take it to them, let them sort it out....

"Mom?"

"What, dear?"

"If...if I happened to stumble on something that would...that could possibly figure in the case, you'd want me to come forward with it, wouldn't you? Even if it made Dad look as though he might really have—"

"Madison!" her mother interrupted, her voice instantly sharp.

"What?"

"I don't think you understand what that investigation did to me, what it did to your father."

"I do, Mom. That's why I haven't said anything so far."

"Ellis was innocent! I'll go to my grave believing that."

"I loved him, too. I still love him. But—"

"Do you know why your father killed himself?" her mother asked, now openly weeping.

Madison thought she could come up with a few plausible reasons. She certainly knew what his critics would say. But she didn't bother answering. Her mother's question was rhetorical. "Why?"

"To put an end to what you and I were suffering. He hated that he couldn't save us from the harassment we were receiving from the police, the community, even our neighbors. So he ended it." She sniffed and gulped for the breath to continue. "He gave up his life so we could live normally again."

"He's gone now, Mom," Madison said softly. "We don't have to protect him anymore."

"I don't care. I won't betray him. And no daughter of mine would betray him, either."

Tension clawed at Madison's stomach. Her father was gone, couldn't have killed this latest victim. But because of that box there *had* to be a connection, didn't there? "You're not listening. I've found some articles that—"

"You could have a videotape and I wouldn't believe it," Annette cut in, her voice vehement.

Madison covered her eyes. "Faith is one thing, Mom. Sticking your head in the sand is another."

"All I know is what my heart tells me is true," her mother said.

Those words sounded like an echo of Madison's conversation earlier with Caleb. But it wasn't surprising, considering she and her mother had relied on that argument for years. "Can you always trust your heart?" she asked, repeating his question.

"If you can't trust your heart, what can you trust?" her mother said, and hung up.

CHAPTER ELEVEN

MADISON SHIVERED as she stood outside a few minutes later, waiting for Caleb to rouse himself from sleep and answer her knock. She tried to tell herself to go back home and go to bed. But she was too upset. Her mother would never forgive her if she turned that box over to the police.

But Madison wasn't sure she'd be able to forgive herself if she didn't.

It all came down to what *she* really believed, and she no longer knew what that was. Her father wasn't the type to hurt anyone. But if he hadn't murdered Lisa McDonna, why was her locket in the crawl space of his house?

Caleb opened the door wearing a pair of hastily donned jeans, judging by the top button, which was undone, and nothing else. His hair mussed from sleep, he flipped on the porch light and squinted against the sudden brightness. "Madison? Is something wrong?"

Suddenly, she felt awkward. When she was at home, it had seemed natural to come to him. She was so tired of being alone.

"I…" She fell silent because what she was feeling couldn't be distilled into a few simple words.

"Did something happen?" he asked.

She held out her hand to reveal the coin he'd given her. That was really all she'd come for, wasn't it? To collect on his promise that she could call him if she ever needed reassurance?

Taking her by the elbow, he guided her inside, closing the door behind them. They stood in the dim light of the living room, the shutters casting shadowed lines across Caleb's face. "Tell me what's wrong," he said.

"They found another p-poor woman." She shivered again, even though it was warm in the cottage.

Pulling her close, he put his arms around her. "You just heard?"

He seemed so solid and real, so in control at a time when she felt as if she was spinning out into space.

She closed her eyes and nodded, concentrating only on the heat flowing through her cheek, which she'd pressed to his bare chest. This was what she needed. This was all she needed. A few minutes of contact with another human being…

"Just tell me everything's going to be okay," she whispered.

He brushed back her hair and placed a featherlight kiss on her temple. "It might get worse before it gets better, Madison, but…" He hesitated, and she leaned back far enough to look up at him. "I'll be here if you need me," he finished, and she smiled because it sounded so much like a promise.

THE SLIGHTLY FLORAL SCENT of Madison's perfume and the softness of her body beneath the baggy sweats she was wearing kick-started Caleb's libido. He knew he'd be much better off sending her back to her own house—right away—but he couldn't seem to let go of her. She'd come to him for comfort, and he wanted to give her that much. Obviously she wasn't as insensitive about the suffering of others as he'd once believed.

Or maybe he couldn't let go of her because he needed a little comfort himself. The past four days hadn't been easy. He'd had a difficult time grasping the fact that such evil had touched his own life in a very personal way. Holly had been almost childlike in the way she'd clung to him, irritating yet sympathetic in her neediness. Her parents treated him as though he and Holly had never divorced, and had been leaning on him to deal with the police and also with the funeral home regarding Susan's burial. Beyond that, every extra minute had been spent helping Detective Gibbons. Caleb had been tracking down Johnny's friends, from previous schoolmates to cellmates, and some friends and neighbors of Tye's, too. He'd told them he was a private investigator working on a murder case and showed them pictures of Susan. And he'd haunted the pizza parlor and surrounding neighborhood, looking for the driver of that blue Ford in the picture—all to no avail.

He felt exhausted, frustrated, torn. Yet he still had some difficult decisions to make. Like how far he was willing to go to manipulate Madison into lending him Ellis's truck. He knew Gibbons would be calling him—if not tomorrow, then the next day.

"I just don't understand it," Madison murmured. The movement of her lips, tickling his bare skin, was enough to make his heart race. "I don't understand why anyone would want to hurt and humiliate another human being."

Caleb pressed her closer, enjoying the sensation of her against him while consciously working to keep his thoughts from turning sexual. Having Madison in his bed would give *him* a lot of comfort, but he was pretty sure sex wasn't the type of comfort *she* had in mind—and it certainly wasn't a memory she'd appreciate once she learned who he was. "Psychologists claim most violence is about power."

"I don't see how hurting someone or something weaker makes a man feel better about himself."

"Neither do I," he said, admiring the slight tilt at the end of her nose and the fullness of her lips. He remembered the softness of those lips all too well....

Before the temptation to abandon his morals could strike again, he stepped back, grabbed a sweatshirt he'd left on the couch earlier and held it out to her. "Put this on, and I'll walk you over to your place."

She pulled the sweatshirt over her head while he held the door.

"I'm sorry for waking you," she said as they crossed the drive.

Caleb jammed his hands in his pockets so that he wouldn't touch her. Now that he'd created some space between them, he needed to maintain it. If she cozied up to him again, he doubted he'd be able to stop himself from at least testing how she might respond to his desire for deeper intimacy. When the truth came out, she'd end up hating him for making love to her under such deception. But there *was* the argument that she was going to hate him anyway....

"No worries," he said. "My door's always open."

She smiled. "I like you, Caleb Trovato," she said. "I'm glad you moved in."

They'd reached her door. Caleb leaned a shoulder against the front of the house while she stood at the threshold.

He liked her, too. Which only made his next question that much more difficult to ask.

Fixing a picture of Susan's battered body in his mind, he called up the rage he felt at whoever had hurt her. "By the way,'' he said. ''Any chance you know someone who owns a truck I could borrow?''

''What for?''

''I have a friend who's moving and could really use some help.''

''When do you need it?''

''Tomorrow or Saturday, if possible.''

She seemed somewhat hesitant, as though she was going to refuse him. But then her smile returned. ''My dad's truck is just sitting in the garage. I'll see what I can do.''

IT RAINED THE FOLLOWING day, tiny drops that quickly turned into a constant drizzle.

Madison grumbled at the damp, foggy weather, wishing she didn't have to drive over to the mainland to get her father's truck. But the memory of Caleb taking her into his arms when she was so upset last night made her want to go to the extra trouble. He'd been there for her. She wanted to be there for him.

''That's what friends are for,'' she muttered, and dashed out of the office building that housed her business, ducking beneath her briefcase until she could reach her car.

After starting the motor, she turned on her wiper blades, then backed out of her parking space. As soon as she was in line to catch the next ferry, she forced herself to do what she'd been dreading all morning—call her mother.

''Madison, is it you?'' her mother asked. After their conversation the night before, Annette's voice was noticeably cool. ''You're cutting in and out.''

A moment later, Madison inched forward along with the other cars, and her cell reception improved. ''Can you hear me now?''

''Yes. Are you in the car?''

"I'm about to cross over to the mainland. I'm on my way to your place."

"Are you showing the house?"

Madison felt a twinge of guilt, because she'd had several calls on her mother's house from both agents and buyers. Just as she'd feared, some of her callers seemed more interested in the house's dramatic history and getting a peek at it than in purchasing the property. Still, there'd been some legitimate calls, as well. Legitimate calls she hadn't returned. And she'd put off the people she'd already talked to, trying to avoid selling the house until she could decide what to do with the box hidden in the crawl space. "Not today," she said. "I'm getting some interest on it, though. Maybe I'll be able set up a tour for tomorrow or Sunday."

"So why are you coming here? Brianna's in school, isn't she?"

"I'm just dropping off the comps I said I'd put together for you."

"The comps?"

"The list of homes in your area that have sold in the past few months, along with the price of each."

"Oh, right. Okay."

"And—" Madison took a deep breath "—and I was hoping to borrow Dad's truck."

Dead silence. Madison knew it was her imagination, but it felt as though the temperature had dropped another ten degrees. "Mom?" she said, cranking up her heater.

"What's going on?" her mother demanded. "Why are you suddenly interested in the truck?"

"Nothing's going on. I want to lend it to a friend, that's all."

"You know how your father felt about that vehicle."

"Of course I know." Once that witness had placed Ellis's truck at Anna Tyler's apartment, he'd become increasingly afraid to drive it. He'd parked the truck in his garage to be sure no one had access to it. At the time, the police were so determined that Ellis was their strangler and so desperate to solve the case, Madison had believed her father's concerns to be legitimate. But now she had to wonder if his paranoia revolved around a fear that Seattle detectives would plant evidence—or find it.

"This has nothing to do with the police or anything else," she continued. "I'm just trying to help Caleb, my new renter."

Another long pause. "Do you have to help him like this?"

"Mom, I'm tired of being paranoid," Madison said. "Caleb needs the truck for only a few hours. For once I'd like to respond as a *normal* person would. For once I'd like to say, 'Sure, no problem,' as if we don't have anything to hide."

"We *don't* have anything to hide," her mother replied.

"Then why can't he borrow the truck?"

Madison could tell Annette didn't like being cornered, but she'd already decided to throw her support Caleb's way. She couldn't see how it would hurt anything to help him out.

"I'll leave the keys on the front porch," her mother said. Then, without a further word, she hung up.

MADISON STARED DOWN at the bulge beneath the mat on her mother's stoop. Evidently her mother wasn't going to soften and come to the door. Well, Madison wasn't about to let Annette's disapproval change her mind. She'd spent the past twelve years supporting and protecting her parents. Surely she could do a friend a favor.

She just wished that favor didn't entail entering the

garage where her father had ended his life. Situated at the very back of the property, the garage opened onto the alley. It was hidden by trees and overgrown with ivy. She hadn't been anywhere near it, or the workshop inside, since her father had shot himself. There hadn't been any reason to go there. Tye had cleaned up the mess, and her mother always parked in the front drive, closer to the house.

Bending, she left the folder of information she'd gathered for her mother on the step and removed the keys from beneath the mat. Then she rounded the house, opened the gate and stared out over the wide expanse of lawn dotted with ivy-covered trees.

This was where she'd grown up knowing a father who loved her....

A father who might have murdered eleven women.

She thought of the photo album Brianna had dragged out from under her bed, and felt her throat begin to burn. She simply couldn't reconcile those memories with what she'd found in the crawl space. She and Ellis might have had occasional differences while she was growing up, but those differences were nothing out of the ordinary. When she was a child, he'd let her follow him around all day and help him in the yard. He'd bought her a big piggy bank and always gave her his change. He'd even spent his "hard-earned money" on a swing set when she begged for the shiny metal kind that came from the store instead of the wooden one he'd planned to build. When she was a teenager, he'd provided her with a car and helped her maintain it. Sometimes he'd surprised her by filling it with gas.

A man like that couldn't be evil. He couldn't be a loving father *and* a twisted killer—could he? Wouldn't she have seen some evidence before now that her father was capable of such things? Wouldn't she have *known?*

Maybe the friends and relatives of killers like Ted Bundy felt the same way....

Whether Annette was really at the window or not, her mother's eyes seemed to bore holes in her back as Madison started across the yard. Her heels sank in the wet earth, slowing her progress, but she reached the safety of the overhang before the misty rain turned into pellet-size drops.

Unlocking the padlock, she turned the handle and used her shoulder to open the stiff, creaky door.

As she'd anticipated, it was mostly dark inside—dark and damp and close.

Leaving the padlock hanging, she stepped hesitantly across the threshold of her father's workshop and closed the door to keep out the rain. But what she found wasn't what she'd been expecting.

A wheel of jars containing various nails and screws hung from the ceiling. Her father's old black radio sat on the dusty window ledge, its antennae bent but still extended. A gray filing cabinet stood in the far corner, next to a scarred wooden desk. Which wasn't unusual. But there was also garbage tossed around, mostly sacks and cups from various fast-food restaurants. A dirty old pillow and blanket had been discarded on the floor. There were cigarette butts all over and a plastic lid teeming with ashes. And the whole place reeked of cigarette smoke and—marijuana.

What was going on? From the look of things, someone had recently been living inside the workshop. But how did he get in? Who was he? And what had happened to her father's guns? The rack that normally held his rifles and the shotgun that had ended his life was empty.

Her heart pounding in her ears, Madison opened the door she'd just come through and left it ajar, so she could make a quick exit if necessary. Then she peeked through the door that led to the two-stall garage.

There was no noise or movement. Whoever had been living in the workshop seemed to be gone now.

Slipping into the garage, she flipped the switch to the fluorescent light hanging from the ceiling. It buzzed and flickered, but even before it came on she could see that the window on the far side of the garage, facing away from the house, had been broken and was letting in the wind and rain.

So now she knew how whoever it was had gotten in....

Madison surveyed the place, taking in the empty stall to the right, the blue Ford parked on the left. Not far from the window she saw what appeared to be a filthy pair of jeans lying on the cement floor—and something else. Madison couldn't tell exactly what. She was just moving closer, trying to identify it, when the garage door suddenly rolled up.

Whirling, she found herself staring at Johnny.

"Johnny, you scared me to death," she said, putting her hand to her chest. "What are you doing here?"

He looked her up and down, then glanced beyond her. "Are you alone?"

Madison was breathing heavily, but she managed to nod. "Why?"

"I don't want your mother snooping around out here, hassling me."

Madison arched her brows. "She happens to own the place, remember?"

He shrugged. "My father was the one who paid the mortgage. I figure putting me up for a few weeks is the least he can do. It's tough for a guy like me to find a house these days."

Maybe that would change—if he was willing to work. "How have you been getting by?" she asked.

"One day at a time."

Madison thought of Ellis's guns and was willing to bet Johnny had pawned them. He'd probably taken other things that had belonged to their father, as well. "Did you ever get hold of Tye?"

"He doesn't want anything to do with me," he answered shortly. He crossed to the object she'd been trying to make out a few seconds earlier, and she immediately realized it was a small pipe, obviously for drugs. Of course.

"Why not?" she asked.

"I told you before, he and Sharon aren't getting along."

"You never told me why."

"Beats the hell out of me." He dug through the pockets of the discarded jeans and came up with a lighter. "Hey, you don't have twenty bucks, do ya?"

Madison felt a sinking sensation as she looked at her brother. He was never going to be in control of his life. He wouldn't even try. "No."

"Well, don't say anything about me being here to your mother."

Madison pinched the bridge of her nose, trying to quell her irritation. "Just tell me you're not on the run."

"What, you think I busted out of prison or something?" he said with a laugh. "I got out on good behavior. You can even call and check if you want."

She decided she believed him. "I'll give you a week. After that, you've got to find somewhere else. Mom's selling the house, and I'll be showing people through it."

"No shit." He shoved his straggly bangs out of his eyes, stuffed his pipe in the pocket of his jean jacket and searched for a cigarette. "And I was just growing fond of this place."

"Then you're the only one," she said, eager to leave. She didn't like being in Johnny's presence. She wanted to love him, did love him because he was her brother, but she couldn't relate to the type of person he'd become. He was throwing his life away, which was a terrible tragedy—but unless he *wanted* to change, she couldn't help him.

"So what brings you out here, all dressed up?" He spoke around the cigarette he was lighting.

Madison glanced down at her suit and the keys in her hand. "I need to use the truck."

"Oh, yeah?" He shoved his lighter back into his pocket and took a long drag. "Well, sorry it's a little low on gas. I didn't have the money to fill it up."

"You've been driving Dad's truck?"

"Why not?" he said. "Nobody else does."

"Where'd you get the keys?"

Smoked curled toward the ceiling from his cigarette as he clasped it between two dirty fingers and took another drag. "He always kept a spare out here. You didn't know?"

She shook her head.

"I guess there are a lot of things you never knew about dear old Dad, right?" He put his hands around his throat in a choking gesture and started making jerking motions and guttural noises, then laughed.

"I've got to go. I'm late for an important meeting," she said, and hurried to climb into the truck. She'd been planning to search it extensively, but she just wanted to get away. Besides, it looked completely clean. Leaving her own car parked out front, she backed out of the drive without bothering to wave.

CHAPTER TWELVE

CALEB SPENT THE MORNING trying to console Holly—who was still taking her sister's death very hard—and the afternoon with Gibbons, going over the evidence that had been found at the site of Susan's body. When he finally pulled into Madison's driveway, he found a shiny black Jaguar sitting in his parking spot. He might have wondered who drove such an expensive vehicle, but the license plate, "Lieber 1," gave him a pretty good indication.

The Jag's window slid smoothly down as he approached, and he immediately recognized the pasty-faced man he'd seen in Brianna's baby book.

"Can I help you?" Caleb asked.

Danny leaned away from the open window to save his expensive suit from the light rain as he studied Caleb. "Don't tell me *you're* the renter."

"Why not?" Caleb asked.

"Because a man your age ought to be able to afford his own place, that's why."

"I like it here," Caleb said carelessly.

"Where's Madison?"

"I'm assuming she's at work."

He made a show of checking his Rolex watch. "I pick up Brianna every other Friday at this time. She's supposed to be here."

"Did you try Madison's cell?"

"She's not answering."

"She must have caller ID," Caleb said.

Because he'd spoken with a smile, it took Danny a moment to realize he'd been insulted. When he caught on, a muscle jumped in his cheek. "If there's one thing I hate, it's a wise ass."

Caleb crouched down, so they'd be nearly at eye level, and rested his arms on the door. "That's interesting," he said, keeping his voice congenial, "because the one thing I hate is a man who bullies a woman."

"I don't know what you're talking about."

"I think you do."

Danny's eyes narrowed. "What happens between Madison and me is none of your business."

"You're right," Caleb said. "And if you want to keep it that way, I suggest you start treating her with some respect."

"You know nothing about our relationship."

"I know she's the mother of your child. That's enough to tell me you should be treating her better than you do."

"She won't have Brianna much longer," Danny said, but before Caleb could respond, Madison pulled into the drive—in her father's truck.

She did it, Caleb thought, standing. She got the truck. And now he had to take it to Gibbons....

His gaze automatically shifted toward the tires. He'd seen the plaster mold Gibbons had made of the track left near Susan's body, but he couldn't tell anything from this distance, especially in the rain. Comparing tire treads was usually a very difficult, laborious process. Only the fact that the mold revealed unique damage created by something sharp gave him any hope that Gibbons might be able to make a determination simply by looking.

"Sorry I'm late," she said, hurrying to help Brianna

out of the cab. "The ferry was backed up when I came across earlier, and that threw off my schedule for the whole afternoon."

"What are you doing with your father's truck?" Danny demanded, getting out of his car.

At the irritation in his voice, Brianna glanced uncertainly from her father to her mother. "Hi, Caleb," she said, sidling closer to him.

Caleb laid a reassuring hand on her shoulder.

"Caleb needs to borrow it," Madison said.

"For what?" Danny asked.

"He has a friend who's moving."

"I guess he's never heard of U-Haul."

"There's no need to rent a truck when I've got one available," she argued.

"Caleb gave me a magic rock," Brianna piped up.

Danny looked her way, and his face reddened when he saw her standing so close to Caleb. "Get your things, Brianna," he said curtly. "Leslie's waiting for us."

Madison's little girl hesitated briefly before running off.

"Please try to have her home earlier this Sunday," Madison said as her ex-husband slid into the Jag's soft-looking leather interior. "You've been bringing her back too late, which makes it hard for her to get up for school."

"I'll do as I damn well please," he snapped.

Madison leaned down to see through his open window. "The visitation papers say five o'clock, Danny."

He opened his mouth to make some sort of retort, but Brianna came charging out of the house at that moment. He glanced at his daughter, then at Caleb, and barely waited for Brianna to climb in before he threw the car into Reverse. Narrowly missing Caleb's Mustang and Madison's father's truck, he whipped out of the drive, leaving Caleb and Madison staring after him.

"THAT WENT WELL, don't you think?" Madison said sarcastically, wondering what was going to happen next.

"I don't think Brianna should spend any time with that guy," Caleb replied, his eyebrows lowered.

Madison chuckled as she watched Danny's car disappear. "He's normally not that bad. He's just bugged that I let you move in. When I do things he doesn't approve of, it reminds him that he no longer has control over me, which means he no longer has complete control of Brianna. That's why he's always coaxing Brianna to come and live with him. His new wife is pregnant, and Danny keeps trying to use the baby as a draw. 'Don't you want to live with your little sister? She's going to miss you when you're gone.'"

"In that photo album, he didn't even seem excited about her birth," Caleb said.

"He wasn't ready for children when we had her. He never got up with Brianna once during the night. Never baby-sat her on his own."

"So what's changed?"

"I guess he's grown up. He seems to be a much better father now."

"You can't tell he's grown up from the way he treats you."

"Like I said, he usually isn't quite *that* bad. I think he was showing off for your benefit."

"I'm not impressed."

"That's just how he is. Don't let him bother you. All I can do is save my dollars and cents for when he takes me back to court."

"Which might be sooner than you think," Caleb said. "He mentioned you might not have Brianna much longer."

"He always says that. But I'll fight him until my dying

day, if that's what it takes, and he knows it." She shifted her briefcase to her other hand, feeling eager to get out of her nylons. She couldn't let herself obsess over Brianna going with Danny. He'd brought Brianna home safely every time. She had to trust that he'd do so again.

Still, she said a silent prayer for her daughter's well-being and promised herself she'd call later and check up. "In any case, I'm free for the weekend," she said. "And the break couldn't have come at a better time. What do you want me to make us for dinner?"

"I was thinking steak and lobster."

"I don't have any lobster."

He slung an arm around her shoulders. "That's why I'm taking you out."

MADISON STARED AT HERSELF in the mirror, wondering if she was really daring enough to wear the tight little black dress. She'd bought it two years ago. She'd hoped it would help her and Danny's love life, their marriage in general, if she transformed herself from "tired mom" to "tempting siren." But Danny hadn't given her much of a chance to try before dropping his "I'm in love with someone else" bomb. Then the years of struggling to please him, to keep the family together, were over.

It really wasn't a "Danny" sort of dress, anyway. Formfitting and rather short, with spaghetti straps, it said "sleek and sophisticated," not "hard-core and raunchy," which was much more in line with Danny's sexual tastes.

Caleb, on the other hand, seemed like a man who'd appreciate a dress like this—and that made wearing it a little risky. But in some ways Madison didn't care. She was feeling better than she'd felt in ages, probably because she was opening herself up to new friendships. She'd won a small battle with the past when she'd taken her father's truck today. And she was actually able to laugh at Danny this evening instead of letting him upset her. Certainly that was progress, and it deserved some reward. What more appropriate reward was there than to feel five years younger and momentarily free from all the emotional baggage she'd been carrying?

She applied some glossy pink lipstick, stood back to assess the effect, and decided it was exactly the look she was going for. Then she began digging around in her makeup drawer for a matching shade of nail polish. Tonight she was going to paint her fingers and her toes, go barelegged and dab perfume right between her breasts.

"I'm getting hungry. Are you ready yet?" Caleb called from the living room. "You looked good before you went back there. What could be taking so long?"

What could be taking so long? Madison smiled at herself. It was just about time to show him.

CALEB KNEW HE WAS in trouble the second Madison emerged from the back of the house. She was all feminine curves, creamy skin and warm smiles, with a little shiny lipstick thrown in for good measure. And he'd been susceptible to her beauty *before* she'd gone and dressed like some kind of sex goddess.

He allowed himself to indulge in a brief fantasy— where he peeled down one of those skinny straps and let his lips skim her bare shoulder. But then he told himself to get a grip, and shoved his hands in his pockets to hide the fact that she'd had a very immediate effect on him.

"All set?" he said.

"I think so. I just need to find my house keys so I can lock up."

She crossed in front of him on her way to the kitchen,

and he breathed deeply as he caught a whiff of her perfume.

"You don't think I'm too dressed up, do you?" she asked, returning to the living room after she'd found her house keys.

He let his eyes climb her legs to the clingy black dress, her creamy shoulders, pouty lips and wide eyes, and began to say she might want to put on something that wouldn't interfere with his thinking. But that wasn't what came out. "You look perfect," he said.

"Good." Her smile seemed to have a direct link to his groin.

Just don't do anything your mother wouldn't approve of, he told himself. Fair-minded and conservative as Justine was, he knew that adhering to her standards would keep him well on this side of ethical. But he'd never been very good at listening to other people, even his mother.

Clearing his throat, he opened the door for Madison. "Let's go."

THE CANDLELIGHT at the restaurant cast everything in a golden glow that added to the surreal quality of the night. Madison reveled in the romantic lighting, the expensive wine Caleb had selected and the intimacy of their little table in the outer reaches of Rudy's Lobster Bay, an excellent seafood restaurant in downtown Seattle. Waiters and waitresses bustled past in tuxedos, yet she and Caleb seemed almost alone.

"Tell me about your childhood," Madison said, taking a bite of filet mignon smothered with mushrooms. "You told me you grew up on Fidalgo Island, but you haven't mentioned much about your family. Do you have siblings?"

"Just an older sister, Tamara. And believe me, with Tamara one sibling is more than enough."

"Why?"

"I never liked her much." He smiled ruefully.

Madison sipped her wine. "Seriously?"

"Maybe not completely, but she was a pain. She was one of those kids who had to tattle at every opportunity. No matter what I did, she ran to tell our parents."

"What did you do that made her want to tell on you?"

"Nothing big," he said, separating the meat of his lobster tail from the shell. "I once kicked a hole in the wall with my cowboy boots and tried to say I didn't know how it got there, but she didn't hesitate to set my parents straight."

"Why'd you kick the wall?"

"She was trying to make me dress up as a girl for Halloween and I wanted to be a cowboy," he said with a laugh. "I had the boots and everything, obviously."

"How old were you?"

"Five."

Madison enjoyed envisioning the rough-and-tumble little boy Caleb had probably been. A cowboy was definitely the better choice for his personality. "I see. Then you were perfectly justified."

He nodded as he began cutting his lobster. "My point exactly."

"Did you get in trouble for it?" she asked.

"Not as much trouble as I got in for other things."

"Like…"

"Like the time my sister was baby-sitting and told me I couldn't have any frogs in the house."

Madison held her glass while the waitress came around with more water. "I take it you didn't listen," she said to Caleb.

"I snuck several into my room because I couldn't see how a few frogs would hurt anything."

"And?"

He dipped some lobster meat in butter and offered it to her. She wasn't typically fond of seafood, which was why she'd ordered a steak. But he made lobster look downright tasty. Leaning over, she ate from his hand, enjoying the fact that he'd thought to share with her, more than the sweet tenderness of the meat.

His eyes lingered on her mouth, and it took him a moment to get back to his story. "And then the frogs got loose and when my mother came home, she stepped on one in the laundry room."

"Ick," Madison said with a shudder. "But I don't see how Tamara had anything to do with that."

"Oh, she was right there, saying, 'I told him not to do it, Mother, I told him you wouldn't like it.'"

Madison chuckled at his imitation of his tattletale sister and tried her steamed vegetables. They were as delicious as the rest of the food. "You must have been a little hellion."

"I don't think I was a hellion. Trouble just followed me around."

"What about your father?" she asked, taking a bite of her garlic mashed potatoes. "Didn't he ever stick up for you?"

"My mother's pretty formidable. He generally doesn't go against her, even for me."

"So she wears the pants in the family?"

"Not really. The power play between my parents isn't too out of whack. My mother's just so…organized and sure of herself, everyone naturally falls in line behind her. Sometimes I call her the Oracle."

"Because she's the font of all wisdom?"

"Exactly. She's always right, no matter what."

Madison couldn't help wishing her own mother was more "organized," more confident, so she wouldn't have to worry about her as much. But then, Caleb's mom hadn't been forced to deal with what Annette had.

"What do you think about that woman they found?" she asked, suddenly changing the subject.

"What woman?"

"The strangled woman."

He stopped eating for a moment. "What do you mean?"

"Have you been following the story?"

"A little."

"Do you think it's a copycat?"

He offered her another bite of lobster, but she waved it away. "I guess anything's possible," he said.

She nodded, thinking about the box waiting for her at her mother's house. She had to do something about it tonight. Tomorrow was Saturday morning—a likely time to have Toby start work.

But for now she was going to forget that her father had ever been involved in a murder investigation, and continue to enjoy herself.

"You're slowing down," Caleb said, nodding toward her plate. "Don't tell me you're full."

"I can't fit anything else inside this dress."

His eyes flicked over her. "It's worth it."

Madison felt a liquid warmth swirl through her. "I'm glad I finally had the chance to wear it. I bought it two years ago, but it's been buried at the back of my closet ever since."

"Sort of like carrying a concealed weapon, huh?"

"What?"

"Never mind," he said, chuckling. He paused for a

minute, then tipped his wineglass toward her. "You're sending me mixed signals. You know that, don't you?"

She leaned back, crossed her legs and took another sip of wine. "Mixed signals?" she repeated, as though she didn't already know perfectly well what he meant.

"You tell me you don't want a relationship, but you wear something that's—" he hesitated, then whistled softly "—guaranteed to stop me dead in my tracks."

"I didn't know this dress came with guarantees like that," she teased.

"It should have. Are you going to tell me what's up?"

She drank the last of her wine. "Okay, I admit to wanting to turn your head," she said. "I like the way you make me feel when you look at me, as though…"

"As though what?"

His voice was a little deeper, rougher than usual, and Madison had to work hard not to think about that kiss he'd given her at her door.

"Just 'as though,'" she said, slightly embarrassed. "But a little flirting is harmless, right? I mean, you're not interested in a relationship any more than I am. You're moving to San Francisco at the end of your lease. This is just a temporary…friendship."

He ate the last bite of his lobster. "I should probably tell you that this isn't feeling very much like friends to me."

"I'm not sure what it's feeling like to me," she said. "I was more or less robbed of the past twelve years. Maybe I'm trying to recapture some of the carefree fun I missed, some of the fun other people generally enjoy in their early twenties."

He held her gaze. "I guess I can understand that."

"Great." She smiled, eager to talk about something else. She didn't want to categorize their relationship or commit herself to any one mode of behavior. She liked looking at the night as an empty canvas, and refused to let the prudence that governed all her actions intercede at this juncture. "Then you won't mind taking me dancing."

He considered her for a few seconds. "Dancing."

"I want to have a night on the town, take a walk on the wild side for a change."

His eyebrows lifted. "How wild are you talking?"

Madison felt a sudden heady rush of excitement. "How wild are you willing to get?"

CHAPTER THIRTEEN

SHE WANTED TO GET *WILD*?

Caleb sat at the table he'd been lucky enough to snag as a small group left the crowded bar, which was pulsing with music and movement, and watched Madison walk away from him toward the ladies' room. He admired her legs for probably the millionth time, noticed a few other guys doing it, too, and knew there wasn't any way he'd be able to live up to his mother's standard of decency tonight. Ever since he'd seen Madison in that dress, he'd been interested in only one thing.

The waitress came by, but he waved her away because he was going to end the evening right now. If he allowed himself to show Madison Lieberman the meaning of wild as he saw it, he'd be taking misrepresentation to a whole new level. And when she eventually found out who he was, she wouldn't thank him. To say the least…

She emerged from the bathroom, and he stood up, planning to guide her out and drive her home. It was the right thing to do. If she wanted to go dancing, she could go with someone else. But when she reached him, she slipped her hand in his and said, ''They're playing John Mayer's 'Wonderland.' I love that song. Can we dance?''

Caleb hesitated. He really didn't want to make the situation any more complicated than it already was. But she was looking up at him with those wide eyes, wearing an expression of such hopeful expectation that he couldn't bring himself to deny her.

Knowing he'd probably pay a high price for the next few minutes, he nodded and led her out onto the dance floor, where she put her arms around his neck and snuggled up to him. He could feel her breasts against his chest as John sang about the wonder of discovering a woman, and at that point he couldn't even *think* about leaving.

There was unethical…and then there was irresistible.

MADISON WAS EXHAUSTED when Caleb brought her home, but she'd had a wonderful time. She hadn't laughed so much since before she'd married Danny, and she didn't want the evening to end. Not yet. After Caleb went home she'd have to revert to her old life—become Ellis Purcell's daughter again and deal with the contents of the box beneath her mother's house. She still wasn't sure what to do with it. But she couldn't leave it where it was.

"Would you like to come in for a nightcap?" she asked as he walked her to the door, hoping to hold reality at bay a little longer.

He shook his head. "Not tonight."

"Why not?"

"It's late."

"You're going to be home by midnight, and you drank nothing but soda at the club," she said with a laugh. "I guess your idea of wild is about as tame as mine."

"I doubt it," he said dryly.

She raised her eyebrows. "What's that supposed to mean?"

"It means if I'd had anything stronger, or the situation was different, I wouldn't be going home right now. At least not by *my* choice."

She studied his handsome face, wondering at the

thoughts behind the dark eyes that had watched her so closely all night. "So you *do* want to stay?"

He didn't answer but extended his hand to her.

Butterflies filled Madison's stomach as she accepted it—a sensation that only grew more pronounced when he pulled her against him. "What do *you* think?" he breathed. Then he kissed her, much more powerfully than he had the first time.

Madison liked the barely leashed tension she felt in Caleb. She also liked the taste and smell of him. She immediately began to imagine his bare chest as she'd seen it that day in her yard, and couldn't resist slipping a hand beneath his shirt to feel the smooth skin at his waist.

As the wet warmth of his tongue moved against her own, her knees went weak and the butterflies in her stomach spread throughout her body. But before she could decide whether or not to let things go any further, he pushed her gently away from him.

"I want to stay, but not because I'm interested in a nightcap," he said, and walked toward his cottage.

Madison stared after him, too surprised to respond. She liked Caleb. She enjoyed his company and found him incredibly attractive. But she didn't know him very well, and her own life was…complicated.

"Caleb?" she called, torn between letting him go and asking him to stay.

He stopped a few feet away and turned.

"I—you're leaving at the end of your lease."

"I know," he said, and started moving again.

"If we were to make love, it would probably be a mistake."

He reached the cottage, opened his door and flipped on the light. "I know."

"That doesn't mean I'm not tempted."

It was difficult to tell from a distance, but she thought she saw him grin. "I know," he said and stepped inside.

"You could have acted a *little* more excited," Madison mumbled, chuckling as he closed the door. He hadn't pressed her or indicated in any way that being with her tonight was important to him. He'd only admitted that he wanted something significantly more intimate than meals and laundry, and it was probably a sad commentary on the state of her psyche that such nominal interest tempted her as much as it did.

"He's too disruptive to my peace of mind," she murmured to herself. She needed to be thinking about other things—like the women's shoes and underwear, and the locket, lurking beneath her mother's house. She'd decided she'd take care of that problem tonight, while Brianna was at Danny's. But the thought of driving there in the dark and sneaking into the damp crawl space while her mother slept and Johnny camped out in the garage chilled her blood.

The telephone rang. Madison glanced at it, surprised that anyone would call her so late, then hurried to pick up for fear it was something to do with Brianna.

"Hello?"

"Everything okay over there?"

Caleb. Madison smiled in spite of herself. "Everything's fine. Why wouldn't it be?"

"Just checking."

"I should've let old Mr. Sanderson move in. You know that, don't you?" She peeked outside to see him standing at his window again. The light in his living room provided a backdrop.

"You're probably right."

"Except that you've shown me a few things he never could have," she said.

"Like?"

"That I'm not dead from the neck down."

His chuckle was soft and stirring. "You seem perfectly vital and healthy to me."

"So tell me why you want to go back to San Francisco," she said. "What's there?"

"A whole other life."

"What does that entail? Friends? A job? A woman?"

"A view of the bay."

"That's it?"

"Pretty much."

"We have a good view of the water here, if you just walk across the street to the beach."

"I've noticed that," he said. "But to be honest, I'm partial to the view from this window."

Madison smiled. "What can you see?"

"Whatever you're willing to show me."

With his flirting, the feeling of weak knees and liquid warmth she'd experienced earlier, while he was kissing her, returned. Madison would never have thought herself bold enough to play along with him. But he was in his house and she was in hers and loosening up a bit seemed almost…safe. At least it was safer than having him any closer.

"So, if I were to unzip my dress and let it slip down a little, like this—" she lowered her zipper and let her dress fall to just above her breasts "—you could probably see that?"

"I could definitely see that." His voice had grown deeper, his expression—or what she could see of it—more intense. Somehow guessing at his reaction made what she was doing that much more titillating.

"And…if I were to lower it a little more, say to here—" she dropped her dress several inches more, to just *below* her breasts "—you could tell what kind of bra I'm wearing?"

"Black lace," he breathed. "My favorite."

The depth of his attention, which she could feel despite the distance, made her giddy. "And if I were to go a little farther…" she heard him suck air between his teeth as she followed suit "…you'd be able to tell if my panties match my bra?"

He groaned. "It's a thong. What are you doing wearing a thong?"

She laughed. "It sort of went with the dress."

"Oh, yeah? Turn around for me," he said. "Let me get a better look."

Taking a deep breath, she let the dress fall to the floor, stepped out of it and turned slowly in a circle.

"You're killing me," he said.

"Are you sure you don't want that nightcap?" she asked, scarcely able to get the words out for the pounding of her heart.

He didn't answer right away. Pressing his forehead to the glass, he closed his eyes. After a few seconds he finally said, "I can't."

"Why not?"

"Because…"

"Caleb?"

When he looked up, she took hold of the front clasp that fastened her lacy bra. She didn't know if she had the nerve to do what she wanted to. She'd never done a striptease in her life. But neither had she ever experienced such wanton desire. "Are you sure?" she asked. Before he could answer, she unsnapped the clasp and let her bra drop onto the floor with her dress.

Caleb's mouth fell open. He obviously hadn't expected

what she'd just done. But she didn't regret it. The appreciation on his face was worth it.

"Beautiful," he whispered. Then, after a brief silence, he added, "Throw on a robe and come over here."

The pounding of Madison's heart seemed to tap out, *Hurry over there…hurry over there…not every girl gets to be with a man like Caleb…don't miss out.* But she'd promised herself she'd make good decisions. She had a six-year-old to think about.

"I know this will probably punch a big hole in my sexy siren act," she said, "but I have no birth control. I haven't been with anybody since Danny."

"I bought some when we stopped for gas."

"You knew it might come to this *tonight?*" she asked, feeling slightly indignant.

He chuckled softly. "On some level."

She said nothing. She was thinking. *Make good decisions, avoid emotional upset, take no risks? Or go to Caleb?*

Somehow, making good decisions and avoiding unnecessary risk had never seemed so hopelessly unappealing. "You come over here," she said.

"I'm on my way." He hung up, and then it was too late to change her mind.

Suddenly far too nervous to remain as she was, Madison put on her bra and got her robe. She was just tying it when Caleb knocked.

That didn't take long. She wondered if she had the nerve to answer. She walked down the hall, backed away, bit her knuckle and, when he knocked again, finally opened the door.

He loomed above her, his face shadowed, the moon directly behind him. For the first time, she found his height a little intimidating. Or maybe it was the intensity of his expression. It seemed to suggest they'd gone too far to turn back now, even though they weren't even touching.

What am I doing? she asked herself. But she didn't wonder long. She stood back in silent invitation for him to enter, and the moment she closed the door, he slipped his hands inside her robe and around her waist, staring into her eyes as he drew her up against his hard length. He kissed her neck, curled one hand around her bottom, and she couldn't wait for his lips to find her mouth and his hands to seek all the places that begged to be touched.

"Caleb?"

"Hmm?" He sounded distracted as he pushed her robe off her shoulders and gazed down at what his hands revealed.

"If you're used to being with really experienced women, I'm not sure I—"

He caressed her lace-covered breasts, and she sucked in a quick breath. "You don't have anything to worry about," he said.

Lowering his head, he kissed the indentation beneath her collarbone, his breath hot, his lips barely grazing her skin. Then his hands sought the clasp of her bra, and Madison squeezed her eyes closed, waiting expectantly for that moment when he'd slip off her bra and actually touch her. But he didn't immediately do so.

She opened her eyes to look up at him. "What is it?" she asked, every nerve taut. She thought she might die if he backed out now.

"I want to go slow, but I don't think I have enough control right now." Surprise echoed through his voice. "I've never wanted anyone so much."

She was shaking; surely that told him how she felt.

"I'm already burning from the inside out, Caleb. And I want you to burn, too. Burn for me."

What had started out slow now moved very fast. "We'll do it again—slower—afterward, okay?" he promised. "Tell me I'll have another chance."

Madison would have told him almost anything. She murmured something and he said, "I know you might hate me for this later, Maddy, but I have to have you."

Madison smiled at the sound of her childhood name on his lips. "Why would I hate you?"

He didn't answer. He kicked her robe aside and removed her bra, leaving it where it landed. Her panties soon followed. Scooping her into his arms, he started toward the back of the house, but her bedroom seemed too far away. She made him stop so she could remove his clothes—his shirt, his pants, everything. And when she pressed against him, both of them fully naked, and felt him shaking like she was, she knew they weren't going to make it another foot. Arching into him, she breathed, "Take me now, Caleb. Right now."

She didn't need to ask twice. He waited only long enough to put on a condom before leaning her against the wall in the dark hallway and burying himself inside her. She cried out, clenching her hands in his hair. She felt herself stretch almost painfully to accept him, yet she wanted to draw him deeper, cling to him, lock her legs around him.

He lifted her and bore the bulk of her weight between him and the wall as he began to move, and the way he looked at her, the way he kissed her, made her feel as though more than their bodies touched.

Suddenly, Caleb was the *only* thing that mattered. Almost immediately Madison felt a spiraling sensation inside her, something she hadn't experienced for a long,

long time. She couldn't believe Caleb had the power to arouse her like this, so easily, so completely. But when she felt her body tense and that first wave roll through her, she cried out his name, determined that he wouldn't retain any more control than she had, and took him with her.

A moment later, they were breathing heavily, their hearts thudding in unison, their skin slick with sweat.

Caleb's eyes were closed, his forehead resting against hers. With his large body pressing her into the wall, Madison felt completely safe. And content… "That was incredible, Maddy," he whispered.

She could have said the same thing. But she was too busy reveling in the feel of him against her, inside her, everywhere.

He gathered her in his arms, as if to carry her to the bedroom, but before they'd moved an inch, he straightened. "Uh-oh."

Madison blinked up at him. "Uh-oh" wasn't what she'd expected.

"What is it?" she asked, suddenly a little self-conscious about her wild abandon.

He kissed her on the shoulder and gently lowered her to her feet. "Hurry and get dressed. Someone's here."

It took a few seconds for that piece of information to register, but when she listened, Madison could hear a car's engine. "Not now!"

She started to collect her clothes, but Caleb moved more quickly. He handed them to her on his way to the bathroom. She heard the toilet flush, then he reappeared and thrust his legs into his pants.

"I'll see who it is," he said.

"This late, it's got to be Johnny," she told him. "And—and you can't answer my door. It'll be too obvious that I'm…that we're… I don't want him to say anything to Danny or Brianna."

"I'll go out the back and walk around, as if I'm coming from the cottage," he said. "Keep your doors locked until I know it's safe."

"Okay." Hearing the back door close, she hurried to her room and pulled on some sweats so she could go to the kitchen and look out at the drive. What she saw when she got there was a new Ford Explorer. A short man with a neatly trimmed goatee and a stocky build had gotten out. It wasn't Johnny. It was Tye.

What was Tye doing here? He hadn't been over since she'd moved in and needed his help to set up her new television. Taking a moment to slow the pounding of her heart, she went to the door and threw it open. "Tye? What's going on?"

"Who the hell is this?" her brother said, jerking his head toward Caleb, who'd met him in the drive.

Madison didn't dare glance in Caleb's direction, afraid the look in her eyes would give away the fact that they'd just made love—or the fact that she wanted to make love with him again. "It's Caleb Trovato."

"Who's Caleb Trovato?"

"My, um, renter," she said, even though calling Caleb her renter suddenly seemed a remote term for a man she now knew more intimately than any other, except Danny.

"You didn't tell me you'd taken in a renter."

"I didn't think about it. The last time we talked, it was just after we'd moved Dad's grave, and I, um, had a lot on my mind." Her throat suddenly dry, she swallowed. "What are you doing here, anyway?" she asked, hoping to deflect his attention.

Tye shot Caleb a look that said he could leave, but Caleb propped his hands on his hips and stood his ground.

Madison's cheeks began to burn as she felt Caleb watching her. Falling into bed with a man she'd known only two weeks wasn't characteristic of her. She focused on her brother to avoid Caleb's possessive glance. "Is something wrong?"

"Isn't that Dad's truck?" he asked, motioning to the blue Ford parked in the drive.

She looked over to see the Ford sitting dark and empty as it had for the past few years, and felt an eerie chill down her spine. She didn't want her father's truck there, parked in the middle of the new life she was trying to build. But she liked the fact that she could overcome her fears enough to lend it to Caleb. That said something. "Yes. I'm borrowing it," she said, to keep things simple.

"Borrowing it," he repeated. "After all the time it's been locked up in that garage."

"Anything wrong with that?"

"I guess not," he said, but he didn't sound happy about it. "Have you heard from Sharon?" he asked.

"Sharon?" She could smell Caleb's cologne on her skin as she raised a hand to scratch her forehead, and quickly lowered her arm. "Don't you know where she is?"

"I can't find her."

"As in, something might have happened to her or—"

"Nothing happened," he interrupted irritably. "She left, that's all."

"But why?"

He waved a hand toward Caleb. "Can't you tell him to go home?"

"He is home," she said, but because she was afraid of what Tye might say or do, she asked Caleb for a few moments alone. "I'll call you later," she told him.

Despite the darkness where Caleb stood, she could see

that his mouth formed a grim line. He didn't answer. He just turned and walked away, and she was grateful for the space. She needed a chance to handle Tye on her own.

"Are you sleeping with that guy?" he asked as soon as she let him in.

Madison would bet the truth was written all over her face. Her body still tingled from Caleb's touch, but she said, "That's none of your business, Tye."

He followed her down the hall to the living room, prowling around once they got there as though he had too much pent-up energy.

"Do you want to tell me what's going on with Sharon?" she asked.

"We're having a little trouble at home," he admitted. "But it isn't anything we can't work out—if I could just find her."

Madison walked over and closed the shutters on the window that looked toward the cottage, as if she could separate Caleb from her regular life that easily. He was fantasy. Tye was part of reality. "Did she file for separation?" she asked.

He picked up the paper flower bouquet Brianna had made her for Mother's Day. "I don't know. I think she's trying to get a restraining order. I tell you, she's lost it. She's gone nuts or something."

"What about the kids?"

He put the arrangement back on the table. "She took them with her."

"When?"

"Yesterday morning. I thought she'd be home by now. But I haven't heard from her."

Madison sat in her overstuffed chair, still trying to recover from what had happened just before Tye arrived. How had she gone from "I'm not going to get involved with you'' to hot, sweaty sex with Caleb in such a short time? "Have you called her parents?"

"I've tried. They won't talk to me. She told them I attacked her." He shook his head in disgust.

Madison couldn't picture her easygoing sister-in-law obsessing over something that wasn't true. "*Did* you attack her, Tye?"

He whirled to face her, his eyebrows knotted. "I can't believe you asked me that! Of course not."

She remembered how aloof and difficult he'd been as a teenager, and hated the fact that she didn't quite believe him. Somehow she doubted Sharon would take the kids and disappear without a good reason. Sharon had always talked as though she really loved Tye. "So where do you think she is?"

"I told you, I don't know. She's imagining things." He walked to the window and peered out through a crack in the shutters.

Madison could feel his pensive mood from across the room. Finally, he turned to face her. "I don't like that guy," he said.

He was talking about Caleb, but Madison didn't want to discuss Caleb with him, so changed the subject. "Have you seen Johnny lately?"

"No, have you?"

"This morning. He's living in my mother's garage."

He moved away from the window. "I never dreamed the old bitch would let him do that."

"She hasn't *let* him. She doesn't even know he's there. And don't call her an old bitch. She has her shortcomings, but she's not as bad as you think."

"She's worse," he muttered.

Madison chose to ignore that comment. "Anyway, Johnny can't stay there for long. She's selling the house and, judging by the number of interested parties, I think it's going to move very fast.''

''Why would anyone want that place?''

''It's a prime piece of real estate.''

Tyc's forehead creased in consternation. ''Isn't your mother terrified that once she moves the police will find some evidence that'll finally prove Ellis really did kill all those women? Then she won't be able to play the persecuted wife of a falsely accused man.''

Madison threw a lap blanket over her legs, feeling a little chilled. ''She believes Dad's innocent. You know that.''

He rubbed his neck, disgusted or upset in some new way. ''But surely she's found that box in the crawl space by now.''

Madison thought for a moment that her heart had stopped beating.

''Madison?'' he said when she didn't respond.

''How do you know about that box?'' she breathed.

He paused, then said, ''I'm the one who put it there.''

CHAPTER FOURTEEN

SO MANY THOUGHTS converged in Madison's mind that at first she could only stare at her half brother. "What are you saying?" she asked when she'd recovered her voice.

"Nothing earth-shattering," Tye said with a shrug. "I found that stuff out in the workshop the day Dad died."

Had he really? But what other explanation could there be? Madison wasn't sure she wanted to ask herself that question, or confront the answer that came so readily to mind. She'd given the house keys to Tye when he agreed to clean up after Ellis shot himself. She'd gotten them back, of course, but he could easily have made copies. Which meant her father wasn't the only one who'd had access to the crawl space beneath the house. Ellis wasn't the only one familiar with the campus area. Ellis wasn't even the only one who drove the blue Ford. If Johnny knew about the spare key, certainly Tye did as well. And Tye hated their father. He probably wouldn't mind if Ellis took the blame for a crime he'd committed himself.

Even more chilling, what about her missing sister-in-law?

That Tye might have had something to do with the women who were murdered was a horrible possibility, one Madison couldn't quite bring herself to believe. Especially because he had no reason to tell her about the box if he thought it might implicate him in some way. Yet his calm acceptance of what was hidden beneath the house disturbed her.

"Why—" Madison began, but her voice broke, so she tried again. "Why didn't you say something before?"

"I knew it wouldn't be welcome news. Not when you and your mother had stood by Ellis through the whole thing."

"Didn't you feel you had a duty to go to the police?" she asked.

"What was the point? Dad wasn't going to hurt anyone else."

Faced with her own logic, Madison winced at how selfish it sounded. Even if Tye *hadn't* murdered those women, he'd shown no consideration for the victims, and she'd done her best to shove them out of her mind, too.

"How long have you known about the box?" he asked.

"Just a couple of weeks."

"So why didn't *you* report it?"

She'd thought it was to shelter Brianna and her mother from any further repercussions of the past. Now she knew there was more to it than that. Deep down, even though she'd seen the contents of that box, she couldn't believe her father had killed those women.

If you can't trust your heart, what can you trust? Maybe she wasn't so different from her mother, after all. "I still don't think he did it," she said.

"What?"

Madison's heart was not only beating again, it felt as though it might jump out of her chest. "I don't understand where that stuff came from, Tye," she said, trying to give him the benefit of the doubt. "But our father didn't kill those women."

He shook his head. "My God, what would it take to convince you?"

"Haven't you heard? Another woman was murdered."

"I know that. It's a copycat killing," he said.

"I don't think so." She hesitated, trying to search within the intuition that had kept her strong through the past—the same intuition she'd switched to "off" once she'd found that locket. "The original Sandpoint Strangler is still out there. I can *feel* it." She watched him closely, waiting for his response, and was greatly relieved when he merely scowled.

"But the evidence—"

"I don't care about the evidence." Throwing off the blanket, she got up.

"How can you say that?" he asked.

"Because I knew Dad."

"Where are you going?"

"To find my shoes so I can walk you out. Then I'm driving over to the house to get that box."

"What are you planning to do with it?"

"I'm going to destroy it," she said, in case he might object to anything else. But she wasn't going to destroy it. She was going to take it to the police.

THE HOUSE WAS AS DARK as Madison hoped it would be. She knew her mother sometimes had trouble sleeping and would lie on the couch and watch television until dawn. But there was no flicker in the window indicating a television might be in use—thank goodness.

After driving past the house twice, just to be sure, Madison parked in front of the neighbor's. She didn't want to risk waking her mother with the sound of her father's truck, which was the only vehicle available, since she'd left her own car here yesterday. And Madison certainly didn't want to go through the alley by the garage and risk waking Johnny. It was spooky back there.

Turning off her lights, she cut the engine and got out. It wasn't raining anymore, but the pavement shone like a mirror beneath the streetlights. Puddles filled every low spot and the entire area smelled of clean air and damp wood. She liked both scents. She just didn't like creeping up to her parents' house in the middle of the night.

It'll only take a few minutes, she told herself, fighting off the sick feeling in her stomach.

Shivering in spite of her warm-up suit, she rubbed her arms as she hurried to the house, moving as silently as possible. Her mother's car was where she always parked it, but there was steam coming off the hood, which told Madison it probably hadn't been sitting there long.

Where would Annette have gone so late at night? She pressed her palm to the hood. It was warm, all right. If her mother had been out, it was entirely possible that she'd just gone to bed and wasn't asleep yet. Madison would need to be extra cautious....

Good thing she'd decided to wait until Caleb's lights were off before she left. She might have arrived only to find her mother gone, with no clue as to when Annette might return.

Caleb... God, she'd made love to her sexy tenant, and was just beginning to realize that the ramifications could stretch far beyond one night, whether she wanted them to or not. That was why, when she called him after Tye had gone home, she'd told him she wanted to pretend it hadn't happened.

That he'd agreed so readily came as a surprise. She wasn't sure if she was relieved about that or upset. But she wouldn't think about him right now. She *couldn't* think about him. She needed to keep her mind on what she was doing.

Slipping through the gate and into the soggy backyard,

she glanced toward the garage to check for any hint of light—and saw nothing. She paused to listen as well, and heard only the steady drip, drip, drip coming from the downspouts.

With a bolstering breath, she searched her keys for the one to the back door—and dropped them in her hurry. The loud jangle as they hit the cement made panic clutch her insides.

She leaned against the house, waiting to see if perhaps a light would come on. When nothing happened, she squatted slowly and recovered her keys, going through them even more quickly this time. The sudden noise, exaggerated in the quiet night, had obviously rattled her because she was beginning to feel as though she was being watched.

She cast another furtive glance at the garage as she found the right key and inserted it into the lock. She was anxious to get inside. The thick clouds that had been covering the moon had rolled away and her shadow now fell across the lawn, looking strangely grotesque, like someone sneaking up on her from behind.

Bracing for the click, she turned the handle and slipped inside.

The heater was on. She could hear the steady hum of air blowing through vents as she closed the door behind her, but she heard nothing else. Her mother was asleep. There wasn't anyone around. She was fine. It would all be over in a few minutes.

Cutting through the kitchen, she headed for the stairs and took them as fast as she dared, quickly descending into the cool, pitch-black basement.

She blew on her hands to warm her cold fingers as she came around the foot of the stairs and stood in front of the door to the crawl space. She'd conquered the garage and her father's truck. She would conquer this, too. She just needed some light. She wished she had enough nerve to scramble under the house and drag that box out with only the bulb in the crawl space to guide her, but she couldn't make herself so much as open the door without first getting her bearings. Even if her mother woke up, she wouldn't see the light from here.

Madison felt a little less spooked once she'd dispelled the darkness. The room appeared as it always had, especially with that photograph of her father looking on. ''Tell me I'm right to believe in you,'' she whispered, and crawled under the house.

It's almost over…it's almost over…

She made her way past the boxes and storage items she'd seen before. Her knees hurt as they knocked against the plank floor. She could hear her own breathing and movement, but then something else scurried off to her right, and she froze. What was it? A mouse? A rat? God, this place gave her the creeps.

But she *had* to get that box.

Finally she reached the end of the makeshift path, where the smell of mildew was strongest, and encountered the moist dirt that spread beneath the rest of the house. She heard another rustle, this one sounding as though it was caused by something much bigger than the average rodent. A squirrel? A possum? Surely it was her imagination that it sounded even bigger than that.…

Madison caught her breath, listening. Drip, drip, drip, coming from somewhere beneath the house. She strained her eyes as she stared into the dark void before her. She couldn't see *anything*. But she had no doubt that anyone out there could see her.

Fear made her palms grow moist, but she refused to let

her imagination run away with her. The house had been locked. The sounds she heard were simply settling noises.

She quit trying to see where there was only blackness, and started shoving things out of the way. But the box wasn't where she'd left it. She had to search through the junk piled around her before she spotted it a few feet away, turned on its side.

The moment she touched it, she knew something was different. It felt light, far *too* light.

She didn't dare take the time to look. Not right then. Not when she was so close to the rustling and the dark.

She pulled it to the door, beneath the light, and opened the flaps to find—nothing. No women's underwear or shoes. No locket. And certainly no rope.

The box was empty.

"Tye?" she whispered, wondering if he'd beaten her to it, wondering if that scurrying was him.

No answer.

"Tye, if it's you, answer me."

Again, no response. The hair was standing up on the back of her neck. But she wasn't willing to ask a third time. Quickly shoving the empty box back under the house, she closed the door to the crawl space, flipped off the light and hurried away.

THE MOMENT CALEB HEARD a car pull into the drive, he yanked on his sweatshirt and headed for the door. He had no idea where Madison had been for the past two hours, but he was certainly going to find out. It was nearly three in the morning, for crying out loud. And there was a serial killer on the loose.

When he knew she'd caught sight of him standing at the edge of the drive, he slid his hands in his pockets and waited.

''Why are you awake?'' she asked as soon as she'd killed the engine and climbed out of her father's truck.

Caleb hadn't realized until he saw Madison safe and whole just how worried he'd been. Maybe what had happened to Susan, along with all the atrocities he'd chronicled in the past, had skewered his perception of violent crime. But he hadn't been able to think of anything except the possibility that someone might hurt her while she was out so late at night. ''I've been waiting for you,'' he said.

A perplexed expression crossed her face, replacing the tense, nervous look that had been there before. ''What for?''

''You didn't tell me you were going out. Where have you been?''

There was more accusation in his words than Caleb had intended, and for a moment she looked as though she didn't know how to react. He thought she might come back with something like, ''None of your business.'' They'd agreed to pretend their sexual encounter had never taken place. Considering his position, he was especially grateful for that. So why he was pushing things with her now, he didn't know. He just didn't want to lose anyone else he cared about.

''Am I *supposed* to let you know when I go out?'' she asked. Her tone was measured, but she didn't fly off the handle the way Holly would have. Madison seemed to be giving him the benefit of the doubt.

He raked a hand through his hair and softened his voice. ''I was worried,'' he said.

Her eyebrows drew together. ''You're sending *me* mixed signals, you know that?'' she said, stealing his line from the restaurant. ''What's going on?''

Caleb tried to tell himself that making love to her had been a slip-up, the result of having been too long without a woman. But deep down he knew it wasn't that simple. If he'd had his way, she'd still be in his bed.

Briefly he considered telling her who he really was, but things had gone too far; he couldn't. Making her hate him wouldn't improve the situation. "Nothing," he said. "It's late, and we're both tired. That's all."

He started toward the cottage house, but she called him back. "Caleb?"

"Yeah?"

"Thanks for waiting up," she said. "It...it helped to have you here."

"I'd like to know where you went," he said.

She hesitated. "I'd...rather not say."

He wanted to press her, but now that he knew she was safe, the desire to touch her again felt much more immediate. "Are we still pretending what happened earlier didn't happen?" he asked.

She nodded.

Too bad. He figured that enjoying the rest of the night couldn't make matters any worse. Jerking his head toward the cottage house, he said, "Do you think we could start pretending in the morning?"

Her eyes met his. "Are you asking me to spend the night with you, Caleb?"

He was really climbing out on a limb. He might be able to attribute what had already happened to a thoughtless mistake, but that wouldn't explain the premeditation involved in asking her to stay with him now. "I am."

When she didn't answer right away, he was tempted to move closer to her, to convince her with his mouth and his hands. After her response to him earlier, he knew he'd stand a better chance that way. But, considering the circumstances, he needed her to come to him without coaxing.

"Just for tonight?" she asked.

"Just for tonight," he promised.

Finally, she said, "Okay," and Caleb closed his eyes in relief. He hadn't known until that moment just how much her answer meant to him.

MADISON BLINKED several times, trying to get her bearings. She felt satiated, content, but lonely without Caleb's warm body curled around her. Still, it was her own fault he wasn't there. She'd insisted on returning to her own bed at dawn. She knew better than to stay with Caleb any longer. The more time she spent with him, the more she wanted to spend with him. The more he touched her, the more she craved his touch.

But she couldn't help smiling as she remembered the many times he'd made love to her during the night. He'd been passionate and all-consuming one moment, gentle and loving the next. With him she'd experienced things she'd never experienced with anyone else—a mutual meeting of the mind, spirit and body. Somehow he already knew her better than Danny ever had.

The phone rang. She rolled over so she could reach the handset, hoping to hear his voice. She'd only been away from him for four hours, but it felt like four days. "Hello?" she answered sleepily.

"It's nearly ten o'clock," her mother said, sounding surprised. "What are you doing in bed? I want you to have an open house for me today, remember?"

Madison grimaced and tried not to yawn. "I thought you were mad at me."

"What gave you that idea?"

Um, the fact that you wouldn't come to the door yesterday? "Forget it," she said. If her mother wanted to pretend nothing had happened between them, Madison was more than game. She wasn't even surprised. It would've taken Annette more effort to do without her than to get past their little disagreement. "Can't we start next week?" she asked. She hadn't advertised it yet—and she couldn't show people around the property with her dead-beat brother sleeping in the garage.

"Next *week?*" her mother said.

Obviously not. "Never mind," Madison grumbled. She could always throw up a few signs. Unless she wanted to risk upsetting her mom again, she was stuck doing the open house. Which meant she'd have to visit the garage and tell Johnny to stay away for the day. "I'm getting up right now."

"But your car's here, remember? When will your friend be finished with the truck?"

Madison had almost forgotten that Caleb was going to be using the truck. "I'm not sure," she said. "I haven't even given him the keys yet."

Almost on cue, the doorbell rang. "I bet that's him right now," she said. She was sleeping in Caleb's T-shirt and a pair of his boxers. She liked the smell and feel of them because they reminded her of him. But she quickly stripped them off and put on her robe so he wouldn't know that.

When she reached the front door, a glance through the peek hole confirmed that it *was* Caleb. He was standing on the stoop, crisp and ready for the day.

Suddenly aware that she had nothing on beneath her robe, she tightened the belt and ran a self-conscious hand through her hair, trying to get it to lie down. "I'm talking to my mother," she explained as she let him in. "I'll be off the phone in a second, okay?"

"Who's that?" her mother asked.

"It's Caleb."

"The man who's living in the cottage?"

"Yes."

"How old is he?"

"He's…'' Madison was about to hazard a guess—she knew Caleb wasn't far from her own twenty-eight—but he answered for her.

"Thirty-four."

It was then that Madison realized he could hear her mother, so she was a little embarrassed when Annette asked, "Is he single?" Especially because Caleb seemed different today than he had last night—more aloof, reserved, preoccupied. And he kept his distance. That was good, right? Her goals for today were to pull herself together, control her rampant emotions, get on track with her life. She was a responsible single mother, not a woman who had wild affairs with her tenant.

"He's divorced," she told her mother, because Annette would just ask again if she didn't answer. "These are for the truck," she said to Caleb, handing him the keys.

"Thanks." He moved to the counter. "I'll leave you my Mustang, in case you need to go anywhere while I'm gone."

"How long has he been divorced?" her mother asked.

Madison pressed the phone closer to her ear, wishing her mother would shut up. "I don't know."

"Two years," he said.

"Is he handsome?" Annette wanted to know.

God, was he, Madison thought. Handsome everywhere. After last night, she could definitely state that with authority. Not that she'd ever admit she possessed such intimate knowledge—not to her mother. "He's, um, never mind," she said. "I'll be over in a little bit. There's something I need to talk to you about."

"What's that?" her mother asked.

She'd assumed Caleb would leave, but he didn't. He was waiting for her to get off the phone. "We'll talk about it later."

"Tell me now."

Madison chose her words carefully. "I was wondering if…if you happened to find anything…strange under the house."

"I don't know what you're talking about."

She would if she'd found the contents of that box. "Has Toby started to help you pack?"

"Not yet."

"Has he been over at all?"

"No, why?"

"Never mind." It had to be Tye who'd taken that stuff, then. Madison felt her blood run cold as she remembered the scurrying under the house last night. What would Tye have done if she'd bumped into him in the dark?

Caleb was watching her closely, but Madison couldn't help murmuring a warning to her mother. "Mom, I think it might be time to get the locks changed on the house."

"Why?"

"Just get the locks changed. Right away, okay?"

"But—"

"Caleb's here," she interrupted. "I can't talk about this now." She covered the phone. "How long will you need the truck?"

"Just a couple of hours."

"I'll see you about one o'clock," she told her mother, and hung up before Annette could respond.

"Madison, are you okay?" Caleb asked, breaking into her thoughts. "You look…worried."

She let her eyes settle on him and, for once, decided to trust someone. "I'm afraid Tye might have had something to do with that woman who was murdered," she said.

CHAPTER FIFTEEN

CALEB GAPED IN SURPRISE at what Madison had just said. He knew he was getting close to her. In fact, after last night, they were considerably closer than his conscience could bear. He had to do something about that—apologize, move out, put some distance between them. But this took precedence. "What makes you think Tye might be involved?" he asked.

"I found something in the crawl space of my mother's house a couple of weeks ago."

Caleb's heart began to pound. This was exactly what he'd been hoping to learn from the beginning—inside information. He pictured Susan's pale face as he'd seen her lying in the morgue, and imagined he might be one step closer to avenging her murder. At the same time, he felt lousy about the means he was using to accomplish that goal. He seriously doubted Madison would have trusted him this much if they hadn't just slept together. "What was it?" he asked, angry that he'd put himself in such a situation.

"A box filled with women's shoes and underwear."

"Whose?"

"I think they belonged to those women who were murdered."

Caleb let his breath go in a rush. "What makes you think so?"

"There was a locket, too." Madison nibbled her lip

and, even as he waited with baited breath to hear what she was about to say, he couldn't help thinking about the way she'd kissed him last night, with such complete abandon. Neither could he forget her body moving beneath his, accepting him, exciting him, fulfilling him as she entwined her arms and legs with his and let him know she was enjoying their lovemaking as much as he was.

Willing his gaze away from her mouth, he looked into her eyes. He had to forget about last night, keep his distance before he made things any worse. "You say that as though it wasn't just any locket."

"It wasn't. It had Lisa and Joe McDonna's picture inside. Lisa was the Sandpoint Strangler's second victim."

She didn't have to tell him that. He knew exactly who Lisa McDonna was. He'd interviewed her husband and many of her friends. "Do you know where the locket and the other stuff came from? How it got under your mother's house?"

She suddenly looked alone and miserable, and he hated himself for betraying her. "Tye put it there the day my father…died. He said he found it in the workshop."

"What did you do with it?"

"Nothing. I was going to turn it over to the police, but when I went back to get it last night, everything inside the box was gone."

No! Caleb felt his muscles tense with frustration. "Where did it go?"

"Tye must've gotten to it before me. It had to be him. He's the only other person who knows about it."

"But how's he getting in and out of your mother's house? Does he have a key?"

"He could have one easily enough."

"Have you asked him?"

"I called him on his cell when I was driving home, but he didn't pick up."

Caleb wanted to move toward Madison, but he didn't dare. He was afraid he'd take her in his arms, and what had occurred in the hall last night would happen all over again. "Why would you doubt his word, Maddy? Why would you think him capable of murder?"

She frowned. "Because I know his dark side."

LESS THAN AN HOUR LATER, Caleb's cell phone rang while he was driving Ellis Purcell's truck to a bakery not far from the University of Washington, where he was to meet Detective Gibbons. He scowled as he looked down at the phone lying innocently on the seat beside him, and refused to answer. He couldn't believe he'd made the situation with Madison exponentially worse by sleeping with her.

Whoever was calling hung up, and silence fell. But a few minutes later, the ringing started again. Finally glancing at the LED readout, he realized it was his mother, and punched the talk button. He couldn't avoid her forever. She'd already left him several messages he hadn't returned because he didn't want to hear all the reasons he shouldn't be doing what he was doing. After last night, he was beginning to figure out a few of those reasons on his own.

Unfortunately, his hunch about Ellis's daughter possessing key information was also turning out to be right.

"Caleb?"

"Hi, Mom, what's up?"

"It's about time I got through to you," she said. "We talked more often when you were living in San Francisco."

"Sorry, I've been busy."

"With Ellis Purcell's daughter?"

He shook his head as guilt washed through him. "I'm meeting Detective Gibbons in a few minutes," he said, purposely sidestepping an answer.

"Holly called here last night," she said, switching subjects.

"She did? What for?"

"She'd just said goodbye to her parents at the airport and was feeling a little bereft. She's taking this all so hard." He heard the sympathy in his mother's voice. Caleb knew Justine was aware of Holly's shortcomings, but the ties they'd forged when they were a family didn't simply evaporate. "She said she dropped by your new place, but you weren't home."

Probably when he'd been out to dinner with Madison. "I'll give her a call," he said.

"That would be nice."

His call-waiting beeped. "I'd better go. Someone's trying to get through."

"Wait," she said. "I was hoping you could come to dinner this evening."

He thought about the contents of the box Madison had described last night. He wanted her to take him to her mother's house and let him search for it—or at least look for indications of who might have removed it. From what he'd overheard earlier, Madison's mother claimed she didn't know anything about that stuff. But Caleb wasn't completely convinced she was telling the truth. Annette was so loyal to Ellis he could easily imagine her destroying evidence that might prove her husband's guilt. And he wanted to question Tye and, of course, Johnny because he was living so close.

"Thanks for the invitation," he said. "I'd really like to see you and Dad, but I have other plans."

"With whom?"

"A friend."

"I'd like to meet Madison," his mother said, without skipping a beat. "Why don't you bring her over?"

Caleb pulled the phone away from his ear so he could catch the number of the person trying to reach him. It was Madison.

"I'm getting another call, Mom."

"So are you coming?"

"I can't bring Madison. Someone—Tamara or Dad—is bound to give me away."

"I'll talk to them before you get here, make sure that doesn't happen."

"I'll get back to you," he said and took Madison's call. "Hello?"

"Caleb?"

"Everything okay?"

"I think so. I wanted to tell you that Brianna called me from her father's house."

"What'd she have to say?"

"She asked me to tell you that the magic rock really works."

Caleb was glad he'd thought of Brianna when he'd found that piece of pyrite on the ground. But he was a little concerned that Brianna had felt the need to use its "magic." "What happened?"

"I guess she spilled her milk, and Leslie got upset," Madison said, worry creeping into her voice. "Brianna didn't get a chance to explain more than that because Danny walked in on the middle of the conversation and made her hang up."

"Did Brianna seem okay when she called?"

"For the most part."

"Is there any chance Danny would let us pick her up early?"

"No. I've tried that before."

"I wanted to bring her with us tonight."

"Are we going somewhere?"

Caleb knew they should avoid each other. He certainly had no business taking her to meet his family. But he couldn't resist. "My mother invited us over for dinner. I told her I'd ask you."

There was a slight hesitation. "Caleb…"

"Just as friends," he said.

"If Johnny's still living in the garage and won't leave, or my mother finds out he's ever been there, today might not go as smoothly as I'd like," she responded.

"Why don't I go there with you, make sure you don't run into any problems?"

"You really want to risk getting involved?"

He didn't want to risk having Johnny recognize him from that long-ago interview, but he couldn't let Madison go over to her mother's place alone, just in case her brother gave her trouble. On the hopeful side, Caleb had a hard time believing Johnny would be sitting inside the Purcells' garage in the middle of the day. "I'm not worried about it."

"If you're sure."

"I'm sure." He reached the Grateful Bread Company on 24th Street and could see Detective Gibbons, wearing his customary cheap suit, sitting inside with a cup of coffee. The detective got up and started toward him as soon as he spotted Caleb pulling into the small lot.

Caleb waved him away until he could hang up with Madison. "So will you come?"

"What time?" she asked.

"My parents usually eat around six, but I'll need to confirm. Do you think we can be finished at your mother's by then?"

"Unless we have Johnny problems."

"We'll hope for the best. I'll see you in a couple of hours." He ended the call and hopped out to find Detective Gibbons already circling the truck, checking each tire. "What do you think?" he asked. "Do they match the track you found near Susan's body?"

Gibbons had him get back in the truck and back up, then circled it again. Finally, he straightened and scratched his scalp. "I don't think so."

Caleb was surprised by the relief that flooded through him. He wanted to find Susan's killer, but he wanted that killer to have no connection with Madison. "You're sure?"

"I'm positive."

Crossing his arms and leaning against the truck, Caleb let some of the tension leave his body. "Then what do you make of the blue Ford that was spotted outside the pizza place?"

Gibbons waved his hand in a dismissive motion. "The make and model of Purcell's truck has been in all the papers. Our copycat's playing games, that's all."

"Our copycat doesn't have to read the paper for information, remember? From the way Susan's body was positioned, he already knows more than we ever revealed."

"I'm afraid our killer is close," Gibbons said. "Close to the investigation. Close to us."

Caleb thought of the trophies Madison had found under her mother's house. Johnny was close. So was Tye. "What about Madison's brothers?" he asked. "Have you learned any more about them than I was able to dig up?"

Gibbons shook his head. "Not really."

"They have alibis?"

"Tye's wife said he was home with her the night Susan was killed."

"When did you talk to her?"

"Two days ago. I talked to him, too. Showed him a picture of Susan. Said he's never seen her."

"Of course he'd say that."

"My thought exactly. So I visited some of the guys where he works, and some of the people who hang out at the same bar he does on weekends, just to get a general feel for what he's like."

Caleb knew Tye worked in construction the way his father had, and made a decent living as project manager for Stoddard Construction, one of the larger developers in the area. "Anybody have anything interesting to say?"

"Seems he has an explosive temper. Gets in fights all the time. But he's a hard worker and good at what he does, so they put up with him at Stoddard. Anyway, I don't see our perpetrator letting others see his temper."

"What about Johnny?"

"I still haven't tracked him down, but he's an unlikely suspect. I've confirmed that he was behind bars when at least two of the strangler's victims were killed."

Caleb considered this piece of information. "Are we sure they were the strangler's victims? The remains of some of those women weren't discovered until months after they died."

"Either way, I've decided he doesn't fit the profile." The detective straightened his tie, which was too short for a man his size. "His parole officer says he's not capable of executing such an organized, methodical murder."

Caleb had to agree. "What about Susan's autopsy? Have we learned anything there?"

"Asphyxiation was the cause of death, just as we expected. She was sexually assaulted with a broom handle or something similar. Only surprising thing was that the coroner couldn't find any Rohypnol in her blood."

"So she wasn't drugged like the others."

"The question is why."

"Maybe she wasn't an intended target."

"Or our copycat isn't as worried about his ability to overpower his victims as the original strangler was."

Pushing away from the truck, Caleb climbed behind the wheel. He hated that they weren't any closer to solving Susan's murder. He could barely think of her without feeling a terrible heaviness in his chest. But at least now he didn't have to worry about taking Madison to meet his mother. The investigation was heading in another direction entirely. She wasn't going to feel the heat of it. Which eased some of the guilt he felt about last night.

He rolled down his window. "So where do we go from here, Chief?"

"We keep searching," Gibbons said. "The news isn't all bleak. I found a message on my desk this morning from the lab. The DNA beneath Susan's nails is somewhat corrupted because of all the filth under there, too. Boy, did she put up a fight. But with time, they think they'll be able to create a profile."

"Really?" Maybe his promise to Susan wouldn't be an empty one, after all. Maybe, with a small amount of luck… "If they come through, we'll need the right suspect."

"Exactly." Gibbons thumped the door panel. "Thanks for getting the truck."

Caleb watched the detective heave himself into a nondescript beige sedan and drive out of the lot. They were making progress, but he was afraid it might be too little, too late. Their killer could strike again if he wasn't stopped soon. Where could they find the answers they needed?

Caleb's eyes lingered on the glove box before dropping

to the floor, which was bare except for a crushed paper cup. If the truck held any secrets, he wasn't sure he wanted to know them. But he felt obligated to search while he had the chance. Obligated to himself, the investigation and Susan.

Opening the glove box, he quickly rifled through its contents: an owner's manual, a service record, a stack of napkins and several receipts for gas, all from several years ago. Beneath the seat, he found a sack that still contained some french fries. The fries didn't appear to be very old, which suggested they were probably Johnny's trash—along with the cigarette butts in the ashtray.

Now Caleb just had to check beneath and behind the seat. He pulled out a coat with a Chinese dragon on the back, but it was a size small; that meant it probably belonged to Johnny, too.

Shoving it behind the seat again, he finally put the truck in reverse. He'd done what he needed to do and, thankfully, Madison was still in the clear.

TWO HOURS LATER, Caleb felt almost euphoric as he drove Madison over to her mother's place in Ellis's truck. The tires didn't seem to match the imprint left at the site of Susan's body. And Johnny and Tye were looking less like suspects than they had before. Which meant the shadow of violence that had so deeply affected Madison's life in the past probably wasn't going to overtake her again. It also meant that what Caleb had done in the name of justice should be forgivable, since there wouldn't be any negative consequences from his actions. He'd simply explain the truth to Madison and apologize. And make sure she understood that last night had nothing to do with any ulterior motives.

He'd tell her tonight, he decided, while there was still a chance she might forgive him.

"So who was the friend you helped move?" she asked, breaking the silence.

Caleb glanced over at her. She was dressed for business in a navy-blue suit, with her hair pulled back, and looked almost too cool and professional to be such a passionate lover. A grin tempted the corners of his lips as he remembered just how erotically she'd behaved. He'd never experienced sexual hunger like he had that first time at her place—unless it was later, at the cottage. But her question about the "move" he'd supposedly helped with this morning put him in an awkward position.

"Just someone I used to work with," he said, thinking of Gibbons. He didn't want to make up any more lies, but he couldn't tell her the truth right now. They were about to arrive at her mother's house, and the way Madison kept fidgeting with her purse strap told him she was nervous about what they might encounter. He'd wait until later, when he had her complete attention and plenty of time to convince her that last night was never part of his plan.

"When?" she asked.

"A couple of years ago."

"When you lived on Fidalgo?"

He cleared his throat. "No, I was just divorced and living in Seattle." He launched into another subject before she could press him for more details. "What do you think your mother will do if she finds out about Johnny staying in the garage?"

"She'll be furious with me for not kicking him out."

"But you didn't give Johnny permission to move in, did you?"

"No, his being there came as a complete surprise to

me. But I should've made him leave right away instead of giving him time.''

''He might not have taken too kindly to that,'' Caleb said.

''I know. I was a little uncomfortable confronting him. But I can't show the house if he's living there, and my mother's getting really anxious to move.''

Caleb wondered if Annette had taken those panties and shoes. And that locket. Lately he went back and forth about whether or not Ellis Purcell was really the Sandpoint Strangler. Susan's murder was too similar to the others to be a new killer, but what about the sightings of Purcell's truck at the scene of two of the previous murders? Either way, Caleb longed to know for sure—at last. He wanted to find out *how* the strangler had done what he'd done and managed to get away with it.

But whether or not Caleb ever learned the truth, Purcell's story was one he'd never write. He knew now that he would never capitalize on his relationship with Madison that way.

Reaching across the seat, he let his fingers close around hers. ''Whatever's waiting for us at your mother's, we'll work it out,'' he said, and hoped his words would prove prophetic about the future in general.

CHAPTER SIXTEEN

THE GARAGE WAS EMPTY. Madison couldn't tell if Johnny was still living there or not. If he'd moved on, he certainly hadn't cleaned up after himself.

Caleb was in front of her. He'd insisted on going in first, and stood with his hands on his hips, surveying the mess. They'd entered from the alley so her mother wouldn't know they'd arrived. The autumn sun, streaming in behind them, warmed Madison's back, but she still didn't like the building's shadowy corners.

"What are you going to tell your mother about the broken window?" Caleb asked, using one foot to shove the glass into some semblance of a pile.

Madison frowned at the glittering shards on the cement. "Nothing. She won't come out here, so I don't have to worry about her seeing it before I have it replaced. I'm only trying to make sure a prospective buyer doesn't run into Johnny and mention him to her."

"How do you know she won't walk out here with someone who's taking a look at the yard?"

"Easy." She motioned toward the workshop and had to take a deep breath to be able to finish what she was about to say. "That's where my father shot himself."

The gravity in Caleb's gaze when it shifted to her face let her know that pumping her voice full of bravado hadn't concealed the fact that her father's suicide still hurt. If you'd loved someone who took his or her own life, did you ever really get over it? Did you ever get over the feeling of waste and betrayal?

"I'm sorry," he said. "You told me he'd shot himself in the backyard, or I'd read it somewhere, but I didn't realize it had happened in here."

She stared through the open door to the workshop, remembering the roar of the ball games her father had always listened to when he was there. "I never dreamed he'd be the type. My father made his share of mistakes, of course, especially when he was young. But he seemed so…stable. When I knew him, anyway."

"The investigation put him under a lot of pressure," Caleb pointed out.

She hiked her purse higher on her shoulder. "It upset him, sure. But not like it upset my mother and me."

"Maybe he just didn't let it show."

"That's what some people say. They assume he believed the police were about to arrest him and make him pay for his crimes. I…" She bit her lip and shook her head.

"You what?"

"I disagree. He didn't think the police were that close to an arrest. The D.A. was still refusing to prosecute because he didn't believe the state had a strong enough case."

"So why *would* your father do what he did?"

She shook her head again. "I guess he was just tired of the fight, or…" The ideas that had been percolating in her mind ever since Tye's visit bubbled to the forefront. "Or maybe he learned something he couldn't face."

"Like…"

"Maybe he stumbled on that box of underwear and shoes, found that locket and figured it had to be Tye who was killing those women."

Caleb walked back to her and placed his hands on her shoulders. "I realize it can't be easy to think your father could have committed such horrendous acts, Maddy. But I'm pretty sure Tye wasn't to blame."

"Why not?"

He seemed to search for the right words. "There's never been any evidence that it was him. At least that I've heard."

"What about the stuff in that box? He had access to my father's truck and...and the house, and he knows the area because he's lived here. He's also much angrier than my father ever was. As much as I'd rather not admit this, I could actually imagine him hurting someone. But the police have never even considered him."

"That you know of," he said.

"I don't think they ever really investigated anyone but my father."

"There must be a reason they kept coming back to him."

Madison sensed that Caleb was trying to be understanding, but she didn't feel he was listening to her with an open mind. "Finding that box is about the only scenario I can imagine that would make my father do something so...permanent," she said. "For one thing, he wouldn't willingly leave my mother. They were close, and she depended on him. He lived to take care of her. The last thing he did was sell the old car he'd been restoring so she'd have plenty of cash on hand. And...he loved me and Brianna. He wouldn't have wanted to do something that would hurt us, too."

"Madison, you're searching for reasons to explain a reality that's very painful for you. It's a natural reaction, and I understand how you feel, but—"

"No!" She grabbed his arms in a beseeching movement. "Think about it, Caleb. Could you go on, knowing that because of you, because of your early neglect, your son had turned into a brutal monster and raped and murdered eleven women?"

He opened his mouth to respond, but she pressed a finger over his lips. "Don't answer yet," she said. "My father was no killer. I need you to believe me."

Madison had never asked anyone to believe her. But it suddenly seemed terribly important that *someone* trust her instincts. And she wanted that someone to be Caleb. Maybe because Danny had never doubted that her father was as guilty as the police said. He'd patronized her occasionally, especially at first. He'd been upset about the inconveniences the investigation had brought him. But he'd never once validated her feelings on the matter, never once said, "You should know your own father."

"He wasn't a killer," she repeated.

The air between them seemed to crackle with the intensity of her emotions. *Please feel what I feel,* she wanted to add. But she refused to say more. She was probably asking too much as it was.

He tilted up her chin and gazed into her eyes, his expression skeptical, more of the same old "you're simply avoiding the truth" she got from everyone. But then something changed. "How can you be so sure," he asked, "when everything that's been found says you're wrong?"

The beat of Madison's heart reverberated in her fingertips. "The same way I'd know, if they ever accused you of such a heinous crime, that you didn't do it. I could *feel* it."

That made an impact, started a smoldering in his eyes. Lowering his head, he lightly brushed his lips against hers.

Madison let her eyelids close, reveling in the strength

of the arms that slid around her and the solidness of his chest as he gathered her to him. Caleb hadn't said he suddenly believed her father was innocent, but she could tell he *wanted* to side with her, which was a great deal more than she'd ever gotten from Danny. Caleb acted as though he believed in her, just like she believed in him.

"If I'm not careful, you're going to cost me my view of the bay," he murmured, kissing the side of her mouth, the indentation behind her ear, the column of her neck.

"Rent *is* pretty cheap at my place," she whispered.

"And the food is good."

"When I cook."

"There are other benefits." His hand came around to part her jacket and close over one breast.

Madison caught her breath. "We can't do this again, remember? I'm not ready for a relationship," she said, but the warmth of his hand was filtering through her thin blouse and lacy bra, and he was beginning to circle his thumb across the fabric directly covering her nipple, which made it pretty difficult to remember *why* she wasn't ready.

"What if we take it slow?" he said.

"Take *what* slow?" she asked, somehow confusing their conversation with the physical sensations that were drawing all of her body's energy into its very center.

"Anything you want," he answered with a lazy grin.

CALEB WAS RELUCTANT to let Madison go, but he certainly didn't want Johnny or someone else walking in on them. And he didn't want to take things any further in the garage where her father had killed himself. He hadn't meant to make any sexual advances. He'd only wanted to comfort her.

"We'd better clean up this place so we can let your mother know we're here," he said.

Madison didn't move. "Caleb, I have a six-year-old daughter and an ex-husband who will probably always do his best to make my life miserable."

He arched an eyebrow, wondering where she was going with this. "Okay."

"I also have an emotionally weak and rather clingy mother who has no one else and can be difficult sometimes."

He was beginning to catch on. What had passed between them had frightened her, and now she was running scared. "Are you making a point?" He handed her one of the black garbage bags he found on a shelf.

"Of course. My point is that you don't want to get involved with me. I failed miserably in my first marriage. Danny was unhappy with me from almost the first week."

Caleb located a broom in the corner next to a few garden utensils and started sweeping up the glass. He didn't have a very high opinion of Danny, so what Danny had thought or felt meant absolutely nothing to him. But that wasn't the issue. "Well, I failed at my first marriage *twice*, so if it makes you feel any better, I've got you beat," he said.

"How does someone fail twice at the same marriage?"

"It's easy. You remarry the person you just divorced and end up divorcing again."

"Were you still in love with her?"

"No, I made a stupid mistake. She wasn't willing to let our relationship go. She kept calling me, coming over, trying to seduce me. And it was too easy to fall back into the same routine."

Madison made a face that told him the mental picture

he'd just created wasn't a pleasant one. "You went on sleeping with her?"

He shook his head. "Not on a regular basis. I had a little too much to drink one night after our first divorce. She came over, it was late, and we ended up in bed together." He sighed and leaned on his broom. "She wound up pregnant, Maddy."

"So you married her again?"

"It was what she wanted," he said, searching the garage for a dustpan. "And with the baby coming…I thought it might make a difference. I wanted to at least try."

"But you told me when you moved in that you don't have any children."

"I don't." He took a deep breath because it wasn't easy for him to talk about the baby. When Holly miscarried, he'd been wanting kids for nearly five years, but she'd kept putting him off. "She lost the baby only a few weeks after the wedding. It happened while I was away on business."

"I'm sorry."

"Now I know it was for the best. We couldn't get along no matter how hard we tried. It's better that a child wasn't involved."

Madison twisted the empty garbage bag around her hands. "How long were you together after she lost the baby?"

"Almost a year, on and off." He gave up looking for a dustpan and swept the glass onto some paper. "So now you know why your failed marriage hardly frightens me."

"But I just pulled my life together again, Caleb, and I really can't get involved, with you or anyone else," she said. "It's simply not what's best for me or Brianna right now."

"How do you know what's best, Maddy? Have you got a crystal ball somewhere?" He rested the broom against the wall and moved toward her. "You can't exactly schedule the people who come into your life, you know. What, did you write in your day planner that three years from now you can meet someone?"

The fact that he didn't immediately back off, as he had earlier, seemed to take her by surprise. Her mouth opened and closed, twice, but nothing came out, and finally she began gathering up the wadded wrappers, napkins, empty paper cups and cigarette butts. "Maybe I did," she said at last. "In any case, you need to quit."

He tried to look puzzled. "Quit what?"

"Quit making me think about getting naked with you."

He laughed outright. "I wasn't the first one to take off my clothes last night."

"You took your clothes off quickly enough once you got the chance."

"True."

"And you goaded me into that little striptease in the first place."

"I won't deny that, either, but I'm certainly not going to help you run away from me just because you're a big chicken."

"I'm not a chicken. I'm being smart."

"If you can call letting fear get the best of you 'being smart.'"

Her brows knitted. "Stop twisting everything I say. I'm not going to sleep with you again."

He motioned for her to move away from the middle of the floor so he could pull the truck into one stall. "We'll see."

She caught him by the arm as he walked past her, her

hand cool against his skin. "*We'll see?* I can't believe you just said that."

He stared down at the freckles he liked so much. "Am I supposed to pretend I don't know what you want?"

She immediately released him. "You're supposed to respect my wishes."

"Okay," he said. "I'll respect your wishes. The next time anything happens between us, it'll be your move." He gave in to the smile tugging at his lips. "But that's not going to change a single thing."

CALEB WASN'T WEARING anything special. After they'd finished the open house and gone back home, he'd showered and changed from his faded jeans into a pair of chinos and a button-down shirt. But he looked so good and smelled so good that Madison couldn't keep her eyes from him as they left home in his Mustang and headed toward Highway 20, which would take them north to Fidalgo Island. After their conversation in her mother's garage, she didn't want to be so preoccupied with her tenant, but something significant had happened in those few moments, something even more monumental than last night. He'd offered her the emotional support she'd needed for so long, and that was a powerful aphrodisiac.

At least thinking about him kept her from dwelling on what had happened during the open house. Most of those who'd come through were more interested in the fact that Ellis Purcell had once lived in the house, and died in the backyard, than they were in actually making an offer. One woman had even said that he was eternally damned and his ghost would probably linger on the premises for generations.

That woman's rudeness hadn't been easy to tolerate. But it was Annette who'd nearly driven Madison crazy.

Her mother either fretted at her elbow, trying to defend Ellis at every opportunity, or fawned over Caleb, who'd been nice enough to mow the lawn and fix the fence while they were there. Annette had insisted on making him some lemonade, even though he'd told her water would be fine. She'd served him cake he'd initially refused. And after he came in from the yard, she had him relax in their most comfortable chair—and look through all of Madison's old photo albums.

"Wasn't she a cute baby?" her mother had gushed, over and over again.

Madison would roll her eyes and Caleb would grin because he knew perfectly well that she was squirming in her seat.

"You might have mowed my mother's lawn and suffered through my old photo album, but don't think that's going to change my mind," she said as they turned left onto the highway.

He cocked an eyebrow. "Did I miss the first half of this conversation? Because I don't have a clue what you're talking about."

"I'm saying I'm not going to sleep with you again."

His chuckle was a low rumble. "Sounds as though you can't think of anything else."

Maddy felt her face flush hot. He was right. She was completely infatuated with him. "It's the first time I've thought about it since the garage."

His smile said he knew she was lying, but he didn't call her on it, and she changed the subject before she could give any more away. "Did you see Johnny while you were out back?"

"No sign of him. But I did place a call to the police about the possibility that one of your brothers might have some tie to the murders."

Anxiety immediately tightened the muscles in Madison's shoulders and neck. "Did you tell them about the box?"

"No. I spoke to a Detective Gibbons, and said you had some suspicions from the way Tye and Johnny have been acting."

She grimaced, recognizing the name. "Gibbons was one of the detectives on my father's case. What did he say?"

Caleb reached out and squeezed her hand. "That they've already checked out Johnny *and* Tye and crossed them off the list of suspects."

"Only because they're sure it was my father!"

"Not anymore, they're not. Not after that other woman was strangled."

Madison missed the warmth of Caleb's hand when he returned it to the steering wheel. "So I don't have anything to worry about."

"That's what they told me."

"But who else could've taken the stuff out of that box?"

He seemed to consider the question. "Let's not worry about that stuff until we find it again, okay? Do you think you could get your mother out of the house tomorrow so I could look around?"

"I don't know. I'll try."

He switched radio stations, then leaned an elbow on the window ledge. "I was hoping for the chance to go under the house and take a look today. But your poor mother needed a distraction from all those strangers pouring through the door into what is normally her private space."

Madison blinked at him, surprised by his sensitivity. He hadn't seen Annette as overbearing, as she'd expected. He'd seen her as an insecure woman trying to cope with certain change, and he'd tried to help. "That's why you let her corner you?" she asked.

He shrugged. "I liked looking at your baby pictures."

Madison felt a flicker of guilt for not being more understanding of her mother. "I should've been more patient with her. It's not easy for her to open herself up to the kind of scrutiny she's received over the past decade or so."

"You should know," he said. "You were right there with her."

"That's probably why she wasn't willing to sell the house before now. Living with what's familiar, even if it's not good, is sometimes easier than taking a risk on the unknown."

Caleb cast Madison a meaningful look. "Seems I know someone else who's struggling with that."

"I'm just being cautious," she said. "It's not the same."

"Whatever you say." He turned his attention back to the road until they reached Deception Pass, the bridge that linked the two islands. Then they started winding around to the north side of Fidalgo Island, and he looked over at her again. "So why aren't you going to sleep with me tonight?"

"I thought you were thinking about other things," she said curtly.

He chuckled. "You've piqued my curiosity."

"Sleeping with you confuses me. I'm not planning to let myself get attached. And I don't do casual sex."

"Judging by last night, there wouldn't be anything casual about it."

And that would be the real reason. "Will I meet your sister today?" she asked, steering the conversation back to safe ground.

"I'm sure there won't be any way to avoid it. She lives next door."

Madison couldn't help laughing. "Tell me what she's like as an adult."

"Not much different than she was as a kid. She's still looking for a chance to run my life. My mother lovingly calls her a 'mother hen' but, believe me, Tamara takes the concept to new heights."

"Does she know how you feel about her?"

"No. And she wouldn't believe me even if I told her. That's one thing I *do* like about my sister. She's sort of indestructible."

Madison gazed out the window at Fidalgo Bay and a small cluster of fishing boats off in the distance. "It's pretty here."

"I've always liked it," he said as they stopped at a red light. They were approaching the small, quaint city of Anacortes.

"Then why did you leave?"

He turned from Commercial onto 12th Street. After a few blocks, Madison saw old, well-maintained homes on the left and Guemes Channel on the right. "I needed some space."

CHAPTER SEVENTEEN

CALEB'S PARENTS' HOUSE was a large white Victorian facing Guemes Channel. Madison loved it at first sight, especially the wraparound porch and the gingerbread that dripped from the eaves. As she got out of Caleb's car, she could see an arbor with climbing roses to the left. Stepping-stones led through it to what promised to be a very natural, beautiful yard.

"*This* is where you grew up?" she asked.

He waited for her to join him at the head of a redbrick walkway. "Yes. And if it looks like the kind of place where the children of the house would be forced to take piano lessons, it was."

Madison glanced at his hands, which were large and devoid of any jewelry. They didn't look like a musician's hands; they looked a lot more solid—like a quarterback's hands. "You can play the piano?"

"I didn't say I could play, only that I was forced to take lessons."

"For how long?"

"Five years. And they were the longest five years of my life. I'd have to sit and practice for forty-five minutes a day while all my buddies were out playing baseball. I hated it."

"How terrible to be so unloved," she said with a mocking smile.

He returned her grin. "I knew you'd understand."

"Just tell me one thing," she said. "How could you *not* learn to play in five years?"

His expression turned sheepish. "Unfortunately, I can be as stubborn as my mother. After all that time, my crowning achievement was a rather mediocre rendition of *Swan Lake*. I still have it memorized."

"What an accomplishment. You'll have to play it for me later."

"I don't think so. For me, that's sort of the equivalent of serenading you outside your window."

Madison feigned disappointment. "That isn't going to happen, either?"

"How'd you guess?"

She didn't have a chance to respond. A thin woman with beautiful white hair swept up with a gold clip had come to the door and was watching their advance. She smiled as soon as Madison looked at her, and Madison could immediately see the similarities between Caleb's facial features and those of his mother. She had the same sharp cheekbones, the same kind but shrewd eyes, the same generous mouth.

Madison particularly appreciated Caleb's mouth....

"Mom, this is Madison Lieberman," he said, embracing his mother as they stepped onto the porch. "Madison, this is Justine, the woman who scarred me with those piano lessons I was telling you about."

Justine rolled her eyes and took hold of Madison's hands. "Don't listen to that ungrateful boy. We're so glad you could come."

Her grip was warm and reassuring, her smile just short of radiant. She struck Madison as self-possessed and dignified. "I'm glad to be here." Caleb brushed past them and strolled inside.

"Then come in," Justine said. "My husband is just

getting cleaned up. He's been working in the back all day, trying to get the weeds pulled, but we'll have dinner soon. I hope you like salmon.''

''That's my favorite fish.'' Madison followed her hostess into a house that smelled of broiled fish, mushrooms, onions and furniture polish—to find Caleb coming out of the kitchen with his mouth full.

''What are you eating?'' his mother demanded. ''You haven't been here ten seconds.''

Caleb didn't look the least bit abashed. ''Want a crescent roll?'' he asked Madison, offering her the rest of what he'd momentarily tried to hide behind his back.

''No, thanks,'' she said, laughing. ''I'll wait.''

''Where are your manners?'' Justine asked him, shaking her head. ''We're waiting for Tamara and the kids.''

''What'd I tell you?'' Caleb said to Madison, finishing off his roll.

His mother's eyebrows lifted. ''What's that supposed to mean?''

''Nothing,'' he said.

Madison could tell his mom knew better. ''Tamara has always loved and pampered you,'' she insisted.

''When she wasn't getting me grounded for ditching school,'' he muttered.

Justine sighed and jerked her head toward Caleb. ''It took all of us to manage this one.''

''I can imagine,'' Madison said.

''But please don't assume that anything he does reflects on me,'' Justine replied drolly, leading her into a sitting room with wide front windows and an antique settee.

A knock at the door preceded two calls of ''Grandma, we're here!'' Then the screen door slammed shut. Little feet pounded down the hallway, and identical twin boys who seemed about eight years old came skidding around the corner, crying, "Uncle Caleb!"

Madison thought they were bent on tackling Caleb right there in front of the Russian tea set and lace draperies. But Caleb tossed the first boy over his shoulder and got the other in a headlock. "Well, if it isn't trouble," he said.

Turning so that Madison could see the boy dangling halfway down his back, he said, "This is my nephew Jacob."

Jacob didn't bother looking up at her. He was half-heartedly trying to free himself from his uncle's grasp. Like his brother, he was on the thin, gangly side and had the usual jumble of large and small teeth so characteristic of the age. But Madison suspected they'd grow up to be almost as handsome as their uncle.

Almost. Madison was beginning to believe no one was or ever would be as handsome as Caleb.

"And—" Caleb brought the red-faced boy in the headlock around "—this is Joey."

"I'm not Joey," the boy complained. The other was laughing too hard to care whether or not his uncle had gotten his name wrong.

"Don't believe 'em," Caleb warned in a conspiratorial whisper. "They love to screw with your mind."

Madison had the impression that it was Caleb who was trying to confuse her. "Hi, Joey," she said to the one he'd introduced as Jacob.

"She got you, Uncle Caleb," Joey squealed.

"So there's my long-lost brother," a tall, large-boned woman interrupted from the doorway. With her facial structure, dark hair and dark eyes, Madison knew it could only be Tamara. But the features that served Caleb so well looked too exaggerated for real beauty on his sister. "He's living in town now, but does he ever spend any time with us?'' she asked facetiously. ''Nooo. Does he ever come by? Nooo. Not unless he needs something.''

Caleb gave her a grudging smile. ''And here we have the woman responsible for having my new bicycle impounded just two days after my thirteenth birthday.''

''You were riding in the street without using your handlebars,'' she said as primly as a schoolteacher.

''A crime if ever I heard one,'' Caleb responded.

''She won't let us ride without handlebars, either,'' one of the twins complained. ''We lost our bikes for a whole month just for riding without helmets. And she still won't let us have skateboards. We're the only two kids in the whole school who don't have skateboards.''

''Skateboards are dangerous,'' Tamara said.

''You're the *only* ones? I doubt it,'' Caleb said, surprising Madison by supporting his sister. He set Tamara's children down and hugged her, and Madison sensed that he didn't dislike her half as much as he pretended to. ''Where's Mac?''

''He's running late,'' she said. ''You know how he is, always on the phone. Most wives worry about losing their husbands to another woman. I've already lost mine to computers and cell phones.'' She glanced at Madison. ''Is this your new lady friend?''

Madison stood and smiled. ''I'm Madison Lieberman.''

''I'm glad he's finally decided to bring home someone besides that crackpot he married,'' Tamara said. ''After this past week I thought he was moving on to marriage and divorce number three.'' She flipped her long brown hair out of her eyes. ''Holly's come by here twice over the last couple of days, Caleb.''

''Tamara, let's not discuss Holly in front of Madison,

please,'' Justine said. "And unless you can say something nice, don't talk about her at all.''

"I can't help it if the truth hurts,'' Tamara muttered as an older, raw-boned man entered the room.

"Ah, there you are, dear,'' Justine said, and introduced Madison to Caleb's father, Logan.

Logan shook her hand, but was far more reserved in his greeting than Justine had been. From beneath the ledge of a prominent brow, his eyes seemed to look right through her, and the lines on his forehead indicated that his intense expression was habitual. She decided it probably took a great deal to impress this man—or figure in his affections at all.

"You're Purcell's daughter, eh?'' He rubbed his chin with a large callused hand, making a scratching sound.

She nodded, feeling a bit apprehensive about what he might ask her next. But when Justine took his hand, his face immediately mellowed. "That whole thing couldn't have been easy on you,'' he said. "We're happy to have you here.''

Madison was pretty sure Justine was behind that sentiment. But Madison muttered the same polite remarks she'd been saying since she'd arrived, then had to repeat them one more time when Tamara's husband, Mac, finally showed up. Mac had just started to say, "Nice to meet you,'' when his cell phone rang, and he stepped out to take the call.

"See what I mean?'' Tamara complained.

Caleb gave one of the twins a raspberry on the head. "What's this I hear about you having a girlfriend?''

"I don't have a girlfriend,'' the boy argued. "Joey's the one who has a girlfriend. He likes Sarah.''

"I don't like Sarah!'' Joey cried.

"Then why do you always give her your chocolate milk at lunch?" he challenged.

"Because I don't want it."

"Right," Jacob said. "I ask you for it every day, and you won't give it to me."

"That's because you're my stupid brother."

"Everyone knows you like her."

Joey's face went even redder than when Caleb had held him in that headlock. "Only because you told them."

"Did not."

"Did, too."

"Hey, what's wrong with liking a girl?" Caleb broke in, putting an arm around both children's waists and dragging them up against him. "Occasionally you meet one who's not half-bad," he added, winking at Madison.

"They just...they can't even play tetherball," Jacob said with disdain. "They spend their whole recess walking around the playground *talking*."

"So? Talking's bad?" Joey said.

"It's boring," Jacob retorted.

Justine gestured them to silence. "That's enough, boys. Your uncle Caleb tells me that Madison has a daughter who's just a bit younger than the two of you. I was sad that she couldn't make it tonight, but now I'm beginning to wonder if she isn't better off."

"You don't have to worry about Brianna," Caleb said, with what sounded suspiciously like pride. "She's tough. She could take these two, no problem. One look down her dainty little nose, and they'd be knocking themselves out trying to please her."

Madison thought of her daughter opening the door to Caleb that first morning and saying, "Oh, it's you," and nearly laughed. Her daughter *was* tough. She'd faced down an adult and let him know, in no uncertain terms, that she didn't approve. Of course, Caleb had won her over pretty easily since then. But Madison had difficulty believing any female could withstand his charm for long.

"If she's anything like her mother, she's probably darling," Justine said.

Madison felt a blush of pleasure at the compliment, but she liked Caleb's mother for more than her impeccable manners. She liked the air of authority Justine carried, and the high place she held in her family's esteem. Madison wished her own family hadn't been torn apart, especially in such an unusual way. The suspicion surrounding her father had separated her from almost everyone else, even friends of hers who'd suffered through calamities such as divorce, abuse or the death of a loved one.

"I'm ready for dinner. Can we eat?" Tamara said.

"Shouldn't we wait for Mac?" Justine asked.

"We can't do that or we'll all starve," her daughter replied.

THROUGH THE FIRST PART of dinner, Madison felt Caleb's eyes on her often and glanced up to see him smile. She loved that smile, even though it seemed to make a mockery of her puny attempts to hang on to her heart.

As the meal progressed, Caleb began looking out into the hallway, where Mac was talking to a client or someone else on his phone. Tamara had been carrying on as though her husband's extended absence from the table didn't bother her, but her smile had grown brittle and Madison was starting to realize how much it upset her. She could tell Caleb was coming to the same conclusion. Especially when, just before coffee and dessert, he excused himself from the dinner table and slipped out.

A few seconds later, he came back, and this time Mac was with him.

"Sorry that took so long," Tamara's husband said, completely nonchalant in his tardiness. "It was pretty important."

"On a Saturday?" Tamara said.

He shrugged. "Business is business."

Madison caught a subtle glance between Justine and Logan, but neither parent made any comment. Justine simply smiled and asked Mac if she could reheat his plate.

"No, thanks," he told her and turned to Caleb. "So how are things going on the case?"

Case? *What* case? Madison waited for Caleb's response, but everything became a little stilted at that point. Justine's fingers seemed to tighten on her wineglass. Tamara put down her fork, and Logan hesitated with his water halfway to his mouth.

Caleb was the only one who continued eating. "Work's going well, as usual. How about you, Mac? You getting that business you were telling me about off the ground?"

Everyone's eyes went to Mac, and the tension eased as he launched into a zealous explanation of why the next few months were going to make him a rich man in the import-export business. He rambled on and on, while everyone sat quietly, waiting for him to come to an end— or realize that he was going into far more detail than anyone cared to know.

Madison watched Tamara, mostly, and noticed the way her eyes flicked from her sons to her brother and finally to her husband. She was obviously struggling with some emotion, and Madison didn't have to be psychic to know that it was because of her husband's preoccupation with himself and his business.

"Are we all ready for coffee and ice cream?" Justine asked when Mac had finally finished eating.

"I don't think so," Tamara said. "Mac and I had better

get back. I have a lot of laundry to do and…and I was going to finish painting the downspouts before it got dark.''

Mac's cell phone had vibrated twice while he ate. Each time he'd paused to check the caller ID, obviously tempted by what he might be missing. But each time, he'd looked at Caleb and pushed the End button. It was then that Madison knew Caleb had said more to him than a simple, ''Your dinner's getting cold.''

''*I* want dessert,'' Mac said. Then his phone vibrated again, and he changed his mind about dessert and left the room.

His ''Hello, this is Mac Bly'' floated back to them as he moved away.

Caleb reached over and took his sister's hand.

Madison saw that Tamara was fighting tears, and the sympathy of her family was only making it worse, so she quickly stood. ''Maybe you wouldn't mind showing me your house, Tamara,'' she said, to offer the other woman an easy retreat.

Tamara glanced up at her in surprise. ''Sure. Excuse us for a few minutes, will you?'' she managed to say, and immediately ducked out of the room.

Madison hesitated, giving her a few seconds' lead.

''Is something wrong with Mom?'' Jacob asked. At least Madison thought it was Jacob. The boys looked so much alike it was difficult to tell, but she was reasonably sure Jacob was the one in the blue shirt. Thank goodness Tamara hadn't dressed them alike.

''She's fine, dear,'' Justine said. ''She's just eager to show Madison your pretty house. She's put a lot of work into that house, you know.''

The way Justine said it indicated Tamara was the only

one working on the house, but she was certain the boys didn't pick up on that.

"Uh-oh," Joey groaned, nudging Jacob. "She's gonna be mad at us for not cleaning our rooms."

"I promise not to notice, okay?" Madison said at the door, and followed Tamara out.

She found Caleb's sister waiting for her on the back porch, wiping her eyes with her hand. "You going to be okay?" Madison asked, sitting down on the step next to her.

Tamara tried to shrug and ended up sniffing instead and wiping her eyes again. "Do you really want to see my house?"

"If you feel like showing it to me. Otherwise, we can just sit here until you're ready to go back inside, and you can give me a tour some other day." *If I'm ever invited back...* Strangely, Madison was disappointed by the thought that she might not have another opportunity to come to this place and be with these people.

Tamara nodded but didn't move, so Madison assumed the tour wasn't going to happen today.

"It shouldn't bother me, you know," Tamara muttered, sniffling again. "It's just...I can't get his attention for five minutes without an interruption, and the boys aren't having much better luck. If he says he'll come to one of their baseball games, he shows up when it's nearly over and then he spends the short time he's there standing in the background, where he can't even see, talking on the damn phone."

"My ex-husband was like that," Madison said.

Caleb's sister propped her chin in one hand, looking dejected. "Is that why you divorced him?"

"No, I was going through some other stuff at the time and didn't get around to considering our relationship, let alone acknowledging that I'd become very dissatisfied with it. He left me for another woman.''

''I'm sorry.''

Madison was surprised to find that it didn't bother her nearly as much as it used to. ''Don't be. In many ways, he did me a favor. Now I'm not saddled with the guilt of calling it quits, which I would've had to do at some point.''

''Maybe that's true for me, too, huh?'' Tamara eyed her as though fearful she might agree.

''I don't get that impression,'' Madison said. ''I think you and your husband still have a good chance of working out your relationship. He's just a little…preoccupied and needs to realize what he's taking for granted.''

The door opened behind them and they both turned as Caleb stepped outside, looking as sexy as always, despite the dark scowl on his face.

''What did you say to Mac?'' Tamara asked when she saw it was her brother.

Caleb leaned on the railing. ''Obviously not enough.''

''You kept him off the phone for nearly fifteen minutes. That's more of an accomplishment than you know.''

''What's the problem between you two?'' he asked. ''I thought things were going well. That's what you always tell me.''

''Isn't that what you want to hear?''

''When I ask, I'm looking for the truth.''

''In a way, things are going well. He hasn't been unfaithful to me that I know of. He says he loves the boys and me. He just works twenty-four–seven, and in a good year he earns a living.''

''In a good year?''

''Not every year is a good year.''

''What about spending time with Jacob and Joey?''

"What about it?" She sniffed, looking resentful of her own tears. "I take care of them."

"That's what I thought." Caleb sighed as he gazed out over the backyard. "When did it get so bad?"

Tamara shrugged. "I can't name a particular time. It's something that's gotten progressively worse. He's just so intent on becoming rich."

"At the sacrifice of everything else?"

"I don't know," she said. "I haven't tested him on that yet."

A large tabby cat hopped up the steps and started purring as it rubbed against Caleb's legs. "Is that where the problems between you are going?" he asked.

Tamara didn't answer. "Look at that," she said, motioning to the cat. "Even my Tabby likes you better than me. Isn't that the story of my life?"

She'd said it jokingly, but Madison felt there might be a kernel of jealousy in those words.

"Are you serious?" Caleb said. "If you felt that way, why were you always working so hard to make sure nothing ever happened to me? 'Don't ride your bike in the street.' 'You're not tall enough to go on that roller coaster.' 'Don't go swimming in the creek without your life preserver.' 'Mom and Dad, Caleb snuck out again last night.'"

"You know why," she said gruffly.

He nudged her with his knee. "I don't think I do."

"What a bonehead," Tamara muttered to Madison. "Because I love you, silly. First you were my baby brother, the very center of our family. Then you became the standard for everything I wanted in a husband."

Caleb blinked, then pinched the back of his neck. "Ah, Tammy. How am I supposed to hold all that tattling against you when you say things like that?"

Madison was beginning to feel she was part of a conversation better suited to privacy. She got up to head back inside, but Caleb hooked an arm around her shoulders and pulled her to him as casually as though they'd been dating for months. "Will you tell my poor sister that I've been a jerk and I'm sorry?" he said.

Madison grinned down at Tamara. "Caleb says he's going to make up for all the grief he's put you through in the past. He'll stay with the boys next weekend and baby-sit while you and Mac get away and, hopefully, talk. He promises to keep in better touch in the future. And..." She paused to think, purposefully ignoring the are-you-nuts? expression on Caleb's face "...oh yes, if you ever need money, you know right where to come."

"Do you have any idea how hard it is to take care of those two boys?" he asked. In the face of baby-sitting, the promise of money was evidently minor, but she could tell he was only teasing, and it went far toward lightening the mood.

Tamara chuckled as she stood up, her tears now gone. "This girl's something special," she said. "I think you should hang on to her."

"Wait a second," he said as his sister started back inside the house. "You've hated every woman I've ever brought home."

"So has everyone else," she said.

"Not Mom and Dad."

"*Especially* Mom and Dad." She cast a know-it-all smile over her shoulder just before the screen door slammed shut.

CHAPTER EIGHTEEN

"THAT CAN'T BE TRUE," Caleb said in the wake of his sister's departure. "I have good taste in women."

Madison laughed at his hurt-little-boy expression. "What don't they like about your first wife?"

He pulled her down on the steps with him, keeping his arm around her, and Madison couldn't bring herself to move away, not when sitting so close allowed her to breathe in the aroma of his clean warm skin. "Let's see...I guess we could start with the fact that she's insecure and clingy."

"And?"

"Temperamental. Basically high-maintenance."

"So you married her because..."

"I was young and stupid."

Madison playfully elbowed him in the ribs. "Come on, there has to be *something* you liked about her."

He pretended to think hard. "I liked being needed for a change. As the baby of the family, I'd spent my life being raised by two more-than-capable women."

"Your mother and your sister."

"Exactly. I was ready to assert myself as the caregiver, and Holly wanted someone to take care of her. It seemed like the perfect fit—at first. But I guess you're right. I liked other things about her, too. I still do. I like the way she throws herself into everything wholeheartedly, usually without looking first. She's childlike in her exuberance for the things and people she loves."

Madison was beginning to regret she'd asked. She no longer felt she had the luxury of throwing herself into anything, least of all a relationship. She had to be cautious. Unlike Holly, she had to look before she leaped. Certainly she didn't compare well to the impetuous, trusting woman he'd married before....

"But I couldn't live with the moodiness," he continued. "And she became so obsessive. She'd get jealous when anyone, male or female, wanted a few minutes of my time. She'd even throw a fit if I spoke to my mother more than once a month on the phone. She was just too insecure. I kept thinking that if I changed or she changed or we both did, it might work. But we're just not compatible. I know that now."

"Why didn't you try for another kid? It sounds as though you were together long enough after the miscarriage. And from what I saw with your nephews, you like children."

He smiled wistfully. "I love kids. I always have. But—" he found a small pebble on the step beside him and tossed it into the yard "—things weren't right between us and I knew it."

"You'll have other opportunities," Madison said.

He turned to look at her. His eyes lingered on her face, then lowered to her breasts, and Madison felt her nipples tighten and tingle as though he'd touched her. "I hope so."

She cleared her throat. "How many children do you want?"

Lightly rubbing the side of her face with his thumb, he continued to gaze down at her. "Three. Maybe four. Unless my wife wants a dozen or so. That would be okay, too."

She laughed. "A *dozen?*"

"Think of all the Little League games," he said.

"I am! And the homework and dentist appointments and science projects and weddings—"

He waved airily. "Piece of cake."

She rolled her eyes. "You just complained about having to baby-sit your two nephews."

"You're not buying it, huh?"

"No, I'm not."

"Okay, I'd have to draw the line at six. What about you?"

"I'm happy with Brianna," she said. "I think I'm done."

His grin was slightly crooked, and the look in his eyes mocked her. "Liar. You want at least one or two more."

She shouldn't have continued smiling, because he'd caught her. But she couldn't help it. She smiled a lot when she was with Caleb. Most of the time he didn't even have to say anything funny. He just had to look at her. But he was right. She did want more babies. She wanted them with a man she loved and respected, a man who loved and respected her. She didn't want to risk another divorce, more heartache, a difficult childhood for those children.

She pursed her lips, bent on a little teasing of her own. "Okay, let me see. If I remember correctly, I've got a baby slotted for five years from now. But that's only if I happen to meet someone in three, as you mentioned earlier."

"I'm going to have to burn that damn day planner of yours," he said, getting up.

"Don't you do anything according to a schedule?" she asked.

Mac came hurrying out of the house, still on the phone. Caleb stepped aside to let him pass, but his gaze followed his brother-in-law across the lawn, and his expression wasn't a happy one. "And wind up like that?" he said, jerking his head toward Mac's retreating back. "Not if I can help it."

"CALEB, WHAT ARE YOU thinking?" Justine asked, her voice a harsh whisper as she trailed him into the kitchen.

He glanced longingly toward the door that led to the living room, where his sister, nephews, father and Madison were waiting so they could finish the game of dominoes they'd been playing together. "That I shouldn't have snuck in here for a second piece of cake and let you corner me," he grumbled.

She stood in front of the exit and folded her arms. "Don't try to be funny. I'm your mother, remember? I'm impervious to your charm."

"Oh, come on," he said with a grin.

"Obviously, you didn't learn anything from having lived in my house for eighteen years of your life," she said without so much as a responding smile. "Can't you see what's happening here?"

"Nothing's happening." He'd been having such a great time, he refused to think seriously about anything else right now. "We're playing bones. That's it. And I'm about to win."

"That's not it, Caleb. You can't look anywhere in the room except at Madison."

"So I like looking at her. She's an attractive woman."

"It's more than that," she argued. "Not only do you watch every move she makes, you touch her at every opportunity. And—"

"Mom, I don't want to talk about this," he said, and immediately started to walk around her.

She caught his arm. "I'm trying to tell you that you're falling in love with the very woman you set out to deceive, Caleb, and I can't imagine that it'll end well. What's Madison going to say when she finds out who you are? When she learns what your real motives have been?"

"Quit worrying, Mom. I don't plan to finish my book on her father, so there's no conflict of interest anymore. And this copycat we've been chasing isn't as close to Madison as we first thought. The way things are now, there's no reason not to tell her the truth."

"Then by all means get to it."

"I will."

"When?"

Soon. When it was safe. When he was sure it wouldn't turn her against him. "I'll know when the time is right."

Justine let him go, but sighed and shook her head. "Just tell me you haven't slept with her."

"Okay, I haven't slept with her," he said.

His mother dropped her head in one hand and began to rub her temples. "I don't deserve this."

"You're quiet," Caleb said on the drive home. "You sleepy?"

Madison roused herself enough to smile, even though the steady *warp, warp, warp* of the tires was sending her into a contented trance. *Contented...* It had been a long time since she'd thought of herself that way. "I was just thinking," she said.

Lights from oncoming traffic illuminated Caleb's chiseled face, and she admired the hollow of his cheeks, the strong jaw.

"About what?"

"Everything. Your sister and her husband. Your parents. Your nephews."

He passed a slower moving car ahead of them while there was a break in the traffic. "What about them?"

"I like them. They're good people."

"Sorry about all that stuff with my sister," he said. "I had no idea Mac had become so neglectful of her and the kids."

"I was a little disappointed in him that he didn't come back and play dominoes with us," she said. "I know Tamara was hoping he would."

"Wasn't beating the rest of us enough?" he teased.

She proudly lifted her chin. "I told you I was good at dominoes."

"And you certainly proved it. I thought I had you right up until the last."

She adjusted her seat belt so she could lean against the door and watch him. "Do you think Tamara and Mac will work things out?"

"With time."

"Do you like Mac?"

"He's never been one of my favorites. But then I don't like Tamara, either, remember?"

Catching a flash of white teeth as he smiled, Madison laughed. "Which is why you rushed to her rescue when she was upset during dinner."

"I didn't rush to her rescue." He sounded offended at being so easily found out.

Maybe he didn't want to admit it, but he'd done exactly that. Perhaps he hadn't said *a lot* to Mac—he probably didn't feel it was his place to go too far—but he'd definitely taken steps to alleviate his sister's suffering.

"I think it's big of you to baby-sit the boys this next

weekend,'' she added, infusing her voice with a little arrogance.

''And I think it's big of you to help me,'' he retorted. ''Because if I get stranded at my sister's house for the weekend, that's exactly where you'll be.''

''Sorry, I'll have Brianna,'' she said breezily.

''I'm afraid that's not good enough. We can baby-sit together.''

She considered him for several seconds, going through her options, then gave in. She didn't mind. As a matter of fact, she was looking forward to it. ''Fine. Brianna will probably be so smitten with those boys she'll follow them around like a puppy.''

''Her company will be good for them. The way they talk, you'd think girls were an alien species.''

''You probably weren't like that,'' she joked.

''Maybe just a little,'' he admitted, but then his eyes took on a devilish light. ''I don't think girls have cooties anymore, though.''

Madison felt the heightened awareness that seemed to wash over at Caleb's slightest provocation. She wished he'd hold her hand. She was dying to touch him—anywhere. But he didn't, and it took her a full five minutes to gather enough nerve to make the first move. Clearing her throat to distract him, she slid closer and rested her hand on his thigh.

She was hoping he'd let her actions go unremarked, or simply respond by taking her hand. But she should have known he wasn't going to make anything easy on her. Arching a brow, he gazed down at his thigh, and her hand suddenly felt like a foreign object. ''What's this?'' he said.

''What's what?'' she replied, groaning inside and feeling her face grow warm.

"Tell me what's going on."

She pulled her hand away. "Nothing's going on." Except an absolute fascination with him.

He chuckled softly. "You're not very good at hiding your emotions, you know that?"

"*You're* pretty good at it," she complained. "I think it must be a guy thing."

"Wait a second," he countered. "I'm not trying to hide anything." He made a point of reaching for her hand and tightly entwining their fingers, which satisfied her enough to make her feel significantly better. "I've made it perfectly clear what I want."

She batted her eyelashes at him. "A dozen babies? If that isn't enough to scare a woman, I don't know what is."

"How would you feel about one or two babies?" he asked.

"One or two doesn't scare me," she admitted. The prospect of having *his* baby excited her. Which was absolutely crazy. She'd known him only a few weeks, and already she was tempted to forget life's harder lessons.

"So what about it?" he asked, kissing her hand.

"What about what?" she responded, stalling, absolutely riveted to the sensation of his lips brushing across her knuckles.

"Will you come home with me tonight?"

No! Yes! Should she go with what she'd learned...or what she wanted?

"Well?"

The moment of truth. As she met his gaze, her entire body began to yearn. "Okay."

MADISON'S ANSWER STOLE Caleb's breath. He'd been half teasing, still expecting her to dodge him. But if he could trust the commitment in her eyes, she was serious.

Evidently he was getting a little ahead of himself. Rubbing the back of her hand against his cheek, he wondered how and when he was going to break the news of who he really was. Considering how quickly things were progressing, he needed to do it soon.

Just tell me you haven't slept with her.

Madison settled closer to him, despite the bucket seats, and laid her head on his shoulder. She was so near, so pliable and willing... And he wanted her.

If he didn't tell her, it might make everything worse later on.

If he did tell her, she might never speak to him again.

He drove for nearly twenty minutes, wrestling with himself. "Madison?" he finally said when they were nearly home.

"Hmm?"

She was half asleep, smelling like heaven and feeling like a dream come true. "Have you ever heard of Thomas L. Wagner?"

With a yawn, she sat up straight and combed her fingers through her hair. "That's the name of that crime-writer guy, isn't it?"

"He's written a few books. The one about Dahmer was probably his best." Caleb glanced at her to ascertain her reaction, and found her frowning.

"I've heard of him," she said, her voice completely flat.

"Have you ever read one of his books?"

"No, but I'll never forget him. He's slime."

Slime? "He's not that bad, is he?"

"Are you kidding? He's like a vulture, swooping in

after a catastrophe to pick the bones of any survivors. He gets rich off other people's pain."

He could see he'd definitely made a positive impression. "He just writes true-crime books. Some people like them. It gets the truth out in the open and sheds some light on the criminal mind."

"I guess," she said in a way that indicated she didn't agree but was playing neutral. "What about him?"

Caleb wasn't sure where to go next. *I'm that vulture?* "I heard he was doing a book about your father."

She shook her head. "He tried, but when the police were never able to solve the case, I think he dropped it. Thank goodness."

"Would a book about your father be so bad? Even if Wagner doesn't write one, someone else might someday."

"Maybe—or maybe not," she said. "In any case, I can wait. Fortunately, Wagner stopped contacting me. I think he moved out of the area."

"How do you know?"

"I happened to be standing in line at a little bookstore downtown when the guy in front of me was buying one of his books. I heard the cashier say Wagner is no longer local. He was lamenting the fact, of course. But I say good riddance."

"Right." Caleb cracked open his window because it was suddenly getting a little stuffy. Good riddance was the *last* thing he wanted her to say. Especially tonight. Which was why he decided that the truth could wait until morning.

"SOMETHING'S WRONG." Madison leaned forward as Caleb pulled into the drive. She was trying to figure out what it was about her house that seemed so…out of place. But a thick fog had descended just after they crossed Deception Pass, and it was so heavy she could barely make out the shape of the house, let alone any details.

"What do you mean?" Caleb asked.

"I didn't leave a light on, for one. I thought about it, but it was still daytime when we left, and I knew I wouldn't be coming home alone."

"Maybe it was already on and you just didn't realize it."

"Maybe," she said, but she didn't think so. Especially since there seemed to be several lights on, and… "Oh, my gosh. Is that my…is my window broken?"

"Where?"

She pointed to the kitchen window, the one that faced the cottage instead of the front lawn, and Caleb shifted to get a better look. "You're right," he said, and jammed the gearshift into park. The car lurched because he hadn't yet come to a complete stop, but that didn't keep him from jumping out and jogging over.

"Looks like someone tried to break in," he said as she hurried after him.

"*Tried* to break in or *did* break in?"

"I'm not sure. Give me your keys." He held out his hand, and she immediately relinquished her house key. "Get in the car and lock the doors," he said. "My cell phone's in there. Call the police if I don't come out in a minute or two."

"Maybe we should stay out here and call the police together," she said, thinking it might be smarter to play it safe. "I don't want you going in there if—"

"Whoever was here is probably long gone. Even if he was still inside when we arrived, I'm sure he heard the car and took off,'' Caleb said as he walked cautiously around to the front.

Madison didn't do as he told her. She ran to grab Caleb's cell and followed him, afraid to discover what might have been damaged or stolen. She hadn't been able to turn the real estate brokerage around as quickly as she'd expected when she bought it, and she wasn't sure she could withstand the financial setback of having to replace a lot of her belongings.

But everything looked as it always did—until Johnny came down the hall to confront them.

"Have a nice time?" he asked.

In what was obviously a knee-jerk reaction, Caleb nearly leveled him, but Madison managed to catch his arm before he let his fist fly. "It's okay. It's only my brother."

"What the *hell* is he doing breaking into your house?" Caleb demanded.

"Somebody cleaned up the garage," Johnny said. "I figured your mother was onto me, so I had a friend drop me off here."

"The same guy who brought you last time?"

"No, he got picked up for grand theft auto." He indicated Caleb with a nod of his head. "Who's this, anyway?"

Madison put a hand to her chest, trying to even out her pulse. "It's Caleb Trovato, my tenant."

"Caleb who?"

"Trovato."

"Like hell it is," Johnny said. "I've met this guy before."

"Johnny, you couldn't possibly know Caleb. He—"

"I'm telling you I know him. He came to the prison once, to interview me. But his name wasn't Caleb... whatever you said."

"What?" Madison thought she must have heard wrong. How could Johnny have met Caleb while he was in prison? "You must be confusing him with someone else. Caleb's from San Francisco."

"That's bullshit," Johnny muttered. "He's from right here in Seattle. He's—" he snapped his fingers impatiently "—I can't remember the name. But he's that big crime writer who made a mint off Dahmer's story. He was hoping to do the same with Dad, remember?"

"Thomas L. Wagner," Madison whispered, feeling numb. Sucker-punched. After her conversation with Caleb in the car, her words sounded like an echo and, when she turned to Caleb, she didn't have to ask if it was true. She knew from the look on his face.

"You lied to me," she said, and suddenly understood why a man like Caleb, who seemed to have it all, would be so interested in a struggling single mother who just happened to be the daughter of an accused murderer.

And she'd slept with him…. God, she was a fool, a dreamer, despite all previous reality checks!

"Madison, listen to me," Caleb said. "Give me a chance to explain."

"A chance to explain what?" she replied. "You knew who I was when you moved in, didn't you?"

"Of course. But then—"

"And you thought it was the perfect opportunity to find out everything you ever wanted to know about my father. You thought you'd slip in, see what you could learn while paying for a few weeks' rent, and the joke would be on me. Well, aren't you clever."

"It was never a joke," he said. "Sure, I thought it would be one way around your refusal to help me. I believed the people who've been hurt by the Sandpoint Strangler deserved some answers. I still believe that."

He reached out to grab her arm, but she knocked his hand away.

"What about *me?*" she asked. "Don't I deserve anything, Caleb? Not even the truth?"

"Because of you, I'm not going to write the book, Madison. I decided that almost the day I met you."

She closed her eyes, determined to fight the tears that seemed to be her heart's only recourse. "You offered to be my friend," she said hoarsely. "I trusted you."

"I *am* your friend."

She shook her head, scarcely able to swallow for the lump in her throat. "You're no friend of mine, Caleb or Thomas or—or whoever you are." She motioned toward the door. "Get your things from the cottage and get out of my life."

CHAPTER NINETEEN

CALEB HAD BEEN STANDING at his window, watching Madison's house ever since he'd left it. He'd seen her cover the broken window with plastic, but he hadn't seen Johnny come out yet. Madison was probably letting her brother stay the night. Caleb hated the thought of that. He didn't believe Johnny presented any real danger to her, but he knew Madison was already struggling to keep her business afloat and, with recent events, she didn't need anything else to worry about.

Who would've guessed Johnny still had enough brain cells to recognize him?

Damn. Caleb should have told her who he really was on the way home. But he'd mistakenly thought he'd have all night—and he'd let his libido get in the way. Now he wasn't sure she'd ever give him a chance to explain. He wasn't even sure explaining would do any good. He'd done exactly what she'd accused him of doing.

Only he'd come to care about her in the process. Didn't that count for something?

Turning to the television, which was on very low so he could hear anything that might happen outside, he stretched his neck. The stark expression in Madison's eyes when she'd heard his pseudonym and understood the truth still haunted him. He wanted to talk to her, didn't feel he could go to bed until he did. But he knew she was much less likely to listen to him while Johnny was there.

LONG AFTER JOHNNY went to sleep in Brianna's room, Madison sat in front of the television. But it wasn't on. Nothing was on except a lamp by the window. She knew she should've sent Johnny on his way. On one level, she was as frightened of him now as she'd been when she was just a kid and he and Tye were smoking pot out behind the garage and coaxing her to join them.

But how could she send her own brother away when he was broke and needed a place to spend the night? Besides, if she made Johnny leave or took him somewhere else, she'd be alone. And she didn't want to be alone right now. Her frustration and discomfort with Johnny seemed pretty minor in light of what she'd just learned about Caleb.

Drawing her knees up to her chest, she shivered against the cold. A ship's horn sounded outside, far off in the distance, and the dampness from the fog drifting in off the bay seemed to filter through the plastic covering the broken window and through every crevice in the house. But she didn't have the energy to get up and turn on the heat or even fetch herself a blanket. She was too busy replaying bits and pieces of conversation in her head, and remembering other things that should've given her some indication that Caleb wasn't what he'd said he was. His probing questions. His unusual work hours. The time he'd kissed her and said, "I never dreamed you, of all people, could do this to me."

Of all people… Damn him! He'd known who she was and what he wanted from her. And if he could get a little sex on the side, that made the joke even better, right?

She stiffened, feeling a renewed sense of betrayal when she thought of him borrowing her father's truck. He no doubt had ulterior motives for that, too. He'd probably gone through it with tweezers and a magnifying glass, looking for evidence. Exactly what her father had once feared might happen...

How could he?

Picking up the phone, she dialed his number.

He answered on the second ring.

"Caleb?"

"Madison! God, I'm glad it's you. Listen, I'm coming over there—"

"Just tell me something," she interrupted, keeping her voice as cold as her fingers and toes.

He hesitated, obviously leery. "What?"

"Did you really help a friend move when you borrowed my father's truck? Or did you make me walk into that garage—" her voice wobbled, so she paused until she could control it again "—and get that truck so you could search it?"

He didn't answer, but that was answer enough. Closing her eyes, she rubbed her forehead. "That's what I thought," she said and hung up.

The phone rang, but she just stared at it dully, as though the sound came from far away. She'd braved the place where her father had shot himself. She'd risked her mother's fragile peace of mind. All because she'd stupidly believed that Caleb was her friend. No, more than her friend...

The phone kept ringing. Madison refused to pick it up. She thought maybe the noise would wake Johnny, but she shouldn't have worried. As far as she could tell, he didn't stir.

Finally, silence fell. She thought Caleb had given up,

but the quiet didn't last long. A few minutes later, he knocked at the door.

"Madison, come on. I want to talk to you."

Madison felt wounded, exposed. She'd trusted Caleb. Yet their relationship had meant nothing to him. He'd merely been using her.

Bang, bang, bang. "I'm not going away, Madison. You might as well answer."

"Leave me alone," she called.

"Open up."

"Hey, I'm trying to sleep here," Johnny cried. "Who's making so much damn noise?"

"No one you need to worry about," Madison told him. Then, because she was tired of always being polite, she added, "So just stay out of it!"

To her surprise, he didn't respond.

"Madison?" Caleb hollered.

"Go away!"

"Not until you talk to me."

She could hear the determination in his voice, so she marched down the hall and threw open the door. "What do you want from me?"

He shoved a hand through his hair, which was sticking up as though he'd ruffled it a few times already. "I want you to calm down for a minute so we can work this out."

"There's nothing to work out, Caleb. I told you in the beginning that I wasn't ready for a relationship. I don't know how I let you change my mind. I guess it was too easy to have someone here who seemed to offer me some support. And then we were going out and dancing and…and I was meeting your mother…and—" closing her eyes, she shook her head "—I liked her. I liked your whole family."

"What went on between us wasn't something either

one of us decided to make happen, Madison." He tried to take her chin so she'd have to look at him, but as much as she craved physical contact, she jerked away.

"If you'll just think for a minute, you'll know what I'm saying is true," he said. "I didn't set out to seduce you."

"But you were certainly willing to take advantage of the unexpected windfall!"

His eyebrows drew together. "Last night was...it just got away from me."

"And tonight?"

"I would've made love to you tonight, too. I won't deny that. But I was planning on telling you the truth—soon. I tried to tell you in the car, remember? Only the minute I mentioned my pseudonym you reacted so negatively...." He sighed and dropped his hands. "It was stupid of me. I see that now. But I decided to wait for a better time."

"A better time would've been the day we met," she said.

"And you would have turned me away in a heartbeat."

"Exactly! I should have had that chance!"

He shifted on the balls of his feet, as though he was too edgy to stand still. "Madison, I know how you must feel, but the woman who went missing, the one who was just found dead, used to be my sister-in-law."

His what? Before Madison could respond, a car pulled into the drive. Caleb fell silent as he turned toward it, and Madison blinked against the sudden glare of headlights. When the engine died and the lights snapped off, she could make out a late-model Honda. The same tall blond woman who'd visited Caleb before was getting out of it.

"Shit," Caleb muttered.

The sick feeling in Madison's stomach intensified. "Don't tell me—it's your wife or girlfriend."

He gave her a look that said he wasn't *that* low. "I haven't been cheating on anyone. It's Holly, my *ex*-wife. Her sister's the woman who was just murdered."

That Caleb had personally known one of the victims somehow changed things, but Madison was still too upset to sort out why.

"Caleb, where have you been?" his ex-wife demanded, striding confidently up the drive in a black leather jacket and jeans. "I've been calling and calling you."

Caleb glanced at Madison, obviously eager to finish their conversation. But Holly demanded his attention. "Caleb?"

His eyebrows lowered into a dark line as she drew closer, but he turned to Madison. "Let me take care of whatever she wants, then I'll come over later and we'll talk some more, okay?"

Madison held up her hand, palm out. Some of her anger had dissipated. But something else was quickly replacing it—a sort of dull acceptance, a sense of inevitability. Had she really thought she'd found her prince at last? That she'd do any better the second time around? "Caleb, maybe—in your mind—you had good reason for using me," she said. "I think I can even understand it. But I just want to be left alone, okay?"

"Madison—"

"Good night," she said softly, and closed the door. Then she sagged against the wall and slid all the way to the floor. She had to take a hard line with Caleb. Softening would only get her hurt—again.

"WHAT WERE YOU DOING talking to Purcell's daughter this time of night?" Holly asked, scowling at Madison's closed door.

Caleb zipped up his windbreaker, wondering whether to knock again or give Madison time to cool off.

"Caleb?"

His muscles felt so taut he could barely move. "We had some business to take care of," he said.

"What kind of business? What was that about you using her?"

He didn't answer. Because of Holly's presence, he decided to give Madison the night to herself, and stepped off the porch. Maybe after she'd had a chance to rest and—

"It's nearly eleven." Holly's voice broke into his thoughts again. "What were you doing at her house at this time of night? Don't tell me you needed her to come over and fix a leaky faucet."

The bigger question, to Caleb, was what Holly thought *she* was doing appearing at his house so late. "I can handle my own leaky faucets," he grumbled. But he wasn't sure he could handle Madison cutting him out of her life.

He cast Holly a quick glance. "What do you want?"

She stiffened, obviously offended by his curt tone. "Is that any way to greet me?"

Caleb felt his jaw tighten and reminded himself that Holly's sister had just been murdered. He wanted to be sensitive to her loss. But she was using the investigation to call him day and night, usually for no good reason. *What are you doing? Where are you going? Can you stop by?* Surely there had to be someone else she could lean on. He was her *ex*-husband, for crying out loud. What about her parents? Her friends?

"It's the middle of the night, Holly," he said. "I wasn't expecting you." *And you interrupted at a really bad time.*

"But I've been trying and trying to reach you."

He'd turned off his cell phone because he hadn't wanted to hear from her.

She had to hurry to keep up with him as he trudged over to the cottage. "Are you going to tell me what you need?" he asked, and he'd insist on a good answer this time. He'd had it with, "I couldn't sleep," and "I miss you." He'd made it perfectly clear that their relationship was over.

She didn't answer right away, so he arched a brow to let her know he was waiting. "You're acting like you don't want me here," she said, pouting.

Her tone was accusatory enough to make him believe she was about to start an argument, and Caleb felt his control slipping. "Holly, I'm not capable of walking on eggshells tonight. If you have something to say, say it. But it had better be good. I'm not in the mood to—" he was about to say, "put up with you," but in deference to what had happened to Susan, he caught himself "—pry it out of you."

"What's bothering *you?*" She grabbed his arm and pulled him to a stop only a few steps from his front door.

He couldn't help looking back at Madison's house, to see that the shutters were tightly closed. Holly wanted to know what was bothering him? Losing Madison bothered him, even more than he'd thought it would.

Holly followed his gaze. "Wait a minute. Don't tell me there's something going on between you and…and Purcell's daughter. Are you sleeping with her?"

Caleb tensed at Holly's proprietary tone. "You act as though you have a right to ask me that, Hol."

"I do! You came here to help *me*. You're supposed to be searching for Susan's killer, not…not climbing into bed with Ellis Purcell's daughter!"

A muscle began to tick in Caleb's cheek. "Holly, don't push me, okay?" He jerked out of her grasp. "Now, I'm really tired. If you don't mind, I'm going inside to get some sleep. I'll call you tomorrow."

He started to move beyond her, but she reached for his jacket. "Wait…Caleb, don't be angry. I only came here tonight because Detective Gibbons called my place, looking for you."

He'd opened his door, but this succeeded in gaining his attention. "Why?" he asked, rounding on her.

"They've found Susan's car."

Caleb's jaw dropped. *"Where?"*

"Parked only a few blocks from Lance's place. Can you believe it? I think Lance has been lying the whole time. I think he killed Susan because she found out about his fiancée and threatened to tell her about their affair."

"Holly, Lance isn't even a plausible suspect. Our killer knows too much, which means he has to be someone closer to the case. Remember the Ford truck outside the pizzeria?"

"That could've been a coincidence."

"The way Susan's body was positioned was no coincidence. And if Lance did kill her, he'd have to be an idiot to park Susan's car so close to his house. But come in," he said, holding the door. "I'll give Gibbons a call. I want to see that car."

She didn't move right away. "You've changed, you know that?"

"Are you coming in?" he asked, refusing to spar with her.

Grudgingly, she stepped past him. "I think I was wrong about you. I don't think you're going to find this killer. He's much too smart."

MADISON COULDN'T SLEEP. She stared at the ceiling, tossed and turned, took a hot bath and went back to bed. But Caleb's face still lingered in her mind, and her heart threatened to break. They hadn't known each other long, but when they'd made love she'd felt like she was part of him. And tonight, when she'd met his family, it had seemed as though she belonged....

How could she have been so wrong?

Eventually, she gave up trying to drift off on her own and took two sleeping pills. She didn't have Brianna to worry about tonight. And, judging by the snoring in the next room, Johnny was so deeply asleep she doubted he'd wake before noon.

The medication was just starting to take effect when the doorbell rang. She heard it as a faint echo in the distance and eyed the digital clock near her bed. Two o'clock.

Caleb again, no doubt. With Johnny already here, it was too late to be anyone else. Except maybe Tye...

Madison wanted whoever it was to go away so she could sink into the oblivion that finally hovered so close. She needed to sleep, forget and wake with renewed perspective and resolve. But the bell rang again, accompanied by a loud knock, and she began to wonder if, by some chance, Danny had decided to bring Brianna home early.

"Johnny? Can you answer the door?" she called.

No reply. Just more snoring.

"Johnny?" Madison feared she was slurring her words. It required real effort to lift her eyelids, but picturing Brianna out in the cold got her up and moving.

She managed to find her robe. She had trouble shoving her arms into the sleeves and couldn't tie the belt, but she didn't care.

Another knock. Only now did Madison realize that

whoever stood at her door was actually giving it more of a light rap than a pounding. If not for being a mother, she probably wouldn't have heard it at all.

"Just a minute!" she called, and stumbled down the hall.

"Madison? It's me." It was a female voice, a voice Madison recognized.

Sharon? Quickly unfastening the latch, Madison opened the door and drew her sister-in-law inside. Then she poked her head out to see if Tye's wife was alone or if she'd brought the kids.

Madison couldn't see so much as a car in the drive—and she was fairly certain the sleeping pills had nothing to do with that.

"Are you okay?" she asked.

"I'm fine," Sharon replied, but it was misty and cold, and she wasn't wearing a coat. She hugged herself, rubbing her arms, as she trailed Madison into the kitchen.

Madison gave her a curious glance. "How did you get here?"

"I drove. My car's parked around the corner."

"Why'd you park it there?"

Sharon didn't answer, but the adrenaline boost of finding Tye's wife at the door helped counteract the sleeping pills. Madison smoothed down her hair, righted her robe and offered to make some tea.

Sharon accepted with a nod, and Madison put on the water.

"You're probably wondering what I'm doing here," she said when Madison didn't speak right away.

"I'm guessing you want to talk about Tye, but let's get you warm before we do that—or anything else." She went to the living room to retrieve the lap blanket, which she brought to the kitchen and draped over Sharon's shoulders. "Can I make you something to eat?"

Sharon gazed longingly at the refrigerator. "No, I'm not staying more than—"

"It'll only take a second."

"Okay," she said, and pulled the blanket more tightly around her. "I'd like that."

Madison collected the mayonnaise, mustard, lettuce, tomato, sliced meat and Swiss cheese from the refrigerator and set about making a sandwich. "What happened?" Sharon asked, eyeing the black plastic covering the window.

Madison followed her gaze. "Oh, that. We…had a little accident earlier." She turned her attention back to what she was doing. "Where are the kids?"

"They're—" Sharon dug at her cuticles, her expression furtive "—somewhere safe."

"*Safe?*" Madison glanced over her shoulder. "Why wouldn't they be safe here?"

Sharon's eyes met hers, but they looked haunted, worried. "I…I overheard something, Madison. Something that has me really scared."

Madison's pulse kicked up a notch. "Of what?" She finished making the sandwich, set it on a plate and put tea bags in two mugs of hot water. After carrying it all to the table, she pulled her chair close.

"Of Tye. And Johnny."

Madison peered down the hall to make sure it was empty. "Why?"

Sharon stared miserably at her food. "You know Tye's always had problems—a…a temper. When he gets angry, he sometimes says or does things he doesn't mean. It stems from what happened to him when he was a kid.

I've tried to be understanding about that. But last week, he…he just went too far.''

Madison wished she'd never taken those sleeping pills. She was feeling more alert than she had a few minutes earlier, but her senses still seemed slightly dull. ''In what way?''

Her sister-in-law took a bite of her sandwich. ''The police came by several days ago,'' she said when she'd swallowed. ''I heard them at the door, talking to Tye.''

''What did they want?''

''To know if he'd seen Johnny.''

Madison considered telling Sharon that Johnny was sleeping in Brianna's bedroom, but she was afraid the news might make her sister-in-law hurry away before she had a chance to say what she'd come to say. And Madison was hoping she'd be able to help her. This was the first time Tye's wife had ever reached out to her. ''What did he tell them?''

''That he hadn't.'' She put the sandwich down. ''But he *had,* Madison. Johnny came by the house several times. He even stopped in the day he got out of jail.''

Madison remembered her conversation with Tye that Saturday morning when she'd cooked for Caleb. *I can't believe Johnny's out. When did they release him?* He'd lied to her, too.

''Why would Tye feel he needs to lie about whether or not he's seen Johnny?'' she asked.

''I think it's because Johnny had something to do with that woman who was murdered. What else could it be?''

Madison twisted to glance down the hall again. ''Johnny wouldn't hurt anyone,'' she said, lowering her voice. But she was remembering another conversation in which she'd told Caleb her father wouldn't have killed himself unless he'd found that box and thought Tye had murdered those women. What if it had actually been Johnny?

"You don't understand," Sharon said. "I heard them talking, just a few days after Johnny got out of prison. Tye was saying, 'Why'd you do it, man? That's stupid.' And Johnny said that something inside him just snapped. When I came in the room, they exchanged a look and shut up, and later Tye wouldn't tell me what they'd been talking about." She twisted her long, sandy-colored hair into a knot and pulled it over one shoulder. "But I knew whatever they were talking about wasn't good. Tye gave Johnny a pile of cash, told him to buy a car and get out of town."

Madison felt a shiver go down her spine. Johnny had been desperate for a mere twenty bucks when he first came to her place, which meant the money Tye had given him had already gone up his nose. Drugs made a person do crazy things. Could Sharon's story be true? "Is that why you left Tye?" she asked.

"No." Sharon stared at her food. "After the police talked to Tye, they wanted to talk to *me*."

"What'd you tell them?"

Sharon pressed her palms over her eyes before looking at Madison again. "Tye warned me to say I hadn't seen Johnny, either. I told him I didn't want to lie, that we could get into trouble doing that. And he grabbed my arm so hard, I thought he might break it. I've never seen such a fierce look on his face." She started to cry. "I told him he was hurting me, and he said it was nothing to what he'd do if I didn't tell the police exactly what he told me to say."

"So Tye's covering for Johnny?" Madison said. Was that why he'd visited the crawl space of her mother's house?

"Of course," Sharon continued after a sniffle. "I told the police what he forced me to say, but I wasn't sticking around. Not if my husband was going to risk himself and our whole family to cover for a murderer. Tye wasn't acting like himself. He was tense, angry. I was afraid he might hurt me or one of the kids."

"So you took them and disappeared." Madison stood up to get some tissues. "What made you come here?"

Sharon accepted the tissues and dabbed at her eyes. "I keep hearing television reports about that woman who was killed, wondering if I'm endangering someone else's life by not coming forward with what I know." She dug at her cuticles some more, even though they were already red and sore. "I don't want to turn on Tye. But I don't want to be responsible for—" Her voice caught and broke, and she buried her face in her hands.

Madison tried to comfort her. But she couldn't seem to do anything more than awkwardly pat her shoulder. She felt numb. "We have to go to the police," she said, sick at the thought. Johnny had had such a bad childhood. And despite all her negative memories, she had a few good ones of him, too. When Perry Little across the street made fun of her because she wasn't as developed as the other girls, Johnny had given him a fat lip. She remembered feeling quite vindicated when the other kids started teasing Perry because he couldn't talk right. And there'd been that time when Tye was so angry with her for leaving the rabbit cage open, and Johnny had stepped in to defend her. Johnny rarely stood up to Tye. That day Tye had been so surprised he'd stared blankly at them both, then simply turned and left.

It had to be the drugs, Madison decided. She knew Johnny had problems, but she also knew he wasn't innately violent.

"I can't go to the police," Sharon said. "What if...what if Tye does something to the children? I have to let him see the kids eventually. I'm afraid he might try to get back at me through them."

"The police will protect them," Madison said, and hoped beyond hope that it was true.

"You didn't see the look on his face."

Madison wished she hadn't taken those sleeping pills. They were making everything fuzzy again. "Don't worry. I'll turn him in myself." She had to, before anyone else was hurt. "Just do me one favor." She checked the hall a third time. Empty. "Write down the address where you're staying and a number where I can get in touch with you if I need to."

Sharon hesitated, but in the end gave Madison the information.

Madison let her sister-in-law out, and watched her disappear into the darkness, toward a car that was apparently parked around the corner. Then she walked as quietly as possible down the hall toward her bedroom. She had to get dressed so she could go to the police. She dared not call, not from here. Not with Johnny in the house. She wanted to get away from him while he was still sleeping soundly....

Only she didn't think he was sleeping anymore. When she reached his door, it was open, and she could no longer hear him snoring.

CHAPTER TWENTY

CALEB STOOD with Holly and Gibbons at Lance's front door. After Susan's car had been towed away around midnight, Gibbons had tried to get him and Holly to go home. It was late, past two o'clock. They probably should've listened. After what had happened with Madison earlier, Caleb wasn't in the mood to be out. But Detective Thomas's wife had just had a baby, so Gibbons would've been alone if they hadn't stayed with him. And Susan's car had been found so close to Lance's house that Caleb was as eager to catch him off guard as Gibbons was. He was beginning to wonder if he'd overrated the guy's intelligence.

According to Gibbons, Lance now lived with a buddy from work. Caleb wasn't particularly impressed by their small Renton neighborhood, but it seemed quiet enough. He'd seen a thousand streets exactly like this one, filled with inexpensive tract homes that alternated between four basic models. Most of the residences on Riley Way were well-maintained. But Lance and his roommate obviously didn't possess the same domestic ambitions as their neighbors. The front window had been broken and was covered with tape and newspaper. The yard was overgrown. And what sounded like a very large dog jumped against a wobbly fence, barking wildly in the backyard.

Caleb glanced at Gibbons when they received no response to their knock and banged again.

When the door finally opened a crack, the wafflelike imprint on Lance's face suggested they'd succeeded in surprising him. And the way he groaned as soon as he saw Gibbons left them in no doubt that he wasn't happy about it. "Oh, man! Not you again. What are you doing here? I've already answered all your questions."

"We need to speak with you again, if you have a minute," Gibbons said politely.

"Now?" He squinted in the porch light, which he'd flipped on only moments before. His short dark hair was bleached at the ends and that, taken together with his fake tan and slouchy posture, made him look like a misplaced beach boy. He was young—maybe twenty-five. "You can't go around waking people up in the middle of the night, you know," he said, his voice petulant.

"Who is it?" called another male voice from somewhere in the house.

"Don't worry, Ross, it's for me." The night was cold and he was wearing only a pair of jeans, but he stepped outside and closed the door behind him. "You know, I really don't like how you guys keep poking around in my life. I haven't done anything. I already told you that."

"You don't call *using* my sister something?" Holly said, immediately going on the offensive. "You don't call *killing* her something?"

Gibbons held up one hand. "I'll take care of this—"

"Look, I had a fling, okay?" Lance interrupted, scowling at Holly. "Screwing around on the side might not be right, but it doesn't make me a murderer!"

"What's the matter?" Holly retorted, leaning closer. "Did Susan find out about your fiancée and threaten to tell her about the two of you?"

"Holly," Caleb snapped, moving between them, "maybe you should wait in the car."

Holly lifted her chin and glared at him.

"Not another word or that's exactly where you'll be," he told her, using the weight of his gaze to get her to back off.

After a moment, she clamped her mouth shut and folded her arms, but continued to glare at all of them.

"I'm miserable, okay?" Lance said, changing his focus to Caleb and Gibbons. "I can't eat. I have trouble sleeping. I miss my fiancée, and I hate the fact that Susan's dead. But I'm telling you again, I never hurt her."

"Susan's car was found only two streets from here, on Lassiter," Gibbons said. "Any idea how it got there?"

Lance seemed honestly surprised. "That's not possible."

"Why not?" Gibbons asked.

"I would've seen it. I drive down that street every day. Where'd it come from?"

"That's what we're trying to find out," Caleb said.

"I wish I could help you," Lance replied. "But I don't know anything about it. I only know I didn't murder anyone."

"Then you probably wouldn't mind providing us with a DNA sample," Gibbons said.

Lance looked a little fearful at that suggestion. "What does it involve?"

The detective handed him his business card. "It's not difficult and it only takes a minute. Call me in the morning. We'll talk about it then."

Goose bumps rose on Lance's arms as he stood in the chill wind, staring down at Gibbons's card. "This is insane," he said. "I liked Susan. I never would've hurt her."

"Like hell! If it wasn't for you, she'd still be here,"

Holly said, but Caleb dragged her away before Lance could respond.

"Calm down," he told her.

"I'm telling you he's the one," she said. "He killed her because he didn't want her to tell his fiancée."

"He has an alibi," Gibbons pointed out.

"His fiancée's mother could be lying," she retorted.

"It's not him," Caleb said. Whoever murdered Susan had copied the strangler *too* well. And twelve years ago, Lance would've been only about thirteen.

MADISON HOVERED in the hall, wondering what to do. She needed to get dressed. She knew she'd feel much more secure and mobile if she had clothes on. But she was afraid to go to her room. She didn't want to pass Johnny's door on the way, didn't want to put herself in a place where she couldn't easily get out of the house if he came after her.

Except he wouldn't come after her. Madison wasn't even convinced that Sharon was right. If he'd killed Caleb's sister-in-law, he'd probably killed all the other women, too. Only he couldn't have. Johnny had been in jail when some of those women died—hadn't he? Without double-checking, there was no way to know for sure. He'd always drifted in and out of her life, and she didn't always know where he was. But he'd never tried to hurt her before, would have no reason to hurt her now.

Unless he knew she was going to the police. But he couldn't have heard her say anything about that. He'd been clear down the hall. She'd checked several times.

The floor creaked as she inched closer.

"Madison?"

She froze, heart pounding so loudly she was afraid he could hear it. What now? Should she answer him?

She didn't want him to get up, so she said, "Yes?"

"Who was that?"

"A friend of mine," she said, and cursed the false note in her own voice.

There was a moment of silence. "What did she want?"

Madison's legs were feeling peculiar, weak. She clung to the door frame to keep from sinking to the ground. "Just to talk."

"This late?"

"She couldn't sleep."

Madison licked dry lips, preparing for a "why?" or "what friend?" But he didn't say anything else.

Gathering her nerve, she said, "Good night."

Again he didn't respond. But he seemed to be going back to sleep, so she forced her legs to carry her to the bedroom as though nothing had changed. She'd get dressed and wait for a while, *then* she'd leave.

Unfortunately, finding the right clothes and getting them on proved more of a challenge than she had anticipated. The adrenaline running through her body was making her hands shake, and the pills she'd taken were starting to compound the problem. "Come on, come on," she whispered to herself.

She managed to don a pair of jeans and a sweater. But only with great concentration did she tie her tennis shoes. When she was finally dressed, she sat on the floor, trying to calm down while watching her digital alarm clock flip from one glowing numeral to the next: 2:43...2:44... 2:45....

She made herself wait a full fifteen minutes. Then she shoved Sharon's number in her back pocket, grabbed a lightweight jacket and hurried into the hall—only to run full-tilt into Johnny.

MADISON TRIED TO DODGE Johnny and run. She couldn't see him in the pitch-black hallway, but she'd certainly felt their collision and could hear his ragged breathing. He was close. Probably too close. But if she could only get around him…

Bumping into the wall, she stumbled and nearly brushed past him. She had to get her keys, open the door, reach her car. But he clutched her by the shoulders before she could go anywhere, and yanked her back, surprising her with the strength of his grip.

"Johnny, let me go," she cried, twisting and pushing at him.

"I can't." His fingers curved painfully into her flesh. "Not until you tell me what Sharon wanted."

He knew. He'd known all along that it was Sharon. He'd been baiting her.

Madison tried not to panic. "Nothing. She didn't want anything except to…to talk about her problems with Tye." Again Madison attempted to wrench free, but the sleeping pills were making her light-headed. She felt dizzy, weak…terrified.

"You expect me to believe that's why you're creeping around?" His grip tightened. "Where are you going?"

"Nowhere. I—I couldn't sleep and—"

He gave her a little shake. "That's bullshit. What did Sharon say?"

"She's worried about you, Johnny."

"Don't lie to me! She's never liked me. Is she running to the police? Is that what's going on? Or is that what *you're* doing?"

"No, I—"

"Tye told me some detectives came around, asking questions about the night that woman was murdered. Now that Dad's gone, they're looking at me. Isn't that right? They think I had something to do with it.''

Madison's mind raced, searching for options. But she knew he'd never trust a denial. ''Sharon knows the truth, Johnny. It's over.''

He went deathly still. ''What truth? I didn't kill anyone. You have to believe me, Maddy.''

Tears stung Madison's eyes. She *wanted* to believe him, but mere wanting didn't count. ''All I know is that we have to make sure nobody else gets hurt. You…you need help.''

''But it wasn't me! I swear I didn't do it.'' His voice sounded gravelly, torn.

''Johnny—''

''Maddy, listen to me.''

She felt his grip weaken, knew she should take the opportunity to break away and dash for the door. But his denial and her memories of him from when she was a child were crowding close, confusing her.

Unless you want another fat lip, don't ever talk to my sister like that again….

Tye, she's just a kid. Leave her alone….

Haven't you ever seen a tadpole, Maddy? Want me to catch you one?

''Maddy?'' he said.

Madison squeezed her eyes shut. She couldn't let herself remember those things. Johnny was a killer, *the* killer. At least that was what Sharon thought. And in some ways it made sense. His childhood had warped him, scarred him, and somehow their father had realized the truth. That was why Ellis shot himself….

''Dad thought it was you, too, didn't he?'' she asked, making no effort to restrain her tears.

She felt his chest shudder against her and knew, despite the lack of light, that he was crying, too.

"He wouldn't believe me," he said. "I tried to tell him I'd never seen the stuff in that box, that I had nothing to do with it. But he…he just looked at me. And his face—" He shuddered again. "You have no idea what it was like seeing him that way. I'd always known he was disappointed in me, but right then I knew I was worse than dead to him."

Tears dripped off Madison's chin as she imagined the scene—the guilt her father must have experienced for not loving Johnny better. The pain Johnny must have known when confronted with their father's pure contempt.

"So you did what?" Madison could barely say the words for fear of Johnny's response because another, even more insidious thought had entered her mind. What if her father hadn't killed himself at all?

"I didn't do *anything*," Johnny insisted. "I told him he could go to hell if he didn't believe me, and I left."

"Then where did that box come from?"

"Dad said he found it buried in the woodpile. He figured I'd left it there, but I didn't. I wasn't lying—I'd never seen it before. Anyone could've hidden it there. Anyone!"

His grip was lax enough now that Madison could have gotten away. She knew that. But something made her hesitate. Maybe the sleeping pills were interfering with her thinking. Or maybe compassion wouldn't allow her to condemn her brother quite so soon. "Sharon overheard you and Tye—"

"I know, but we weren't talking about murder. We were talking about what I did the day I got out of prison. Tye was angry. He knew that since I'm on probation, they'd put me back in prison if anyone ever found out."

"Found out what?"

She couldn't see him, but she could imagine the tortured expression on his face. "That I...that I went to the cemetery."

His arms fell away from her, and he stepped back. But Madison didn't run. She didn't so much as flip on the light. Somehow she knew they both needed the darkness right now. "It was you who dug up Dad's coffin?" she said, her voice barely a whisper. "Why?"

"I was so angry, Madison. So...damn angry at him. Why wouldn't he believe me? I told him I didn't do it. For once, couldn't he have listened to me?"

She didn't answer. She couldn't speak, couldn't move. The passion in his voice was so real.

"I just wanted him to believe me," he said. "I *hate* going to sleep at night and seeing that...that damn look on his face." He drew a ragged breath that testified to the depth of his emotion. "I was high when I went to the cemetery. I wasn't thinking straight. Or I would've known it was far too late." His tone turned deadpan. "I couldn't convince him even when he was alive."

Poor Johnny. He lived with so many demons. Even now drugs stood between him and any kind of recovery. But he was no killer. He just didn't have it in him.

Putting her arms around him, Madison tried to draw him close, to offer him some of the support and comfort he'd never had.

At first he stiffened, tried to push her away. But then she said, "It's okay, Johnny. I believe you." And after a few moments, he was sobbing on her shoulder.

CALEB SAT AT HIS kitchen table with a cup of coffee and watched the sun rise. He'd arrived home nearly three hours ago, but he hadn't gone to bed. He had too much on his mind. Mostly Madison. And the investigation. Neither of which were going the way he'd hoped.

Did you really help a friend move when you borrowed my father's truck? Or did you make me walk into that garage and get that truck so you could search it?

He'd done worse than that. He'd made her walk into that garage so he could search Ellis's truck *and* have Gibbons check the tires. And it had all been for nothing.

With a yawn, he rubbed his tired eyes. After spending most of the night thinking about Madison, he'd finally decided that what had happened between them yesterday was probably for the best. Their relationship couldn't have gone anywhere. She wasn't emotionally available; she'd told him that several times. And he was going back to San Francisco. Better to get over his fascination with her now and focus on what he needed to do before he could return home.

Shoving his coffee away because the caffeine seemed to be making him sick, he called Gibbons.

"Shit, Trovato, don't you ever sleep?" Gibbons complained, picking up after the answering machine had come on.

Caleb felt a pang of guilt for waking him. Gibbons had already put in far more than his share of overtime. But Caleb was impatient. If he wasn't going to pursue a relationship with Madison, he wanted to get the hell out of Seattle. "I don't think—"

"Wait until the machine goes off."

They fell silent until Caleb heard a click, then it was Gibbons' turn to yawn, which he did loudly. "What is it?"

"I don't think we should waste any time with Lance Perkins."

Gibbons snorted. "Hell, I hope you didn't wake me up

just to tell me that. I know Lance isn't our man. He stood right in front of us, bare-chested. He didn't have a scratch on him. And I know Susan left marks.''

"So where do we go from here?" Caleb asked.

"We get some sleep and recoup when we can think straight.''

Caleb was too discouraged, too frustrated to sleep. But he didn't have any right to demand superhuman hours from Gibbons. This was just another case to him. There'd been plenty of such cases before, and there'd be plenty after.

"Call me when you get up," Caleb said, and disconnected. Then he slouched back in his chair, scowling at the gray clouds already scudding across the sky outside.

He'd wanted to search Madison's mother's house today, had hoped to find the contents of that box. He wasn't sure it would relate to Susan's disappearance in any way, but he knew it couldn't hurt to have a look. Maybe it would help the police finally solve the old case, finally prove Madison right—or wrong—about her father. But he'd lost her cooperation.

He'd lost a hell of a lot more than her cooperation....

The case. He needed to move on. What was he missing? What small detail had the killer left behind that would eventually be his undoing? Surely there had to be *something*.

According to the FBI profiler, the perpetrator was methodical, obsessive, manipulative. Like John Wayne Gacy, he probably managed to appear functional. Maybe he held a steady job, participated in community events. Which meant he could be one of a million different men living in Seattle.

Except this killer was probably impotent, judging by the way his victims had been sexually assaulted. And the profiler had given them one limiting physical factor—she'd said the killer wasn't very large. He was attacking small women to be sure he could physically overpower them, and he was using the date rape drug, Rohypnol, to improve his odds.

Caleb drummed his fingers on the table, asking himself the same questions he'd been asking all along. Who knew enough about the case to set up the crime scene? And who had the cunning, the complete self-absorption required to commit such crimes?

Johnny knew an awful lot about the case. He'd seen some of the crime-scene pictures. In an effort to get someone to talk, the police had shown the whole Purcell family those shocking photos. But Johnny's thinking was simply too disorganized. He lacked the control to get away with something like this.

Tye, on the other hand, appeared functional, even capable, and knew as much about the case as Johnny. But Caleb didn't believe he was their man, either. For one thing, he couldn't see Tye limiting his attacks to small women. Tye wasn't particularly tall, but he was muscular. And from what Gibbons had said, Madison's oldest brother had an explosive temper. An explosive temper would too easily tempt him beyond the veil of secrecy and premeditation required to commit the kind of murders they were dealing with.

Caleb took the picture of Susan standing outside the pizza place out of his wallet and stared down at her blurry profile. He knew Gibbons would be contacting Tye Purcell to ask him about the contents of the box missing from under the house. But Caleb didn't want to wait. Now that Madison knew who he really was, maybe the time had come to confront her brother face-to-face.

TYE LIVED IN AN OLDER, rather depressed neighborhood of small, cookie-cutter houses, very few of which had a garage. Here and there, a carport had been finished off by homeowners seeking more living space. Tye's carport was still open, however, and housed a weight bench, which he happened to be using when Caleb arrived.

Pausing when he heard the car, Tye rested the barbells in the stand over his head and sat up, letting his hands dangle between his legs. "What are you doing here?" he asked as he watched Caleb approach.

It was nearly eight o'clock, which wasn't too early for a workday. But this was Sunday. Caleb had expected to find Tye in bed, but had wanted to catch him before he went out. "I have a few questions for you," he said.

"What kind of questions?" Suddenly indifferent, Tye started bench-pressing another set. It was chilly out, gray, overcast and a little windy, but Tye wore only a pair of karate pants and a T-shirt with the sleeves cut out. He had a Chinese dragon tattooed on his right biceps, very similar to the one embroidered on the jacket in his father's Ford, making Caleb wonder if he'd been wrong about the owner of that jacket. In any case, judging by the tattoo and the pants, Caleb guessed Tye was either taking or teaching karate. Which supported his gut feeling that if Tye wanted to hurt a woman, he wouldn't feel the need to use drugs....

Folding his arms, Caleb leaned against the corner of the house. He'd expected to see some sign of Tye's wife and kids. His wife had provided his alibi, after all. But except for Tye, the place seemed deserted. The only vehicle was Tye's Explorer parked out at the curb.

"Where's the wife and kids?" Caleb asked, noting the bikes, scooters and baseball gloves tossed against the shed that comprised the back wall of Tye's carport.

Tye paused with the barbell straight over his head. "Is

that one of your questions?'' he asked, his muscles straining. ''Because it's none of your damn business.'' The barbell clanged as he shoved it roughly into the stand and sat up, his eyes narrower than before. ''Why don't you just tell me what the hell you're doing out here?''

''I know about the box of women's underwear and trinkets under the house,'' Caleb said.

Tye's eyebrows raised a notch. ''So? What does that box mean to you?''

''My sister-in-law was just murdered, strangled like the women your father was accused of killing. I think there might be some connection.''

Tye's face was devoid of emotion. ''Was she killed before or after you moved in with Madison?''

''Before.''

Tye swore softly under his breath. ''Did Madison know that when she let you move in?''

''She knows it now.''

''I hope she kicked your ass out,'' Tye said.

''Once I get the answers I need, I'm leaving anyway.''

Tye stared at him for a moment. ''Well, much as I'd like to help, that stuff belonged to my father. And if you know anything about the case, which I'm guessing you do, you know he's dead. You're wasting your time here.''

''Humor me,'' Caleb said.

''How?''

''Where's the stuff in that box?''

Tye scowled darkly. ''You said yourself that it was under the house.''

''Until a couple weeks ago. Now it's gone.'' Caleb couldn't tell if Tye was surprised or not. He just kept stroking his goatee with his thumb and index finger.

''Well, I don't give a shit,'' he said at last. ''That box has nothing to do with me.''

"Then why didn't you take it to police?"

"Kiss my ass." Rolling back, he started yet another set, but Caleb didn't leave as he was obviously expected to. He dug into his pocket and retrieved the picture of Susan outside the pizzeria.

"Do you know this woman?" he asked, shoving the picture in front of Tye's face.

Tye grunted as he lifted the barbell for the twelfth time, arms shaking. When he put the weights away, he grabbed the photograph but only glanced at it briefly before handing it back. "What are you, a cop?"

"I used to be."

"Then you're a civilian just like me, which means you're trespassing and you've got no right to be here." Caleb didn't respond because it was true.

"I'll tell you what I told the detectives who already came by," Tye said in a disgruntled voice. "I've never seen her before."

"Is that the truth?"

"What do you think?"

Caleb thought he was lying. He'd never considered Tye a real suspect in the killings, but there was something suspicious about his belligerent attitude and his reluctance to really look at Caleb.

"I have a woman who says she saw you there," Caleb said, folding the picture neatly. He meant Jennifer, but he was bluffing. When Caleb had met with Jennifer, he'd shown her a picture of Tye and been told she'd never seen him before. But that didn't prove Tye wasn't at the pizza place. She'd admitted she hadn't been able to tell *who* Susan was arguing with.

A muscle jumped in Tye's cheek. "What woman?"

"Someone who was there that night, too."

A door shut discreetly over at the neighbor's, but Caleb

didn't even look in that direction. He was too busy studying Tye's face.

"That's bullshit, man," Tye said.

"Is it?"

Silence. Tye stood, obviously agitated, but his mouth remained firmly closed.

"Have you had possession of your father's truck in the past few weeks, Tye?"

Now Madison's half brother looked positively furtive. He curled his fingers into fists, and Caleb straightened, preparing for anything…just in case. "No, I haven't," Tye muttered.

"I have a witness who says you drove your father's truck to the pizzeria that night," Caleb said, taking it one step further.

Tye's chest rose as if he'd inhaled deeply. Caleb got the impression he was about to reveal…something. But he didn't. "Get out of here," he said instead. "Get out of here right now or you'll be damn sorry you ever showed up."

Shit. Caleb's bluff hadn't paid off. He stared at Tye's angry face another long moment, then turned to leave.

He was only a few miles from Tye's neighborhood when an old Dodge came screaming up behind him. A chubby, middle-aged man honked and yelled for him to pull over.

Caleb rolled down his window. "What do you want?" he called above the wind as the man drove alongside him.

"Are you a detective?"

To keep things simple, Caleb nodded.

"That's what I thought." The guy braked to avoid a collision with the car ahead, and Caleb slowed to stay even with him. "I live right next to Tye Purcell," he hollered when it was safe to glance over again. "Pull off the road. I have some information for you."

"WHAT ARE YOU DOING?" Holly asked the moment Caleb answered his cell phone.

Caleb grimaced at the sound of her voice and changed lanes so he could speed up. "Heading home." *Racing home...*

"Where have you been?"

"Nowhere important," he said. After her behavior at Lance's last night, he was reluctant to share the grim information he'd just received. "Did you call for a reason?"

The phone went silent for a few seconds, then she said, "I left my purse in your car."

"I haven't seen it."

"It has to be there. I had it with me last night, and I haven't gone anywhere since."

Keeping one hand on the wheel, Caleb reached over to feel around the passenger seat. He found a few gum wrappers and a quarter wedged next to the console, but no purse. "It's not here, Holly."

"Then I must've left it at your house."

Wonderful. Another excuse to visit. "If it's there, I'll bring it over later, okay?" he said.

"Caleb, I need it right now."

"Holly, I'm tired." And he had to talk to Madison.... "Why—"

"I won't stay long," she promised.

He ground his teeth. He didn't want to see his ex-wife; he wanted to deal with what he'd found out. But he thought he'd be able to get rid of Holly more quickly and easily if he just gave her the damn purse. "Okay," he said. "But don't come for an hour or so. I'm in south Seattle and the ferry to Whidbey always takes awhile."

MADISON SCRUBBED HER FACE with her hand and blinked, trying to clear the blurriness from her eyes. Once she'd finally gone to sleep, she hadn't stirred for hours, thanks to the natural letdown of her emotions, combined with the effect of those sleeping pills. But then someone had knocked at the door, and she'd dragged herself out of bed to find the sun peeking through rain clouds and Caleb's ex-wife standing on her stoop.

"Can I help you?" Madison said, steadying herself with a hand on the lintel.

Holly didn't answer right away. Her gaze traveled slowly over Madison's robe to her well-worn slippers before returning to her face. "I left my purse at Caleb's house last night, but he isn't home."

Madison waited for her to make some sort of request, but Holly didn't add anything else. "I have an extra key," Madison said, "but I'm afraid I can't let you in without Caleb's permission. Have you tried calling him?"

Holly smiled. "Of course. He said he'd be here in a minute. I was just hoping you and I could have a little talk while I wait."

"A little talk about what?"

"Just a few things I think you should be aware of."

There was something about Holly's manner Madison didn't like or trust. And she wasn't eager to face any more unpleasant surprises. She felt sick every time she thought about her visit with Caleb at his parents' house and how wonderful it had been compared to the confrontation that had occurred afterward.

But basic good manners demanded she hear Holly out. She was certainly curious. "Come inside," she said, because it was beginning to sprinkle.

Feeling she needed a jolt of caffeine to help restore her

faculties, Madison led the way to the kitchen so she could make a pot of coffee.

"Nice place," Holly said, scratching one arm through her leather jacket as she came down the hall. "Did you decorate it yourself?"

"Yes." Madison motioned to the kitchen table. "Would you like to sit down?"

"No thanks." Caleb's ex-wife circled the room, gazing at the cupboards and appliances, examining the magnets and pictures on the fridge. "How long have you lived here?" she asked.

"Not quite a year."

"Since your divorce from Danny, the engineer?"

Madison was about to fill the coffeemaker with fresh grounds, but turned to stare at Holly instead. "How do you know anything about Danny? Or my divorce?"

"You're Ellis Purcell's daughter, aren't you?"

Madison curled her fingernails into her palms, feeling doubly betrayed that Caleb hadn't even bothered to keep quiet about the fact that he was playing her for a fool. "Did Caleb tell you that?"

"Of course. We're still *very* close." She took a picture off the refrigerator. "Is this your daughter?"

Holly held a photo of Brianna at the zoo. "Yes."

"What a cute little girl."

Her words were nice enough, but they were spoken almost tonelessly. And the way Holly stared at the picture made Madison want to yank it away. "She's a good girl. Most of the time, anyway," she said, watching Holly closely.

"I've always wanted a child."

Madison remembered Caleb telling her that he and Holly had lost a baby due to miscarriage. She would have felt sympathy except that Holly seemed so emotionally detached. Her comment had sounded like a casual observation.

"What is it you came to tell me, Holly?" Madison asked, anxious to bring their "little talk" to a close.

Holly tacked the picture back onto the fridge and turned. "Caleb's only interested in you because of who are you are," she said. "He thinks if he can solve this case, he'll finally reel in the one that got away. The big one. You know what I mean? That's all it is. It isn't you or—" she waved at the pictures of Brianna "—or your little girl that he likes."

Madison hated hearing what Holly was saying, but she couldn't argue with it because Holly was right. Caleb had only moved into the cottage because she was Ellis Purcell's daughter. But common sense told her that Holly wouldn't have shown up at her door unless she was feeling threatened in some way. "Holly, since you've been so candid with me, I think I'll do you the same favor," she said.

Holly's eyebrows shot up and she straightened, giving Madison the impression that she was surprised her revelation hadn't reduced Madison to tears. "What?"

"Caleb's over you. If you're smart, you'll forget him and move on with your life."

Which is exactly what I plan to do. But she knew forgetting Caleb was going to be much easier said than done. Especially when she heard a car turn in at the drive and her heart leaped into her throat at the thought that it was probably him.

CHAPTER TWENTY-ONE

THE IMPATIENCE CALEB FELT whenever Holly contacted him lately returned with a vengeance the moment he saw her car. Since it was Sunday, the ferry had been moving more quickly than usual. He'd made the drive from south Seattle in less than forty minutes, yet she'd beaten him here. Even after he'd told her to give him an hour. No wonder he'd moved to San Francisco.

Scowling, he put the Mustang in Park and cut the engine. He needed a few minutes alone with Madison, but he had to get rid of Holly first—wherever she was. He was fairly certain he'd locked the door to the cottage, so she couldn't be inside. And she wasn't sitting in her car.

He got out and started across the drive. When he'd cleared the arbor, he could see more of the cottage, where he expected to find Holly hunched against the rain, waiting for him under the eaves. But he saw no one until he was just a few feet away from Madison's house. Then the door opened and Holly dashed out, nearly running into him.

"Whoa, take it easy," he said, dodging her.

She glanced from him to Madison, who was standing in the doorway behind her. "You wouldn't even be here if it wasn't for me, Caleb," she said, her face full of fury.

"Holly—"

"I don't want to talk about it," she said, and marched to her car.

"What about your purse?" he called after her, but she'd already slammed her door and started the engine. Throwing the transmission in reverse, she gave it far more gas than necessary and tore out of the drive.

"THANKS FOR DETAILING my identity and your plans for me to your ex-wife," Madison said as the echo of Holly's squealing tires died away. "I guess I was the only one who didn't know, huh?"

"It wasn't like that," Caleb said.

"What was it like?"

"Would it make a difference if I told you?"

"Should it?"

He raked a hand through his hair. "I don't know," he said with a sigh. "But we need to talk." His somber expression and his tone told Madison that he wanted to discuss more than just their relationship.

Prickles of fear raced down her spine. Had he found something? Something she wouldn't like?

"Okay," she said, and held open the door, steeling herself for whatever would follow. But then Danny's Jaguar pulled into the drive, and Brianna got out.

"Hi, Caleb," she called and ran over the lawn to give him a big hug. "I'm home early!"

Madison waited her turn for a hug from Brianna, then crossed the wet lawn to collect Brianna's bag from Danny. "It's only ten o'clock," she said when he handed it to her. "What's going on?"

"I decided I'd better go in to the office today. I'm behind at work."

"You couldn't have called to let me know you were bringing Brianna home now?"

"You *asked* me to bring her home early," he said.

Madison sighed. "It would have been nice if you'd arranged it."

He shrugged and got back in his car. "I knew you'd be here," he said simply, and drove off.

Madison turned, trudging back to Caleb and Brianna. Caleb had lifted Brianna into his arms, and she was busy telling him all about the new fish her father had bought this weekend to add to her aquarium.

"Let's get out of the rain," Madison suggested, and felt the pressure of Caleb's hand on her back as they hurried inside. He pulled away to close the door, but not before she recognized that, no matter what he'd done, she still longed for his touch.

Evidently she was an even bigger fool than she'd thought.

"Well?" she said as he put Brianna down.

Caleb gave a subtle nod that let Madison know he was concerned about Brianna overhearing what he had to say. "Is there someplace we could be alone?"

"Johnny's here, too," she said.

"Then maybe I should go home. We can talk on the phone." But he didn't turn to leave right away. He stood there staring at her, making her feel self-conscious about her damp, tangled hair and hastily donned robe, even though he was mostly looking at her lips.

"Why's everyone up so early?" Johnny asked, stumbling into the living room with a yawn.

Grateful for the interruption, Madison broke eye contact with Caleb. "Brianna's home," she told him.

CALEB PEELED OFF his clothes on the way to his bedroom, planning to climb beneath the sheets and pass out for a few hours. But he still had to call Madison, prepare her for the fact that Tye would probably be arrested. He knew she'd have divided feelings. Horror that her own half brother could be capable of such violence. Sympathy for the way it was going to affect his wife and children. Vindication that she'd been right about her father all along.

Kicking off his jeans, he tossed them aside without caring where they landed, scooped the cordless phone off the nightstand and sank into bed in his boxers. Never had a mattress felt so good....

But he didn't have long to relax. Madison answered almost immediately. "Hello?"

He stared at the ceiling, picturing her almond-shaped eyes gazing up at him and her mouth curved into the same seductive smile as the night they'd gone dancing. "It's me."

She was silent for a moment, a silence fraught with tension. "What's happened?" she asked.

Closing his eyes, Caleb tried to separate what he felt for Madison from what he felt in general. "I'm afraid I have some news you might not want to hear."

"What is it?"

He could tell by the sound of her voice that she was bracing for the worst. "Tye might have a connection to my sister-in-law's murder."

His statement was met with silence. "I was afraid of that," she finally whispered. There was another long pause before she continued. "How did you find out?"

"I have a picture of Susan the night she disappeared. A blue Ford truck just like your father's is parked right next to her."

"There are a lot of trucks like my father's."

"Not with the same license plate. Tye's neighbor saw him driving your father's truck the night Susan disappeared. He said Tye brought it home and parked it out front for a while."

"Driving my dad's truck doesn't prove he hurt anyone," she said, but her voice held no conviction, and because of the locket and other things that had disappeared from under the house, Caleb knew she believed Tye was involved.

"We'll learn more later. I'll call you as soon as I hear anything."

"Does that mean he killed those other women, too?" she asked.

"Nothing's definite, yet. But it's possible."

He heard her sigh. "If so, he got away with it because of my father," she said. "Why would he kill again?"

"Sometimes there's no good explanation for homicidal behavior. To a psychopath, killing becomes a craving, an addiction. Serial killers feed on the power. Maybe the compulsion overcame him."

"Would he go to prison or..."

She let her words drift away, and Caleb knew she was thinking about the death penalty. "I won't lie to you. If the lab is able to come up with the DNA profile they've been working on, and it happens to match Tye's DNA, the district attorney will have a pretty strong case. And there'll probably be other evidence." He punched his pillow and rolled over. "I've called Gibbons. The police will be heading over to your brother's place as soon as they can procure a search warrant."

"I suspected Tye and yet...I can't believe it," she said. "When will we find out for sure?"

"Depends on the lab, but it shouldn't take more than another few days, maybe a week."

"Poor Sharon."

"Are *you* going to be okay?" he asked.

"I don't know. I'm relieved no one else will be hurt. And I'm numb enough right now that I just want it all to end. It's been part of my life, in one way or another, for far too long.''

''I hope it'll be over soon.''

''So you can write another book?'' she said, her voice caustic.

''So I can go home,'' he said truthfully. He didn't need the headache of trying to sort out his feelings for her. He was torn between wanting to pursue a relationship and, now that things had turned sour, wanting to back away entirely. Holly had been a big mistake. He had no desire to make another.

''When will you leave?'' Madison asked.

''Sometime soon.''

Caleb sensed that she was softening toward him, and couldn't help taking advantage of it. ''Madison, I want you to know that I didn't intend for what happened between us to—''

''Don't,'' she said. ''I know. When we made love it was too honest for either of us to be pretending. But it's all too much right now. I—I don't know what to think about anything anymore.''

He bit back the rest of what he wanted to say. He needed to give her time. She'd just learned that her brother might be going to prison—or worse. ''What happened with Holly?'' he asked when several seconds had passed in silence. ''She was supposed to pick up her purse, but it's still here.''

His call-waiting beeped, and he pulled the phone away to see who was trying to get through. He was eager to hear from Gibbons, to find out for sure that Tye was their man. But it was Holly.

''Speak of the devil,'' he said. ''Holly's calling me on the other line.''

''Then I'll let her explain.''

"Okay."

He felt a nagging reluctance to let Madison go, even though there was nothing left to say. "I'll call you when I hear from Detective Gibbons," he said, forcing some finality into his voice.

"Caleb?"

"Yes?"

"Will you do me one favor?"

"What's that?"

"Don't leave without saying goodbye. After my father... Well, I hate that. I hate that I never got to say goodbye."

He closed his eyes. Despite his best efforts to push the memory away, he could still feel her body beneath his the night they'd made love. "I won't leave without saying goodbye," he said, although he knew it wouldn't be an easy moment.

She hung up and Caleb switched lines. "You never got your purse," he told Holly.

"I couldn't. I couldn't stand being around that woman another minute."

Caleb used one hand to rub both temples while he talked. "You mean Madison?"

"Who else?"

"There's nothing wrong with Madison, Holly."

"She thinks she has some sort of hold on you, Caleb. Can you believe she had the nerve to tell me you don't love me anymore, that I should move on?"

She laughed incredulously, but that only annoyed Caleb further. He'd told Holly the same thing in a million different ways. The fact that he'd divorced her for the second time and moved to another state wasn't enough? What he'd said in the cottage, when he'd told her they were over for good—that wasn't enough?

Maybe he'd been too gentle. Obviously, Holly didn't get it.

He gave up rubbing his temples. He was never going to relieve the tension humming through his body as long as he was talking to his ex-wife. "Holly, Madison's right," he said frankly.

"*What?*"

"We've talked about this before. We're finished. For good. Do you understand?"

"No, Caleb, I don't. You...you don't mean it. You came back to me last time."

"Last time there were—" he thought of the baby, dared not mention it "—other issues involved."

"I don't care. You came all the way back here, just because I needed you."

"Holly, I came back to help you out as a *friend*. I'll be going home in the next few days."

"You can't leave! What about finding Susan's killer?"

"I think we might have done that today."

He could tell by the sudden break in the conversation that this surprised her as much as he'd expected it to. "Who is it?" she asked.

"Tye Purcell."

"Madison's brother?"

"You remember him?"

"I remember everyone involved in the case, Caleb. I've been with you every step of the way since we first met. But then, *I* believe in 'till death do us part.'"

Hearing her voice rise, he hurried to cut her off before emotions could escalate any further. "I'm really tired. I've got to go, okay?"

"But you love me, Caleb. Admit it, *please*. You'll always love me."

"I don't love you, Holly. Not like you think."

He heard her sniff. "It's Madison, isn't it? You've fallen in love with her."

Caleb willed her words out of his head, willed Madison out of his heart. "What I feel for Madison is none of your business, Holly," he said, and disconnected.

MADISON TOUCHED Johnny's arm. He was sitting on the living room floor next to her, playing Candyland with Brianna, but he wasn't having an easy time relaxing. He kept glancing at the clock and jiggling his leg.

"You okay?" she asked.

"I'm fine."

Brianna squealed at getting a card with double red squares. "I'm going ahead of you," she taunted Johnny.

He shrugged, obviously indifferent to the game, agitation rolling off him in waves, but he took his turn. Madison supposed she had to admire her brother for even playing. She knew he'd only agreed because Brianna had begged him. But Madison had enough on her mind today without worrying about Johnny. Ever since Caleb had told her about Tye this morning, she'd been guessing and second-guessing about whether or not her brother could really have committed those horrible acts. And no matter how shocking, disturbing or overwhelming she found that possibility, her mind kept returning to Caleb.

Caleb's so handsome, Maddy. How did your date go last night? Her mother had asked her that on the phone earlier.

It wasn't really a date.

Did he kiss you?

I didn't call about Caleb. I called to tell you that I've got Brianna home, so I won't be showing the house today.

That's fine, dear. Do you think this Caleb is ready to find a wife?

Mom, that's enough!

But it was so nice of him to mow the lawn. They just don't make men like that anymore. You've got to snap him up while you can.

He's moving back to San Francisco.

When?

Soon. Too soon…

Don't let him get away, Maddy.

She'd known she could shut her mother up very quickly simply by telling Annette who Caleb really was. But something—misguided loyalty, no doubt—made her reluctant to ruin her mother's good opinion of him. She hadn't told Annette that Johnny had been the one to visit the cemetery, either, or that the police were now investigating Tye. What Johnny had done would hardly improve his relationship with her mother. And she didn't want to break the news about Tye, even to Johnny, until they knew for sure.

"What are you thinking?" Johnny asked.

She blinked and brought her attention back to the game. "Nothing. Is it my turn?"

He scrubbed his face, his palm rasping over several days' worth of whiskers. "It was your turn thirty seconds ago," he said as she drew a purple card and moved her plastic gingerbread man.

When they were talking privately earlier that day, she'd told Johnny she'd help him get on his feet. She'd promised to let him stay in the cottage after Caleb left, if he'd clean up and begin a rigorous rehabilitation program. But he hadn't made any commitments. To Madison's disappointment, the closeness and understanding they'd achieved the night before hadn't lasted. If anything, she felt Johnny resented her even more for having seen his weakness.

"Come on, Mom, go!" Brianna said.

"Sorry." Realizing it was her turn *again,* Madison offered her daughter a quick smile and picked up another card. "Oh, no!" She managed a groan for Brianna's benefit. "I have to go back."

Brianna laughed as she watched Madison move back to the purple "Plumpy" pictured on the card. "I'm going to win," her daughter cried gleefully, clapping her hands.

Madison knew she was *way* behind Brianna, and even Johnny, on their journey to the king's candy, but she wasn't worried about losing the game. She was afraid that, amidst the turmoil in her life, she was about to lose something much more important.

"It's your turn again, Mommy," Brianna said, her voice full of fresh impatience.

A honk sounded outside and Johnny scrambled to his feet. "That's my ride."

Madison frowned at him. He'd made a few calls earlier. She'd heard the drone of his voice in the other room while she was reading to Brianna, but he hadn't mentioned anything about leaving. "I didn't know you were going anywhere," she said. "Will you be coming back?"

"Not tonight. I'm gonna chill with a friend," he said, heading out.

Madison opened her mouth to tell him he might want to stay close, that they might have a family crisis on their hands. But she knew it wouldn't change his mind. He was his own walking crisis. And she didn't want to discuss what was happening with Tye until she heard more from Caleb.

"You're not quitting the game, too, are you, Mommy?" Brianna asked, clearly not pleased with Johnny's defection.

Madison sighed as the door slammed behind her half

brother, wondering when, if ever, she'd see him again. "No, I'm not going to quit," she said, and took her turn, only to land on the square labeled "Gooey Gumdrop—Stay Here until a Yellow Card is Drawn."

On her next three turns, she drew a green, a purple and then a red card. Brianna giggled each time she couldn't move, but Madison didn't think it was funny. The game felt a lot like her life. She couldn't continue happily on her way until she got over Caleb.

Unfortunately, she'd done exactly what she'd told herself not to do—and fallen in love.

HOLLY TURNED OFF her headlights and let the engine of her Honda idle as she sat behind the wheel, staring at the sleepy little house where Madison lived. Rain thrummed softly on her hood and beaded on her windshield, pearl-like in those fleeting moments when the moon's pale glow managed to slip through the clouds. Eventually, the drops began to quiver, then roll down the glass like tears. But there were no other sights or sounds to distract her. Only the beacon of light in Madison's kitchen where she sat alone at the table, bent over something Holly couldn't see because of the black plastic that covered half the window.

Madison Lieberman... Who would've thought Ellis Purcell's daughter would exact such perfect, if unwitting, revenge? Pretty, *petite* Madison.

Shaking her head, Holly laughed bitterly. Men liked their women small because it made them feel strong, powerful. Small women were *desirable.* Holly had large bones and height to rival most men's. The exact opposite of the petted girl she'd grown up with as her stepsister. Different from Susan in every way...

But that was nothing new. Holly had long since learned

that luck was never in her corner. If she wanted *anything,* she had to take matters into her own hands.

Getting out of the car, she pulled the black hood of her sweatshirt up over her hair. It wasn't easy to see through the trees that partially blocked her view of the house, but she dared not move the car any closer. Caleb wasn't a fool. After hearing his impatience with her on the phone, she was afraid of what he'd do if he caught her here.

But she needed to look things over. To think. To plan. Madison was something new, something she hadn't anticipated....

The smell of the sea hit her with the first blast of wind. She inhaled deeply as she made her way up the drive, crouching between the cars, moving steadily, deliberately, while gathering her calm and controlling her rage.

Caleb's car was to the right, Madison's to the left. They were parked side by side, as if they belonged to a married couple.

Holly grimaced and felt the hood of each car with the back of her hand. Cold. Just as she'd expected. It was nearly midnight.

With a frown, she hid in the arbor that concealed her from Madison's house, and craned her head to see Caleb's cottage. It was dark. He was there, in bed, without her.

She felt a sudden wave of debilitating sadness. Why did Caleb have to betray her like this? Why was he forcing her hand? It didn't make sense. She'd done everything for him, even going so far as to arrange her sister's death for his next book!

Absently rubbing the scratches on her arms where a few scabs remained, she closed her eyes, trying to shut out her last memories of Susan. If it hadn't been for Lance, the cheating bastard, her sister would never have shown up at her house so late at night. Susan would never have seen what she'd seen. But she *had* shown up and left Holly no choice. Susan was too perceptive, too persistent and inquisitive. She wouldn't let it go.

Still, Holly regretted that Susan was gone. Her stepsister was the only person in her life who'd stuck by her through thick and thin.

It's okay, she told herself when her throat started to tighten and burn. *I only did what I had to do.* And she'd been clever enough to make it all work to her advantage. She wasn't going to let Caleb slip away from her now. Madison would be a figure in his next book, nothing more, and Holly and Caleb would finally be together again.

Except Holly's rival wasn't only a woman. It was a child, too. She'd seen that picture on the fridge, known instantly how much Madison's daughter would appeal to Caleb. He'd wanted children for years....

Holly remembered the time she'd pretended to be pregnant. Sometimes it helped to pretend. Having a child would have made her life so much easier. Caleb wouldn't have left her if there'd been a baby.

Only she couldn't conceive. The abortion she'd given herself at sixteen had ruined any chance of that. But she wouldn't allow Madison to offer him what she couldn't.

Reality, as cold and harsh as the wind stinging her face, was too strong for pretending tonight. Holly knew she had to face the truth and deal with the gut-roiling jealousy that caused her real, physical pain—pain so acute she doubled over, barely biting back a groan.

"I'll fix it...I'll fix it...." She whispered those words like an incantation until she could believe her own promise. Until she could stand again. Until she could breathe.

She *would* fix it, she decided. She'd fix everything.

But how? Holly bit her lip as she tried to think. She could lure Caleb away from the house with a lie about some new piece of evidence. If she said Margie White, a friend of Susan's they'd already interviewed, had found something in her car, Caleb would rush right over to her house. Margie wouldn't know what he was talking about once he got there, of course, but Holly didn't need Margie to support the lie. She just needed time. When she saw Caleb again, she'd tell him that whoever had called her with the information had sounded just like Margie. She must have been mistaken, she'd say. Anyone could call based on that flyer they'd distributed, right? Maybe she'd even try to make it seem like a crank. And once Caleb was gone, she'd cut Madison's phone line, just in case things didn't go as smoothly as planned.

That was it, she decided. That was a good plan. With *that* plan, Madison and Brianna wouldn't figure in Caleb's affections for long.

CHAPTER TWENTY-TWO

THE RINGING OF the telephone interrupted a particularly good dream. Caleb was reluctant to wake fully, but he thought it might be Madison. *Why* he thought it might be her, he wasn't sure. Probably just wishful thinking.

"Hello?" Hearing the scratchy quality of his own voice, he cleared his throat and tried again. "Hello?"

"Wake up, Trovato."

Gibbons. Caleb tried not to feel disappointed. Shoving himself into a sitting position, he shot a glance at the clock to see that it was only one in the morning and not dawn, as he'd first assumed. "What is it? Did you arrest Tye Purcell?"

"No."

Caleb's disappointment grew exponentially. He'd been so sure they'd finally reached the end of the road, achieved resolution. "Why not?"

"Several reasons. Remember that drop of blood we found on the sheet beneath Susan's body?"

"Yeah."

"It's Type O, and Tye's Type B. It might take a few weeks to do a DNA comparison, but it only takes a minute to get a blood type."

"So that's it? We're back to square one?" Caleb propped the phone against his shoulder, got out of bed and yanked on his jeans. He needed a cup of coffee. He'd slept most of the day and half the night, but he still felt groggy as hell.

"Not yet. Holly just called me."

"Thank God she didn't call me," Caleb muttered, heading to the kitchen. He was so sick of hearing from his ex-wife he thought he could live the rest of his life without contact and be the better for it.

"You two having a lovers' quarrel?"

Caleb flipped on the kitchen light, wincing at the sudden brightness. "We don't have a lovers' anything. What'd she want?"

"She said a friend of Susan's named Margie called her and—"

"This late? Don't people do things in the middle of the day anymore?"

"That's what I'd like to know. According to Holly, Margie just found a note in her car signed by a man named Tye. She thinks it must've fallen out of Susan's purse a week or so before she died, when Margie and Susan went to lunch."

"Holly and I met Margie," Caleb said, scratching his bare chest with one hand while filling the coffeepot with the other. "She seemed pretty straight up, but—"

"Whether she's straight up or not, handwriting samples and maybe fingerprints should tell us whether the note is really from Tye," Gibbons interjected.

Caleb set the coffeepot on the counter. "But a note from Tye doesn't make sense. I thought you just said his blood type doesn't match the blood found on the sheet. Yet suddenly we have proof that he and Susan knew each other?"

"I'm as confused as you are."

Something didn't feel right. Caleb shook his head.

"You wanna meet me at Margie's house?" Gibbons asked.

Caleb changed the phone to his left hand so he could button his jeans with his right. "Are you *asking* me to come? When you found Susan's car, I had to twist your arm to let me join you."

"Yeah, well, you know I'm not supposed to bring civilians. An ex-cop is one thing. Holly's another. But Holly claims this woman won't talk to me tonight unless you're there. And I'd really like things to be easy for a change. If Tye *is* our killer, we've got to close in before he runs or hurts someone else."

"Why won't Margie talk to you without me?" Caleb asked. That didn't sound right, either. He'd only met her once, and they hadn't spoken since then.

"Who knows? Holly said Margie trusts you because she's met you before. I told her Margie shouldn't have any problem trusting me, but she repeated that she'd promised Margie you'd be there. You know how a woman thinks. If telling you once is good, repeating it fifty times is better, even if it doesn't make sense from the get-go."

"Where's Holly now?" Caleb asked.

"At home. She wanted to come, too, but I told her there was no way, not after the kind of behavior she exhibited at Lance Perkin's the other night."

"Did she give up?"

"Yeah. She said she'd stay out of it so long as you're going to be there. And believe me, I'd much rather have you present than her."

"Thanks, but I'm not dumb enough to believe that's much of a compliment," Caleb said dryly.

Gibbons chuckled. "We'll get this woman's statement and the note. That's it. If I need to arrest Tye, I'll take a couple of uniforms. When we questioned him today he nearly went ballistic.''

"This note doesn't add up," Caleb muttered again.

"I've got to check it out whether it adds up or not," Gibbons said. "Are you coming?"

"I'm on my way." Lord knows he wasn't going to be able to sleep anymore tonight.

MADISON EXAMINED the sketch she'd just finished of Caleb's chest and shoulders, and scowled in frustration. His sculpted body easily lent itself to an artist's pencil. So did the raw-boned beauty of his face. But she'd been drawing for more than two hours and simply couldn't match the vision of him she held in her head.

She was still such an amateur, she thought in disgust, and dropped her pencil. But she'd drawn Caleb's mouth earlier, and felt she'd done a better job there. That sketch sat on the table at her elbow, tempting her eye again and again because his lips looked almost as sensual on paper as they did in real life. Almost. With Caleb, it was pretty tough to compete with reality.

Why she continued to torture herself by sketching him, Madison didn't know. She had so much work she needed to do. But drawing was the only thing that kept her from thinking too much about Tye and whether or not he'd be going to prison—or facing an even worse punishment.

Tomorrow would probably tell....

Pushing away from the table, she stood and stretched. She'd stayed up far too late. Her life might be in upheaval, but responsibilities didn't disappear. Tomorrow was Monday. Brianna had school, and Madison had to work. She'd checked earlier and already knew her voice mail was loaded with messages. Which was good. If business didn't pick up soon, she'd have a lot more to worry about than Tye getting arrested, or moving on without Caleb in her life.

Gathering her pads and pencils, Madison piled them neatly on the counter. Then she lingered in the kitchen, wiping off the faucet, cleaning the microwave and watering her plants, dreading the moment she actually had to call it a night. Everything seemed so quiet, so still, like the calm before a storm.

When she ran out of things to do, she started down the hall. But the crunch of tires on gravel outside drew her back. She'd heard Caleb leave about twenty minutes ago. She couldn't help hoping he was back. She liked knowing he was around.

Or maybe it was someone dropping off Johnny....

Standing to the side of the window, Madison watched a tall blond woman climb out of a familiar white Honda.

It wasn't Caleb or Johnny. It was Holly.

HOLLY SMILED WHEN Madison passed the window on her way to the door. She hadn't even had a chance to knock. Obviously Madison wasn't afraid of her. Not that Holly had expected her to be. Women weren't typically afraid of other women. Even during the media blitz following the other murders, Holly had never had trouble getting young women, complete strangers, to meet her somewhere or even come to her apartment. She'd bumped into Tatiana Harris at the grocery store and, simply by striking up a conversation and laughing at the stupid little comments Tatiana made about her husband, had talked her into going to a movie with her instead of straight home. Rosey Martin had gone home with her from the Laundromat to watch a video. Lori Schiller had agreed to meet her at a park. And there were others, including Anna Tyler, who'd lived next door.

Want to come over? We can do makeovers…manicures…have a drink…grab a bite to eat.…

Women were so gullible—and catty and deceitful. They pretended to be your friend only to stab you in the back the moment you confided in them. Just like Rosie Wheeler and Paige Todd had done to her in high school.

Holly winced at the memory of the morning she'd shown up at school to find Baby Killer and Whore written in nail polish across her locker. She could still hear the whispers and muffled laughter, still feel the scorn that had nearly smothered her for months afterward. The other girls wouldn't include her, or even speak to her. But she'd show them.

She'd show Madison, too. Madison wouldn't take away the one person who made her feel complete. She hadn't felt the same anger when she believed Caleb loved her, hadn't bothered anyone the whole time they were married. There wasn't any reason to. When she had Caleb she had what all the other girls wanted and could simply laugh in their faces.

But if she was going to hang on to Caleb, she had to move fast. He wouldn't stay gone forever.

She reached the front step and heard the scrape of the deadbolt as Madison unlocked the door. "Is something wrong, Holly?" she asked, opening it slightly.

"Sorry to stop by so late," Holly said. "I wasn't going to bother you. I was just hoping to catch Caleb. But I don't see his car. I guess he's not home, huh?"

"He left about twenty minutes ago."

"That's too bad." She laughed. "I'm so out of it. I forgot my purse at his place again. Do you have any idea when he'll be back?"

"I'm afraid not. It might be smarter to call him tomorrow." She started to close the door.

Holly quickly put out a hand to stop her. "I'll do that. But before you go, I have something to tell you."

Madison seemed to hesitate. Holly could see only a slice of her face and body through the door, but it was enough to know she was wearing a pair of sweatpants and a cropped T-shirt. The T-shirt was faded and worn, but the way it hugged Madison's small breasts made Holly even angrier. She was trying to steal Caleb, tempt him. Women—they were always up to something.

"Holly, I don't think—" Madison began, but Holly cut her off.

"It's nothing like before. I would like to come in for a minute, though, if you don't mind. It's a little cold and damp out here." She rubbed her arms and shivered for added effect.

Madison still seemed skeptical. "Tomorrow would be better."

Holly backed up as though she was about to leave, purposely acting as nonconfrontational as possible. "Okay. I understand. I just wanted to tell you I've been out all night thinking. And you should know you were right earlier. I have to let go of Caleb. It's time. Past time, really, but—" she let her voice break, and swiped at the false tears gathering in her eyes "—sometimes it just hurts so badly. I still love him. I'll always love him. And…" She gulped as though the words were difficult for her. "And I'm afraid if he can't love me, no one else will be able to, either."

Compassion softened Madison's features. "I understand how you feel. Anyone who's gone through a divorce experiences some of the same insecurities. But you'll get over it and find your feet again."

"I'm not so sure of that," Holly said, and buried her face in her hands, sobbing brokenly.

Madison opened the door wider. "It takes time, Holly."

"You're probably right," she muttered. "I'm just so alone."

"You're not alone…. Why don't you come in, and I'll make us both some tea?"

"I wouldn't want to wake your little girl." Holly sniffed, finally lowering her hands from her face. "Or anyone else who might be staying with you."

"There's no one else, just Brianna. And we won't wake her."

Wiping her eyes, Holly followed Madison inside. The house smelled like homemade cookies. Madison was *so* domestic, with her pretty little girl, her natural beauty and charming house.

"Maybe Caleb will be home by the time you finish your tea, so you can get your purse," Madison was saying, her back to Holly now.

Holly felt in her pocket to make sure she hadn't lost the pills. She'd only be able to use them if she could get Madison to drink something. But Susan had proved that she didn't really need drugs. The shock would be enough.

"Maybe," Holly said. But she knew she'd be long gone by the time Caleb returned. She'd leave a surprise for him, though. And no one would suspect her.

No one ever suspected a woman.

FRUSTRATED, CALEB PUNCHED Holly's number into his cell phone again. He'd already called twice since leaving Whidbey Island and had gotten her answering machine both times. Where was she? She'd obviously been awake when she'd called Detective Gibbons only a half hour or so earlier. Even if she'd gone to bed, she wasn't a heavy sleeper. He knew that from when they were married. There were plenty of nights he'd awakened to find her staring at the ceiling or gone, off to the corner convenience store or out driving.

He glanced at her purse in the seat next to him and considered delivering it to her tomorrow, then decided against it. Her place was on the way to this Margie White's house, where he was supposed to meet Detective Gibbons. Taking it to her now, while it was so late and he was in a hurry, would be perfect. They'd have no time to talk, and she'd have no reason to contact him tomorrow. Especially if the police ended up proving that Tye *was* the one who'd murdered Susan. Then Caleb's obligation to the relationships of his past would be fulfilled; his trip to Seattle would be over.

He could easily conjure up the smell of San Francisco's crusty sourdough bread and the crabs and other seafood sold along the wharf, could feel the wind coming in off the bay. If picturing himself in his new home also felt a little lonely, he refused to acknowledge it. He just had to get back to work. At that point everything would be good again.

Slowing for the next off ramp, he exited Interstate 99 at Mill Creek and turned toward Alderwood Manor, where he used to live with Holly. The house they'd shared, which he'd given her as part of the divorce settlement, was nothing like the big estates on Mercer Island. But it had been new when they moved in and comfortable for a young couple just starting out. They'd both had great hopes when they'd bought that house.

He gazed at the quiet streets he'd frequented on and off for so long, feeling like a stranger now. Funny how things changed.

His cell phone rang. He glanced at the caller ID to see it was Gibbons before punching the Talk button.

"Where the hell are you?" the detective asked, nearly blasting out his eardrum.

Caleb jerked the phone back a few inches. Couldn't Gibbons say anything without shouting? "I've got to drop something by Holly's. I'll be there in a minute."

"I'll wait ten. Then I'm going to the door with or without you. I want to sleep sometime tonight."

"Good enough," Caleb said, and ended the call. But when he finally reached the small stucco, two-story home he'd shared with Holly, he found it dark. Evidently she'd gone to bed.

Shoving his phone in his pocket, he grabbed her purse and went to the door, leaving his car idling in the drive.

Susan's dogs barked as he waited impatiently for Holly to answer the bell, but seconds turned into minutes and she didn't appear.

He pushed the doorbell again, then knocked. Finally he tried the door handle. It was locked, but the small lockbox he'd bought to secure their spare key back when they were together was still right where he'd left it, inside the front flower planter. He doubted Holly knew how to change the combination. He'd always done that sort of thing. So he wasn't surprised when he pushed 1-9-4-3, the year of his mother's birth, and it opened.

"Holly, you home?" he called, poking his head inside the foyer as soon as he'd unlocked the door.

Susan's schnauzers growled low in their throats, but when he bent down and offered his hand for them to sniff, they remembered him. One even licked him. But there was no response from his ex-wife.

"Holly?" He stepped inside, immediately noticing that the house smelled different than it had when they were living together. He supposed that was normal, since his cologne, hair products and clothes were no longer part of the equation—since *he* was no longer part of the equation. But it didn't smell of perfume, like Susan's place, or feel-good food and crayons, like Madison's. Or even like the dogs. This scent was more…musty.

Once he flipped on a light, Caleb could see why. Piles of everything from clothes to magazines to books to papers covered all horizontal surfaces—even most of the floor—along with a thick layer of dust. The clutter seemed to be growing from the walls like some kind of space-eating plant, until only a narrow pathway remained, leading from room to room.

With Susan's murder, he could certainly understand why Holly wouldn't be worried about cleaning. But what he saw wasn't the result of days or weeks of neglect. It would take months, maybe even years, to collect so much junk. Holly must not have thrown anything away since he'd left her.

"Jeez, Holly," he muttered. She'd always been a pack-rat. They'd had a million arguments over cleaning out the garage and the closets. But now that she was living alone, without anyone to check her tendency to hang on to absolutely everything, she seemed to be taking it to new extremes.

He pulled a newspaper from the bottom of a stack of papers and grimaced at the date. It was thirteen months old.

Setting her purse on top of a box of envelopes and copy paper on the dining room table, he turned to go, counting himself lucky that he'd managed to miss her. But it seemed odd that she wouldn't be home when she'd told Gibbons she would be. There was something strange about the house in general. The mess, the shut-up feeling… What was going on with her?

Grudgingly, he turned back. He should at least let her

know he'd returned her purse. He'd placed it in a prominent spot, but there was still a good chance she'd never see it in the mess.

"Hello?" He rapped on the walls as he made his way up the stairs and down the hall toward the master suite.

Again, no answer.

The bedroom door stood ajar. "Holly?" He turned on the light, just in case she'd managed to sleep through the dogs barking, the bell-ringing and calling.

The bed was empty. Clothes were piled everywhere, and boxes of God-only-knew-what were stacked on the dresser, the nightstand, the cedar chest and the floor, making her room as difficult to navigate as the rest of the house. Next to a heap of what looked like clean laundry, he even found toys—a giant box of dolls and jump ropes and roller skates.

What was Holly doing with children's toys? And why was there so much paper, wadded into tight balls, strewn across the floor?

Curious, he picked one up and smoothed it out. Holly had written "Madison" over and over in red ink, scribbled it out until the paper tore, and started again. He ironed out another one to find more of the same. And another. And another. He was just wondering what the hell this was all about when Susan's dogs caught his eye. Growling playfully, they were fighting over some kind of leopard-print fabric.

Caleb's blood suddenly ran cold. That fabric looked like…

Bending closer, he took the article away, and saw that it was exactly what he'd feared—a halter top. Exactly like the one Susan had been wearing the night she disappeared. Exactly like the one Holly had said she'd never seen before.

Caleb's phone broke the silence. It was Detective Gibbons. "I don't know what's going on here," he said, "but I just dragged Margie White out of bed for nothing. She claims she never called Holly and doesn't know anything about a note from anyone named Tye."

CALEB'S HEART jackhammered against his chest as he dashed out of Holly's bedroom and pounded down the stairs. He took the halter top with him, but didn't bother locking the front door. Slamming it behind him, he jumped into his Mustang, popped the transmission into reverse and squealed out of the driveway.

He was at least thirty minutes away from Madison's, and Gibbons was even farther. Gibbons had just contacted the station. A car was on its way. But fear that they were already too late made it difficult for Caleb to breathe.

Holly says this woman won't talk to me tonight unless you're there....

She'd purposely drawn him away.

It's Madison, isn't it? You've fallen in love with her....

Madison...Madison...Madison, written all over those sheets in red ink...

Holly was crazy, obsessed.

He rounded the corner, then looked both ways before running a stoplight. "I'm coming, Maddy. I'm coming," he muttered, but he couldn't avoid the images dancing in his mind—images of finding Madison like Susan had looked.

Holly had seen pictures of the crime scene. She'd poured over every bit of evidence, right along with him. She could definitely have copied the Sandpoint Strangler, but now that he saw her as capable of doing what she'd done to Susan, bits and pieces of memories assaulted him one after the other, making him sick. He had a terrible

feeling that Holly had been lying and manipulating him
and everyone else for a long, long time, using the fact
that she was a woman to evoke sympathy instead of suspicion.

*He was driving a blue Ford truck with a white camper
shell....*

Holly had said that the first day they'd met. Now Caleb
wondered if she'd been lying from the start. All the papers
had mentioned the Ford. Cunning as she was, she could
even have tracked down Purcell in order to come up with
the partial plate number. She'd been the main reason the
investigation had focused on Purcell.

I'm afraid our killer is close, Gibbons had said. *Close
to the investigation. Close to us.*

Holly was close, all right. She'd stuck to Caleb like
glue since he'd first knocked on her door about Anna
Tyler's murder. Anna, the ninth victim, had been living
next door to her. Talk about opportunity.

*I think I was wrong about you. I don't think you're
going to find this killer. He's much too smart....*

Such calm, cool confidence wasn't the result of one
freak, accidental murder. Caleb thought of all the pretending Holly had done, all the setting up. A person didn't
turn into a cold-blooded killer overnight. She never
would've been able to pull it off if she'd felt even a mor-
sel of regret. She'd fed him misinformation, manipulated
his emotions, used him to stay one step ahead of the investigation the whole time. And he'd looked everywhere
but right in front of him.

"God!" he said, and smacked the steering wheel.

Only she'd finally slipped up. If she hadn't kept that
halter top...

Did you see anything like this in her apartment, Holly?

No, I've never seen a halter top like that before in my life. I'd definitely remember it....

Grabbing his cell phone, he tried Madison's house again. "Pick up," he pleaded. "Pick up."

But it just rang and rang and rang....

CHAPTER TWENTY-THREE

"SO HOW MANY TIMES have you slept with Caleb?" Holly asked.

Startled by the question, which had come out of nowhere after fifteen minutes of small talk, Madison set her cup in its saucer with a clumsy *clank*. She blinked several times because Holly was no longer in clear focus, and shook her head. "I'm…I'm not going to answer that," she said, but her speech seemed hopelessly slurred. She wanted to tell Holly to leave, but the words eluded her. Probably because the room was spinning, scrambling her brain.

"*Have* you slept with him?" Holly persisted. "Has he made you shudder in ecstasy like he does me?"

Madison grimaced. The image of Caleb with Holly, especially in the present tense, made her nauseous.

"What? Don't you like thinking about what I'm going to do with Caleb later, when I console him over your death?" Holly said.

Her *death?* Was that supposed to be some kind of joke? If Madison wasn't mistaken, Holly was smiling faintly. But her eyes seemed strangely blank. They didn't act like windows to her soul; they were more like mirrors, reflecting Madison's image back at her.

And Holly didn't make sense. Nothing did. Madison could see Holly's words shimmering in the air between them, floating in space as though she could reach out and capture them with her hands.

Summoning all her mental energy, she focused hard on the question, because it seemed important that she reply. "Why are you trying to upset me?" she asked, and tried to take another sip of tea, but the cup was too heavy to lift.

"I'm not trying to upset you. I don't care about you at all. I'm just saying that Caleb takes making love pretty seriously. Once he goes to bed with me again, things will be different."

"Diff… differ…" Giving up on the longer word, Madison went for the more important one. "How?"

"He doesn't sleep with just anyone, like some men I know. Sex has meaning to him. He makes you feel as though you're the only woman in the world. It's very erotic."

Madison knew how erotic it was. She felt flushed just remembering. Or maybe she was coming down with the flu. Certainly something was wrong.…

"Madison? Are you still with me?" Holly snapped her fingers in Madison's face.

Madison closed her eyes to stop the room from shifting. "Yes. Yes, I think so."

"Aren't you going to finish your tea?"

"No, I—" She used her hand to prop up her head, which suddenly seemed too large for her body. "I think it's time…for you…to go." There. She'd said it. It had taken supreme effort to remember all the words and string them together in the appropriate sequence. But she'd managed to say what needed to be said. She had to get back into bed, had to sleep until she felt better.

"To *go?*" Holly echoed. "That isn't very polite of you, now is it?"

Holly's laughter grew loud, then soft, then loud again. When her chair scraped the floor, Madison knew she'd gotten up, but she couldn't figure out what Holly was doing.

"Are…are you leaving?" she asked, having to take several breaths to get the whole sentence out.

"Of course not. At least not yet," Holly said. "I need to get my rope before I visit your daughter's room. But don't worry, it's just out in the car."

"Holly?" Madison felt disoriented, confused. Silence fell for an interminable time. Holly was gone, evidently. But then she was back and moving down the hall. Holly wanted to visit Brianna's room. Why? Holly was no friend….

At first Madison told herself it was all right; Brianna was at her father's. But then she heard Brianna's frightened voice calling, "Mommy? Mommy, who is this? Where are you?"

She lurched to her feet. "Brianna? Brianna, run, hide!" Madison used the table, the refrigerator, the wall to help her reach the hallway. She would have called out to her daughter again, warned her, but blackness was closing in on her fast, rolling toward her like a sudden storm.

BRIANNA SLIPPED UNDER her covers, away from the unfamiliar image of a stranger in her doorway. Her mother had said to run, to hide, but Brianna didn't know where to go. Her room had always been safe. What was happening? Why should she run?

She wanted to cry out for her mother again, but the blankets were thick and it was hard to breathe. She lay perfectly still, listening, trying to decide if Mommy was playing some kind of new game. But Mommy usually didn't trick her. And it was very late to be playing a game.

"Brianna? That's your name, isn't it? Come here, sweetheart." It was the stranger, a woman. Or maybe it was a monster with a woman's voice. That would be a very mean monster. Her mother *had* said to run and hide....

Brianna held her breath and squeezed her eyes shut as the she-monster patted the bed, searching for her among the blankets. She was drawing closer. Her hand nearly touched Brianna's arm, but Brianna slithered away and slipped into the crack between the bed and the wall, where she sometimes liked to stuff Elizabeth. It was their little hideout.

"Damn it! Come here." The monster grabbed her arm through the covers, and Brianna screamed. Jerking hard, she twisted free because of the blankets, and scooted under the bed. She stayed there on the floor in the corner, crying now because she knew this was no game. The she-monster was pulling away the bed, and there wasn't anywhere else to go.

BRIANNA'S SCREAM HELPED Madison force back the blackness, gave her the strength to keep fighting. She had to make her legs work, had to remain conscious long enough to be sure Brianna was all right.

Never had a hall seemed so long. Madison didn't think she was going to make it. She could hear her daughter whimpering, "Mommy...Mommy...Mommy..." and clung to that small voice.

"Shut up!" The woman. Angry. In Brianna's room.

Madison had to get there. And she had to do it *now*.

Now...now...now... The words inside her head echoed with urgency, but Madison could no longer walk. The world was spinning, tilting out of control. She was going to throw up. She wanted to sink to the floor and rest her head in her hands, let whatever lapped at her ankles suck her completely away.

Only she wouldn't give up until she knew her daughter was safe.

Falling to her knees, she crawled closer. She heard the squeak of the bed as someone pushed it around, heard low muttering, Brianna's crying....

Brianna, hang on. I'm coming. Mommy's coming.

Madison was breathless by the time she dragged herself into the doorway of Brianna's room. She could see a shape that had to be Holly down on her knees, trying to reach Brianna, who'd apparently crawled under the bed.

Gathering all her strength, Madison managed to find her feet again. *Get away from her. Get...away from...my daughter!* she shouted, but only inside her head. Then she launched herself at Holly.

Madison's movements weren't coordinated enough to do much damage, but she pushed Holly to the ground and their arms tangled. Holly tried to shove her off, to get up, but Madison used the weight of her body to pin her down. She could sense Holly's interest in Brianna, her desire to return to her daughter's bed.

Not at any cost, Madison told herself. Grabbing a fistful of Holly's long hair, she kept hold, focusing on only one thing, even as the darkness overcame her.

Don't let go...don't let go...don't ever *let go....*

She was just drifting off when she heard footsteps tramping down the hall and a male voice calling to her. Then Holly was wrenched away from her, screaming as she lost two fistfuls of hair, and the blackness became both silent and complete.

CALEB SAT NEXT TO Madison's hospital bed, a rectangle of pale yellow falling through the open door the only light. He was tense with worry despite the doctors' promises that she was going to be fine. Madison had been through so much. So much she didn't deserve. They all had.

Because of Holly.

Shaking his head, he swore under his breath, angry with himself for not realizing his ex-wife was insane. Gibbons had called to tell him he'd found a bunch of other things in Holly's attic—his own attic at one time—many of them belonging to women they'd long believed to be victims of Ellis Purcell.

He should have realized *somehow,* figured it out sooner. He'd known she had emotional problems. He'd just never imagined they were so severe, never imagined she was capable of doing what she'd done. He'd been too busy blaming himself for her problems because he couldn't love her the way she said she needed to be loved. Even after writing that book about the female serial killer Aileen Wuornos, he'd never considered that the Sandpoint Strangler could be a woman. What had happened was a classic example of looking beyond the mark. If a woman was going to kill, she typically used poison.

Holly *had* sedated her victims with drugs, he mused, which made it easy to sexually assault them with whatever she chose, whatever was handy at the time, and strangle them afterward. She was cunning, far more cunning than anyone he'd written about so far. She knew exactly how to make it look like a man's crime, how to cover her tracks.

Damn! He'd known there was some sort of link between the killer and Madison's family. He'd just never dreamed it was him....

Light crept through the window as the sun began to

rise. In the hallway, Caleb could hear movement, creaking wheels, the smooth voice of a woman over the intercom. Holding Madison's hand, he gently rubbed her delicate fingers. The effects of Rohypnol typically lasted for several hours, but according to blood tests run by the doctor when Madison first arrived, she hadn't ingested very much.

She'd been stirring for the past few minutes, so he wasn't surprised when she finally opened her eyes.

"Welcome back," he whispered, feeling relief pour through him.

"Caleb."

He squeezed her hand.

"Where's—" her eyebrows drew together "—where's Brianna?"

"She's with your mother." He pressed the back of her hand against his lips, enjoying the warm, reassuring feel of her skin. "They just left. Thanks to you, she's fine."

Tears trickled from the corners of Madison's eyes. "What happened? I—I can only remember Holly sitting at my kitchen table, drinking tea. And then...Brianna needing me."

Before he could answer, Caleb felt a presence at the door and turned to see that Johnny had returned from his trip to the cafeteria.

"She awake?" Johnny asked.

Caleb nodded.

"Johnny, you came back," Madison said.

"And it's a good thing," Caleb told her. "He arrived at your place before I could get there. He came before the police arrived. If it wasn't for him—" Caleb didn't want to think about what might have happened if Johnny hadn't shown up when he did.

"I didn't do much," Johnny said, chafing beneath the praise. "The cops came almost right away."

It would've taken Holly only a few minutes to add two more victims to her tally. But Caleb wasn't pointing out that grisly truth. He wanted to focus on the fact that everything was going to be okay. It was over. Holly was in jail. Even if she didn't get the death penalty for reason of insanity, she'd never set foot outside prison. She'd murdered nine women before he ever met her, another two while they were divorced the first time, and a woman in Spokane, as well as Susan, since he'd moved.

He felt terrible for her parents. After all they'd done to raise her and love her… And he felt even worse for her victims and their families.

"How long will I be here?" Madison asked, her eyes circling the room.

"Not long," Caleb assured her. "Holly slipped some date rape drug in your tea. The doctor wants to make sure you come out of it okay. Then he'll release you."

Her eyelashes fluttered to her cheeks. "Are you sure Brianna's okay?"

"I'm positive. But I want you to know something else before you fall asleep."

He watched her fight the weariness. "What's that?"

"You were right, Maddy. Your father never killed anyone."

Madison managed a fleeting smile, but he could tell she was struggling to remain conscious. "I'm so tired."

"Go ahead and sleep."

"Will you be here when I wake up?" With obvious effort, she raised her eyelids once again and met his gaze.

"Yes." He glanced at Johnny. "Tye and your mother are on their way. Your family will be waiting right here."

"My family," she said, and that faint smile returned as she drifted away.

THE NEXT TIME Madison woke, a nurse helped her dre[ss] and Caleb drove her home. There were so many question[s] she wanted to ask about what had happened, so many nuances she didn't understand. But she felt as though she was living inside a bubble, or swimming underwater, completely out of touch with her normal environment and those around her. She knew Brianna was safe, Johnny was back and Caleb was with her. The rest could wait.

When they reached her place, Caleb insisted on carrying her inside. Leaning against his chest, she turned her face into his neck, comforted by the scent of him and the ease with which he bore her weight. As he tucked her into bed, she knew everything was going to be fine. Everything was going to be *better*. A feeling of hope and excitement told her she had something special to be happy about. She couldn't remember why—until she started to dream.

She was five and her father was pushing her on a swing in the backyard…. She was ten and finding a candy bar her father had slipped into her drawer to surprise her…. She was sixteen and getting into her car to find her father had filled it with gas, even though her mother had sworn she'd have to buy her own….

Simple things, but Ellis Purcell had been a simple man. He'd never asked for thanks or a great deal of attention. Not in life, not in her dreams. He was just there. And he was the man she'd always known—not a perfect man, but an innocent man, and a father who'd loved her.

Then her dream changed. Her father was walking toward her across the grass and she was going to meet him. He looked just as he had before he died, with his barrel chest and thick shoulders, salt-and-pepper flattop, calm brown eyes. He didn't wave or speak. But a lump grew in her throat as she reached him and put her arms around his neck. "I love you, Daddy," she murmured, and woke to find that she was crying.

"TAMARA WANTS TO TALK to you, too," Justine said. "Tamara, pick up the other line."

Caleb tossed the towel he'd been using to dry dishes across the kitchen to land on Madison's counter, and rolled his eyes. He didn't want to repeat everything he'd just told his mother, but his family was understandably shocked at the truth about Holly. *He* was shocked. There were moments when he still couldn't believe that the woman he'd lived with on and off for seven years had tried to kill Madison and Brianna, had succeeded in killing Susan, and had taken the lives of at least twelve others.

"My God, Caleb. What's happened is so unreal," Tamara said. "Poor Susan."

Caleb thought of Susan lying in the morgue. He'd been completely convinced by Holly's grief that day they'd identified the body. Her sadness had been so palpable, so real. Obviously she hadn't been grieving for the reasons he'd assumed.

"I should've known somehow," he said, finally speaking his thoughts aloud.

"Caleb, quit beating yourself up," Tamara said. "How could you have known? You never saw any proof of it, did you?"

"That depends on what you mean by proof. She was off balance. We all knew that. She was manipulative, obsessive."

"So? You were trained since you were small to shield and protect women. Of course you wouldn't even think of suspecting her. Lots of people are off balance, manipulative, obsessive, even certifiably insane, yet *they* don't become serial killers."

"She loved you, Caleb," his mother added, on the extension. "Make no mistake about that. I've never seen a woman so head over heels."

"Maybe she ingratiated herself with you because you were working on the case," Tamara said, "but it quickly turned into more than that."

No kidding, Caleb thought. Almost as soon as he and Holly had started dating, he'd tried to break if off and hadn't been able to.

"You were particularly susceptible to a needy woman like her," his mother said. "You've always been drawn to people you think you can help, and you tried to help her. Only she was too broken. I feel almost as sorry for her as I do for the people whose lives she destroyed. What would make a woman do what she's done?"

"Who can say?" he said. "I know she blames other women for almost every problem she's had in her life—her adoption, her unhappy childhood, her sister always stealing the limelight. She's always hated other women, distrusted them. But I never guessed that what she felt would be enough to turn her into a homicidal maniac."

"Caleb, at what point does any man look at his wife and wonder if she could be a cold-blooded killer?" Tamara asked. "No one is all good or all bad. We don't walk around with signs posted on our foreheads that label us good or evil, because we're all a mix to one degree or another. And Holly was so adept at pretending to be something she wasn't. Which is why I never liked her."

Cognitively, Caleb knew women were capable of violence. He'd done that book on Aileen Wuornos. But he'd also written a few other books about women who'd killed for more immediate reasons—because they'd been severely abused or stood to benefit financially. A violent woman who killed for power and control had never been part of his personal reality. And when he researched the crimes he wrote about, he was always dealing with a perpetrator who was a stranger to him, someone *else's* father, brother, cousin.

"What's going to happen to her now?" his mother asked.

"She'll go to prison."

"You're sure?"

He thought of the halter top in Holly's bedroom, the DNA evidence that should be forthcoming, and the tire imprint. Gibbons had called to tell him it matched an old Chevy belonging to Holly's neighbor. Evidently, she'd borrowed his truck when she'd dumped Susan's body. "There's plenty of evidence, so much that she knows she doesn't have a chance of fighting. Gibbons told me she confessed."

Madison's telephone beeped. Caleb glanced at the caller ID to see that her own mother was calling.

"I've got to go," he said.

"Does this mean you won't be baby-sitting for me this weekend?" Tamara asked.

Caleb smiled because he could tell she was joking, trying to lighten the mood. "Do you think you can get Mac to stay off the phone long enough to make leaving with him worthwhile?"

"He's promised to give up his cell phone for the whole weekend. We had a big fight yesterday. I threatened to leave him, and he swears he's going to do better."

"I like the doing better part. If he'll leave his phone at home, I'll gladly baby-sit. See you later," he said, and switched to the other line.

"How's Madison doing?" Annette Purcell asked.

Caleb went to the window and gazed out at Johnny in the yard. Caleb had promised Madison's brother forty dollars if he'd mow the lawn and trim the bushes. Caleb thought it might help keep his mind off his crack addiction and, for the moment, it seemed to be working. "She's still sleeping, but the doctor checked her just before we left the hospital and said she'll be fine. How's Brianna?"

"She's happy here. We just bought a new coloring book and some washable markers. Later we're going to look at some pictures of Grandpa."

Caleb could hear the pride in Annette's voice when she spoke of Ellis. She'd loved him and stuck by him through the whole thing. Her loyalty was impressive. It was tragic that Ellis had killed himself before this day could come. In a way, he was another of Holly's victims.

"I'm sorry about all you've gone through, Annette," he said. "And for my role in it." When they'd spoken at the hospital earlier, he'd told her who he was. She'd been upset at first, but she was too relieved to have Ellis's name cleared to hold it against him.

She was silent for a few seconds. "Everything's going to be fine now."

"I really thought it was Ellis," he said. "I came back here determined to finally prove myself right, and I nearly got your daughter and granddaughter killed."

"But you *didn't* get them killed. Do you realize that if you hadn't come back, we still wouldn't know the truth? Holly would still be preying on innocent people."

Caleb smiled. There was definitely some solace in that. As much as he hated the fact that he hadn't been able to save her past victims, his returning to Seattle *had* saved any future ones. "Thanks."

"Have you heard from Danny?" she asked.

"No."

"I guess I should call him." She sighed. "No one likes him much, but he *is* Brianna's father and should probably know what's going on."

Caleb chuckled. "Do you think he really intends to take Madison back to court for custody?"

"He might. He threatens often enough. But after what Madison just did for that child, I don't think there's a court in the country that would take Brianna away."

"I hope not," he said.

"Well, I've made some chicken soup for the both of you. I just wanted to let you know I'm on my way over."

"I'm sure it'll be good for Madison to see you—and Brianna."

"She's been asking about her mother. But she's been asking about you, too," Annette said. "Seems she's growing quite attached to you."

"You might mention to her that—" Caleb was about to tell Annette he was going back to San Francisco right away, as originally planned. But Madison called to him just then and suddenly San Francisco seemed very far from home.

"Never mind." He wasn't sure he could gain Madison's confidence again. He'd betrayed her trust and unwittingly put her in danger. But he did have a lease on the cottage. And it didn't run out for another five months.

CHAPTER TWENTY-FOUR

MADISON STUDIED CALEB as he came to stand in the doorway of her room. He was wearing a gray polo, a pair of jeans and a Giants cap, and the dark shadow covering his jaw indicated he hadn't shaved this morning. But he looked as good as always—strong, masculine, confident.

"How do you feel?" he asked, the muscles of his arms flexing as he hooked his fingers on the doorjamb over his head.

"I'm still tired," she admitted.

"You want to sleep some more? Or are you ready to eat something?"

She wriggled into a sitting position. "I want to talk."

He cocked an eyebrow, as though he was a little worried about what she might say.

"I need to understand what happened," she explained.

Letting go of the jamb, he moved closer, and she slid over so he could sit on the edge of the bed. "It was Holly," he said simply.

"How could that be? How could she kill her own sister?"

"Obviously she's not right. I arrived here just after the police arrested her. She was hysterical by then, cursing at the top of her lungs and blaming me. I couldn't get any coherent answers out of her. But I called Detective Gibbons from the hospital later, and he filled me in on a few things."

Madison blinked in surprise. Caleb had gone to the hospital with her when he finally had the killer for whom he'd been searching so long? "What did the detective say?" she asked.

"The day before Susan died, Susan and Lance, the guy she was dating, got into an argument. Susan suspected Lance was seeing someone else, which was true. Anyway, she was upset and showed up at Holly's house unexpectedly, late at night. Holly was gone and the door was locked, but Susan managed to fit through a window Holly had forgotten to close. While she was there, she found some Roofies hidden in a Tylenol bottle in the kitchen cupboard."

"Roofies?"

"Date rape drug."

"How did she know what they were?"

"The tablets are marked, and they're not as scarce as you might think. Susan was a partier. I'm sure she'd run into them before. Only, finding them at Holly's worried her. She started poking around, wondering what else she'd find, and discovered a jacket that belonged to the woman who was just murdered in Spokane. The police had made a big deal about it because—"

"It had her initials embroidered on the front," Madison interrupted. "I heard someone talking about it at work."

"Exactly." He leaned across her, propping himself up on one hand. "Susan confronted Holly. Holly said she'd bought the jacket at a garage sale, but she knew Susan would eventually figure it out and possibly even tell someone. She felt she had to do something. So she called Susan and told her she wanted to meet her at the Pie in the Sky Pizzeria the following night."

"Why such a public place?"

"She needed a place where she could convince Tye to meet her."

"Tye?" Madison exclaimed in surprise.

"Don't worry. He was as manipulated as the rest of us. Holly just wanted your father's truck and Susan seen in the same vicinity. She wanted to throw the police off track. And she wanted me back. She knew how interested I was in the old case, and was afraid I might not take enough interest in Susan's disappearance if it didn't tie in somehow."

"But I don't understand why he'd agree to meet her," Madison said. "Weren't they total strangers?"

"She promised to provide Tye with information that would prove your father innocent of the killings."

"Why would he bring the truck?"

"Because that's what the note she sent him said to do, so she'd be able to recognize him. When he arrived, no one came forward to meet him, of course. But Susan nearly backed into him when she was trying to park, which caused an argument between them."

"Tye never said anything about a note or anything else," Madison said.

"Can you blame him? Susan wound up dead, and *he'd* met her the night she was murdered, even argued with her. I'm sure Tye smelled a setup, but he didn't have any idea who'd sent that note, and after what happened to your father, he had no confidence that the police would believe him if he came forward."

"So Holly didn't even go to the pizza place that night."

"No."

"Then how did she kill Susan?"

"She simply called Susan, told her she couldn't make it and asked her to come to the house instead."

A creeping sensation made Madison shiver and pull the

blankets higher. "And Susan went to her house, after finding that jacket?"

Caleb sighed. "Holly's an incredible liar. And Susan had all their years as sisters working against her. She probably couldn't fathom that Holly could really be what the evidence seemed to suggest."

"Like I could never believe it of my father," Madison murmured. "Despite all that evidence."

"Even if Susan thought Holly capable of violence, she probably never dreamed her sister would harm *her*. There wasn't any Rohypnol in her blood, though, which leads us to believe she was leery enough to refuse a drink from Holly. She also put up a damn good fight."

"Poor Susan."

Caleb fell silent for a moment, and Madison knew he was feeling the same sympathy. But then she remembered something else. "Wait, what about the contents of that box under the house?" she asked. "The rope and the locket and—"

"Holly put that stuff in the woodpile behind your father's house after we got married the second time."

"Why?"

"She told Gibbons she'd decided to stop killing. Somehow being with me satisfied that urge, though I certainly wouldn't presume to understand her crazy logic."

"So she dumped those…trophies at my *parents'* place?" Madison asked.

"It was the safest place to put it," he replied. "Everyone already suspected your father. She'd made sure she set him up as her scapegoat years earlier. She'd seen the news reports of Tatiana Harris's neighbor claiming to have seen your father's truck leaving Tatiana's house. At that point, she merely dug up an old phone book that had your father listed, and made a point of driving by the house to get part of his license plate number. She must've done it right before she murdered Anna Tyler, the woman living next door to her, knowing the police would come knocking to see if she'd heard or seen anything."

"But my dad found that box and thought Johnny had killed those women! He—" Madison couldn't finish without breaking into tears. After her dream, she felt so close to her father.

Caleb nodded sadly and took her hand. "I'm sorry about that."

Rage at Holly and what she'd done burned inside Madison. She wondered if she'd ever be able to get over that anger. She knew others would tell her she had to forgive, for her own sake, but she also knew it was going to take time. How did a woman forgive a person who'd caused her father to commit suicide? Who'd tried to murder her daughter? Who'd nearly ruined her life in so many ways?

"Then Tye found it and hid it in the basement," he added, "which is where you found it."

She wiped away her angry tears. "But where did it go from there?"

"Your mother took it," he said. "When you were talking to her on the phone that day, telling her you'd found something, she knew where you must have found it. And she wasn't about to let anything that further implicated your father come to light."

"How do you know?"

"She told me this morning that she's turning it all over to police."

"So she did take it," Madison mumbled. "She was that certain my father was innocent."

"And now everyone else is, too," Caleb said.

Madison let her breath go in a long sigh. "I can't believe the nightmare that started twelve years ago is finally over.''

''It's about time.''

She glanced at the phone. ''We need to tell Sharon.''

''Sharon?''

''Tye's wife. She thinks Johnny was involved with the murders. She left Tye because she believed he was protecting Johnny.''

''That's the only reason?''

Madison considered his question. ''Probably not the only reason. Tye has his problems. But I know she loves him. I think their marriage is worth saving.''

Madison could tell by the way he was looking at her that Caleb's mind was now moving in a different direction. ''What?''

''That makes me think of something else that's worth saving,'' he said.

Hearing the subtle change in his voice, Madison hesitated before responding. ''What's that?''

''I know you're angry about what I did, Maddy.'' He trailed his fingers up her arm, and she shivered at the unexpected pleasure. ''You have every right to be. But I'm thinking you and I had something good. If you can forgive me, I'd like to stick around for a while and see what happens.''

Madison's heart skipped a beat as her eyes met his. She knew what would happen. She'd get completely caught up in him. He was everything she'd ever wanted in a man. But she'd just been through the worst experience imaginable. How could she muster enough faith in the future to take such a risk right now? Especially with a man whose permanent address was three states away? If things went bad between them, he could simply pack up and leave. ''Caleb, I—''

He immediately concealed the hope in his face, letting Madison know he anticipated her rejection. "You what?"

Madison felt as though she had a bowling ball sitting on her chest as she opened her mouth to continue. But she *had* to continue. She'd promised herself that she'd protect Brianna, protect them both. "I have to think about my daughter," she said. "She's dealt with so many changes already. With Danny always waiting in the wings, hoping to take my daughter away from me, I can't take any chances right now. I'm sorry."

Caleb stood, putting some distance between them, and she saw him take a deep breath, as though her answer had stung him. "I understand," he said shortly, his eyes now hooded. Then her mother hollered from the front door and Brianna came running toward the bedroom. The next thing Madison knew, Caleb was gone.

IT DIDN'T TAKE MADISON long to recover. She slept for most of Monday and Tuesday, but by Wednesday, when the glass company arrived to repair the window Johnny had broken, she was ready to take care of herself and Brianna and let her mother go home. She and Annette got along quite well. They'd had to stick together to get through the past, after all. But Madison was ready to be alone, or as alone as she could be with Johnny living in her house. She hadn't seen Caleb for several days, and she was having a tough time pretending it didn't matter.

"Mommy, when did you draw these?" Brianna asked.

Madison turned from admiring the new window as the repairman drove away to see that her daughter had found the sketches she'd done of Caleb's chest and lips. "A few days ago," she said, feeling her cheeks grow warm because her mother had also turned to look. "I was just doodling," she added quickly.

"Can I hang them up?" Brianna asked.

Madison opened her mouth to say no. The last thing she needed was a daily reminder of the man she'd fallen so deeply in love with. But Annette took a closer look and spoke before Madison could.

"I think they should go in your mommy's room," she said. "They're excellent."

"Thanks." Madison started cutting onions for homemade chili and blinked back tears she couldn't blame entirely on her task.

"Where is Caleb, anyway?" Brianna asked, wearing a frown. "I want to see him."

Madison decided the truth was probably best. "I think he moved back to San Francisco." She didn't know for sure because she hadn't been able to make herself go over to the cottage to check. She was afraid she'd find it as empty as she suspected it was.

"Can we go there?" Brianna asked.

"No, it's too far away," Madison said.

Brianna wrinkled her nose. "Why would he want to live there?"

"That's where his home is."

"But we're *here*. When's he coming back?"

Never was too permanent for a child, so Madison mumbled something about "someday."

"Speaking of Caleb," her mother murmured. "He sent you a check to buy out his lease. And his mother called while you were in the shower."

Caleb had sent her a check? Madison didn't feel right about taking his money when she'd asked him to leave. But she was more immediately concerned with the fact that Caleb's mother had called. "What did she say?"

"She wanted to make sure you're all right."

Madison had a definite soft spot where Justine Trovato

was concerned, but she needed to avoid anyone who had anything to do with Caleb, or getting over him would only be more difficult. "Did you tell her I'm fine?"

"No. I told her you'd call her back." Her mother waved at a slip of paper tacked to the fridge. "Her number's right there. And I put Caleb's check in the side pocket of your purse."

"Mom, you know I'd rather not deal with—" Madison started, but Brianna was watching her closely, so she stopped.

"I know what you told me," her mother replied. "But if you're going to shut him out, you're going to do it on your own because I can't help thinking that some risks are worth taking. And Caleb is one of them."

THAT EVENING, Madison sat in her bedroom, staring at the slip of paper with Justine Trovato's number. Annette had finally left. Johnny had gone over to Tye's because Sharon and the kids were back and Tye was trying to make up to his wife by fixing a few things around the house; he'd asked his brother to help. Brianna was in bed. So Madison was alone at last. She had the time and the opportunity to return Caleb's mother's call. But she knew talking to Justine would make her miss Caleb that much more....

After another few minutes, she took a deep breath and picked up the phone. She couldn't be so rude as not to call.

"Hello?"

"Mrs. Trovato?"

"No, it's Tamara."

"Oh, Tamara, I'm sorry I didn't recognize your voice. This is Madison."

"Madison, we've been worried about you. How are you?"

"Better."

"I'm glad to hear it. You must be tremendously relieved that Holly is now behind bars."

"I am." There was an awkward pause. "I'm just returning your mother's call."

"Wonderful. Hang on a second, I'll get Caleb."

"Wait! I said...what...why—" Madison sputtered.

"And you'd better make this count," Tamara added in a low voice. "He flies out in the morning."

"Tamara—"

"Hello?"

Madison's whole body tingled at the sound of Caleb's voice. Gripping the phone much too tightly, she licked suddenly dry lips and closed her eyes, feeling an overwhelming desire to see him again. "Caleb?"

"Maddy?"

She could hear his surprise, wondered what she was going to do now. Tell him that she'd sacrifice her good judgment—anything—to be with him again? How could she, after she'd already thought it through so many times and made her decision? "I, um, just called to tell you that I can't accept your buy-out check. A lessor has to buy out a lease only when he breaks the agreement. And you didn't do that. I'm letting you out of your lease," she said, proud of herself for thinking of an excuse so fast.

"I want you to have the money," he said. "It'll help you get by until you find another tenant."

"But—"

Brianna opened her door and poked her head inside the room. "Mommy?"

Madison jumped as though she'd been caught doing

something wrong. "What are you doing out of bed, Brianna?"

"I'm thirsty. Can I have a drink?"

"Of course." Madison decided she should end the call so she could take care of her daughter. They really had nothing more to discuss. But she couldn't bring herself to say goodbye. "Caleb, can you hang on for—"

"That's *Caleb?*" Brianna squealed, jumping up and down. "When's he coming home? Can I talk to him? I *knew* he'd call!"

Madison hesitated for a moment, wondering what to do now. "Brianna wants to say hello," she finally said.

"Put her on."

Madison handed her daughter the phone and Brianna eagerly clutched it to her ear. "Caleb, where did you go?…Why didn't you say goodbye to me?…When are you coming back?…"

Madison was supposed to be getting Brianna a glass of juice, but she was too caught up in what she was seeing and hearing, especially when Brianna's shoulders began to slump and her questions slowed. "But who's going to mow the grass?… Johnny doesn't even know what a praying mantis is…I don't want you to go to San Francisco…What about *me?* Elizabeth will miss you.…"

Madison's heart ached as she watched and listened. Without even telling Caleb goodbye, her daughter gave her back the phone and started dragging Elizabeth out of the room. Her head was down, her request for a drink completely forgotten.

Brianna's dejection hit Madison hard. She was so busy trying to protect Brianna that she was denying her connection with someone she already cared about. She was denying herself, as well. Was she wrong? What if Caleb turned out to be an important part of their lives? Didn't she owe it to herself, to Brianna, to give him that chance?

Her pulse racing, Madison put the phone to her ear again. "Caleb?"

"Yes?"

She took a deep breath. "If I asked you to, would you come back?"

CALEB NEARLY DROPPED the phone. Shooting a glance at Tamara, who was hovering nearby, pacing and rubbing her hands, he turned his back on his sister, wishing for a moment of privacy. "Maddy, if I hadn't lied to you so I could move in, Holly would never have come after you and Brianna. I can't tell you how responsible I feel for that, how sorry I am."

"Caleb, getting to know you was worth everything that happened," she said. "My mother is happier than I've seen her in years, and Johnny and Tye have something of a fresh start—all because of this. I feel it's brought us closer as a family. Besides, Brianna is fine." She paused. "Except that she's crying in her room right now because she believes you're leaving town."

Caleb tensed. "Is she the only one who cares that I'm leaving?"

"God, you never make things easy for me, do you?"

He chuckled softly. "Say it, Maddy. Say it or I won't stay."

There was a long silence, then she said, "I'm in love with you, Caleb."

The words were almost a whisper, but they carried a tidal wave of emotion. Caleb let it wash over him, filling him with relief. He'd been trying to come to grips with the fact that he might never see her again, but he hadn't been able to do it. He'd thought of nothing but Madison and what she and Brianna had come to mean to him. Even if he'd been capable of forgetting her, his family wouldn't have let him. They talked of her constantly, encouraging him to stay in contact with her, encouraging him to wait until she was ready and then try again.

He grinned at Tamara, who was watching him with a self-satisfied smile. "I suppose I could work on Whidbey Island just as easily as in San Francisco," he said. "But you'd have to make a few concessions."

"Oh, yeah?" Her voice was slightly skeptical, as though she knew he was going to milk her confession for all it was worth. "What concessions would those be?"

Tamara squeezed his arm in support, then rushed to the door of the kitchen to call his mother.

"The cottage is a little drafty," he complained, sitting at the small telephone desk in his mother's kitchen.

"It is?" Madison replied.

He put his feet up. "Terribly."

"Which means…"

Justine Trovato hurried into the room, smiling. She was trailed by his father, who looked slightly amused, which was saying a lot for his father. Together with Tamara, they stood waiting expectantly, silently cheering for him. "I think I'd be much more comfortable living at your place," he said.

"With me?"

"Not without marrying her first, you're not," his mother said, obviously appalled, but he shook his head.

"Of course with you," he replied to Madison.

There was another slight hesitation on Madison's part. "What about Brianna?"

"What about her?" he said into the phone. "I love Brianna."

"And she loves you. But—"

"But what?" Folding his arms, Caleb pictured Madison's pretty face, her brow creased in consternation, and felt his grin broaden. She was backing right into his trap.

"We can't live together," Madison said. "Not unless...unless we get married."

"So you're proposing to me?" he said.

"No!"

He laughed at the embarrassment in her voice. "What if I was proposing to you? Would you say yes?"

His mother released a big sigh and nodded her approval. But he could hear Madison's quick intake of breath and thought maybe he was pushing too hard, too fast.

"You want to get *married?*" she said. "Already?"

"Does that frighten you?"

"It terrifies me. We haven't known each other very long."

"I'd be good to you, Maddy. I promise you that. I'd do my best to make you happy, and I'd love you for the rest of my life," he said, marveling at the fact that he wasn't embarrassed about making such promises despite having his entire family as an audience.

"He's not *too* hard to live with," Tamara chimed in.

Caleb knew Madison had heard her when she laughed. "But this is...this is so sudden," she said. "A moment ago, I thought I was never going to see you again."

"I don't think I could have left it at that," Caleb admitted. "I was hoping you'd call me, but I probably would've broken down and called you as soon as I reached San Francisco."

"I don't know what to say."

"Just say yes," he told her.

"We'll make it a lovely wedding," his mother said.

Madison paused for a second, a heartbeat, but it was

the longest moment of Caleb's life. "Yes," she said at last. "And tell your family yes, too.

"We're getting married," he announced, and they all started hugging each other. His mother began to cry and his father clapped him on the back.

"Now will you come home?" Madison asked.

He gave Tamara a high five. "My bags are already packed."

EPILOGUE

Eight months later...

THE SUN FELT SO WARM on Madison's face that she could scarcely keep her eyes open. The fact that she'd just finished another of Justine's big meals didn't help. They were all moving a little more slowly, even Mac, who had his arm around his wife and was chewing on a blade of grass not far from her and Caleb. He got up every few minutes to answer his cell phone, but overall he seemed to be giving Tamara more attention, which made Madison even happier.

"What did you say?" she murmured to Caleb, feeling his fingers comb gently through her hair while she lay in his lap, completely content just to be near him.

"I said Brianna needs a dog, don't you think?"

"A dog?" She turned to look across the yard, where Brianna was kicking a ball with Jacob and Joey. "She's only seven."

"So?" he said.

"A dog's a big responsibility. That's why we gave Susan's dogs to Tye, remember?"

"We gave Susan's dogs to Tye because he relates better to animals than he does people. And I didn't want to face those dogs every day of my life and think of Susan," he said.

Madison continued to watch the kids play. "But Brianna doesn't need a dog right now. She has a half sister at her father's house, and I'm due in three months, so she'll have another sibling. Do we have to do everything all at once?"

Caleb put a protective hand on her extended abdomen, which he did often. "The siblings are good, but I think she needs a pet, too."

"She has pets at Danny's."

Caleb grimaced. "She has fish at Danny's because Danny and Leslie are so afraid anything else will shed hair on their expensive furniture or stain their Persian rugs. And she only gets to see her fish every other weekend."

"But she's never mentioned wanting a dog to me," Madison pointed out.

Caleb called Brianna over. "Honey, you want a dog, right? You're lonely without a dog."

"I'm what?" Brianna said.

"Lonely."

"Oh, we're doing this now?" She wiped the smile off her face and managed a pleading expression, and it was all Madison could do not to roll her eyes.

"Mommy, I really, really, *really* want a dog. *Please...*"

"See?" Caleb said smugly.

Madison decided to play along. "Will you help take care of a dog?"

"I will," she said. "I'll give him food and water and brush his fur and—" she glanced at Caleb and lowered her voice to a whisper "—what else was I supposed to say, Daddy?"

Madison dropped the charade and cocked an eyebrow at her husband, while Tamara hooted with laughter. "You're busted, buddy," his sister said.

"What?" He spread out his hands, trying to play innocent.

"*Brianna* wants a dog?" Madison said.

"Okay, so she's not the *only* one who wants a dog."

"Our yard isn't equipped for a dog."

A devilish glint entered Caleb's eyes. "Then maybe it's time to move. Our family's outgrowing your little house, anyway. And once we have another baby and another, we're going to need the space."

"Caleb, I've told you, I'm not having six kids," Madison said. "I don't want to give up my business. I still believe I can get it turned around."

He leaned back on his palms. "You don't have to give up anything. I'll help you with the kids. I work from home, remember?"

She rolled onto her side and gazed up at him, admiring his sensual mouth. "You're in the middle of writing Holly's story. Granted, you're closer to this project than any in the past, but—"

"That's what'll make it so riveting."

"—half the time you don't even answer when we speak to you."

"I don't answer? Really?" He seemed genuinely surprised.

"What's going on out here?" Justine said, coming out of the house with Logan.

"Caleb is trying to talk Madison into a new house *and* a dog," Tamara said.

"Oh, is that all?" Justine teased. She took husband's hand and sobered as she looked at Madison. "What would Johnny do if you moved?"

"I think he'd be okay," Madison said. "Every day's a struggle for him, of course. But he's been clean and sober for almost six months, which is really saying something.

And he works with Tye, so Tye can help us keep an eye on him. It's probably time he lived on his own, anyway.''

"So what do you say?'' Caleb said, obviously not willing to let his petition for a dog go unanswered.

Madison gazed up at him, pictured his beautiful body the way she'd seen him when they'd showered together this morning, and grinned. She loved him so much. How could she say no? ''What kind of dog do you want?''

*   *   *   *   *

*Turn the page to read the first chapter of
Brenda Novak's next book, A FAMILY OF
HER OWN, published by Harlequin
Superromance and available in April 2004.*

PROLOGUE

BOOKER ROBINSON SAT in his truck at ten o'clock on a warm Thursday night, staring at the small rental house where Katie Rogers lived and telling himself he was crazy to even be here. He wasn't the type to ask for anything. He'd made it a habit never to need anyone. He'd learned as a child that showing vulnerability was never rewarded.

But he'd heard that Katie and Andy Wolfe were almost engaged, that she was going to leave town with Andy. And he knew if she did, she'd be making a big mistake. Andy wouldn't take care of her the way he would. Andy wouldn't love her as he did. Andy loved only himself.

Taking a deep breath, Booker cut the engine, got out and walked up the drive. He'd hoped Katie would come back to him on her own. For a few short weeks, they'd shared something that was heady, powerful and very mutual. He could tell that she'd felt everything he did. But her family and most of her friends had convinced her she'd be ruining her life to take a risk on someone like him, a man with a criminal past and not much of a future. And now she was running scared and on the verge of marrying someone else.

She might end up marrying Andy, Booker told himself, but she wasn't going to do it without at least knowing how he felt about her. He lived with enough regrets already.

It took several minutes for someone to answer his

knock. When the door finally opened, Katie's best friend, Wanda, peered out at him.

"Oh…uh…hi, Booker."

He could tell she was nervous to see him, so he didn't bother with small talk. Wanda was one of the people telling Katie that he'd never amount to anything. "Is she home?" he asked, not bothering to specify Katie by name because they both knew who "she" was.

"Um…I don't think—"

He broke in before she could finish. "I saw her pull into the garage from the end of the street."

"Right." She chuckled self-consciously. "I wasn't sure if she actually came in or not, but she must have if you saw her. Just a minute."

While he waited, Booker's pulse raced. He'd never laid open his heart to a woman before, wasn't sure where to start now. He hadn't let himself love many people.

You're a fool for even trying, you know that, don't you? Who are you to say you're any better than Andy? At least Andy comes from a good family and has a college degree.… What do you have to offer?

He almost turned to leave, but Katie finally appeared.

"Booker?" She sounded surprised to see him. He'd known she would be. He hadn't contacted her since they'd had that big argument several weeks ago—when she'd told him it was over between them, that she wanted to start seeing Andy, and he'd thought he could let her go.

He took a deep breath. "Can we talk?"

"I don't think so," she replied. "There's really nothing to say."

"You're making a mistake, Katie."

"You don't know that."

Maybe he didn't know it. But he *felt* it. Letting her marry anyone else was a mistake. It had taken him nearly thirty years to fall in love, but the hell of living without Katie for the past few weeks had left little doubt in his mind that he was there now. "What we had was good."

"I—I can't argue with that, but—" she tucked her long blond hair behind her ears in a nervous gesture and glanced over her shoulder "—I'm sorry. I've already made up my mind."

The expression in her large blue eyes looked tortured. He could tell that she was torn between what she thought and felt and what others were telling her. He knew she was afraid of what he'd once been. He wouldn't want a daughter of his to marry an ex-con, either. But he couldn't change his past. He could only change his future.... .

"Katie..." Reaching out, he ran a finger down her jaw. The contact made him yearn to hold her, and she seemed to feel something similar. She closed her eyes and pressed her cheek into the palm of his hand as though she was dying for his touch. "You still care about me," he murmured. "I can tell. Come back to me."

Tears glittered in her eyelashes, reflecting the porch light. "No," she said, pushing his hand away. "Don't confuse me. Andy says I'll feel differently after a few months away. We're going to get married, have a family—"

"But you don't love Andy," Booker said. "I can't even see you with that self-serving Yuppie."

"I'm trying to make a good decision for my future, and yours, too. I've got to go."

"Marry me, Katie," he said suddenly, passionately. "I know I can make you happy."

Her eyes widened, and two tears slipped down her cheeks. "Booker, I can't. You're not ready to be weighed down by a wife and family. You love your freedom too much. I knew that when we first started seeing each other.''

"Katie, maybe it wouldn't have come to this quite so soon if things had worked out another way, but—''

"I'm sorry, Booker. I've got to go,'' she said. Then the door closed in his face. When she drove the bolt home, he knew he'd lost her.

CHAPTER ONE

Two years later

KATIE ROGERS SMELLED smoke coming from the engine of her car.

"Come on, you can make it," she muttered, her fingers tightening on the steering wheel of the old Cadillac, which was pretty much the most valuable possession she had left. She'd purchased the vehicle three days ago after posting a Garage Sale sign near her apartment and selling off the last of her and Andy's furniture. Then she'd packed up what remained of her belongings and headed out of San Francisco before he could come home and beg her to give him one more chance. She couldn't stay with Andy Wolfe anymore. Not with a child on the way. Not when she was the only one who was finally growing up.

The smell of smoke became more pronounced. Katie wrinkled her nose and remembered, with longing, the nice new truck she'd owned when she left Dundee. She and Andy had used that truck to move to San Francisco. But once they'd arrived, Andy had talked her into selling it for the security deposit on a better apartment. "We don't want to stay in a dump," he'd said. "And we don't need a car. We're in the city now, babe. It's easy to get around. As soon as I start making the big bucks we can get another set of wheels...."

As soon as he started making the big bucks... Ha! Katie would've been satisfied had he earned just a *few* bucks. Or at least used some caution when he threw *her* money around.

Because they couldn't afford parking, she'd finally agreed to sell the truck. But it was a decision she'd long since regretted. If she'd had a reliable vehicle, maybe she would've left sooner.

The Welcome to Dundee, Home Of The Annual Bad-To-The-Bone Rodeo, Population 1,438 sign she'd seen thousands of times in her youth appeared in her headlights. Breathing a huge sigh of relief, Katie began to relax. She was going to make it home safely. After traveling 640 miles, she was only another ten or so from her parents' house—

Suddenly, the Cadillac gave a loud *chung,* and the lights on the dashboard blinked out. Katie frantically pumped the gas pedal, hoping to get a little farther, but it didn't do any good. The car slowed, trailing smoke.

"No!" Katie shifted the transmission into neutral so she could crank the starter. Returning to Dundee in her current situation was pathetic enough. She didn't want anyone she knew to see her stranded on the side of the road.

But the car wouldn't start. She was pretty sure it was dead for good.

Her tires crunched on the snow-covered shoulder as she managed to pull over without the power steering that had gone out when everything else did. Then she sat, listening to the hissing of the engine and watching smoke billow out from under her hood. What now? She couldn't walk the rest of the way to her folks' house. The doctor didn't want her on her feet. Just two weeks ago, she'd started experiencing premature labor pains and he'd told her she had to take it easy.

Sitting inside a dead car wasn't getting her anywhere. And for all she knew, the engine was on fire and the car would explode, the way so many seemed to do on television.

Wrestling her luggage out of the back seat, she dragged it a safe distance. Then she sat on the bigger suitcase and shivered in the cold night air as she watched several cars pass. She didn't have the heart to stand or make herself noticed. She'd hit rock bottom. Life had finally gotten as bad as it could be.

And then it started to rain.

BOOKER T. ROBINSON switched on his windshield wipers as he descended into Dundee. It was a chilly Monday night, cool enough that he expected the rain to turn into snow before morning. Dundee typically saw a lot more snow in February. But Booker didn't mind. He was comfortable living in the farmhouse he'd inherited from Grandma Hatfield. And any kind of extreme weather was good for business.

Sticking one of the toothpicks from his ashtray into his mouth, a habit he'd developed when he quit smoking over a year ago, he calculated how much longer it would be before he had Lionel Richman paid off.

Another six months, he decided. Then he'd own Lionel & Sons Auto Repair free and clear and could buy the lot next door and expand. Maybe he'd even give the business his name. He'd kept Lionel & Sons because it had been that way for fifty years and the people of Dundee didn't like change any more than they'd liked him when he first moved to town. But since he'd taken over, he'd developed a solid reputation for knowing cars and—

The sight of an old banged-up sedan, parked mostly off the highway up ahead, piqued Booker's curiosity enough to make him brake. He had the only tow truck in the area, which was currently at his shop. But he hadn't received a distress call on his radio. Yet.

Where was the driver? He couldn't see anyone inside or around the vehicle. Whoever owned the Cadillac had probably already headed into town, looking for help. But judging by the smoke pouring out from beneath the hood, he doubted the car had been sitting too long.

Chewing thoughtfully on his toothpick, he pulled up behind the stranded vehicle, left his lights on so he could see and got out. If the car was unlocked and he could get beneath the hood, it would probably be smart to take a look while he was here. Chances were the car had a busted hose—a problem he could solve easily without going to the trouble of towing the Cadillac to his shop in the middle of town.

The moment he stepped out of his truck, however, he realized he wasn't as alone as he'd thought. A woman peered at him from around the front of the car. She was wearing a man-size sweatshirt with a hood that shielded her face from the rain, a pair of faded jeans with bottoms a little wider than he typically saw in these parts and—his eyes darted back to her feet—*sandals? In February?*

The car had California plates. Leave it to someone from sunny California to run around in sandals all winter.

He shrugged on his leather jacket as he walked over, stopping well short of her. He didn't want to frighten her. He only wanted to get her car going so he'd be able to meet Rebecca and Josh for a drink at the Honky Tonk and not be interrupted later. "Having trouble?" he asked above the sound of the wind.

"No." She pulled the hood of her sweatshirt farther forward. "Everything's fine."

The wind whipped her words away and made it difficult for him to hear. He took the toothpick out of his mouth and stepped closer. "Did you say everything's fine?"

She moved back a distance equal to his advance. "Yes. You can go on your way."

Booker glanced at the smoke rising from her car. He might've figured it was just steam coming off a warm engine on a cold night. Except steam didn't explain the luggage or why this woman was standing on the side of the road in a sweatshirt so wet it dripped along the hem. And it sure as hell didn't explain the distinctive odor of a burned-up engine.

"Everything doesn't *smell* fine," he said.

"I'm just letting the engine cool."

The engine was going to need a lot more than cooling. He could tell that without even looking at it. But Booker didn't say so because this time when she'd spoken, something about her voice had sparked a flicker of recognition.

The California license plate flashed through his mind. He didn't know anyone from California, except—God, it couldn't be....

"Katie?" he said, trying to make out her face despite the shadow of her hood.

He saw her shoulders droop. "It's me," she said. "Go ahead and gloat."

Booker didn't respond right away. He didn't know what to say. Or how to feel. But gloating was pretty far down his list. Mostly he wanted to leave so he wouldn't have to see her again. Only, he couldn't abandon her, or any woman, on the side of the road. Especially in this rain. "You need a lift?"

She hesitated briefly. Then her chin came up. "No, that's okay. My dad's good with cars. He'll help me."

"Does he know you're out here?"

A slight hesitation, then, "Yeah, he's expecting me. When I don't show up, he'll realize I had car trouble."

Booker put the toothpick back in his mouth. Part of him suspected she was lying. The other part, the stronger part, felt immediate relief that she was somebody else's problem. "I'll take off, then. Your dad can call me if he has any questions."

He strode briskly to his truck, but she followed him before he could make good his escape.

With a sigh, he rolled down his window. "Is there something else?"

"Actually, I got here a little earlier than I planned and—" she rubbed her arms, shivering "—well, it's possible that my parents won't miss me for a while. I think I'd be better off taking that ride you offered, if you don't mind."

Everything's fine.... She'd said so when he first pulled up. Why couldn't he have taken her at her word and let her remain anonymous?

The pain and resentment he'd felt two years ago, when she'd closed the door in his face, threatened to consume him again. But considering the circumstances, he had to help her. What choice did he have?

"What's with the sandals?" he asked.

Hugging herself for warmth, she stared down at her soaked feet. "I bought them in San Francisco. They're one of a kind, designed especially for me."

They were still only sandals, and it was raining, for Pete's sake. She must have realized that he didn't understand the full significance of what she'd just said because she added, "The day Andy and I bought these was the best day of the past two years. And the only day that turned out anything like I'd planned.''

So they were a symbol of her lost illusions. Well, thanks to her, Booker had a few lost illusions of his own. Not that he'd possessed many to begin with. His parents had taken care of that early on. "Hop in," he said. "I'll get your luggage."

KATIE SAT WITHOUT talking, listening to the hum of the heater and the beat of the windshield wipers as Booker drove into town. Of all the people in Dundee, he was the last person she'd wanted to see. So, of course, he'd been the one to come along. It was that kind of day—no, *year*.

Clasping her hands in her lap, Katie stared glumly out at the familiar buildings they passed. The Honky Tonk, where she used to hang out on the weekends. The library, where her friend Delaney, who was now married to Conner Armstrong, used to work. Finley's Grocery, where Katie had once knocked over a whole display of Campbell's Soup cans while trying to get a better look at Mike Hill, a boy she'd had a crush on all the time she was growing up.

"You warm enough?" Booker asked.

She nodded even though she was still chilled, and he turned down the heat.

"So," she said, hoping to ease the tension between them, "how've things been since I went away?"

She could see the scar on his face that ran from his eye to his chin—something he'd obtained in a knife fight, he once told her—and the tattoo on his right bicep. It moved as his hands clenched the steering wheel more tightly. But he didn't respond.

"Booker?"

"Don't pretend we're friends, Katie," he said shortly.

"Why?"

"Because we're not."

"Oh." Booker's list of friends had always been short. He regarded everyone, except maybe Rebecca Wells— Rebecca *Hill* since she'd married Josh—with a certain amount of distrust. So Katie knew that, with the history between them, she shouldn't be surprised. She'd lost his good opinion along with everything else. If she'd ever really possessed it. Even when they were spending so much time together before she left, she'd never felt completely confident that he cared about her. He'd driven her around on his Harley and shown her one heck of a good time. But he was somewhat remote, and she'd always approached their relationship with a sense of inevitability, believing that it wouldn't, *couldn't,* last. Then he'd shown up at her door and *proposed!* She didn't know how to explain it, except that his widowed grandmother, Hatty, had just died. He and Hatty had been so close throughout her final years that Katie could only suppose his sudden marriage proposal was triggered by his loss.

Now he was obviously holding a grudge that she'd turned him down at a difficult time, or been the one to break things off between them. "I make a left at 500 South?" he asked after several minutes.

She pulled her attention away from the rain beading on the windshield. "What?"

"Your parents still live in the same place, don't they?"

Last she'd heard they did. But she didn't *know.* She hadn't talked to them since a year ago Christmas when they'd told her not to call again. "They've been on Las siter nearly thirty years," she said, infusing her voice with as much confidence as she could muster. "Knowing them they'll be there another thirty."

"Seems I heard your father say something about build

ing a cabin a few miles outside of town.'' He shifted his gaze from the road to study her. "They gave up on that?"

Apprehension clawed at Katie's insides. Her folks had the same telephone number. She'd definitely heard her mother answer when she used the pay phone yesterday. She'd wanted to tell her family that she was on her way home. Only, she'd lost her nerve at the last minute and hung up.

"Yeah." Having the same number didn't necessarily mean they hadn't moved within a certain geographic area, but Katie was sticking with the gamble. Doing anything else would reveal a rift she preferred to keep private. "They like living so close to their bakery. That bakery is their life," she added.

The Arctic Flyer came up on the right, evoking bittersweet memories. Katie had worked there the summer of her junior year, because she'd wanted to try something besides her parents' bakery, and she'd broken the ice cream machine her very first week. Harvey, the owner, had complained every day about the money she was costing him, until the part to repair the darn thing finally arrived.

Booker turned up the radio, and she glanced at him surreptitiously. Her memories of him didn't go back nearly as far as her Arctic Flyer days. She'd heard talk of him visiting for several months when he was about fifteen; he'd raised enough hell that the entire town still regarded him as trouble. Later he'd mentioned a few things about that visit himself, like stealing Eugene Humphries's truck and driving it into the river. But Katie was only nine years old then. She hadn't met him until years later when he moved in with Hatty.

"Aren't you curious to know what I'm doing back?" she asked, turning to conversation to stanch the memories.

He looked pointedly at her two suitcases, which he'd wedged into the back seat of his extended cab. "I think that's pretty obvious."

"Actually, it's probably not what you think. San Francisco was fabulous, for the most part," she said. Which was true—if she confined her comments to the city itself.

When he made no reply, she plunged ahead. "It's just that I'm a country girl at heart, you know? I decided that San Francisco is a great place to visit, but no where I want to stay."

He slung one arm over the steering wheel, and she supposed it was his rebel attitude that made it possible for him to look both bored and on edge at the same time.

"Don't you have *anything* to say?" she asked.

His toothpick moved as he chewed on it. "Where's Andy?"

"He—" she scrambled for something to crack Booker' reserve "—he's laid up and couldn't come along."

Booker arched an eyebrow. "Laid up?"

"He was hit by a cable car."

She'd hoped to elicit a smile, but the line of Booker' lips remained as grim as ever. Slowly, he moved th toothpick to the other side of his mouth. "You mean lif in San Francisco wasn't the nirvana you were lookin, for."

She resisted the urge to squirm in her seat. "We a make mistakes," she muttered as he pulled up in front c her parents' white-brick rambler.

He easily yanked the suitcases she could barely lift o of his truck, carried them to the door and punched th doorbell. Then he pivoted and headed back, leaving he on the doorstep without so much as a goodbye or a goo luck.

"Haven't you ever done anything you regret?" sh

called after him. She knew he'd done plenty of outrageous things; she just didn't know if he regretted any of them. He'd certainly never acted as though he felt any remorse.

But she didn't listen for a reply. The door to her parents' home opened almost immediately, and her stomach knotted at seeing her mother's face for the first time in two years.

"Hi, Mom," she said, praying that Tami Rogers would be more forgiving than Booker.

Her mother's expression didn't look promising. And when Tami glanced at Booker and his truck, her features became even more pinched. "What are you doing here?"

Katie peeked over her shoulder at Booker, too, wishing him away, well out of earshot. "I…" The pain inside her suddenly swelled. She couldn't even remember, let alone recite, the eloquent apology she'd prepared on the way from San Francisco. All she wanted was for her mother to reach out and hug her. *Please…*

Her mouth like cotton, she searched for the right words. "I…I need to come home, Mom…just for a little bit," she added because she thought it might make a difference if her mother understood she didn't expect any long-term help. Just a place to stay and some kind of welcome until she could find a job that wouldn't require her to be on her feet.

"Oh, *now* you want to come home," her mother replied.

"I know you're angry—"

"Andy called here looking for you," she interrupted.

"He did?"

"He told us you never got married." She folded her arms and leaned against the lintel. "Is that true?"

"Yes, but only because—"

"He also said you're five months pregnant."

Instinctively, Katie's hand went to her abdomen. She hadn't gained much weight yet, so the pregnancy wasn't apparent, especially in Andy's baggy sweatshirt. "It—it wasn't something I planned. But once it happened I thought that maybe Andy would finally see—"

Her mother held up a hand to stop her. "I don't want to hear it. I raised you better than this, Katie Lynne Rogers. You used to be a good girl, the sweetest there was."

Katie tried not to blanch as her mother's rejection lashed a part of her that was already raw. "I'm still the same person, Mom."

"No, you're not the girl I knew."

Katie didn't know how to combat that statement, so she switched topics. "Andy had no right to tell you anything. He's the one who—"

"He's a bum, just like we said. Right?"

Andy was handsome and debonair. He certainly looked the part of a stand-up guy. But he was full of empty promises and false apologies. She couldn't refute that, so she nodded.

"We tried to tell you," Tami went on. "But you wouldn't listen. Now that you've made your bed, I guess you can sleep in it."

The door closed with a decisive *click*.

Katie blinked at the solid panel, feeling numb, incredulous. Home was the place that *had* to take you in, right? She'd hung on to that thought for miles and miles. She didn't have anywhere else to go. She'd spent nearly every dime she possessed reaching Dundee.

She thought of the last twenty bucks in her wallet and knew it would never be enough to get a room. She couldn't even walk back to town, where there was a motel, without risking the baby.

Slowly it dawned on her that she hadn't heard Booke

pull away from the curb. Which meant he'd probably heard the whole thing.

Embarrassment, so powerful it hurt, swept through her as she turned. Sure enough, he was standing at the end of the walk, leaning against his truck with the rain dripping off him, staring at her with those shiny black eyes of his.

His learning about the baby this way, seeing what Andy had reduced her to—it was more humiliating than Katie had ever imagined. She'd broken off her relationship with Booker because she wanted more than what he could give her. And here she was....

A lump formed in her throat and her eyes began to burn. But she had a few shreds of pride left.

Bending she picked up her small suitcase. She couldn't lift the large one. It was too heavy to carry with any kind of dignity, and she wouldn't get far trying to drag it. So she sucked in a quick, ragged breath in an effort to hold herself together a little longer, threw back her shoulders and started down the street.

She didn't know where she was going. But, at the moment, anywhere was better than here.

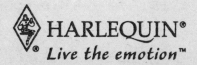

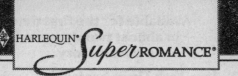

Nothing Sacred
by Tara Taylor Quinn

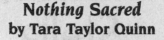

Welcome back to
Shelter Valley, Arizona.
This is the kind of town
everyone dreams about,
the kind of place
everyone wants to live.
Meet your friends from
previous visits—including
Martha Moore, divorced
mother of teenagers. And
meet the new minister,
David Cole Marks.

Martha's still burdened
by the bitterness of a
husband's betrayal. And
there are secrets hidden
in David's past.

Can they find in each
other the shelter they
seek? The happiness?

By the author of *Where the Road Ends*,
Born in the Valley and *For the Children*.

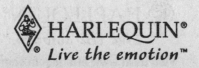

HARLEQUIN®
Live the emotion™

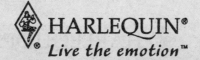

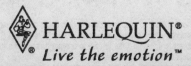

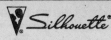

Carnival Elation
7-Day Exotic Western Caribbean Itinerary

DAY	PORT	ARRIVE	DEPART
Sun	Galveston		4:00 P.M.
Mon	"Fun Day" at Sea		
Tue	Progreso/Mérida	8:00 A.M.	4:00 P.M.
Wed	Cozumel	9:00 A.M.	5:00 P.M.
Thu	Belize	8:00 A.M.	6:00 P.M.
Fri	"Fun Day" at Sea		
Sat	"Fun Day" at Sea		
Sun	Galveston	8:00 A.M.	

TERMS AND CONDITIONS

PAYMENT SCHEDULE:
50% due upon booking. Full and final payment due by July 26, 2004.
Acceptable forms of payment are Visa, MasterCard, American Express, Discover and checks.
The cardholder must be one of the passengers traveling. A fee of $25 will apply for all returned checks. Check payments must be made payable to **Advantage International, LLC and sent to: Advantage International, LLC, 195 North Harbor Drive, Suite 4206, Chicago, IL 60601.**

CHANGE/CANCELLATION:
Notice of change/cancellation must be made in writing to Advantage International, LLC.

Change:
Changes in cabin category may be requested and can result in increased rate and penalties. A name change is permitted 60 days or more prior to departure and will incur a penalty of $50 per name change. Deviation from the group schedule and package is a cancellation.

Cancellation:
181 days or more prior to departure	$250 per person
121—180 days or more prior to departure	50% of the package price
120—61 days prior to departure	75% of the package price
60 days or less prior to departure	100% of the package price (nonrefundable)

U.S. and Canadian citizens are required to present a valid passport or the original birth certificate and state issued photo ID (driver's license). All other nationalities must contact the consulate of the various ports that are visited for verification of documentation.

<u>**We strongly recommend trip cancellation insurance!**</u>

For further details call 1-877-ADV-NTGE or visit www.GetCaughtReadingatSea.com

---

For booking form and complete information
go to www.getcaughtreadingatsea.com
or call 1-877-ADV-NTGE

Complete coupon and booking form and mail both to:
Advantage International, LLC
195 North Harbor Drive, Suite 4206, Chicago, IL 60601

Harlequin Enterprises Ltd. is a paid participant in this promotion.

Visit us at www.eHarlequin.com

GCRSEA2